Cold

Alison Carpenter

RENAISSANCE ALLIANCE PUBLISHING, INC.
Nederland, Texas

ISBN 1-930928-85-8

First Printing 2003

9 8 7 6 5 4 3 2 1

Cover design by Mary D. Brooks

Published by:

Renaissance Alliance Publishing, Inc.
PMB 238, 8691 9th Avenue
Port Arthur, Texas 77642-8025

Find us on the World Wide Web at
http://www.rapbooks.biz

Printed in the United States of America

I'd like to take this moment to thank some very special friends of mine.

Stephanie Solomon, who has always encouraged me, and refused to read *Cold* until it was finished, thus ensuring its completion.

Barbara Davies, who helped me with the online version of this story, and helped it to make sense.

Blayne Cooper, who wasn't satisfied until I'd submitted *Cold* for consideration. If not for her, this book would probably have never made it to print.

I'm lucky to have such friends.

And, of course, my thanks to RAP, for their faith in my little tale.

— Alison Carpenter

Chapter
1

The Rolls Royce seemed to glide silently into the small court-yard. Once the car came to a halt outside one of the black-glossed doors, the engine was silenced. The driver's door opened, and a smartly uniformed man walked around the front of the car to the rear passenger door and opened it. An exquisitely dressed woman unfolded herself from the rear seat. She stood for a moment straightening her coat, which was still in perfect order.

"Thank you, Jonathan," she said, reaching back into the car for her handbag. "I should only be a few minutes."

"Madam," the chauffeur acknowledged, bowing slightly at the waist. He pushed the door closed and went back to his place at the front of the car.

Marianna Holbrook-Sutherland, or, to give her correct title, Lady Collingford, keyed in the number in the security panel she knew would give her access to her daughter's small abode. The dark-haired woman pulled her coat closer about her, warding off the extreme cold of the English December day. She had called her daughter on the journey to the small town house in Kensington that she and her husband, Lord Collingford, had bought for the girl. After receiving no more than a grunt from her offspring, she knew she was in for a struggle to rouse her.

Joanna Holbrook-Sutherland was their youngest child. They expected nothing of her and she didn't disappoint by exceeding their expectations. Joanna had spent the last few years of her life enjoying the privilege of title and wealth, with her parents' approval. Their son, Jeremy, heir to the family title, helped run the huge house that was the family seat in Cumbria. It opened from April to September to the public, and during that time, Marianna and her husband lived in London. Their eldest daughter, Olivia, had married the head of a large corporation and now lived in Seattle, USA.

Joanna had shown no ambition to marry or to make a career for herself. She was content to party, to shop, and to break the record for visiting every alcohol-dispensing establishment in London before she was twenty-five.

The small courtyard had once been home to half a dozen stables. They had been bought some ten years previously and converted into luxury living accommodations. The lower level housed a large garage, with a small laundry room behind. Marianna made her way up the short flight of stairs to the living quarters. At the top of the stairs was another door, which she pushed open. In the short hallway was a telephone table, and on the wall above that, an entry intercom. To her left was a door which led to the kitchen and to her right the door to the lounge. Right next to the kitchen door another flight of stairs led to what used to be the loft, but now housed two bedrooms and a bathroom.

Joanna recognised the voice that was becoming increasingly annoying. She turned onto her back, shielding her eyes as her mother pulled the cord and opened the blind that was across the window in the roof.

Marianna regarded her youngest daughter. The telephone was still held in one hand, resting on the pillow beside the dark head, which was just visible beneath the ivory coloured quilt. Joanna had inherited her father's height and blue eyes and her mother's Greek colouring, which made for an interesting and stunning mix.

"Joanna, dear. There's a strange woman on your futon."

Blue eyes blinked at her from beneath the quilt. "What does she look like?"

Marianna strained to hear the muffled voice of her daughter. "Really, Joanna." Marianna tutted and sat on the edge of the bed. She looked at her daughter and then at her watch.

"Am I forgetting something?" the sleepy woman asked. She eased herself to a sitting position, her back resting against the headboard.

"Really, Joanna," she said again, the phrase becoming a favourite. "I told you last week. I'm hosting an exhibition of Charles DeBurgh's photography at The Gallery."

The Gallery had been Lord Collingford's gift to his wife when she complained of boredom. She had hosted exhibitions, parties, and fashion shows at the venue, and it had become one of the fashionable places to be seen in.

"And you're telling me this...why?" the younger woman asked, reaching for the half-finished glass of orange juice on the bedside cabinet.

Marianna stood so quickly that Joanna jumped, spilling some of the juice across her chest. "Really, Joanna." The phrase actually made the girl wince this time. "You promised you would make an appearance this time." She stood in front of the mirror, taking in her own appearance. Giving a small nod, she turned back to her daughter. "I want to show you off, dear. Is that so terrible?"

Joanna sighed and scrubbed at her face. She looked at the clock on the cabinet beside the bed. It showed that it was 8.32am; she'd had four hours of sleep.

"I'll wait in the car for you, dear." She opened the door to the bedroom but turned back before leaving the room. Joanna was out of bed now, and her mother took in the lean form of her youngest child. "A little blonde."

Joanna had just pulled a towelling robe on. "What?" she asked.

"The girl on the futon." She gave her daughter a lopsided smile, something else the younger woman had inherited from her. "I see your tastes haven't changed."

Half an hour later, Joanna was sitting next to her mother in the back of the Rolls.

"You're twenty-four, Jo." Marianna had remained quiet for a good twenty minutes. She'd sighed deeply when it had taken her daughter nearly half an hour to appear through her front door. Though she appreciated that the younger woman looked stunning in a little black dress with a hemline that reached mid thigh. She wore a thick black coat over it, and black stilettos that added to her already imposing height. Her long, dark hair fell loose about her shoulders.

Joanna ignored her mother and watched the passing buildings, occasionally catching the gaze of the chauffeur in the rear view mirror. He winked at her.

"Your point is?" Joanna asked after another long period of silence.

Marianna patted her daughter on her thigh. "Your father and

I have always done everything we can for you. You know that, don't you?"

Joanna turned to face her mother. "Yes, you have. And yes, I know it, and I'm grateful." There was a wariness in her voice.

Marianna pursed her lips. "Who was that girl, Joanna? Another of your conquests?"

Jo shrugged. "I suppose so." She smiled. "Why?"

"Are you happy...the way you are?"

The laugh that exploded from Jo's throat startled her mother and caused Jonathan's eyes to switch from the road to the rear view mirror. "'The way I am.' What the hell's that supposed to mean?" She ran a hand through her long hair, another habit she shared with her mother.

"This life you lead, dear. It seems so...empty."

"Jon, stop the car," she called to the driver. He looked for confirmation from the older woman.

"Drive on, Jonathan."

Joanna slumped back in her seat. "Mother, I'm not looking for a permanent relationship right now. I'm quite happy. I have friends. I have my family. I have no ambition to find a good man, which I know is what you're expecting from me."

The older woman was quiet for a moment. "This...phase you're going through."

"I've told you before, it's not a phase. I'm not going to wake one morning and have an overwhelming desire to find a husband. I told you when I was eighteen that I preferred the company of women. Lots of women. That isn't going to change anytime soon."

"I only thought—"

"Well don't, Mother, you could be dangerous."

Marianna decided to drop the subject. For now.

The gallery doors opened at 10am, and Joanna was there beside her mother to welcome the invited throng into the fashionable venue.

By noon, the small gallery was heaving with the young, famous, and hangers on.

"Jo!"

Joanna turned when she heard her name being called. Her relief was evident when she saw her friend pushing towards her through the crowd. She smiled easily, seeing the tousled blonde head and the wide grin of the woman coming towards her. "Harry, I'm so glad you made it." She bent and embraced her friend. Harriet James was the daughter of her father's business partner.

"They wouldn't let me in. You didn't leave my name on the door."

Joanna shook her head. "I forgot. Four hours sleep," she explained.

"Yeah, I saw you leave. Good night?" Harry asked, grinning up at her taller friend.

Joanna put an arm across the shorter woman's shoulders. "You know me," she whispered into her ear. "Come on, let's get a drink." They managed to find a quiet corner with a small sofa, and both collapsed onto it with a glass of Bucks Fizz each.

"So what's this all about?" Harry asked, indicating the milling crowd with her glass.

"Mother's latest discovery." Jo looked through the crowd. "There." She pointed to a tall willowy man, deep in conversation with two women. "That's Charles DeBurgh. She thinks he's the next David Bailey or something."

"So what does he photograph?"

Jo shook her head. "No idea."

Choking on Bucks Fizz was probably not the most attractive look, Harry decided, as the orange liquid threatened to exit her nose. "You've been here for two hours and you haven't looked at the bloody pictures?" she managed, after she'd recovered.

Jo was leaning back against the arm of the sofa, keeping her drink out of the range of her coughing friend. She shrugged.

"Come on, let's go see." Harry stood and hauled her friend to her feet.

Joanna stood in front of the first set of pictures. "Oh...my...God."

"What?" Harry walked over from the photos she was looking at to see what Joanna was finding so interesting.

"I can't believe my mother dragged me out of a perfectly good bed on a Saturday morning to look at pictures of..." she leaned closer, peering at the black-and-white pictures, then straightened up and turned to face her friend, "vagrants."

"I guess it's what they call art," said Harry while peering at a picture.

"No, art is the body that I left back on my futon."

"The futon?"

"That was as far as we got."

"And you left her there?"

"Not my fault if she lost the ability to walk." Joanna looked pleased with herself. "I have a reputation to uphold."

Harry chuckled, and both women enjoyed a moment of silence as they studied the photos.

Jo moved ahead and turned a corner, looking at a set of pictures that were on another wall.

Harry caught up with her. "I really don't see the attraction of a picture that shows some guy sitting in a pool of vomit," said the shorter woman. "Jo?" she asked, when she received no reply.

Joanna was staring at a picture, and Harry went to stand beside the taller woman.

The picture her friend was looking at was one of the larger ones in the display. The subject was a woman, no more than a girl, from what Harry could make out. Some sort of scarf was about the girl's neck, partially covering her chin. The lips were full but unsmiling. But it was the eyes that were so striking, even though the picture was a black-and-white portrait. The eyes stared unrelentingly from the picture almost defiantly. Blonde hair fell haphazardly across the girl's forehead, just reaching her eyelids.

"Makes you realise how lucky we are," Harry said without looking up. When she received no answer, she looked up at the angular profile of her friend. "Jo?"

The taller woman turned towards her, confusion clouding her gaze.

Joanna saw her friend, saw her lips moving, but couldn't hear the noise that Harry was obviously making. Then Harry's face seemed to grow smaller and smaller, and blackness encroached from the edge of her vision.

Harry tried to grab her friend when she saw Jo's knees buckle, but the taller woman's weight bore them both to the ground. She watched in horrified fascination as Jo's head fell back against her arm. Harry was aware of people rushing to see what was happening, but she just heard her friend whisper as she lost consciousness.

"It's her."

Chapter
2

An hour after the incident in the gallery, Jo was sitting in the back of the Rolls next to a very quiet Harry. "Jonathan, I think I'll go home," Jo said wearily.

The chauffeur didn't take his eyes off the road. "Lady Collingford instructed me to take you to Castleton Lodge."

"I know what my mother said, but I want to go home."

Jonathan gave a short nod and immediately took a sharp left.

Jo now had her eyes closed and was pinching the bridge of her nose between thumb and forefinger.

"Jo?" Harry reached across and laid a hand on her friend's shoulder.

"I'm fine, just a bit of a headache." Jo was remembering coming to awareness and finding herself surrounded by a dozen or more curious faces. "They think I'm either pregnant or drugged up to the eyeballs," she said with a tired sigh.

"Do you know what happened back there?"

Jo shook her head. "No. Just my wild ways catching up with me."

"It scared me a little, Jo," Harry said.

"Scared me too. I'm going to go home and go to bed. I don't think having just four hours of sleep agrees with me." Jo eyed her best friend. "What do you want to do?"

"I'll stay with you." A pause. "If that's okay?"

"Of course it is. I could do with some company." Jo gave the blonde a tired smile and patted Harry's thigh.

"I thought you already had some," Harry said, suddenly finding the passing scenery interesting.

Jo shook her head. "I told her I probably wouldn't be back all day. She's probably gone."

They were silent for a moment.

"Jo?" Harry looked across at her friend who was sitting quietly with her eyes closed. The dark-haired woman didn't answer but turned blue eyes on her. "Doesn't matter," said Harry, just as the Rolls pulled into the courtyard.

As Jo had suspected, the small house was empty. Her guest had left. Harry dropped onto the chair and watched as Jo eased her body onto the sofa. Her back was hurting where she had twisted as she fainted, and her head was thumping.

"Shall I make some tea?" Harry asked, pulling herself up. "And I'll grab you some painkillers." She didn't wait for an answer as she made her way to the kitchen.

Some ten minutes later, Harry emerged from the kitchen with a couple of mugs. Jo was sitting on the sofa, her head resting against the back, and her eyes closed. "Sorry," Harry said as she placed the mug of tea on the coffee table and put a couple of Nurofen in Jo's hand. "Take these, then see if you can get to sleep."

Harry watched her with worried eyes.

They had been friends for many years, but at no time desired to take their relationship any further. Both acknowledged the other's beauty, but neither apparently found the other physically alluring. True, Harry was blonde, and every woman Jo had ever wooed had been blonde, but Jo always thought of Harry as just a good friend. And she didn't want to complicate their very close relationship with sex.

After taking the tablets and drinking her tea, Jo quickly made herself comfortable and started to drift off.

"Jo?"

"Mmm?" was the sleepy response.

"Did you know the girl in the picture?" Harry sank into the plush armchair, taking in her friend's profile, which was barely visible in the darkened room. Though only two-thirty in the afternoon, it was a dull day and was dark in the lounge since the blinds were pulled close. The gas fire, complete with artificial flames, filled the room with warmth and a gentle glow.

Jo was quiet for a long time. "No, I don't think so."

"Well, you had a hell of a reaction to it." Harry studied the contents of her mug for a long moment. "You said something.

Before you passed out, you said something."

It took quite an effort for Jo to open her eyes and turn them back towards her friend. "What are you talking about?" There was a hint of annoyance in the tired voice.

"You said, 'It's her.'"

"'Her'?"

Harry shrugged. "That's what you said. That's why I wondered if you knew her."

"No, I didn't know her. I'm just tired, Harry." Jo stood abruptly. "Look..." She once again pinched the bridge of her nose. Her face was pale, and her eyes were scrunched tightly shut. "Look," she said again, only softer, "I'm going to bed." Her eyes opened and she looked at her friend. "You're welcome to stay. You know that."

"Yeah, I know," Harry said, standing and giving her friend a peck on the cheek. "You give me a shout if you need anything."

Jo smiled down at her. "I will." She gave her a brief squeeze on the shoulder and disappeared up the short flight of stairs and into her bedroom. She was asleep less than five minutes later.

Harry was dozing off and on while on the sofa, the TV remote control hanging precariously from one hand. She flicked through the channels, her tired brain taking in the usual Saturday evening fare of quiz shows and talent shows that terrestrial TV seemed to think its customers preferred. Flicking to satellite, she found American dramas. She came to one particular channel and dwelt a little longer there, admiring the physique of the two leading ladies. Being one who spent most Saturday nights in the bars and nightclubs of London, she wasn't familiar with the usual Saturday night menu of shows. She made a mental note to get out the manual for her VCR and finally master setting the timer.

Whatever it was that she was watching ended, and she proceeded to flick through the channels. She came across a rerun of some quiz show and watched in fascination as one of the contestants struggled with what was, to her, a simple question. The quizmaster oozed self-admiration and posed the question again. A few thousand pounds rested on his answer.

"Princess Anne is older than Prince Charles. True or False? I'm going to have to put the timer on."

"Can I call a friend?" The contestant fidgeted in his seat.

"You can. Do you want to?"

The contestant thought for a moment. "No. I'll answer.

False."

"Is that your final answer?"

"Yes, false."

"You're sure?"

The contestant hesitated, his face draining of all colour.

Harry was caught in the moment. "Come on, dipstick. You're right. Everyone knows that."

"You don't want to change your mind?" The quizmaster tapped on his board with his pen.

The contestant looked to the audience, obviously having family out there somewhere. He looked like a man condemned, about to walk the final short distance. "False," he said again, his voice cracking under the strain.

"You had six thousand pounds," the quizmaster said, his face impassive. There was silence—a long silence. The tapping of the pen on the board was the only sound. "You now have twelve thousand pounds."

The audience erupted and the contestant looked just about ready to faint.

Harry switched channels quickly, unable to stand much more of the torture of the poor man. He was only on twelve thousand pounds. What would happen when he got to bigger figures and more difficult questions? "Who the hell doesn't know that Prince Charles is the oldest of the Royal kids?" Harry asked herself.

She flicked through a few more channels. She watched some real life cop show from the States for a while and then came across *The World's Scariest Police Videos*, which contrary to the show's description seemed to all take place on American highways. It was then that she heard Jo. At first Harry thought Jo was calling for her, but as she neared the bedroom door she realised that her friend was in some kind of distress. She burst into the room to find the naked, dark woman thrashing wildly in her sleep, seemingly trying to disentangle herself from the quilt cover, which was coming loose from the quilt. Cries of pain and anguish came from Jo.

"Jo, stop," she said, climbing onto the bed with her friend and trying to get control of the long arms which threatened to deliver a painful blow in their thrashing.

"No, don't go!" Jo sat bolt upright, her arms reaching for something unseen. Her eyes were wide, scanning the dark of her bedroom, which was lit only by the light from beyond the bedroom door. The blue gaze fell upon her friend, and then Jo's face twisted. She collapsed back onto the bed and curled in on herself. Her arms were crossed across her chest, as if she was in great pain.

"Jo?" It was like the calm after the storm; only the ragged breathing of the tall woman was audible now. Harry reached out and laid a hand on a heaving shoulder. "Are you all right?"

Jo didn't reply for a long moment. "What time is it?" Her voice was hoarse, her breathing just coming under her control.

"Umm..." Harry turned her watch towards the light filtering through the doorway. "Just after nine-thirty."

Jo eased herself out of bed, wondering how she missed running the London marathon earlier that day. Surely she must have; her body was certainly telling her that it had gone through some sort of traumatic event that day. She pulled on a robe and shuffled out of the room, watched all the time by a bemused Harry.

Harry shook her head and followed her friend down to the lounge.

"What is this?" Jo asked, trying to focus sleepy eyes on the TV, which was showing the view from a police car as it followed a motorcyclist across rough ground.

Harry picked up the remote and silenced the TV.

Jo sat on the sofa while Harry sat on the armchair.

"You okay?" the blonde asked.

Jo looked as though she'd been awake a week, instead of asleep for the past few hours. "Nightmare. Christ, I haven't had a nightmare since I was at boarding school. Had them all the time there. Bloody nuns."

"You want to tell me what it was about?"

Jo shrugged. "Can't really remember."

"But you know it was a nightmare?"

"I was scared." Jo shook her head gently. "I know I was scared."

"Was someone chasing you?" Harry leaned forward, her elbows on her knees and her chin cupped in her hands.

Jo thought for a moment. "No, someone was leaving me." She was remembering the dream, remembering the feeling of pain and helplessness. "There was nothing I could do. No way I could reach her."

"Her?" Harry sat upright; now this was getting interesting.

Jo sighed, a long, knowing sigh. Harry must think she was losing her marbles.

"Was it..." Harry began.

Another sigh, and Jo nodded her head. "It was the girl in the picture."

"So, you do know her?"

"I'm sure I don't." She leaned her head against the sofa back. "I mean, I don't think so. I've met a lot of women..." She paused hearing Harry's snort.

"Sorry," the blonde said.

"How would I know someone who lives on the street?"

"Maybe she hasn't been on the street long."

Jo ground the heel of her hand into her forehead, trying to ease the pain that was building there. "She just turned away from me and left me."

Harry was quiet, waiting for her friend to continue.

"I couldn't breathe," Jo said. "My legs wouldn't move. I watched her go and did nothing to stop her."

Harry watched Jo carefully. The woman was distraught. Her hair was stringy and falling in a tangled mess about her shoulders. A sheen of sweat covered her face and chest. Her hands clutched at the material of her robe. "Can you remember how the dream started?"

Jo was silent, and for a while Harry wondered if she was going to answer.

"I was walking through," she thought for a moment, "alleyways, I think. It was somewhere dark and cold."

"And she was there?"

"Not to start with. But then she was."

Harry squirmed on the chair, intrigued. "Did you talk to her?"

One perfectly formed eyebrow rose and blue eyes pinned the blonde. "This is a dream, Harry. I can remember snippets, images, feelings. I can't remember conversations."

"So, what did you feel?"

Jo looked into the artificial flames of the fire. "Cold, I felt cold."

Chapter
3

Breathe, just breathe. Jo bolted upright, once again clutching her chest against the sharp pain that manifested itself right next to her heart.

"Jo?" A sleep-tousled blonde head peeked up from beneath the quilt beside her. "You dreaming again?" Harry asked, looking up at her friend's dark profile, barely seen in the darkness.

For the first time since she was a child, the darkness had disturbed Jo. This feeling resulted in her leaving the landing light on and asking her friend to sleep with her in her bed, rather than in the guestroom.

"Yeah," was all that Jo could manage as she held the flat of her hand against her own wildly beating heart.

"Same thing?" Harry asked, pulling herself to a sitting position and peering around Jo to see the illuminated numbers on the radio alarm—01.37.

Jo nodded.

"Same woman?" Harry waited while her friend composed herself.

Jo swallowed hard, her eyes tightly shut. "I'm going mad, aren't I?" she asked, burying her face in her hands.

"I think maybe you're very tired," Harry said softly, "and the photos in the gallery affected you in some way. A tired mind can play strange tricks on you sometimes."

Jo suddenly threw the quilt back and leaped out of bed. "Where are you going?" Harry asked, pulling the quilt around herself.

"To have a chat with Mother."

"Umm...Jo?" Harry began, but Jo was already heading out of the bedroom, pulling on a robe as she went. By the time Harry reached the lounge, Jo had turned on the gas fire and was arguing with her Mother's chauffeur.

"I really don't care, Jon. I want to talk to her, and I want to talk to her now."

Harry reached out a tentative hand and rested it on Jo's shoulder. "It's really late, Jo," she said quietly.

The tall woman ignored her. "What?" she barked into the phone. "Then I'll come over there. Which would you prefer?"

Harry moved away from the angry woman, realising that she was being ignored, and watched Jo as she sat on the sofa. Jo had the phone hard against her ear.

"Mother?" Jo's eyes were closed, a look of something approaching pain on her face. "Yes, I know." She was obviously fending off an irate woman. "Well, it'll only take a moment. I need a phone number." Harry wordlessly handed Jo a pad of note-paper; the tall woman took it and the pen that was also handed to her.

"Charles DeBurgh. Never mind that. Do you have the number?" Jo scribbled something down and put the phone down without wishing her mother a good night. She punched in the numbers her mother had given her and waited while the phone rang and was answered.

"Charles, Joanna Holbrook-Sutherland. I need to see you...Yes, I do know what the time is...No, not in the morning. Now. I need an address." Jo took a deep breath. "Charles, how long did my mother promise you in the gallery?" Another pause, and the faintest of smiles graced the beautiful face. "Did she now? That long? I could have you out of there on Monday. Now then, give me an address." Jo once again scribbled something on the notepad. "I'll be there shortly."

After slamming the phone down, she passed a dumbstruck Harry and went back to her bedroom. She pulled on some under-wear and jeans and a sweater and then sat on the bed pulling a pair of sturdy ankle boots on.

"D'you want me to come with you?" Harry asked, amazed at how quickly her friend could dress.

"It's up to you. If you want to come, you had better be quick. I'll get the car out. Meet you downstairs."

Harry quickly dressed and ran down the stairs. Jo was waiting outside the front door in the Merk. Harry shivered in the cold winter night. She eased into the passenger side of the convertible, reaching forward as she did so to make sure the heat was turned up to its highest setting. Jo had pulled out of the courtyard and onto the main road before Harry had a chance to secure her seatbelt.

The streets were mostly quiet. The exceptionally cold weather and the late hour combined to keep most people indoors. Only a few cars were about, taking people home from nightclubs and maybe workers home after a long day. The occasional police car passed them as they made their way through the damp and freezing streets.

Harry marvelled at Jo's knowledge of the streets. She herself didn't know the part of London they were entering at all. Before long they arrived on a long street and Jo drove down it slowly, leaning over the steering wheel to see the numbers on the doors.

"There it is," she said and pulled up against the kerb. Quickly, she was out of the car and scanning the names below the six or so bells for the correct name. She rang one of them and waited.

"Yes?" the mechanical voice asked.

She leaned close to the intercom. "Joanna," was all she said.

There was a buzz, and she pushed the door open. Harry trudged along behind her. She was beginning to doubt her desire to follow her friend on this ridiculous chase across London.

Charles DeBurgh was waiting by the open door of his apartment. He was wearing a pair of red pyjama bottoms and holding a glass, which contained an unidentifiable substance. He stood aside and allowed the two women to enter.

"I don't know why I agreed to this," he said, gesturing towards the lounge. "Has this got anything to do with the exhibition?"

Harry looked towards Jo when no answer was forthcoming. The tall woman was standing just inside the doorway, looking around her as if wondering where she was and how she got there.

The blonde woman took hold of Jo's arm, "Jo, are you okay?"

"What the hell am I doing?" she asked, turning away from Harry and facing a bemused photographer.

"Shit! I hope you haven't dragged me out of bed because you're fucking well PMSing." Charles turned away from the two women and stalked into his lounge, slumping down on the sofa and taking a long draught of the drink he held in his hand. The two women followed him into the room. Harry sat in one of the plump armchairs, and Jo wandered aimlessly around the room.

"One of the pictures in the exhibition..." Jo's voice faltered.

"Well?" Charles asked, his patience obviously waning.

Jo closed her eyes. "I can't get her face out of my mind." There it was. Simple. To the point.

Charles was quiet for a long moment, taking in the pale face of the woman standing before him. Then he stood abruptly. "Come with me." He led them to what they assumed was his office. There was a computer and a number of filing cabinets. From one he took a number of folders. He handed them to Jo. "That's all the photographs I have at the gallery."

Jo sat on the small sofa that was in the room and placed the folders on the cushion next to her. With shaking hands, she removed the photos. All were 6x4 colour prints. There were three folders, and Jo carefully looked at each photo before placing it back in the folder. Charles waggled his empty glass at them and left the room. Harry sat on the chair in front of the computer table.

The blonde watched Jo as she went through the pictures, one by one. Then her attention shifted. She surveyed the rest of the small room, and then her gaze fell on the small clock sitting beside the computer. 02.47. Was she really sitting in a virtual stranger's flat, in the small hours of the morning, chasing after...what? What were they doing here? Chasing a dream? And not even her dream. The dream of this woman, who she loved. Like a sister? No, no sister would do the things to a sibling that she had in mind for Jo. But Jo didn't want that with her, and she would abide by her friend's decision.

A gasp brought her out of her musings.

Jo was looking at a photo, holding it in shaking hands. "They're green," she whispered. Jo turned towards Harry. "Her eyes are green, the same as in my dream. How did I know that?"

Harry moved the folders away from Jo's side and sat next to her friend, peering at the picture still held carefully in her hands. Harry took the photograph from Jo and looked long and hard at the face staring back at her. "I thought you didn't see much of her in the dream."

"I didn't." Jo took a handful of her own hair in both hands and pulled sharply. She took in a deep breath. "This is crazy.

What am I going to say to Charles? He's going to think I'm some crazy woman."

There was no answer from her friend who was studying the photo with quiet deliberation.

"You think I'm crazy, don't you?"

Harry didn't look up. For a start, she didn't know how to answer Jo. Yes, she had, on the drive to Charles' flat, decided that her best friend had finally lost her marbles. All the nights of partying and enjoying the attentions of beautiful women had finally taken their toll. But it was the broken sound of Jo's voice that silenced her.

She handed the photo back. "I'm going to talk to Charles. Take a moment to think."

Jo nodded, her shoulders slumped.

Harry found Charles sitting in his lounge, nursing another glass of whatever he was drinking.

"Can I?" Harry asked, pointing towards the small bar.

"Be my guest," Charles said, but there was a touch of sarcasm in his voice.

Harry poured herself a whisky and sat back down on the sofa, facing Charles.

"This isn't like Jo at all." Harry watched him, waiting for the caustic reply she was sure was coming.

"Really?"

"Yeah, really." She paused, gathering her thoughts. "I've never seen her like this before. Jo is the youngest of Lord and Lady Collingford's children. They have never pushed her. And she has no ambition." Harry searched for the right words. "She's a...free spirit. That's the best way I know to describe her. She's never had a worry in her life. Anything she's ever wanted, her parents have bought her. The biggest decision she makes is which restaurant to visit on which night."

Charles looked at her vacantly. "And you're telling me this for some reason?"

"I'm trying to explain how out of character this is for her. Something has shaken her so badly she feels she needs to chase around London, in the small hours, just to try to get to the bottom of it." Harry looked at the man, feeling she was battering her head against a brick wall. However strange her friend's actions were to her, she would still defend Jo to the last.

Charles looked up, and Harry followed his gaze, finding Jo

standing in the doorway.

She walked across the room towards Charles, the picture in her hands. "Can you tell me who this is?" she asked.

Charles couldn't take his eyes from the troubled, blue gaze. He reached out and took the photo. Tearing his eyes from Jo's, he looked down at the face on the photo. "Rocky," he said.

A muted chuckle from Harry was quickly arrested when the blonde saw the confusion on Jo's face.

"Rocky?" the tall woman said.

"I should imagine that wasn't her real name."

"Rocky," Jo said again, feeling the name, deciding something was wrong. "You've spoken to her?"

Charles shrugged. "Briefly. She's not terribly talkative. Very nervous of strangers."

"How did you manage to get her to pose for this then?" Jo asked, taking the picture from Charles. She stared at it. "Rocky"? Even though she didn't know the girl's name, she instinctively knew that wasn't it.

Charles laughed. Not a nice laugh, Jo decided. "She didn't pose. I got that after waiting for hours for her. It became something of a challenge."

"She didn't want her picture taken then?" Harry asked.

"Not likely." Charles drained his glass and rose to get a refill.

"But you took it anyway," Jo said.

Charles turned from the bar, his glass now full. "Look at that face, Jo. I had to capture that."

"So it was like some kind of game for you. A hunt?"

Another shrug from the photographer. "You could call it that, I suppose. I waited for three days before I got that shot."

"Where?" Jo asked, her stomach clenching. She was getting close.

"Where what?" Charles was looking smug now, remembering outwitting the girl who had been so elusive.

"Where did you finally...shoot her?" Jo now had her eyes closed, the events of the past few hours catching up with her.

"Oh, it was around Whitechapel somewhere. There's a regular soup run down there most evenings. I just waited for her to make an appearance."

Jo nodded and turned troubled blue eyes on her friend. "Harry?" Harry stood and moved to Jo's side. "Can I keep this?" Jo asked, waving the photo at the man.

"Be my guest." Charles put his empty glass on the bar and ushered the women out of the lounge. "Now, if you don't mind, I'm going back to bed."

Just as he was about to close the door to his apartment after seeing them out, Jo stopped him. "Charles, I'm sorry, I don't—"

"Whatever," Charles said and shut the door in their faces.

As they got to the Merk gleaming dully in the streetlight, Harry put her hand out. "I'm driving."

"Harry, there's no need," Jo protested.

"I think I'd feel better." Harry was unmoving, holding her hand out until Jo placed in it the keys with the small remote control for the alarm attached. After disarming the alarm, the two women climbed in. Jo still clutched the photograph in her hands. "Home then?" Harry asked quietly.

Jo nodded. "I'm sorry," she whispered. "I don't understand this."

"Me neither."

"Who do you think she is?" Jo was looking at the picture, squinting at it in the artificial light. Jo gave a brief chuckle as a thought occurred to her. "And why do I care?"

Chapter
4

Jo sat on the floor in front of the gas fire in her lounge, staring at the photograph.

The girl's hair was blonde, naturally highlighted by the sun. It looked clean. She remembered seeing footage of homeless people on the news once, and the fact that their hair always looked as though it hadn't seen a drop of water or shampoo in years had struck her. This girl was different. The blonde hair fell across her forehead, the very tips tangling with the dark eyelashes that framed her eyes. Jo took long moments looking into those eyes. If she looked closely she could see other colours mixed with the green. Hazel and gold. The eyes of the girl stared out at her, unflinching, and Jo found herself having to look away from them. She lowered her gaze to the lips, and now Jo could see that they were slightly parted and the very edge of even white teeth could just be seen. Again, Jo was surprised. She expected a person living on the streets to find the everyday toiletries that she took for granted hard to come by. Jo smiled to herself, amazed at the absurdity of the thought that sprang into her mind. It would make kissing her a more pleasurable experience if she'd brushed her teeth in the previous twelve hours or so.

Jo started to laugh. What was she thinking? Her laughing brought Harry from the kitchen where she was watching the milk that was boiling in a saucepan.

"What's funny?"

Jo shrugged. "Just thinking stupid thoughts."

Harry watched her for a moment, and then returned to the kitchen.

"Stupid, stupid thoughts," Jo whispered to herself. "Who are you, Rocky?"

Harry returned some moments later with two mugs of steaming coffee. "What are you going to do now?" Harry sipped her coffee, curling herself into the armchair.

"Well, I thought we'd take a drive around when it gets light, see what we can see. Charles said something about Whitechapel. We'll take a look around down there, maybe ask some questions. If we've found nothing by the evening, we'll see if we can latch on to one of those soup wagons. I think they travel to more than one place. I'll take the photo; someone must have seen her." Jo looked up to see Harry regarding her, open-mouthed. "What?" Jo asked.

"Would you listen to yourself, Jo? What the hell is going on?"

Jo's mouth opened and closed a couple of times; no sound was forthcoming, however.

"You're really going to scour London looking for what is obviously a vagrant." Harry placed her mug on the low table and leaned forward, her elbows on her knees. "And then what? Have you thought about that?"

The colour drained from Jo's face, confusion evident in the blue eyes.

"Didn't think so." Harry continued. "So when you find her you say: 'Oh hi. I'm Jo, and I've been dreaming about you. I'm not crazy, but I want you to come home with me.'" Harry sat back, crossing her arms across her chest, waiting for her friend's response.

"I have to do something," Jo said quietly. "I feel I have to. Need to."

"You're chasing after some kind of fantasy, Jo."

"No. She's real. I'm sure she is."

"I'm real, Jo. I'm here. I don't understand you." Harry's head fell forward, her eyes squeezed shut

"What are you saying?"

"You really don't know, do you?"

"No, I don't." Jo watched her friend with concern, taking in the silent tears that tracked down her cheeks.

Harry let out a long, hitching breath. "I think I should go," she said, standing.

Jo was on her feet quickly, stepping in front of Harry as she made for the door. She placed her hands on the shorter woman's shoulders, forcing Harry to look up. "I'm sorry if I've hurt you.

You're the best friend I've ever had."

"Exactly," the blonde said and shrugged out of Jo's grasp. She collected her coat and left quickly.

Ten minutes later, Harry was walking purposefully along the street when a car pulled alongside her. She recognised the silver Merk immediately. She opened the door and got in without question. "I forgot it was only 4 o'clock," she said, looking down at her hands.

"Me too," Jo said, her voice little more than a whisper. "I didn't realise; I'm sorry."

Harry shook her head gently and ran her fingers through her own dishevelled hair. "I value your friendship, Jo. And I know we've always said there would never be anything...else between us. But I couldn't help myself."

Jo reached over and took her hand. "I love you, Harry. You know that right?"

Harry nodded and sniffed. "Yeah, it's just been really hard watching you the last day or so. Getting crazy over a photo."

"I don't understand it any more than you do."

There was silence for a moment in the car, the glass fogging up. "We'd better go before we attract the attention of the police." Jo reached over and turned Harry's face towards her. "Where do you want to go?"

"Home," she said simply. "I'm sorry, Jo. You're going to have to do this on your own."

Jo nodded. "Yeah, I know."

Joanna had never felt lonely in her small house before. Now, as she walked into her lounge, the hairs on the back of her head stood on end, and she suppressed a shiver.

She'd watched Harry walk away from her and disappear behind the large door of her house. She'd never really considered the fact that her friend had wanted more from her than friendship. They'd discussed that on more than one occasion. Had talked about Jo's cavalier way with women, and how many hearts she'd broken. And now she realised she'd broken her best friend's heart, too. But that was exactly what Harry was, her best friend. And as hard as she tried, Jo just couldn't contemplate their relationship being any more than that.

She slumped down into the armchair. It was 5.30am on a Sunday morning. It was an hour that Jo was not unfamiliar with. Though the other times she had experienced it, she had usually been just arriving home after a particularly excessive night out. Clutched in her right hand was the photograph, and once again her attention was drawn to the face of the woman she'd never met, but who was, strangely, becoming a part of her life. She fought the urge to leave immediately, knowing she was exhausted and would probably crash the car straight into the Thames before she got anywhere. So she closed her eyes, her thumb moving unnoticed across the lips of the blonde girl in the photo.

Jo woke with a pain in her shoulder where she'd slumped against the arm of the chair. Her neck also refused to obey her brain's instructions to support her head, which seemed to have acquired its own bass drum. The drum in question had struck up a monotonous rhythm, which intensified as Jo straightened up in the chair. She'd left the fire on low, and now her mouth felt as if someone had forced a wad of cotton into it. She raised herself slowly, looking more like her mother's mother than her mother's daughter, and made her way to the kitchen.

After draining two large glasses of orange juice, she went back into the lounge, glancing at her watch as she did. It was a little before 8am. She picked up the picture from beside the chair. It had fallen face down from her hand as she slept. She felt the flutter in her chest and the clenching of her abdomen as she looked upon the face again.

As she left the house, she briefly wondered how she would cope with meeting the girl herself since the picture alone was giving her palpitations. Charles had mentioned Whitechapel, and so that was where she'd start.

She'd studied the photograph in great detail. Once she'd managed to tear her eyes away from the face of the girl, she realised there was a shop of some kind in the background of the shot. She saw only the first three letters on the sign: Chi. That was all she could see.

So there she was, on a bleak December morning, searching the foggy streets of Whitechapel for a lost soul. Though at that moment Jo didn't realise just how lost the girl was in the picture and in her dreams. A church clock was chiming the hour of nine as Jo parked the Merk. She'd seen homeless people before, huddling around fires that they'd lit in some dark, damp corner. But now there were none to be found.

Glancing occasionally at the photo, she started walking the streets.

It was cold, and Jo pulled the collar of her coat up against the biting wind, which howled gently around the corners and into the alleys that made up much of that part of London. Ahead of her, out of what looked like an old church building, a number of people were filing into the cold morning dampness. She looked at the faded blue-and-yellow sign above the ancient door. "St Augustus Hostel for the Homeless."

A number of men shuffled towards her, their belongings clutched in a few tattered bags. Each one eyed her as she stood, letting them pass, unable to ask any of them the question that burned in her throat.

She looked over at the door as it was being pulled closed. "Wait a minute!" she called.

The young man opened the door a little. "Yes?" The man had a pleasant face. His hair was cut fashionably short with a small tuft just above his forehead. He wore a plain white t-shirt and faded jeans. "Can I help you?"

"Maybe," Jo said. "I'm looking for someone."

He didn't try to hide the incredulous look on his face. A woman of her obvious standing wasn't usually the kind to be seeking one of his guests.

Jo pulled out the picture. "Have you ever seen her?" she asked, as he took the picture from her.

He shook his head. "We don't take women in here. They cause too much trouble with the guys."

Jo experienced her first failure, and it must have shown on her face. The man sighed. "Is she family?" he asked.

Jo hesitated. The answer that screamed in her head was "yes."

"No, she isn't," Jo said as she took the picture from him. "I just...I need to find her." Jo shook her head, unable to explain even to herself the reason for her quest.

"The Salvation Army runs a hostel for homeless women. It's on Argyll Street. Maybe someone there can help you." The young man smiled, closing the door quietly and leaving the tall woman standing on the doorstep.

Jo turned back to the street. Most of the men that had exited from the hostel had left the area, but one or two had only made it as far as a couple of benches. She approached them cautiously, trying to discern which one might be amenable to a few questions.

A younger man caught her attention. His hair was dirty, as were his clothes. He appeared to have anything that could be pierced on his face adorned with some kind of jewellery. He was rummaging through a large bag when she appeared in front of him. He looked up quickly and dismissed her just as quickly.

"Excuse me," she said, waiting for him to look up again. He didn't. Jo cleared her throat.

"You wanna give me money?" he asked, his voice slurred.

"Well, I don't..." Jo took a step back as he stood suddenly.

"So what do you want?" He reached out a hand, feeling the edge of her leather collar.

"I...I'm looking for someone."

"Baby sister run away from home?" He walked around her, before appearing in front of her once again. "Or maybe your old man preferred the streets to you." He turned away from her and collected his belongings from the bench. "A lot of people out here don't want to be found. Go back to your TV and your washing machine. Leave us alone."

Jo watched the man walk away from her without a backward glance. She was shocked. Shouldn't she be the one disgusted? Yet it was she who felt dirty, felt as if she were imposing on someone else's privacy. This was their world. The same city, but a different world entirely. And if she were to survive here and learn about these people, she would have to be more careful.

She made her way along the street in the direction that the young helper at the hostel had pointed her. Argyll Street appeared out of the mist, and, as at the men's hostel, a number of women were milling aimlessly around the entrance. She regarded them carefully. Shuffling away slowly was an elderly woman pushing a shopping trolley ahead of her. Quickening her pace, Jo caught up with the woman and fell into step beside her.

"Hello," Jo said when the woman cast her a sideways glance, not really taking in her face. The woman dismissed her and carried on shuffling along. "I was wondering if you could help me?" Jo said, trying to ignore the fact that the woman was making a good job of ignoring her.

"Public loo is round the corner, cop shop two streets away." The woman waved her arm dismissively.

"I'm looking for someone."

"Then you want the cop shop."

"Would you look at this picture please?"

The elderly woman stopped, turning aggressively towards her. "Look..." she began, then her eyes found Jo's and she faltered, grabbing onto the younger woman as her world tilted.

"Are you all right?" Jo asked, as the colour drained from the woman's face. She took her arm and led her to a low wall, not letting go until the woman was settled on the cold damp stone. "Should I call someone?"

The woman shook her head. "Takes me like that sometimes," she said as she watched Jo retrieve her trolley and bring it to her. "You're looking for someone?"

Jo sat beside her on the wall and pulled out the photo, silently handing it to the woman. "Do you know her?"

The grey head nodded, and Jo noticed tears filling the old grey eyes. Unmindful of the damp grass, Jo knelt in front of the woman, gently pulling the photo from her hands. "What? You know her?"

"I did."

"What do you mean? Was she here?" Jo's heart was thundering in her chest. "D'you know where she is now?"

The old woman nodded, the tears now dripping from her chin. "Rocky died, about three weeks ago."

Jo couldn't remember driving home, but that's where she found herself. She felt out of breath, as though she'd run home rather than driven a top of the range Merk. She staggered out of the car after leaving it in the garage and made her way up the stairs into her house. She went into the lounge and poured herself a large whiskey. And then another. Cradling the glass in her hands, she slumped onto the sofa and reached into her pocket for the picture that had become her most treasured possession. It wasn't there.

The glass slipped from her fingers, its contents staining the carpet. She sobbed as the realisation hit her. She'd lost everything. Not just the picture, but the dream. This woman had invaded her dreams, her soul. And she'd not even been given the chance to know her. She had felt her calling to her. Why? Had she died alone, in pain?

"I don't believe in ghosts," Jo said out loud, as if to convince herself. She closed her eyes, picturing the gentle face. "And I don't believe you're dead." She gathered her coat and gloves again, and set out for the only link she had to the woman in the picture. This time the old woman (Don't know her name yet) would tell her the truth.

Chapter
5

Jo began to doubt the wisdom of her foray into the realm of the homeless when she was asked to buy a "Big Issue" for the fifth time. The magazine was printed and distributed to those with no other means of earning money in an effort to cut down on begging in London and all over the country.

The people she found beneath the railway arches waved soggy copies of the magazine at her as she stepped over the debris that they left. Her jeans were now splashed with the muddy water that the people who called this dank place home seemed to accept without question. As she scanned the faces for one of the two people she was seeking, she found an emptiness that seemed to duplicate itself in every face she saw. It was despair and helplessness which led to hopelessness. In many of the faces she saw defeat, a final acceptance of their plight. It had been the same in the gallery when she first viewed the pictures. Empty eyes. And that was the reason the photograph of Rocky had affected her so completely. The eyes held life and pride. There was no illusion of defeat there, only challenge. And Jo wanted to take the girl up on that challenge, wanted to see beyond the grime and the stigma, wanted to know the woman.

And that want, that need brought her to a part of London she barely knew existed.

It was only a few minutes from the hostel where she had first encountered the old woman, and it was as good a place as any to begin her search. She spotted the shopping trolley first, though it was by no means the only one there. The woman was rummaging furiously through the contents of the wire basket of the trolley.

"Hello again," Jo said, her eyes flitting from the woman to a couple of men who were approaching from her right.

The grey head rose and the equally grey eyes took in the smartly dressed, aristocratic form. The woman looked past Jo at the two men and, with a flick of her hand, sent them on their way.

"They're scared of you?" Jo asked, a look of amusement on her face.

"Probably," she turned back to her trolley. "What do you want now?"

Jo folded her arms across her chest. "I want to know why you lied to me."

"About Rocky?"

Jo nodded. "I don't believe she's dead."

The old woman nodded towards a couple of tyres and sat on one, waiting for Jo to join her. "It's cold," the old woman said as Jo eased herself down onto the dirty tyre.

"Coldest winter for over fifty years," Jo agreed, wondering why they were carrying on this ridiculous conversation.

"My name's Edna." The old woman thrust a dirty, withered hand towards Jo and was surprised when the younger woman took it without reservation.

"Jo," the younger woman said simply.

Edna held onto the hand, feeling the strength there. "You have strong hands."

"From my father, I think."

Edna nodded and released the hand. "Your colouring comes from your mother. She's not English."

"That's right. She has Greek parentage, but was born in England." Jo was running on automatic, her upbringing forcing her politeness.

Another nod from the grey head. "I didn't lie to you about Rocky, only about when she died."

Jo was sure there was a serpent in her chest, squeezing the life from her heart, as it pounded, making her head throb in unison. "She's not..."

"Oh, she is dead," the old woman said. "Died just over five years ago."

"No, I saw the picture. It was taken a couple of months ago."

"You saw what is left. It's just a shell. Rocky is dead."

Two pairs of pale eyes held each other for a long moment as the younger woman took in what she was hearing. Then the dark head began to shake slowly. "No, I saw something. I saw..."

"Nothing. There is nothing. She arrived here five years ago. Too young to claim benefit. Terrified of being sent back."

"Back where?" Jo ran a shaking hand through her damp hair.

"We don't ask. It's nobody's business. She was a child, and she was afraid. We helped her until she could help herself."

"Edna, how old was she?" Jo was shivering now, her leather jacket not enough to keep out the bitter cold.

"She was just fifteen, I think." Edna watched the angular face across from her, seeing the sorrow there.

"Jesus. Why?"

"We all have reasons for being here, Jo. What's yours?"

"I'm looking for Rocky." The answer came to Jo's lips easily. It was simple.

"And you don't know why, do you?"

Jo pulled the collar of the jacket up, her hands holding it tightly beneath her chin. "Can you tell me?" she whispered.

Edna seemed to ignore the question. "Why did you come here?" she waved her hand. "Why this place exactly?"

"I was trying to find you." Jo looked puzzled.

"But why Whitechapel, why outside the hostels?"

"DeBurgh said—"

Edna stood so quickly Jo almost fell off the tyre she was sitting on. "Don't say that bastard's name in my presence." She paced in a small circle. "This is what she was scared of. This is..." She looked back down at the stunned woman, who still sat close to the ground. "I'm sorry." Edna returned to her seat beside Jo.

"So am I. I don't know much about..." Jo was obviously trying to find a word that wouldn't insult the elderly woman.

"The homeless? Displaced? We have many names, most of them not good."

"I'm not here to judge you, Edna. Just to find Rocky."

Edna nodded. "So you are. And as I said before, why here?"

"And I already told you, because—"

"Because you heard the word Whitechapel. Yes, I know. But it goes beyond that, Jo. You are here to find a woman you've never met, never knew existed before yesterday. And you're confused as to why."

Two perfect eyebrows knitted, as Jo's brow furrowed. "Who are you, Edna?"

"You're not stupid, are you, Jo?"

"I like to think not."

Edna's pale eyes caught the blue of Jo's and held them. "I was here when Rocky arrived, and I was here when you did."

"And?" Jo squirmed on the cold tyre, trying hard to understand the woman's cryptic answers.

"And I believe it was meant to be."

"What are you saying, Edna? I don't understand."

"I believe that Rocky has been waiting for you. That's what drew her here."

Now it was Jo's turn to stand and pace. "And you're saying that she's been waiting for me to turn up? Without appearing to be rude, Edna, that's a crock of shit." She walked a few paces away, and then crossed her arms and bent her head. Feeling suddenly tired, she kept her back to the still seated woman. "I saw her picture in a gallery. For some reason I feel compelled to find her." Jo shrugged, hugging herself tightly against the cold breeze. "I don't know, maybe I'm going crazy."

"Not many of us get the chance to find the other half of our souls." Edna waited, watching the woman turn slowly towards her. "You have an ancient soul, Jo. It needs the other half to be fulfilled."

Jo was backing away from her now. "I don't believe this crap."

"Believe it or not, Jo. I see in you something you have kept buried for many years, for centuries in fact." Edna stood and approached the retreating woman. "Let it have its voice."

"Jesus, you're crazy," Jo said as she backed up against a wall.

Edna smiled a gentle smile. "Maybe. Many have called me that. But Rocky never did."

The girl's name seemed to calm Jo somewhat. "Where is she?"

"Not far, we can go there now."

"Now?"

"Of course, come on." Edna turned abruptly and started picking a way through the debris and bodies that littered the alleyway, making a path for her shopping trolley.

Chapter
6

For over fifteen minutes Jo had stood "guarding" Edna's shopping trolley. A number of people had passed her, curious as to why a decently dressed young woman should be there with what appeared to be her worldly possessions in a wheeled supermarket trolley. But the old woman had asked her to watch it, and watch it she would.

Edna had left her near a small park, deserted in the cold winter morning. There was very little in the park, which was ringed by bushes that hid metal railings. A couple of trees stood to one end, a flowerbed to the other. Between the two trees was a picnic table, next to that a waste bin.

Jo looked down at the trolley, full to overflowing with plastic bags, and wondered how this woman survived like this. Would she be able to? She thought not. She sat on the bench that was beside a bus stop, pulling the trolley closer to her. She wished now that she'd chosen something warmer to wear. She had a sweatshirt on under her leather jacket, but it was proving inadequate against the extremely cold weather. Her thoughts strayed to Rocky. Where had she slept the night before? Where had she woken up this morning? Where would she sleep tonight? If she found her, what then?

Harry's words echoed in her head. *Hi, I'm Jo, and I want to take you home*, or words to that effect. So what would she say when she saw her? What if Edna came back alone? What if she refused to see her? A hand on her shoulder shook her out of her rapidly building panic, and she jumped at the contact.

"Hey," Edna took a step back, "it's only me."

Jo stood, looking past the woman. "Is she here?"

Edna shook her head. "No, but she'll come in a while."

"What is it? What's the matter?" Jo was shivering now, blowing her warm breath onto cupped hands.

"Nothing's the matter." She reached out a hand and rested it comfortingly on the younger woman's forearm. "She's just taking her time." Edna pulled back her arm, watching as Jo surveyed the street. She pointed towards the small park. "She'll meet you there."

Jo followed Edna's gaze. "In the park? Is it safe?"

"This time of year, yes. Too cold for your average rapist."

Jo looked doubtfully at her.

"It's safe, Jo. I have a couple of friends watching it, too." Edna took possession of her trolley. "I have to go try to get some breakfast. You wait here."

The old woman began to shuffle away, but Jo took a gentle hold of her arm. "Thank you," Jo said, her voice breaking.

Edna merely nodded and walked away, never looking back.

Jo made her way to the picnic table in the park and sat on the damp wood, swinging one leg across and straddling the narrow bench. Resting her elbow on the table, she massaged her forehead, trying to quell the headache that was beginning. She couldn't feel her feet now. Cowboy boots were great to look at but didn't keep out the cold. But then she'd never needed to before. Where did she go that was cold? She went from her house to her car. From her car to a restaurant. From a restaurant to a club. Then back to the car. She didn't walk anywhere that she could take her car. Suddenly the lack of sleep in the past forty-eight hours seemed to catch up with her. She bent her head forward to rest on her forearm.

"What do you want?" The voice was low, soft. There was a hint of anger in it.

Jo raised her head and found herself pinned by green eyes. "Rocky?" she asked.

The girl said nothing, standing about five feet from the table, still on the stone path that bisected the park.

Jo stood abruptly, causing the girl to stiffen.

The blonde girl seemed to be weighed down by the amount of clothing she was wearing. The trousers Jo could see were khaki, but they seemed to be only the top layer. They were too long, but she could just see roughened boots peeking from beneath the

hems. Her jacket was also khaki and was also huge, the sleeves
turned up a few times, and even then her gloved hands were all but
hidden. On her head she wore a hat. The kind that possessed flaps
that could be let down to cover the ears, which they had been. The
small leather ties that would be used to tie the earflaps on top of
her head hung loosely against her shoulders. Her blonde hair
peeked out from beneath the hat, and once again it seemed to tangle with her eyelashes. At her feet were a couple of large bags, her
hands never left the long carrying straps.

Jo started to walk around the table. As she did so, Rocky bent
and took a hold of the shorter straps on the bags, picked them up
and took a step back. The taller woman raised her hands and
slowed her advance.

"It's okay," Jo said. "I just want to talk."

Rocky said nothing, maintaining the same wary attitude.

Seeing that the girl was skittish, Jo went back to her seat.
"Would you join me?" she asked, nodding to the bench on the
other side of the table.

Rocky advanced slowly, her eyes never quite meeting those of
the other woman. She stopped when her knees hit the bench but
remained standing. "Are you with the police?"

That was unexpected. "No, I'm not." Jo ducked her head, trying to get eye contact with the blonde.

"Did my uncle send you?" The girl was looking around, her
eyes never seeming to connect with those of the taller woman.

"No, I don't know your uncle." Jo watched her, staying very
still, not wanting to frighten the obviously nervous girl away.

Then, suddenly, the pale green eyes were fixed firmly on her
own. "So what do you want?"

Jo suddenly realised she wasn't really sure.

The girl sat cautiously but didn't put her legs right over the
bench. She sat sideways, one arm resting on the damp wood of the
table, the other still keeping a grip on her bags.

"I saw your picture." Jo immediately regretted the statement
when she saw the anger wash over the face of Rocky.

"DeBurgh," Rocky said simply and stood again, her back to
Jo. "I thought I got away from him." She turned backed to the
stunned woman. "Where did you see the picture?"

Jo managed to snap herself out of her haze. "My mother's gallery."

"Not in a paper or anything like that?"

"No." Jo was quiet as she watched the blonde process the information.

"What kind of people would have seen that?"

Jo had had enough of this line of questioning. "What are you afraid of?"

The question seemed to affect Rocky like a physical blow, but she quickly gathered herself. "Nothing. I just want to know why you were looking for me."

"Are you hiding from someone?" Jo persisted.

Rocky gathered her bags and turned away from Jo. "I have to go."

Jo sprang from the bench and ran to catch up with the rapidly walking woman. "Please." She reached out and caught Rocky by the shoulder, turning her to face her. Now that she was up close, she could see the pain in the green eyes, and for a moment she was breathless. This time the eyes did not leave her own, but she could feel the small body trembling. "I'm not going to hurt you," she whispered. "I just want to talk to you."

"About what?"

Jo let her hand fall slowly away from Rocky's shoulder, trusting the girl not to bolt again. "Whatever you like."

"Is this some kind of bet?"

Jo was confused, as the lines on her brow showed. "What?"

"Did your friends put you up to this?"

Jo shook her head. She knew now she had to tell Rocky the truth. "Yesterday I saw your picture at Mother's gallery. I don't know why, but it had a dramatic effect on me. I fainted." Jo chuckled, but her mirth was not echoed in the face of the smaller blonde. The smile left her face quickly. "Anyway, I had the sudden compulsion to find you. I'm not sure why, but the desire to go out and search for you was overwhelming. I went to see DeBurgh..." At the mention of the man's name, Rocky turned away from Jo. "I know he hunted you. He told me. I'm sorry." Again she reached out to the girl and laid her hand on her shoulder.

Jo saw the small form in front of her relax, and then the blonde head shook gently. "I told him no. Why couldn't he take no for an answer?" She reached up and took the hat off, her blonde hair standing on end in its wake. Ruffling her hair with her free hand, she turned back towards the tall woman. "Edna says I should listen to you. I wouldn't be here otherwise."

"Then I have a lot to thank Edna for." Jo graced her with her most dazzling smile. It wasn't returned, however.

"So why do you think you needed to find me?"

Jo considered this. Should she tell the blonde of her attraction towards other women? Her attraction in particular to petite blondes? She stuffed her hands into her pockets. "Believe me, I've been asking myself the same question. I had to come here, for my own sanity as much as anything else."

"You think you're going mad then?" Rocky pulled the hat down onto her head again, pushing aside the hair that was forced into her eyes by doing so.

Jo nodded. "This time yesterday, my life was normal. All I did was to look at a picture in a gallery."

Rocky bent and picked up her bags. "I have to go."

"What?" Jo took a step forward, stopping quickly when the girl flinched and backed away from her. "Can I...can I see you again?"

Rocky shrugged. "Not sure. Can't imagine you being a regular down here."

"Well, if I come down, will you meet with me again?" Jo's voice was taking on a hint of panic.

"I don't know what you want from me," Rocky said quietly.

Jo saw fear in the green eyes, and a stab of guilt pierced her chest. She had put that fear there. "Just to be your friend." Jo maintained the distance between them, and there was a long silent moment, heavy with tension. As Rocky stood silently, Jo made the decision for them both. "I'll be back here this afternoon at 3. Will you meet me here?"

Taking a firmer grip on the straps of her bag, Rocky hoisted one over her shoulder. "Don't know if I'm free." She turned her back on the tall woman. "Don't count on it," she said as she walked out of the park.

Jo watched her walk away, grinning from ear to ear. "I think she likes me," she said to a pigeon, which had alighted on the picnic table.

Jo was inordinately pleased to find her Merk untouched when she returned to it. She got in and quickly started it, making sure the heat was turned up full. But instead of driving away immediately, she sat back in the plush leather seat, her hands resting lightly on the steering wheel.

So I've met her. She was cute, even cuter than her picture. I know she exists, but I knew that anyway. Didn't I? Why was I so sure? She spoke to me. What did she say? Nothing. She told me nothing. We talked about nothing. But we did talk. Didn't we? She's scared. Scared of being found. Scared of me? I hope not. She'll come back later. I know she will. I'll find out more about her then.

Jesus, what am I doing?

With a shake of her head, Jo shifted the Merk into gear and drove away, her freezing feet managing to obey the signals her brain was giving them.

It was nearly 3.30 and actually starting to snow lightly. Jo was a little better dressed this time, having spent the hours since her meeting with Rocky shopping. It was near to Christmas, hence more shops than usual were open on the cold Sunday afternoon. She'd found herself buying two of everything: thermal socks, shirts, and gloves. She bought a pair of arctic proof boots, and a silly hat similar to Rocky's.

So there she sat, in the rapidly failing daylight. The sky was overcast, a gentle snow falling through the bare branches of the trees. On the bench beside her sat a box, her hand resting on its surface. Jo felt more comfortable in the warmer clothes she now wore, but still wondered how people could survive in these severe temperatures. Her cheeks glowed red, and her eyes watered. She heard the muffled sound of her cell phone and fumbled in her pocket for it. She had some difficulty getting a hold of it with the thick gloves she was wearing.

She looked at the caller id on the display and rolled her eyes. "Hi, Trixie."

"Jojo, baby. Where are you?"

"Um, would you believe sitting in a park somewhere in Whitechapel?"

"Jojo?"

"It's difficult to explain."

"I missed you last night."

"Yeah, well."

"Will you be there tonight?"

"Probably not."

"Jojo!"

"I didn't make any promises, Trix."

"You've never missed a Sunday night yet. What's going on?"

"Nothing that I have to explain to you, Trix. Now, I have to go. I'll call you when I can." Jo snapped the cell phone shut, ending the call. She looked at the device in her hand, and after a moment's debate dialled a stored number. "Harry?"

"Hi, Jo."

"Are you okay?"

"Yeah, I'm fine."

"I'm sorry about yesterday."

"Me too." A pause. "So what are you doing?"

Jo considered the question for a moment. Then decided to answer truthfully. "I'm sitting, freezing my rear end to a park bench, and probably being stood up." Nothing but silence was forthcoming from Jo's phone. "Well, aren't you going to say 'told you so'?"

"No, not my style, Jo. You should know that by now... So you haven't found her yet."

"Oh yes, I found her. We arranged to meet here at 3."

"And?"

"And what?"

"Jesus Christ, Jo! What the hell's she like?"

"Um, I only spoke with her for a short while."

"So, she can speak?"

"Of course she can speak."

"What does she look like? Well, I mean, I know what she looks like, but...well, you know what I mean."

"She's gorgeous." The words were out of Jo's mouth before she realised.

"So where is she from?"

"I don't know."

"Okay. Where does she stay?"

"Um, don't know."

"So what do you know about her?"

"Nothing." Jo absentmindedly shut the phone, cutting off the connection. She glanced at her watch. It was nearly 4. The light was fading. And she came to the conclusion that, for the first time in her life, she had been stood up.

Chapter
7

Jo glanced at her watch again—nearly 4.20, and it was just about dark already. She sighed dramatically, watching the cloud as her warm breath hit the frigid air, disturbing a few snowflakes as they floated gently towards her. She looked to her right, to the box that sat on the bench beside her. Shrugging her shoulders, she left it where it was and unfolded herself from the cold seat, swinging her legs stiffly over and stamping her feet on the ground. Jo took a few slow steps towards the small gate at the entrance to the park. After taking one last glance back at the picnic table and bench, she left. Almost immediately, she stopped just beyond the high hedge that surrounded the small green.

Rocky was sitting on the low wall into which the metal railings were set. Her elbows rested on her knees, and she was staring at the ground between her scruffy boots.

"How long have you been here?" Jo asked, a little more sharply than she intended.

The girl's head didn't move. "About half an hour," the girl replied. "Can't be sure though."

"Why didn't you come into the park? I've been freezing my arse off waiting for you."

Rocky looked up, her green eyes finding those of the woman towering over her and immediately looking away. "I'm sorry," she said quietly, returning to contemplating the ground beneath her feet.

"Hey," Jo said, gently. "Look at me."

It took a few moments, but the blonde finally looked up. And she found the taller woman was offering her hand. She watched her own, gloved hand reach for the larger one, and then it was enveloped by a warmth she could feel even through the two pairs of gloves that she wore. She was gently pulled to her feet.

"Look, I'm frozen—" Jo began.

"I'm sorry," Rocky said.

From the look on the girl's face, Jo could tell she truly was sorry. "Yeah well, my car isn't far. Can we go and sit there?" She saw the fear in the girl's eyes as the blonde head jerked up and Rocky took a step back. Jo put her hands up, trying to slow the rapidly retreating woman. "Hey, I just want to warm up, nothing else."

"I haven't...I don't..." Rocky was still backing away.

"I just want to talk with you, nothing else." She stopped and looked back into the darkened park. "I have something back there. Will you wait while I get it?"

Rocky had stopped. She was standing and watching the tall woman, her arms wrapped about her small body against the cold.

"Will you wait?" Jo asked again. Rocky nodded. Jo rushed back into the darkened park, leaning over the picnic table and retrieving the parcel. Rocky was standing where Jo had left her when she returned. "I have some bits in here," Jo said, nodding towards the box in her arms. "Come on." Jo turned away from the smaller woman and started striding purposefully towards the side street in which she had left her car. She glanced back to see if Rocky was following and smiled a small smile when she saw that the blonde was, albeit at a slower pace.

"Here we are," Jo said, putting the box on the ground and rummaging in her pockets for her keys. "I'm going to get one of those things that you whistle at," she said as she transferred her search from her jeans' pockets to her jacket pockets. "Ah, there we go." She unlocked the car and reached through to put the box on the ground. Then she opened up the passenger door and turned towards Rocky. "We can be a little warmer in here."

Rocky gazed into the car and then at the woman beside her. "I'm not..."

"Hey." Jo took a step towards Rocky and placed a gentle hand on her shoulder. "That's fine, you stay here if you'd rather." She released Rocky, pleased to see that she didn't shrink away from her touch this time, and then sat down on the passenger side of the car, her legs still outside. Almost lying backwards across the seats, she managed to get the key into the ignition and started the car up, turning the heating controls onto high.

"I'm freezing. Don't know about you." Jo smiled, leaning down and opening the box. "I have some flasks of hot drinks. Tea and coffee, which do you prefer?"

Rocky was shifting from foot to foot. "Um, tea...please."

"Okay." Jo took out the silver flask and poured some of the steaming liquid into a china mug. "I never could drink tea out of plastic," she said as she handed Rocky the mug. "There's milk and sugar in the box. Didn't know how you'd take your tea."

"I don't get the choice very often," Rocky said as she crouched down and added milk and sugar to her tea.

"I'm sorry?" Jo was pouring herself a mug of coffee.

"I usually get my hot drinks in plastic or polystyrene."

Jo looked up at the girl standing above her and found Rocky staring at her. "What?"

"Why are you here?"

"I told you before, I don't really know."

"What do you want from me?"

"Would you believe nothing?" Jo cupped her hands around the warm mug, and watched as Rocky blew gently on her hot drink.

Rocky began to walk around the car, her oversize boots scuffing the ground as she went. She appeared in front of the car, her form barely visible through the misty windscreen. "What type of car is this?"

"It's a Mercedes CLK 320."

Rocky nodded. "What size engine?"

"Um, no idea. I just get in it and drive it. It goes fast, that's all I know."

Rocky walked back around to the open passenger door. "What do you do? For a living, I mean."

"Ah, well," Jo shifted uncomfortably in the seat. "I don't work."

"You don't?"

Jo shook her head. "No. I may some day, but for now I don't."

"So how do you survive?" Rocky bent at the waist and placed her mug back in the box.

"My parents." Jo couldn't look up at her. She'd never felt ashamed of her wealth and her lifestyle before. Why now?

"I have to go," Rocky said. "Edna's watching my stuff."

Jo nodded, suddenly feeling deflated and foolish. "I'll come back tomorrow."

"Why?" Rocky asked. "Why don't you just go back to your world and forget about me? Whatever it is you think you're looking for isn't here. Find another cause to ease your conscience."

"Is that what you think I'm doing?" Jo stood, throwing the mug into the box with a clatter. "Trying to ease my conscience because I'm some sort of rich bitch?"

Rocky shrugged. "We've seen it before. They come down here, do a few soup runs, and think they've done their bit. If you want to help, put some money in the poor box sometime. There are folks worse off than me." Rocky turned away from her and started walking. She looked back as she walked away. "Go home, Jo."

Jo watched her walk away, watched her thrust her hands into her pockets as she ambled along the road. Just as the blonde turned the corner, she glanced back at the dark haired woman, and Jo was sure she saw something in the green eyes.

"She feels it too," she said to herself and eased herself out of the car. She placed the box on the seat and walked around the car, getting into the driver's side. The car had warmed up nicely in the time she'd been sitting there, so she shifted it into gear and headed home.

When Jo arrived at her small house, she immediately noticed a light on in the lounge. She parked the car in the garage and made her way up the stairs. Just inside the door, she noticed the leather jacket hanging on the stair rail.

"Trix?" she called out, walking into the lounge.

"Were you expecting someone else, Jojo?"

Beatrice James, Trixie to her friends, was draped across Jo's sofa, wearing Jo's bathrobe and a smile. She pushed bleached blonde hair back from an angular face and stood to meet the dark woman half way. "I've been waiting for you, Jojo."

"So I see," Jo said, seeing the half-empty whisky glass on the coffee table.

Trixie snaked her arms around Jo's neck, pulling her down. "I missed you last night," she said and captured soft lips with her own. Maintaining the contact, she brought her hands between them and started to unzip Jo's jacket. Once it was undone, she pushed it back off the tall woman's shoulders. "And I think you missed me."

Jo hesitated for a heartbeat and then pulled the woman against her body, crushing the blonde's lips with her own.

"Oh yeah," Trixie breathed into Jo's mouth, unfastening her jeans and pulling down the fly. "I've got what you want," she husked, as she slipped her hand into the taller woman's jeans and past her underwear. Jo gasped as slim fingers delved into the liquid heat between her legs and allowed herself to be pushed back onto the sofa.

Trixie pulled her hand free and used both hands to pull the sweatshirt off the body she was straddling, making short work of the bra beneath that. "You need this," Trixie whispered, as she dipped her head and took as much of Jo's breast into her mouth as she could, then caught a taut nipple between her teeth. "You need me." The blonde hooked her fingers into the waistband of Jo's jeans and drew them down across her hips, though the dark woman's boots prevented them from being removed altogether. "Tell me what you want, Jo." Trixie sat back, still straddling Jo's hips, her hands fluttering across aroused breasts, then moving downwards.

Jo's hips shot up off the sofa as Trixie's fingers arrived at their destination. "Oh yeah. This is what you want, isn't it?" She watched the woman beneath her through hooded eyes, knowing the power she held. "Tell me what you want, Jo," she said as her fingers stroked the other woman towards release.

"Fuck me," rasped the dark woman, knowing she could no more deny her body this than she could air. Then she reached up and tangled her hands in the blonde hair, pulling the woman's head down to where she needed it most.

It was later—how much later, Jo wasn't sure. She was lying face down on her bed. Beside her, Trixie amused herself by running her hand gently across Jo's back, sometimes dipping down to trace the contours of her hips and buttocks. Jo stared at the wall a few feet from her bed, her mind in another place, certainly not in the room with the blonde. She felt a hand delve into the wetness between her legs.

"Don't," she said, never raising her head.

"Come on, Jojo," Trixie said, not ceasing her stroking.

Without turning her head to look at the woman, Jo growled, "If you don't stop that now, Trix, I'm going to break your fucking wrist."

Maybe it was the low and menacing voice, or maybe the pent up fury she felt in the body beneath her hands, but Trixie wisely removed her hand. "Jojo?"

"Don't 'Jojo' me, Trix." Jo turned onto her back and then swivelled and sat on the edge of the bed.

"You can't tell me you didn't enjoy it, Jo." Trixie placed her hand on Jo's shoulder, rubbing in small gentle circles on the soft, slick skin.

"I don't want to do this anymore." Jo's voice was little more than a whisper, and she shrugged away from the woman's touch. She felt the blonde get off the bed and heard her walk out of the bedroom and down the stairs to the lounge. After a few moments, Trixie appeared in the bedroom again. Jo hadn't moved.

"Call me when you need me," Trixie said from the doorway, doing up the buttons of her blouse.

"Don't hold your breath." Jo didn't look up, her knuckles whitening as she balled the sheet beneath her in her hands.

Trixie took a slow walk towards the naked woman. She raised Jo's face and gazed down into blue eyes turned grey in the darkness. "You've never been able to say no to me, Jo. Don't start trying to now. I'll see you around." She bent and kissed Jo, taking her bottom lip between her teeth and biting down.

Jo pulled away and raised a hand to her mouth, feeling the sting of a small cut and tasting the metallic tang of blood. Trixie laughed and walked out of the bedroom and out of the house.

Jo was furious. She stood and pulled the sheet with the evidence of her weakness from the bed, throwing it into a corner of the room. Then she staggered to the bathroom. Reaching into the shower stall, she turned the water on and stepped into the cleansing spray, sliding down the wall to sit on the floor of the shower. It was only the water running cold that forced the tall woman out of the shower. She returned to the bedroom, grabbing a large towel from a cupboard as she passed it. She lay on the sheetless mattress, pulling the quilt up around her shivering body.

"Oh God, Rocky. What have I done?" She sobbed into the pillow.

Jo had fallen into a fitful sleep, and it was only the persistent ringing of her doorbell that awakened her. She pulled the towel around her still trembling body and made her way down the stairs to the hallway and to the intercom.

"Yeah?" Her voice sounded broken to her own ears, and she cleared her throat and tried again. "Yeah?" she said again, louder this time.

"Harry," was the short reply.

Jo pushed the button next to the intercom to admit her friend and went back up to her bedroom to retrieve her robe. By the time she'd found it and returned to the lounge, Harry was sitting in the chair.

"Well, aren't I the popular one this evening?" She glanced at the clock. It was a little after 9 p.m.

"You look like shit, Jo," Harry said, standing and closing the space between her and her friend. She raised a hand and gently touched Jo's bottom lip, tracing the small cut there. "Who did this?"

Jo shook her head. "Doesn't matter."

"If you say so." Harry shrugged and returned to her seat.

Jo collapsed on the sofa and rubbed her temples with shaking fingers.

"You want to talk about it?" Harry asked.

"No...yes," a big sigh, "I don't know."

"Did the girl show up?"

"In the park? Yes, she did." Jo leaned forward and turned up the heating on the artificial flame fire.

"So...are you going to tell me what happened here tonight?"

Jo pushed herself back into a corner of the sofa, tucking herself into as small a ball as possible. "Nothing happened."

"Strange, I was just in the club. Trixie was there."

Jo closed her eyes.

"She gave you that split lip, didn't she?"

Jo nodded and opened her eyes to see Harry moving towards her and sitting beside her on the sofa.

"Come here," Harry said. She gathered the shaking woman into her arms as Jo crawled towards her. "She uses you," Harry said into dark silken hair.

"I use her too," whispered Jo. "I have no excuse."

"Since when did you need an excuse, Jo? You've used anyone who took your fancy." Harry felt the woman in her arms stiffen. "You know it's true."

The dark head nodded against her chest. "I know."

Harry barely heard her friend's answer. "So why is it different tonight?" Harry asked.

Jo shrugged.

"Come on, Jo. Talk to me." Harry gave her friend a little shake.

"Tonight I felt ashamed," Jo said finally.

"D'you think it has anything to do with Rocky?"

"Maybe."

"Would you like to have a relationship with Rocky?" There was silence from the dark woman. "Jo?" Harry tried to push the larger woman away from her so that she could see into her face. "Jo, look at me." The blue eyes wouldn't meet her own, and once again Harry took Jo's shoulders in her hands and gave her a shake. "Jo? What is it about this girl? Do you know yet?"

Jo shook her head. "I've never felt ashamed before. And tonight I felt both ashamed and dirty. I hated Trix for the power she held over me tonight. I couldn't stop her. I couldn't stop myself. I wanted what she was giving me, and, for a while, it felt good. I'm scared, Harry."

"Jesus, Jo. You've never been scared of anything."

"I'm scared I'll always be like this. I'm scared I'll always need people like Trix. People who want me just for another fuck, want a body, any body. Trix never wanted me. I could have been anyone. I was just always available. I can't—" Jo's voice broke, and she buried her face in Harry's chest once more. "I'm scared, Harry," she said again between sobs.

"Don't be scared, Jo. You'll find a way out of this. And I have a feeling you won't be alone when you do find your way."

Jo raised her head and regarded her friend with bloodshot eyes.

Harry smiled at her. "I hope Rocky realises the change she's made in you."

"Change?"

"Yeah. You've started to turn the corner, Jo. You're too good for parasites like Trix. You're my best friend, Jo. But I have to tell you, the way you've been living your life can't go on. If finding Rocky changes who you are, then I'm glad."

"I felt like I was betraying her," Jo said, obviously surprised at the revelation.

"You felt like you were betraying someone who isn't even

your lover?"

"Not even a friend yet."

"But you'd like her to be your friend."

Jo shook her head in wonderment. "I feel as if I desperately need her to like me, to accept me. And I feel I need to be a different person for her."

"I don't think you need to be anyone but yourself. I like the person you are, I just don't really like the person that needs the Trixes of this world."

"Do you think Rocky would want to know the woman who came home and found Trix here?"

"Probably not. But only you can determine whether that person is gone for good now."

"I want her to be. But what if she's still here?"

"Then you have to control her. You have to push her back down when she wants her way." She watched her friend contemplate what she was saying. "It's up to you, Jo. Do you think you can change?"

"I have to."

Chapter
8

It was Monday morning and, for most, the beginning of another week. But for Lady Joanna Holbrook-Sutherland it was just another day. True, weekends were more memorable, but Joanna's days all started very much the same. Rising in the late morning, if not early afternoon. Then, after showering and dressing, she'd most likely leave to meet with one of her myriad of friends for a liquid lunch.

Jo was asleep—hardly surprising as it was only a little after 8am. She and Harry had talked long into the night. Harry had coaxed out of her the events following her return to the house after her last meeting with Rocky. She had tried hard to understand Jo's inability to resist what Trixie had offered. She'd listened to her friend's tense whispered voice as she tended to the scratches across Jo's shoulders.

"She did this to you?" Harry had asked as she spread an antiseptic cream across the worst of the marks.

Jo nodded, her face buried in the quilt. "She's very physical, likes it rough." Her breath hissed through her teeth as Harry examined what looked like half-crescent punctures in her shoulder.

"Sorry." Harry reached again for the tube of cream and squeezed some directly onto the wounds, rubbing it in with gentle fingers.

"No, I should be sorry." Jo's voice was barely heard, muffled against the quilt.

Harry's fingers stilled and rested lightly on Jo's back. "I'm still your friend, Jo. Your best friend. Right?"

Jo turned her head to look up at the blonde who was kneeling on the bed beside her. "I was beginning to wonder, after the other night. I wasn't thinking about you. I didn't realise—"

"Exactly. My fault too. Jealousy is an ugly thing." She rested back on her heels, taking a towel and wiping the cream from her hands. "I was jealous. But I don't want to lose you as a friend."

"Me neither," Jo said. Reaching out, she curled her hand around Harry's smaller one.

Harry crept into Jo's room and raised the blind a little, allowing some of the grey light into the room. Jo was asleep, lying on her stomach, the quilt covering her up to her shoulders. When Jo asked Harry to stay the night after their talking had gone on beyond 2am, Harry decided to stay in the guestroom. The look on Jo's face almost changed the blonde's mind. But she kept her resolve, walked up to her friend, placed a kiss on her cheek, and left her on her bed. Which was where she found her the next morning. She reached over and gently shook the sleeping woman's shoulder, noticing the dark shadows beneath Jo's closed eyes.

"Hey there." Harry smiled as the blue eyes fluttered open.

"Harry?"

"Yeah. You expecting someone else?"

"What time is it?"

"Time I was going. I have to go home first to change. I'll be late for work if I'm not careful." She eased herself down onto the edge of the bed and watched as Jo gingerly turned onto her back, pulling the quilt around her against the cold. "I just went down and turned the heating on. You don't have it set to come on yet."

"I'm not usually conscious yet, let alone up." She squinted up at the blonde. "Thanks for last night."

"Anytime, you know that."

"Yeah I know." Again she squeezed her friend's hand. "Anyway, your Dad's your boss. You won't get into trouble."

"You wanna bet?" Harry stood and walked towards the door, but turned before leaving. "Take care."

Jo nodded, smiling. "I will."

Jo snuggled down into the quilt, listening to the sound of her friend as she let herself out of the house. Then she heard a car door slam and the car itself pull away. Obviously Harry had called a taxi to take her home to change. Jo pushed the quilt away and swung her legs out of the bed. The cold hit her warm body, and she quickly picked up her robe from the floor, wrapping it around herself against the chill.

She padded downstairs to the lounge, smiling when she saw that Harry had turned on the fire in the lounge. She sat in front of it, warming her hands, and immediately her thoughts went to the blonde that had occupied her dreams the night before. *Would she have a fire to warm her hands on this morning? Would she be able to go to a kitchen and make herself a hot drink?* Jo sat heavily on the sofa, watching the artificial flames. She imagined the girl here with her, sitting in the warm comfort of her home. She imagined holding her as she slept, combing soft hair with her fingers. She imagined waking her with a gentle kiss, and then watching sleepy green eyes find hers and smile in recognition.

But how could that be? Jo's thoughts returned to the previous night, to her inability to resist Trixie. She remembered the feel of the woman's hands on her body and the feel of Trixie's breasts beneath her own hands. Could she really run from the woman she had become? Would trying to ignore the needs she had only make them stronger? Harry's advice had been given without the knowledge of what it was like to have a physical need so great it could gnaw at her very being if it wasn't sated. What would happen the first time her need reared its ugly head in the presence of the small blonde who occupied her sleeping as well as waking thoughts? Jo shook her head and wound her hands in her own hair. What was she thinking here? She was contemplating changing her life for someone who had, so far, made it patently clear she wanted nothing to do with her.

"I'm going crazy," Jo said to herself. She thought of the willing bodies that pressed themselves into her in the many clubs that she frequented. Any one of them would gladly "help her relieve the tension," as she put it. So why was she now returning to her bedroom and dressing in a ridiculous amount of clothes to go out into a cold December day to look for someone who was not exactly reacting to her as she was used to? Is that what made this girl so irresistible? Because that's how Jo felt. As unable as she was to resist Trixie, she now felt she needed to find Rocky. And she knew she would have to put aside her notions of romance for the time being. *Romance? Did I really just think that?* Jo paused, boot in hand, her foot encased in a thermal sock. She still felt something compelling her to go out and find this girl and it wasn't a need to get her into her bed.

It was a need to protect.

The boot fell from Jo's hand, hitting the floor with a thump. Never before had she felt the desire to protect. Wasn't she the woman that mothers should protect their daughters from? So who was she going to protect Rocky from? Herself? Could she expose the nervous girl to the person she could be? The person that had slept with Trixie the previous night. Jo leaned forward, burying her head in her hands.

No, she couldn't.

It was just over an hour later that Jo found herself sitting in a traffic jam, watching the back of a bus. Once again her weak will was overcome by her desire. This time, however, it was her desire to get to know a certain small blonde, rather than her need of the baser actions of the flesh. She found herself bogged down in rush hour traffic made worse by the horrendous weather. Her wipers struggled with the mixture of rain and snow, and her demisters also struggled to keep the screen unfogged.

The parking space she'd used the day before was occupied, as were all the others in the vicinity. So she had to look further afield. Half an hour later, she was selecting a ridiculously expensive option and obtaining a 12-hour ticket from a machine in a multi-storey car park. She hefted the large bag she had stowed in the back of the car and made her way out into the foul weather for the longish trek to Whitechapel. The only place she could think of going to was the park, and it was there that she found herself a half-hour later. Her face was glowing from the cold as she entered the ornate gates, and she stopped dead in her tracks at the sight that greeted her.

Rocky was sitting on the bench, staring intently at the table-top in front of her.

"Hi," Jo said softly and eased herself onto the bench opposite the blonde.

Rocky looked up and stared long and hard into the blue eyes.

Feeling uneasy in the long silence that ensued, Jo started her banal chattering. "It's cold."

Rocky continued to stare.

"I brought some hot drinks again." She bent to retrieve the thermos from the bag. "And I have some other things too," she said, pulling a number of items out and placing them on the table. "I had them yesterday but forgot to give you them. This," Jo pushed a large rolled bundle towards Rocky, "is a sleeping bag. It's the sort they take up in the mountains." She looked for some reaction from the blonde, pleased when the green eyes flicked momentarily to the bag. "And I have thermal socks, vests, gloves, and longjohns."

The green eyes returned to hers. "I'm not stupid enough to turn this down. But I don't want you to buy me anything else." Rocky pulled the items towards her, looking annoyed at her own need of the things that Jo had bought her.

Jo was almost startled by the husky voice. Rocky sounded tired, and when she looked harder she could see dark rings beneath her eyes. "Okay," Jo said quietly and poured two mugs of steaming tea. "Glad the rain's gone off a bit." She handed Rocky a mug, waiting for the girl to pull off one of her thick gloves to take it from her. Then she put the milk and sugar on the table. "Would you let me get you just one other thing?"

Rocky looked up slowly.

"Would you let me buy you breakfast? You look all in."

Rocky laughed, and Jo took in the changes in the face opposite her. The small crease at the bridge of her nose, a flash of white teeth, and the sparkling green eyes. She decided she'd like to see more of that look.

"You going to take me to one of your haunts, then?" Rocky stood, her arms out at her sides. "I'm not exactly dressed for it."

Jo sighed. "I'll take you wherever you want. Do you know anywhere around here?"

Rocky folded her arms across her chest. "Why are you doing this, Jo?"

Jo cupped the warm mug in her hands. "I could ask the same of you. Why did you come here?"

The blonde turned her back on Jo, and it was a few tense moments before she turned back towards her. "I talked for a long time with Edna last night. I wouldn't be here if she didn't say it was for the best."

"And what did you talk about?"

Rocky looked past her, toward the entrance, and Jo turned to follow her gaze. Manoeuvring her trolley across the grass was the woman in question. Jo quickly stood and helped the old woman with her load. Rocky had the same idea but stopped when she saw

Jo reach Edna first.

"Have you two been here long?" she asked, accepting Rocky's untouched mug of tea.

"Not long," the blonde said, returning to her seat.

"So you haven't told her yet?"

While Rocky shot Edna a look that would have been fatal to many others, Jo turned in her seat and faced the woman. "Told me what?"

Edna looked towards the smaller woman, who nodded. "Ever since Rocky arrived on the streets of London she's been having dreams."

Jo looked towards the blonde who had, once again, found the surface of the table incredibly interesting. So she turned back to Edna. "So what occurred in these dreams?" She asked the question of Edna, assuming that Rocky had talked to her at length about them.

"Nothing much," she turned to Rocky. "Did it, Rocky?" Edna took a sip of tea. "No, it was more like a feeling. She'd get a feeling of warmth, of safety. Didn't you, dear?" She looked at Rocky, wanting her to tell her own story. Rocky merely nodded. "She's told me of her dreams on many occasions. I'm no dream reader, but I got the feeling that she drew comfort from the images."

"There were no images, just feelings."

Both Edna and Jo looked at the girl.

"The dreams would come on nights that I felt most alone. Like some sort of message." She shook her head. "It's hard to explain. I've had them ever since I arrived on the streets. They helped me to survive."

"Why—" Jo began, but Edna placed a hand on her knee.

"Why is she telling you this?" She turned to Rocky. "You tell her."

Rocky was silent for a moment. "Last night I had the dream."

"And?"

"And this time I saw you."

Edna couldn't remember the last time she saw a smile such as the one that graced the face of the woman sitting beside her. And she knew then that this woman had come for her friend and would keep her safe. Her job was done, she'd seen the girl survive through the hardest of times, and now she was a strong and independent young woman. From frightened child to adult. She had watched the change and was pleased with the end result. She was sad to see what was obviously the beginning of the end of their life together on the streets. Rocky had been a part of her life for almost five years but would soon be leaving. She knew that the girl herself didn't know that yet and would most probably resist the pull of the dark-haired, charismatic woman. But she knew destiny when she saw it, and this woman was Rocky's destiny. Now it was up to her to persuade her, to persuade both of them, of that fact.

"So I've never been in your dreams before?" Jo asked.

Rocky shook her head, looking up and finding blue eyes boring into her own. "No, but the feeling was the same."

"And you, Jo. Do you dream?" Edna asked the question, though she felt she already knew the answer.

"Not as a rule, no. But the other night..."

"The other night you dreamt of Rocky." It was not a question from the old woman.

"Yes, I did." Jo turned from the blonde to Edna. "But if Rocky has been dreaming of me for just about five years, why haven't I been dreaming of her?"

Edna patted her hand but looked across the table to the blonde. "This is my guess, but maybe Rocky has needed you for that long."

Rocky stood, a look of outrage on her face. "I don't need anyone, certainly not a spoilt, rich..."

"Bitch?" Jo offered.

The blonde paused in her tirade then calmed. She returned to her seat.

Beside Jo, Edna cleared her throat. "I have to go."

Rocky stood again, a look of something approaching panic on her face. She ran around the picnic table and blocked Edna's path to her shopping trolley. "Please, don't go yet."

Edna cupped a chilled cheek. "Rocky, you need to talk with this woman. Listen to what she has to say. Tell her of your dreams." She leaned forward and gave the blonde a kiss on the cheek. "And your nightmares."

"I'm not sure I can. I don't know her," Rocky whispered.

"But you do, sweetheart. You just don't realise that yet."

Edna waved away both women as they tried to help her navigate her way out of the park. With a brief glance at the two women still standing awkwardly beside the table, she left, a satisfied smile on her face.

Jo turned back towards Rocky and took a tentative step

towards her. "Would you let me help you?"

Rocky closed her eyes and took a deep breath. "A long time ago, I learned not to feel, not to hope. It was the only way to survive. To not want anything, then I wouldn't miss anything. And I've been fine for a while now. I've come to terms with what I don't have. Then you come along."

Jo ducked her head, seeing tears forcing themselves from between tightly shut eyelids. "And?" she coaxed.

"And you make me feel." She looked up into blue, the tears falling freely from her eyes. "You make me want. I can't survive wanting. Not out here."

"Then come back with me." Jo took a step towards her, reaching for her.

"No!" Rocky held up her hands, backing away. "Don't promise something you can't give."

"I won't promise anything, and I don't want promises from you. I'd just like to help you. Why won't you let me?"

"Because I've lost so much, and if I have nothing, then I can't lose anything." She lifted her gloved hands to her face and sobbed into them. The feel of hands on her shoulders made her look up again. "Please don't," she said as Jo pulled her towards her.

"Shh," whispered the taller woman, as she pulled the tense body against her own. She felt the resistance slowly dissipate, and the blonde head, hat and all, tucked itself beneath her chin. "There," she said, closing her eyes. "I don't understand it either." She felt the small body shaking in her arms and held on tighter. "I've got you," she whispered. "Here, sit down." Jo pushed Rocky gently towards the bench and eased them both down, never letting go of the girl. "Let's see." She raised the tear-stained face and wiped away the moisture with gentle fingers.

"I haven't...cried for so...long," Rocky said between hiccups.

"Sometimes it's good to cry."

"Do you cry?" Rocky looked up into Jo's face, wiping her own with a dirty sleeve.

Jo's brow creased in thought, and she shook her head. "Can't say I do."

Rocky disengaged herself from the dark woman's embrace. "I'm sorry."

"For what?"

Rocky shrugged. "I should be going. I need to get a hot meal. I have to be down at the church."

"Let me get you something." Jo stood, gathering up her belongings and putting them into the bag.

"No." Rocky put up her hands again, forestalling Jo's protests. "No. I need to think. I need to talk to Edna."

"But Edna said—"

"I know. But I've listened to her a lot. Ever since I've been here. Give me some time. Please."

Jo took a step back and nodded. "Okay." She turned to the items she'd given Rocky. "Will you still take these?"

The blonde gave her a smile, causing Jo to smile right back at her. "Thank you, Jo. I'll look after them."

"Oh!" Jo suddenly remembered another something she had in her pocket. "I want you to have this too." She handed a couple of cards to the girl. "It's a phone card. It has £10 on it. And the other card is my number and my mobile number. If ever you need me, any time, just use it to call me."

Rocky looked long and hard at the cards and then put them in her pocket.

"Can I see you later today?" Jo asked.

"No," Rocky said, looking up and almost flinching at the hurt she saw in the blue eyes. "Just give me today. I'll be back here in the morning."

"Will you?"

Rocky saw the doubt in her eyes. "Like you said, Jo, no promises." She took a deep breath. "I've been out here for a long time. For a while I had to rely on Edna and some of her friends to survive. But the past three years, I've looked after myself. Sure, I have to rely on charity, but that's all. I've never taken money from strangers on the streets. I've never sold my body. I don't run drugs. All of those things could have made my life more comfortable." She tucked the sleeping bag and the other items into her bags. "This is the first time something has been given to me personally. I didn't think I could accept something like that."

"I was worried you wouldn't take it."

"Well, like I said before. I'm not stupid enough to refuse it." Rocky gathered her belongings, slinging the now heavy bag over her shoulder. She turned to leave and then paused, standing for a moment before turning back to the tall woman. "Jo, do you have a boyfriend?"

Jo's mouth opened and closed a couple of times, before she found her voice. "No, I don't. Do you?"

Rocky pursed her lips and shook her head. "See you tomorrow," she said and was gone.

Chapter
9

The rest of the day passed slowly for Jo. She'd gone back to her house after leaving the small park in Whitechapel. She'd made herself a pot of tea and settled down to watch TV, something she rarely did. She couldn't quite bring herself to go down to the pub, which would be her normal course of action. She went back into the kitchen, opening the fridge to see what Rosanna had bought her this week.

Her mother had employed Rosanna shortly after her parents had bought her the small house. Rosanna was the daughter of Marianna's cook at their London home. Jo's mother knew that her youngest daughter didn't know what a supermarket was, let alone what she should buy in it. Rosanna bought food and put it in the refrigerator and cupboards. Most of it she removed a couple of days later, untouched. But there was always food there should she need it.

So Jo peered into the fridge, amazed at the variety of things she found there. She also found bread in another cupboard and made herself a passable ham sandwich. She switched on the TV and settled down to watch. The rather droll TV fare and the warmth from the fire, coupled with the unsettled nights she'd been having, soon took their toll. Within minutes she was asleep.

There's nothing worse than falling asleep during the late morning and then waking, thoroughly confused. Jo looked around, her eyes finding the illuminated clock on the VCR. It was 3.30pm. She wondered what had woken her.

"Hi, Jojo."

She sat up slowly, scrubbing her face with her hands and putting her foot onto the plate with a half eaten sandwich on it. "Dammit," she cursed, leaning over the back of the sofa to the shelf, which held a box of tissues. "What do you want, Trixie?" she asked, wiping off the butter stuck to her heel but never once looking at the woman sitting in the chair opposite her, and bitterly regretting ever giving her the entry code.

"Just wanted to see you," Trixie pouted. "Aren't you glad to see me?"

Jo sighed. "No, Trix. I thought I made myself clear." Jo threw the butter-covered tissue in the waste paper bin and took her cup and plate through to the kitchen. She found a dishwasher there and put both the items into it.

Trixie had followed her into the kitchen and came up behind her, wrapping her arms about the tall woman's waist. She nuzzled Jo's neck, her hands moving up from her waist towards her breasts.

Jo turned in the blonde's embrace and found a hot mouth clamping itself on her own. She reached between them and found the blonde's hands, which were caressing her breasts through her sweatshirt. She forcefully pushed Trixie back, her hands taking a vice-like grip on the blonde's wrists. "I said no, Trix."

Dark brown eyes narrowed. "You got someone else to take care of you?" she asked, pulling her wrists from Jo's grasp.

Jo took a couple of steps back, her hands shaking, until she leaned against the counter top. She reached behind her to steady herself. "I no longer need what you can give me," she said steadily. If she could convince herself of the fact, then she was sure she could convince Trixie.

The blonde took a couple of steps towards her, completely aware of the power she held over the beautiful woman. "Oh, but you do, Jojo." She reached up and hands traced Jo's clenched jaw. "Why so tense?" She pushed dark locks behind Jo's ear. "I can help you with that tension." She took a handful of dark hair and pulled Jo's head towards her, kissing her roughly and biting her bottom lip as she pulled back, reopening the cut she had made before. She pushed Jo back as the tall woman put her hand to her mouth, staring dumbly at the blood she saw on her fingers. "Call me when you grow up, Jo. I'll be waiting."

When Jo looked up, Trixie was gone. She heard the door slam, and then the sound of a car driving away. Almost in a daze, she went downstairs to the security box by the front door and opened it. She changed the entry code and tested it. Then she went back upstairs and poured herself another large drink.

In another part of London in a derelict factory, a lone woman watched the small fire she'd built. She'd managed to build a small lean-to with a large piece of panelling. The snow drifted through the ruined roof and threatened the flickering flames. Rocky fed some more of the wood she had found around and about the structure. There were some more people in the ruined building, too intent on their own survival in the sub-zero temperatures to worry about who else was about.

The blonde looked up, wondering if she had really just heard her name called.

"Rocky? Are you in here?"

Rocky stood, looking into the darkness at the hunched figure stumbling across the debris towards her. "Edna?" She met the old woman halfway, helping her across the fallen walls and ceiling to her little patch of cleared floor. "What are you doing here? Why aren't you in the hostel?"

Edna eased herself onto the floor, warming her hands on Rocky's small fire.

"I wanted to talk to you," she said indignantly.

"You need to be inside tonight," Rocky said, plopping herself down beside her friend.

"So do you, Rocky."

Rocky looked away, finding the fire more interesting than her friend. "You know I can't go to those places."

"Well, if you're going to stay here, so am I."

"Edna," Rocky warned, giving her a sideways glance.

The old woman held her hands up. "They're keeping a place for me at the hostel. I have to be in before midnight." She nudged the grumpy blonde's arm. "Like Cinders."

Rocky turned her attention back to the fire. "So what do you want to talk about?"

"Jo."

Rocky shrugged. "Nothing to tell."

"Hey." Edna reached over with a gloved hand and turned the young woman's face towards her. "This is me you're talking to."

Rocky looked at the woman for long moments, wondering whether she could divulge the thoughts that had refused to leave her during the last couple of days.

"Tell me what you feel when you see her."

Rocky closed her eyes, picturing the tall elegance, the blue eyes. She felt a tingle on the back of her neck as the image was formed in her mind's eye. "Comfort," she said simply. Her forehead creased into a frown. "Why is that?" She shook her head in wonder and looked up at Edna. "I don't know her."

Edna opened her mouth to disagree.

"Yeah, I know," Rocky said. "You tell me I already know her."

"How else can you explain the feelings you have?"

Rocky pulled her coat a little tighter around her cold body. "I can't. You know that."

"So...what do you want to do when you see her?"

Rocky turned towards Edna and smiled then blushed. "I want to hold her. But something tells me I shouldn't. I've never thought about loving a woman, Edna. I've never thought about love, not since..."

"Go on." Edna had never pressed Rocky to tell of the circumstances that drove her to the hell that was her life now.

Rocky shook her head. "I can't. I'm sorry."

Edna patted the hand that was close to her own. "That's all right, sweetheart. Most of us out here have our secrets. One day you'll find someone you feel you can tell them to."

"I'm sorry, Edna." Tears now coursed down the strained face, and the old woman pulled Rocky into her arms. "She makes me feel again." Edna had to strain to hear the whispered voice. "And I'm scared that all the feelings will come back, the bad ones I've fought so long to forget."

"But if they do, she'll be strong enough to help you with them."

Rocky pulled herself out of the frail embrace. "How do you know that?"

"How did I know to be at Victoria Station the day you arrived in London? There are many things I know, Rocky. But I don't know why I know. Some call it a gift. I see in that woman a great strength, the same as I've always seen the beauty in your soul. Somehow, against many odds, she has found you." She wiped away the tears that were flowing unabated from green eyes. "She didn't know she was looking for you, but now her life won't be complete without you."

"I can't believe that." Rocky wiped her face with a dirty sleeve. "She's wealthy. She doesn't need me. She looks like she's never needed anything in her life."

"Up until a couple of days ago, she didn't. You, on the other hand, have always needed her. You just didn't have a face to picture in your dreams."

Rocky held her head in her hands. "I don't know what to do, Edna."

Edna put a bony finger beneath the blonde's chin. "You must do what your heart says is right. You must learn to feel again, to love again. Stop punishing yourself." Edna smiled, seeing the outraged look once again. "I know."

"No, you don't." Rocky stood and stepped a few paces away. "You don't know. You don't know what he did. What he took from me." She walked back and towered over Edna. "I couldn't stop him." She collapsed to her knees next to the old woman, who gathered the weeping woman into her arms again.

"Sshh," Edna whispered. "Tomorrow, you will see Jo. Don't fight your feelings. You can't let the past rule your future. You must learn to trust again. You must learn to trust your heart, and the person who wants to hold your heart." She looked up through the ruined roof of the derelict factory, to see the moon peeking from behind the snow clouds. She would soon have to leave the girl she thought of as a daughter to the cold of the night. But for the moment she would stay, content in the knowledge that this beautiful soul she held in her arms was about to find her destiny.

Jo woke with a start and discovered that spending the night on a sofa that was two feet shorter than you was not a good idea. Her left shoulder screamed at her, as did her neck. The fire was still on, and her mouth, as a consequence, was dry. She stumbled into the kitchen, pulling a carton of orange juice from the fridge, and grimaced as she bumped her wounded bottom lip as she drank directly from the carton.

She went back into the lounge and peered through the darkness at the clock on the mantelpiece. It was just after 5am. She'd been asleep on the sofa since the previous evening. She felt hot and sticky, so she made her way upstairs to the bathroom and started the water running. A shower wouldn't do on this occasion, she needed a bath. She needed a long bath, with some of the Body

Shop's very own aromatherapy oils added to it.

Well over an hour later, she eased herself out of the bath. After pulling on her towelling robe, she went back down to the lounge, plopping herself down on the sofa just as the phone rang. She started to reach for the noisy instrument then suddenly realised just who would be calling her at such an early hour. Her hand shook as she picked up the phone, the sudden silence ringing in her ears.

"Hello?" She waited for what seemed like an eternity, listening to soft breathing. She knew who it was. "Rocky?"

"Um, hi."

"Are you all right? Is anything wrong?"

"No, I'm fine. Did I wake you? I forgot how early it was."

"No, I've been up about an hour. How about you?"

"I've been up a while."

There was silence for a long moment.

"Jo, I need to see you."

Jo's mouth suddenly lost the ability to produce coherent sound. Instead she made a vague croaking noise, which caused her caller some alarm.

"Jo?"

"I'm here," she said after clearing her throat.

"There's a café, not far from the park. It's called Mario's. Can you meet me there?"

"Of course I can. When?"

"As soon as you like."

"I'll be there in half an hour."

"Okay. I'll be outside."

"Rocky..." Jo began, but pulled the phone away from her ear when she heard the dialling tone. Rocky had hung up.

She placed the handset gently back in its cradle and stared at it as if it was about to burst into flames. The she remembered she would need to dress before venturing out into the elements.

Jo found the café quite easily and drove slowly past, trying to see in through the grubby window. She couldn't see Rocky but quickly dismissed the fact and went in search of a parking space. With it being so early, she found a space relatively easily in a side street, without having to pay a fee. She pushed her hands into the pockets of her short leather jacket, pleased that she was finally meeting Rocky in a place that hopefully wouldn't require thermal clothing. She stood outside the café and looked up and down the street, seeing no sign of the blonde.

And then suddenly she was there.

"Good morning," Rocky said softly, dropping her bags onto the pavement beside Jo.

If Jo was startled, she hid it well. She bent and picked up one of Rocky's large bags. "You ready for breakfast?"

Jo didn't wait for an answer but headed into the dingy café, glancing back once to make sure the blonde was following her in. Inside Mario's was almost as grubby as the outside, and it bore no comparison to the trendy Italian eateries that Jo frequented. In fact the name was the only Italian thing about the place. There were about a dozen small tables, just over half of them occupied. Most of the customers looked like early workers, truck drivers, and factory workers stopping off for breakfast on their way to their place of work. Jo took the bag to a table in the corner and placed it on one of the four plain wooden chairs that surrounded it. Rocky had followed her in and put the bag she was carrying on the floor beneath the table.

"What do you fancy then?" Jo asked, eyeing the menu, which was on a blackboard behind the counter. "Do you want the full breakfast?" She read the list: bacon, egg, fried bread, tomato, sausages. She turned to Rocky who was easing herself into one of the chairs.

"I'll just have some toast and some tea," Rocky said quietly.

Jo turned towards the seated woman, the tired voice suddenly becoming apparent to her. "Hey, you okay?" she asked, sitting in the opposite chair and ducking her head to see into the bowed face of the blonde.

"I'm fine, just tired," Rocky said, not looking up.

"Let me get you something substantial to eat. Just this once." She ducked her head again, reaching across and tapping the table just in front of Rocky. "Please?"

Rocky looked up and once again revelled in the soft blue gaze. "Okay," her mouth said. Her brain, on the other hand, was trying to come to terms with the emotions that blue gaze evoked. Jo's smile made Rocky's stomach clench, it was such a beautiful sight. And she knew that smile was for her and her alone. She wanted to see it again; she wanted to cause it again. Rocky watched Jo as she stood and went to the counter to order their food.

"I'll have two of the breakfasts, please," she said to the man in the dirty white t-shirt behind the counter and pulled out her small wallet from the back pocket of her jeans. "And two large teas as well." She handed him her credit card, which he peered at, his hand hovering over the cash register.

"No plastic," he said, crossing his arms.

"Really?" Jo peered at her card and then back at the man. "How does one pay then?" she asked.

The man, a huge hairy man with bushy eyebrows and black moustache, looked at her with obvious amazement. "Cash?" he said, shrugging his shoulders.

"Cash," repeated Jo flatly. She hadn't had any of that for years, since she was a teenager. Everything she paid for, she paid for with plastic. "I'll be right back." She went over to Rocky, who was gazing out of the window. "Don't move a muscle. Be back in a jiffy."

Jo sprinted across the road. She'd seen the bank earlier and just hoped she could remember the PIN number as she fed her card into the cash point. She got it right at the second attempt and drew the notes from the machine, stuffing them into her back pocket. Back in the café, she put two £10 notes on the counter for the man. He handed her one back and then gave her change and two mugs of tea. "I'll bring the food over when it's cooked."

Jo watched him walk into the back room and then returned to her table, absentmindedly looking back at the menu, trying to work out how much breakfast for two had cost her. "£6, that only cost £6?" she asked as she placed the mug in front of Rocky.

The blonde chuckled. "Welcome to the real world, Jo," she said. "What do you usually pay for breakfast?"

"I don't usually have breakfast." Jo spooned sugar into her tea, and then shoved the bowl across to Rocky who added some to hers.

Rocky was studying Jo intently, absently stirring the contents of her mug. "What happened?" she asked nodding towards the small cut on Jo's bottom lip.

Jo's hand flew to her mouth, feeling the small puncture there and the slightly swollen lip. "I bit myself eating a pâté sandwich last night." She blushed, her first lie to Rocky and she felt as if she'd slapped the blonde woman.

Rocky seemed to accept the answer, and the blonde once

again found the rapidly awakening sights and sounds of London beyond the café window fascinating.

Jo took a moment to study the blonde. Rocky had taken her hat off, and her gloves, but still wore the large, heavy coat. The coat appeared to be army surplus, as did the trousers and boots. Jo decided that Rocky must cut her own hair, though she hadn't made a bad job of it. The blonde locks still fell into her eyes, and she would occasionally push it away, running her fingers across her eyebrows as she did so.

Although Jo knew Rocky to be about twenty years of age, she decided that she looked at least three years younger. Jo was amazed that the young woman had survived for five years out on the streets. The hard façade that Rocky wanted to project was softened in the early morning light filtering through the dirty window. Now the girl just looked tired and lost.

"I was surprised when you rang me," Jo said, unable to stand the silence any more.

Rocky closed her eyes. "I talked to Edna last night."

Two plates full of steaming food clattering onto their table made both women jump.

"Good grief!" Jo said, looking wide-eyed at the huge pile of food in front of her.

"Sauces?" the man asked.

Rocky tore her eyes from the startled-looking woman opposite her. "Red and brown," she said with a chuckle.

Both women were silent for a while as they tucked into their breakfast. Jo was pleasantly surprised that the stuff was edible and was also pleased to see Rocky attacking the meal with great enthusiasm.

"You said you spoke to Edna," Jo said, laying her fork down on her plate.

"Yes, I did." Rocky slowed her eating, looking up to see Jo leaning back in her chair, wiping her hands on a napkin. The dark-haired woman then pushed her half-empty plate to one side and leaned forward, her elbows on the table.

"Would you talk to me?" Jo asked, resting her chin on her linked hands.

Rocky looked up from her all but empty plate and carefully put her knife and fork down on it.

"I've been out here for just about five years," Rocky said, so quietly that Jo had to strain to hear her over the conversations of the other patrons in the café. "In the beginning, I was lost. I wouldn't have survived long if it hadn't been for Edna and Tom."

"Tom?" Jo asked, taking a sip of tea, surprised that it tasted like tea.

"He died, about a year ago."

"I'm sorry," Jo said, not really knowing how close this Tom had been to Rocky.

The blonde shrugged. "A lot of people I've known since I've been out here have died. It happens."

Jo was quiet, wanting Rocky to continue.

"I arrived at Victoria Station on an autumn day. I wasn't really sure where I was going or what I was doing." She looked up to find blue eyes regarding her intently. "That's when I saw Edna."

"Why were you there alone, Rocky?" Jo immediately realised her mistake when the blonde stood abruptly and gathered her bags. Jo cursed, realised she'd pushed too much too soon, and caused a couple of the other customers to jump as she pushed the chair back and followed the blonde out of the café.

"Rocky!" she called to the rapidly moving form. She jogged to catch up with the girl and positioned herself in front of her. "I'm sorry," she said, breathing hard. "I didn't mean to push."

Rocky's shoulders slumped, and her head bowed. "It's me," she mumbled. "Not you." Rocky sighed and looked up into Jo's concerned face. "Thanks for the breakfast."

Jo shrugged. "You're welcome. Is there anything else I can do?"

A small smile crossed the blonde's face. "I'd like to see the countryside."

"You would?" Jo's face lit up, a hundred different locations flitting through her mind. "Anywhere in particular?"

"I don't know anywhere around here. I wouldn't want you to have to go too far."

"We could be in Scotland by this afternoon if you wanted," Jo said with enthusiasm.

Rocky chuckled, and Jo, deciding it was the most adorable sound she'd ever heard, followed suit.

"I think Scotland's a little far. Do you know anywhere nearer?"

Jo reached over and took one of Rocky's bags and gestured in the direction they would need to go to find her car. "We can go to

Epping Forest, it shouldn't take much more than an hour. How does that sound?"

"Sounds good," Rocky said. "I haven't been out of the city for over five years; it'll be good to see the countryside again."

"Come on then," Jo said and hoped this would be just the beginning of a longer journey for them.

Chapter 10

The two women arrived back at Jo's car, and the taller woman opened the vehicle using the remote on her key ring. Walking to the rear of the car, she opened the boot and stood to one side as Rocky put her bag in the back. Then she threw in the one she had been carrying. She walked around the Merk to the driver's side and looked at the blonde over the roof of the car. Rocky was standing looking at the silver-grey vehicle with her hand hovering over the door handle.

"You might want to take off your jacket," Jo said as she eased her long frame into the driver's seat.

Rocky still stood unmoving, and Jo leaned across and opened the passenger door. "Are you okay?" she asked. Receiving no answer, she got out of the car and walked around the front, standing before the silent girl and ducking her head to better see the tense face. "What's wrong?"

Rocky shook her head. "I'm not sure. It's been a long time since I was in a car. I suppose that's it."

"Would you rather we didn't—"

"No!" Jo took a step back at the exclamation. "No," Rocky repeated. "I really want to get away, just for a couple of hours."

"We can do that." Jo held her hand out. "Let me take your jacket."

Rocky hesitated for a moment then began lowering the long zip on the army jacket. She pulled it off her shoulders and handed it to her friend. She felt strangely exposed and wrapped her arms about herself before quickly opening the car door and sitting in the passenger seat.

Jo walked around the car, the large jacket folded over her arm. To her, it was a small victory, getting through the first layer of the complex and beautiful young woman. She leaned into the back and put the jacket on the small rear seat, then settled in beside Rocky who was fastening her seat belt. She glanced sideways at her travelling companion. Without the bulky jacket, she looked much smaller. She was wearing a grey sweatshirt, which, Jo decided, was still the top layer of many others. The sweatshirt was cleaner than she thought it would be. The collar of a red check shirt poked out of the top of the sweatshirt. It was frayed and crumpled but again looked clean.

"Right then. Epping," Jo said, starting the car and putting it into gear. She turned the heating on full and the CD player down low. "Is there anywhere else you'd like to go?" she asked, glancing to her left at the girl who was watching the passing cars. Rocky shook her head, not looking across at Jo, who returned her attention to the road. Traffic was heavy now, and she picked her way through it carefully.

Just over half an hour later, Jo had made her way onto the A11 and then onto the A104 more commonly known as the Epping New Road. Some time during the journey, she had noticed Rocky's head bobbing as the blonde fought the pull of sleep. When eventually the tousled fair head fell forward, Jo steered the car off the road into a lay-by and eased the girl against the seat back. She pressed a button on the centre console between the seats and the back of the passenger seat reclined slightly. Making sure that Rocky was still safely secured within her seatbelt, she reached down for the handbrake, only to find that the blonde's hand had slipped off her lap and onto the handbrake lever. Jo picked Rocky's small hand up, turning it over in her own and gently rubbing her thumb against the palm. There was a small amount of dirt beneath the fingernails, but the palm was soft and the fingers closed gently around her own. It took a great effort for Jo to place the sleeping woman's hand back in Rocky's lap. Looking into the peaceful face, she smiled gently and once again put the car into gear.

Jo was watching two workmen enjoying a cup of tea whilst waiting for the lights to change to green. The traffic lights were temporary; some distance back she had passed a sign apologising for the delay due to "essential works." She glanced to her left, a gentle smile forming on her lips as she took in the features of the sleeping girl. She looked so young. The hand that Jo had placed back in her lap was now curled just beneath her chin, the other hand covering it. It almost looked as if she was trying to cover herself, trying to protect herself, even in sleep.

The lights changed to green, and Jo pulled away. Immediately after the lights, she saw a sign indicating the route to take for a picnic area. The small road took her deeper into the forest, the bare trees blocking out what little there was of the dull daylight. There had been a gentle fall of snow as Jo was driving, but now that had stopped, though the clouds still threatened. She pulled into the small car park for the picnic area, and, as she expected, it was empty. She left the engine running, knowing how quickly the car would get cold without the benefit of the heater. And she also wanted to take the opportunity to study the woman sleeping so peacefully next to her.

Not so peacefully, she decided, as Rocky began to mumble in her sleep. The blonde head rocked from side to side, her forehead creasing in her growing alarm. "No." The word seemed torn from Rocky's throat.

"Hey." Jo laid a gentle hand on Rocky's arm. Instead of soothing the girl, however, Rocky lurched away from the touch. She threw herself against the restricting seat belt, her legs coming up and catching the underside of the front console.

"No!" Again the agonising cry tore itself from her lips. She flailed her arms, catching Jo across the bridge of her nose, and struggled against the hands that attempted to calm her.

"Rocky!" cried Jo, an edge of panic in her voice.

Green eyes snapped open, and Jo saw firsthand the panic and terror in them. "Don't touch me!" Rocky screamed. "I can't—" Blue eyes, wide with fear, brought her back to the present from the terrifying place sleep had taken her.

Jo held her hands up, so that the blonde could see them. Then she slowly lowered them to the steering wheel, watching as Rocky brought shaking hands to her face. "Oh God." Her voice was muffled behind her hands, but Jo heard the pain in it and slowly reached down to release the seatbelt that strained as Rocky leaned forward. Jo also pushed the button to bring the back of the girl's seat to the upright position.

"I fell asleep," Rocky said, pushing dishevelled hair back

from her face and wiping away tears that had flowed suddenly.

"It's warm in here." Jo's hands slipped from the steering wheel to her thighs. She wanted nothing more than to reach for the distressed girl and pull her into an embrace. Instead she balled her hands into fists and watched as Rocky struggled with the aftermath of the dream.

Rocky nodded, dropping her head onto her chest, feeling more tired now than before she fell asleep. Then she raised her head and looked around. "Where are we?"

"Epping Forest. It's quiet, no one else about." Jo couldn't take her eyes from the girl, who was managing to get her breathing under control again. "Are you all right?"

"Yeah, sorry." Rocky gave her a weak smile. "Shall we take a look around?"

Jo leaned forward and shut off the engine, then reached in the back and dragged Rocky's jacket across the back of the seats, depositing it in her lap. "You'll be glad you took this off now—it's going to be cold out there."

Rocky took the jacket from her and then stepped out into the cold before putting it on. She looked around her. "It's so peaceful." Her voice was almost a whisper, maybe in reverence to the almost church-like silence around them.

"My nanny used to bring me here when I was a child," Jo said as she shrugged on her own jacket, pulling up the collar against the cold. She activated the door lock and the alarm and then joined Rocky as they headed for one of the dirt paths that led into the woods.

"You had a nanny?" the blonde asked as she fell into step alongside the taller woman.

"Yeah, her name was Catherine. She was nanny to all of us."

Rocky pulled on her two pairs of gloves, and then pulled her hat out of a large pocket, jamming it onto her head. "How many of you are there?"

"I have a sister and a brother, both older than me." She bit her bottom lip then asked, "What about you?"

Rocky's step didn't slow, but she kept her head down, watching her boots as they scuffed through the fallen leaves. "I don't have any brothers or sisters."

Jo looked down at the tense profile. "Sometimes I wished I didn't. Being the youngest, I was picked on by both of them."

"What did your parents do?" Rocky asked quietly. "They

must have been busy to have a nanny."

"Not busy really," admitted Jo. "It was just the done thing."

Rocky stopped. "Jo, I know your parents are wealthy. What exactly do they do?"

Jo had walked a couple of steps ahead of Rocky when the blonde stopped, and she turned to face her, wondering if telling Rocky who exactly she was would have an effect on their friendship. "My father is Lord Collingford."

"Christ. Then you are—" Rocky plunged her hands further into her pockets, her head cocked to one side while regarding the uncomfortable-looking woman standing on the muddy path ahead of her.

"My title is Lady Joanna Holbrook-Sutherland. I rarely use it though."

"It is a mouthful." Rocky resumed her walk along the woodland path.

"So it doesn't bother you?" Jo asked, falling into step alongside the blonde.

"No, should it?" Rocky thought for a moment. "My being a vagrant should bother you more."

"Don't call yourself that."

"Why? It's what I am."

"You are homeless. Not a vagrant."

"A vagrant is homeless."

Jo sighed. "Yeah, but the word paints pictures of drunks sitting around a fire. I can't see you doing that."

"I have done that," Rocky said. "Sometimes, when things get really bad out there, I take a drink or three."

"Why are you out there, Rocky?"

Green eyes found hers, and Jo watched as a hundred different emotions played across the pale face. For a long moment Jo thought that Rocky was going to ignore her, and again she wondered if she'd pushed too much too early.

"I wanted to disappear. I didn't have the strength to be where I was, I couldn't fight. So I decided to disappear." Rocky continued walking along the muddy path, her eyes fixed on the ground a few feet ahead of her. "I knew I could lose myself in London. And I did. I've never claimed a penny in benefit; as far as anyone is concerned, I'm dead."

The last word made Jo shiver, but she put it down to the dipping temperature rather than the emotionless way in which Rocky spoke the word.

"I can't imagine how you manage without money." Jo raised her hands to her mouth and blew on them, cursing the fact that she didn't have gloves.

"There are plenty of organisations that help people like me. Salvation Army, Christians, Buddhists, all sorts. I can get a hot meal at least once a day. And when my clothes become too thread-bare I can get replacements."

"And if you become ill?"

"I don't. I've only had a couple of colds since I've been out here. I've been lucky. Edna gets me some of the things I need." She chuckled. "I think the folks at the Sally Army still wonder what a woman of her age needs tampons for."

Jo chuckled with her, but it faded quickly.

"Would you let me help you?"

Rocky sighed. "I still don't understand why, Jo. What brought you to Whitechapel?"

"Edna says something about destiny." Jo took a step towards the blonde. "Do you feel anything at all?" Jo had listened to Rocky's brief description of her life and found she needed to find a way to get Rocky out of the cold and into her life.

Rocky's head dropped, unable to hold the taller woman's gaze.

"You do, don't you?" Jo asked.

The blonde head nodded. "I don't understand it. And it scares me."

Jo reached out putting a hand on each of Rocky's shoulders. "What is there to be afraid of?"

"I've learned to live with nothing, and not to want anything. Now I want something, and if," She drew in a deep shuddering breath, unable, for the moment, to continue.

"What do you want, Rocky?" Jo lifted the pale face, now wet with tears.

Rocky's eyes were closed, tears forcing themselves from between tightly closed eyelids. "I want you." Her voice broke and her head fell forward onto Jo's chest as the dark woman pulled her close.

Jo was lost for words. She held on tight to the sobbing woman in her arms, resting her chin on the top of Rocky's hat-covered head.

"I can't believe I'm crying again," sniffled Rocky, leaning

heavily into Jo. Her arms tentatively wound around Jo's waist and found a certain comfort. It was the same feeling she got from her dreams. Dreams that were always chased away by the nightmares. "I cried last night as well."

Jo pulled away slightly, looking down at the shorter woman. "You did? Why was that?"

Rocky wiped a sleeve across her face. "I was talking to Edna." She looked up, a slightly embarrassed smile across her face. "About you."

"Really?" Jo asked and turned them both so that they were making their way down the path once more. She kept an arm around the blonde's shoulders as they walked, needing for the time being to have some contact with Rocky.

Rocky leaned into Jo as they walked. "Edna seems to think you're some kind of knight in shining armour, come to save me."

"And what do you think?"

"I don't know what to think. I want..." Rocky chuckled. "There I go breaking my rules again." She rubbed her face vigorously with her hands. "I want to believe you. But like you said. You're a lady. Why do you want to help me?"

Jo squeezed the shoulders of the girl walking alongside her. "I've dreamed about you too. In the dream you turned away from me. I was devastated. I felt so lost. So I decided if I did find you, I wouldn't let you walk away, because I couldn't stand to feel like that again."

"Do you believe in dreams?" Rocky asked, her head now leaning heavily against the solid body beside her.

"I do now. Now I've met you, held you. I know I need to be with you." Rocky stopped suddenly, and Jo turned to face her again. "Is something wrong?" Jo asked.

"There's something I need to do too," Rocky said. She reached up and grabbed the small collar of Jo's jacket, pulling the taller woman down. As Jo's lips approached hers, she stopped pulling, giving the dark woman every opportunity to pull out if she wished. But Jo had no intention of pulling back. She was drawn to the full lips that beckoned her and nothing was going to stop her forward momentum. She closed her eyes as their lips met, bringing her hands up to cup cold cheeks, feeling small hands leave her collar and rest on her hips. The kiss was brief, but none the less monumental. Jo pulled back and looked down into glassy green eyes.

"Thank you," Rocky whispered. "But I need to ask you some-thing, Jo."

"What?" Jo's breath warmed Rocky's chin as she leaned in and kissed chilled lips again.

"I really need a loo."

Jo laughed and pulled the small blonde into an affectionate embrace. "Let's go find one then and hope we don't freeze to the seat."

The two women made their way along the woodland path once more, the taller one inordinately pleased when the smaller reached out a small hand and curled it around her own. They fol-lowed the green signs and before long found a small building which housed a café, behind which were the toilets.

"I need..." Rocky pulled her hand from her tall companion's and pointed towards the new-looking building.

Jo stuffed her hands in her pockets. It had been so peaceful, walking in a comfortable silence with the small blonde. Now she felt the drop in temperature even more as the warm hand left hers. She gestured towards the café with a nod of her head. "I'll go and order some hot drinks."

Rocky looked hesitant for a moment, shuffling from foot to foot. The she took a couple of steps back towards Jo, stood on tip toes, and gave her a peck on the cheek.

"Thanks," she whispered and was gone.

Jo watched her go, delighting in the smile Rocky bestowed on her as she glanced back at her. The grin was still firmly on her face as she entered the empty café.

Behind the counter an elderly woman looked up from wiping down the counter top. "Hello, dear." She wiped her hands on some paper towels, which she threw away. Then she made her way to the end of the counter where Jo was perusing the cakes. "It's a cold day to be out and about," the woman said. "Are you having a hot drink?"

"Yes, thank you. Tea for two, I think."

"I'll make you a nice big pot, dear." She shuffled off, collect-ing the things she needed.

"And a selection of cakes, please."

"Go and sit down, dear. I'll bring them to your table."

There were only three tables in the café. There were more outside on the small deck, but in the present weather the chairs were stacked in a corner, and the tables unused.

Jo looked outside and saw Rocky. The girl had walked back around the front. She was holding her hat in her hands and staring into the café. Jo beckoned her in, but she stood hesitantly on the wooden deck.

The waitress placed a tray with a pot of tea, milk, and sugar on the table. "Is your friend coming in?" she asked, following Jo's gaze.

"I'll get her." Jo stood and pushed through the café door, the cold stinging her face as she left the warmth of the room.

"Come on, I have tea and cakes." She glanced back inside to see the cakes delivered to her table.

"Is it all right?" Rocky asked.

"Is what all right?"

"I...I'm not sure. I'm not..." She looked down at her clothing and then at the café.

Jo took her hands and pulled her in through the doorway. "I've got you tea and cakes."

The waitress looked up to see the oddly matched couple entering the café. If she thought anything of the smaller woman's appearance she didn't mention it, nor did it show on her face. "If you want anything, just shout," she said and moved back behind the counter.

Jo pulled out a chair for Rocky, who slipped out of her jacket. "You should take your jacket off," she told Jo. "You won't feel the benefit of it when we go back out otherwise."

Jo did as she was told and draped her jacket across the back of her chair. "Shall I pour?" Jo asked, turning the cups the right way up before stirring the tea in the pot to make sure it was strong enough.

Rocky watched Jo as she poured the tea, wondering briefly what this beautiful, obviously desirable, woman was doing on a cold winter's day, pouring tea in a deserted café in the middle of a deserted wood for a vagrant. She chuckled to herself, shaking her head lightly.

"What?" Jo asked, her smiling face showing her enjoyment at once again seeing her friend smile.

"Nothing." Rocky said taking the offered cup and adding milk and sugar to it. "Tell me about your childhood."

And Jo did. Telling her about her early years, the boarding school, the scandals at University before she eventually gave up on it. How she lived off her parents and how she found a picture in a gallery, which completely turned her life around.

They were there a couple of hours. For a while the elderly waitress joined them, delighting them with her tales of strange customers and her work in the canteen of one of the police stations in the city. Never once did she make any comment about Rocky's appearance, and she laughed with the pair of them, occasionally reaching across to squeeze Rocky's hand. Jo left a large tip for the woman when they eventually made their way back out into the cold of the afternoon. They took a leisurely walk back to the car. It was growing dark as they reached it.

As Jo fastened her seat belt she saw a flake of snow hit the windscreen, then another.

"It's snowing," she said to Rocky as the blonde buckled herself in.

Rocky said nothing and settled back in the seat. She watched the snow fall through the glow from one of the streetlights that ringed the small car park.

"Rocky—"

"I know what you're going to say, Jo. Please don't."

"I'm scared for you." Jo's eyes were closed, her head hung low, and her hands gripped the steering wheel.

"Don't be," Rocky whispered. "I'll be fine."

"Look, just tonight. I have a spare room."

"No. I'm sorry." She reached across, laying a gentle hand on Jo's forearm, rock hard as she grasped the steering wheel. "I've had a wonderful day with you, Jo. I don't want to fight with you now."

Jo shook her head, drawing in an unsteady breath. Wordlessly she reached down and started the engine. She took one more look at the blonde beside her, trying valiantly to mirror the smile she was receiving, then drove out of the car park and headed back to London.

The snow was falling heavily when she reached Whitechapel some three-and-a-half hours later. She had taken the long route back and deliberately got stuck in heavy traffic. She parked the car, but left the engine running. Rocky had once again fallen asleep, and Jo placed a hand on her shoulder, gently nudged her awake.

"Wow, must be the heater. I'm not used to it," Rocky said as she looked around, working out that she was back in Whitechapel. She reached across and took Jo's left hand in her own. "I've had a great time today."

Jo looked down at their linked hands. "I really hate this." She looked up into green eyes barely visible in the street light filtering through the windscreen, which was rapidly being covered in snow.

Rocky leaned across and kissed the dark woman lightly on the lips and then pulled back. She turned to open the car door and found herself pulled back and turned again. Jo's arms were almost crushing in their need to gather the small blonde up and hold her tightly.

Rocky didn't resist the embrace, rather she sank into it, allowing herself the luxury of letting go, if only briefly. She laid her head on the tall woman's breast, hearing the rapidly beating heart and knowing that she caused the thundering that she heard there. Putting a hand on Jo's chest, she pushed back. Sitting up again, she looked into the distraught face of her new friend. "I'll see you tomorrow." Jo opened her mouth to speak, an objection obviously about to be voiced. Rocky raised her hand. "We both need time to come to terms with this."

"I don't." Jo knew she was pleading.

"I do. I have a lot of things to think about." She patted Jo's hand and opened the car door. Snow blew in, and she quickly reached into the back seat and pulled out her jacket. She put it on as she ran around the front of the car to Jo's side. "No, don't get out," she said as she saw Jo opening her door.

Jo shut the door and pushed the button to lower the window. She waited while Rocky retrieved her bags from the boot and then returned, bending at the waist to speak to the sitting woman.

"Tomorrow then?" Rocky asked, having to raise her voice over the sound of the wind and the traffic.

Jo nodded, not trusting her voice.

Rocky gave her a smile and leaned in, giving her another peck on the cheek. And then she was gone. Disappearing into what was rapidly turning into a blizzard with frightening ease.

Jo leaned her head back against the headrest. "Heaven help me," she said to herself.

Rocky slung her bag over her shoulder and made her way into the factory which had been something like a home to her for the past year or so. Her little lean-to was still there, but she'd need something extra tonight because of the severe weather. She put her bags down beneath the panelling and went in search of something to give her some extra protection against the high winds. As she picked her way across the debris strewn floor, she thought back to her day with Jo. A smile found its way to her face, and she chuckled to herself, remembering one particularly funny story Jo had told. She was glad that the elderly waitress had left them at that point, not knowing what she would have thought about twelve naked young women in a boarding school swimming pool at midnight. Jo's excuse that they were practising synchronised swimming routines fell on deaf ears, and Jo was off to her fourth school in as many years.

The fact that Rocky had survived the past five or so years on the streets bore testament to her vigilance when it came to her own safety. So maybe it was the fact that she'd just spent a day unlike any other since she'd arrived in London that caused her alertness to slip. She was almost upon the five men before she heard their lowered voices. Their two cars were parked at the rear of the derelict building, the boot of one raised. Five faces turned to regard her as she turned the corner, and in the headlights of the two cars, she saw their faces turn towards her.

In the hands of one of the men was a large package, and Rocky's eyes flitted to it before returning to his face. She realised immediately that she had stumbled on some sort of drug deal, and spun quickly, darting back into the shell of the decimated building. She heard the men behind her, their angry shouts loud in the empty building, and flew across the debris, her lightness making easy work of the obstacles in her way. She was further into the body of the factory than she'd ever been, and in parts the floor groaned beneath her feet. She flattened herself against a wall and listened.

She smiled as she heard their howls of outrage as they stumbled on the remains of the factory floor and listened to their mumbles of "It's just some tramp, probably too drunk to know what was going on." They breathed heavily in the cold air, the snow drifting through what was left of the roof onto their heads. She heard the men stand for a while, listening for any movement. Then they shuffled out of the building.

Rocky waited until she heard the car doors slam and the cars drive away. Waiting a few moments more, she made her way cautiously out of her hiding place. She'd taken only a few steps when she felt the floor beneath her feet shift, and then she was twisting in thin air and bracing herself for the impact as the floor gave way.

In another part of the factory two old men heard a cry and then silence. They returned to searching for wood for their fire.

Jo went back into the bathroom, testing the water that was pouring into the tub. She'd had the ridiculously huge tub put in last year, even having to have the floor reinforced to accommodate it. She'd added her aromatherapy oils to the water and had poured herself a large drink. She threw her clothes onto the floor of the bathroom and eased her long frame into the water. Relaxing back against the tub she reached out and grasped her glass, almost dropping it into the bath.

"Oh, bliss," she hissed, and, with a smile on her face, thought back to the wonderful day she'd just spent. Only one thing spoilt the day, of course. The small blonde of her musings wasn't sharing the experience with her now.

"Soon," she said to herself. "Very soon."

Chapter
11

Jo lay in the bath, the water covering her to the tip of her chin. She reached out with her toe and turned the tap, letting some more hot water into the bath. She'd been luxuriating for just over an hour. The cold had got to her, and she was glad of the warmth and comfort that seeped into her bones from the water's heat. But the thought of Rocky out in the cold night was never far away. Taking another sip of her drink, she decided that tomorrow she'd insist upon the girl coming back with her. She'd make up the spare room, not that she really wanted her in there, and would insist that Rocky at least came to look at it.

"No," she said to herself. "I want you with me."

She drained the glass and decided that she should really be getting out. Her skin was pruning, and she was feeling lethargic. She stepped out of the bath and put on a robe that was hanging on the back of the door. Accounting the shiver she felt across the back of her neck down to the cooler air hitting her body as she exited the steamy bathroom, she made her way down the stairs to the lounge.

It was almost 8pm, and she picked up the remote and switched on the TV. She wanted to go to bed. Like a child on Christmas Eve, she wanted tomorrow to come, and quickly. But she knew if she did, she'd lie awake thinking about a small blonde who had felt so right, so naturally right, in her arms. She smiled at the thought and curled her body up on the sofa, laying her head on the arm and hugging a cushion close.

So Rocky felt it, too. She smiled at the thought. *She said she wants me.* She rolled onto her back, staring at the ceiling. The television flickered in the corner, unwatched. Jo closed her eyes and saw in her mind's eye the face of the woman she'd been seeking all her life but had only just come to realise the fact. She'd never before had any compulsion to take one of her relationships with the many women she'd met any further than sexual gratification. She bedded them and, as soon as they started talking about commitment, she called it off. One of the people who understood that and used it to her advantage was Trixie. Trixie knew that she could use Jo and knew damn well that Jo used her.

However, Trixie was finding Jo's recent reluctance to partake of her particular pleasures somewhat hard to accept. Jo knew that. And the thought that she could use Rocky the way she'd used Trixie, the way she'd used many women, sickened her. Suddenly her life, her existence sickened her. And what would Rocky think when she found out? Could she keep her past a secret? Did she want to? At what point did it no longer become fun? She'd enjoyed the hunt, the seduction, and the conquest. Now her main ambition in life was to get one small woman out of the cold and into her life. She wanted to get up and go out. Now. She wanted to go and find Rocky, throw her into her car and bring her home. But she wouldn't. Rocky wouldn't respect her if she imposed her will on the blonde. The decision had to be Rocky's, and she would abide by that decision, however hard it was to take.

She surrounded herself in the warmth that thoughts of Rocky inspired. Drifting off in the comfort of her home, she dreamt of sea-green eyes and the promise of soft skin under her hands. She dreamt of full lips caressing her own and of small hands exploring her body. She dreamt of burying her face in silken hair, drawing in the scent of the blonde as she traced a delicate ear with her tongue. Oh yes, she would love this woman, and she would be anything and everything the blonde wanted.

Some two hours later, Jo awoke with a start. She looked at the clock, and found it to be just after 10pm. She didn't know what had woken her and stared uncomprehendingly at the TV. A particularly violent film was showing—men hanging bloodied and battered from a ceiling. Only half awake, she switched off the TV and made her shuffling way up to bed. She chuckled to herself as she snuggled down into the comfort of her thick quilt. Suddenly realising that, only a week ago, at this time of night, she would just be entering into another night's hunting. Like some sort of predator, she would be stalking her usual hunting grounds, looking for prey.

What a difference a weekend makes.

She was having a beautiful dream. In it she was with Rocky. What she was doing to Rocky was interesting, but the annoying sound she could hear just wouldn't go away. She slapped her hand at the alarm, before she remembered she never set the radio-alarm that sat on the bedside cabinet. Her sleep-fogged brain tried to comprehend what the noise was. Then she realised that it was the phone. She reached over and picked up the handset, listening to the babbling she heard as soon as she lifted the handset.

"... not working, never did like using these newfangled things."

"Hello?" Jo asked. Whoever was on the other end obviously wasn't paying attention. She looked at the glowing numbers on the radio-alarm. 02.26. "Hello!" she shouted.

"Hello, hello," the voice repeated.

"Who is this?"

"Jo?"

"Yes. Edna?" A knot of fear twisted in Jo's chest. "Edna, is Rocky all right?"

"Jo?"

"Yes, Edna. What is it? Is it Rocky?"

"I can't hear you."

Jo sat up, pushing the quilt aside and dragging her hand through her tangled hair. Her heart began to beat quickly, a hundred different scenario's forming in her imagination.

"Edna," she shouted. "Can you hear me?"

"Jo? I can't hear you, Jo. But if you can hear me, come to the old leather works near Bethnal Green—"

The old woman's voice was replaced by the dialling tone, and Jo threw the offending object across the room, flinching when she heard it hit the wall and bounce across the floor.

She picked up the clothes she'd had on earlier that day from where she'd thrown them. Putting them on quickly, she grabbed her jacket, hat, and gloves from their place in the hall and, without tying her bootlaces, rushed down the stairs. She narrowly avoided slipping as she left the warmth of the house and opened the garage door using the remote control. Not waiting for the car to warm up, as her father had always taught her, she reversed out of the garage, narrowly avoiding reversing into another parked car as her tyres refused to grip on the ice.

As she drove through deserted streets, she suddenly realised she had no idea where the old leather works were. She did, however, know where Bethnal Green was. There was a particularly popular nightclub that she frequented occasionally, and so she found herself in Bethnal Green quite quickly. "Old leather works," she said softly. It must be an old factory, probably not used anymore. *Was this where Rocky lived?* She shivered at the thought. She'd never really taken the time to think where Rocky spent her nights. She hoped that maybe she squatted in an empty house or something. Not in a derelict building.

She drove around in circles for a half-hour, looking for something that would point her in the right direction. Then she saw the high fence with a barbed wire top. Signs warning of prosecution for trespassers and of an unsafe structure were present every few yards on the fence. The original, huge iron gates stood in the centre of the fence. She parked her car under a streetlight and, after locking the Merk, made her way to them. Above the gates, cast in wrought iron, were the words: Mitchell Tannery.

She peered through the gates. An old man came shuffling forward from the other side. "You lookin' fer Edna?"

"Yes." Jo gripped the cold metal of the gates, pushing against them in her desperation.

"You won't get through 'ere." He pointed to his right. "Go down about fifty yard. There's a hole in the fence. Slip of a lass like you should get through there no trouble."

Jo was gone before he had the chance to tell her he'd meet her at the opening.

The hand that took her by the arm as she crawled through the fence took her by surprise, but then she looked up into the grizzled face of the old man. He smiled at her, showing a couple of dirty teeth, and then beckoned to her to follow.

"Watch your step," he said as he led her across the old factory floor, startling a couple of pigeons into the air. Only a few bonfires casting a golden glow across the walls lighted the area. A steadily thickening layer of snow covered the ground, making it even more difficult to navigate a safe path through the debris.

Edna stood as she approached, and Jo saw the hunched figure of Rocky slumped against the wall behind her. Edna managed to intercept the rapidly moving woman, putting her hands on her upper arms. "She's hurt, Jo. Be careful."

Jo slowed, took a couple of deep breaths, and nodded. "What

happened?" she asked as she crouched in front of the blonde.

"I'm not sure. Old Bill over there came to the hostel to find me about an hour and a half ago. Seems she had a fall. Floor gave way and she fell through to the cellar. Don't know how long she was down there, but she managed to get out."

Jo reached out a shaking hand and gently lifted Rocky's bowed head. "Hey," she whispered. "What have you been doing to yourself?"

Glazed green eyes found her own, and Jo immediately recognised the pain in them. "Jo?" Rocky tried to move but cried out when the pain became too much.

Even in the firelight, Jo could see the lack of colour in the blonde's face. Her skin was covered by a thin sheen of sweat. Her jacket was draped across her shoulders, and she was hunched over, protecting something it seemed. A small graze marred her left cheek, high up near her eye.

"Where does it hurt, Rocky?" Jo asked, gently parting the front of the blonde's jacket, wanting to find what was causing the pain. But she felt the fear as well, not knowing how she would deal with a serious injury.

"Shoulder," was all Rocky could manage, gasping again as Jo slipped the heavy army jacket off her shoulders.

She could see immediately something was very wrong with Rocky's left shoulder. She placed a gentle hand on it, feeling the obscenely misplaced joint. "Feels dislocated."

"We know," Edna stated from behind her.

"So why didn't you call a bloody ambulance? You had the bloody card." Jo covered Rocky again with the jacket. The blonde, in her misery, was unaware of the argument going on in front of her.

"She won't have it." Edna crossed her arms and stood up straight. "We know better than to force her to do something."

"But it's for her own good." Jo threw her arms in the air in frustration.

"I won't go back on a promise. She won't go to a hospital, that's why Bill tried to put it right."

"He what?" Jo spun to look at the old man, who once again grinned at her.

"He tried to put it back in, but it wouldn't go."

Bill nodded his head. "It's a bad one," he said. The grin never left his face.

"He used to work with horses apparently," Edna said as a means of explanation.

"Jesus Christ! I can't believe you let him do that, Edna," she said, kneeling once again in front of the shivering blonde.

"I wasn't here. I was in the hostel. I knew nothing about this until long after it happened."

Jo wasn't listening. She cupped a sweaty cheek and ducked her head to see into the pale face. "Rocky, we have to take you to the hospital."

Rocky took in a deep breath, wincing as the pain in her shoulder flared. "No, no hospital. Can't go there." She gripped Jo's wrist with her right hand. "Promise me, Jo."

"Sweetheart, you're in agony. I can't let you stay like this."

"Can't go to hospital." She sobbed as the pain got worse. "Please, Jo."

"Okay." Jo stood and pulled out her cell phone. Dialling a number programmed into the memory, she waited a while until it was answered. "Leo?" she paused for a moment, listening to the outraged voice. "I know, I need some help...No, not that kind of help...No, now." She held the phone away from her ear. "I'll meet you in the surgery. Will you tell them we're coming?" She nodded at the answer. "See you there." She flipped the phone closed and pushed it back into her pocket.

She crouched down in front of Rocky again. "Rocky," her voice was barely above a whisper, "I'm going to take you to a friend of mine. He has his own private surgery, and he'll help us."

"No hospital," Rocky managed to say, gasping again when she shifted slightly.

"It's a private hospital, looks more like a hotel. He'll see us in his surgery." She pushed sweat-soaked hair off the pale face. "Sweetheart, you have to get it seen to. Trust me, please."

Rocky drew in a long ragged breath and nodded tightly. "Help me up."

The hardest part was getting Rocky through the low hole in the fence. The manoeuvre caused the small woman considerable pain, and she leaned heavily on Jo and Edna as they led her to the car. Between them they managed to get the blonde settled into the passenger seat of the Merk. Jo leaned across her and fastened the seatbelt, then threw the jacket, which she'd slipped off her shoulders, into the boot.

Edna reached in and gave her friend a brief kiss on her cheek.

"You're going to be fine," she said, reluctantly pulling her hand from Rocky's weak grasp. She shut the door and watched Jo over the roof of the car.

The younger woman finally looked up from the keys she held in her hand. "Edna, I'm sorry I shouted. I'm glad you called me."

Edna nodded, accepting the apology. "It shows you care. I can sleep now, knowing you'll do your best for her."

"I will, Edna, I promise." With that, Jo folded her long frame into the car. After a brief look at the slumped form in the passenger seat, she sped away. Every bump in the road, every turn, elicited a groan from Rocky. As much as Jo wanted to get the injured woman to a doctor, she kept the speed down and eased into the bends.

At last she was parking the car outside the splendid building in central London which housed her friend's surgery. Leo was a friend of her brother's. Older than Jeremy by five years, he had followed the family tradition and studied medicine. He, however, wasn't going to spend long hours working for the National Health. He followed his father into the rapidly growing plastic surgery business. And a business it was. He now had his own very successful practice, catering to the need of wealthy women to keep their looks or to enhance what looks they had. He had flirted unashamedly with Jo every time he had the pleasure to meet her. And this wasn't the first time she had used his attraction to her for her own needs. Though on each occasion the treatment had not been for her.

As she opened her door, Leo arrived, parking his Jaguar in front of Jo's car. She walked around the front of the car and leaned in to unbuckle Rocky's seatbelt. Leo went on into the clinic and had a word with the security guard, who was talking to a nurse behind the reception counter. Jo helped the blonde up the short flight of steps and through the door. She immediately spotted Leo who beckoned her to follow him.

Leo's office was plush, with a huge desk and a long leather couch. There was also an examination table behind a curtain. Certificates mounted the walls, along with photographs. One photograph showed Leo and Jeremy on the summit of some mountain. Jo had never thought to ask which one. Jo eased Rocky across to the couch and lowered them both down onto it.

Leo was sitting on the edge of the table, looking very undoctor-like in jeans and blue sweatshirt.

"She's dislocated her shoulder," Jo said, settling Rocky back onto the cushions.

"I can see that." Leo made no move to approach them. He looked long and hard at the two women, then took a bunch of keys from the chain attached to his belt. "Just one moment," he said and left the room.

"So tired," whispered Rocky.

Jo tore her eyes from the door through which Leo had just left and took in the sight of the pain-wracked girl. "Won't be long now, sweetheart. Leo will put it right." She rubbed gentle circles across the girl's back, being careful to avoid the injured shoulder.

Leo returned with a small cup of water and another smaller plastic cup. "Here, take these." He handed the small cup, which contained a couple of pills, to Rocky. "They're muscle relaxants. It'll help when I put the joint back in place."

Rocky took the pills with a shaking hand. She looked at them and then at Jo. "Go on," her friend urged. Rocky tipped the pills into her mouth, and then took the cup of water from Leo, washing them down.

"They'll take a few moments to take effect." He turned soft brown eyes on Jo. "Can I have a word?" he asked and, without waiting for an answer, walked out of the room.

Jo watched him go and then turned to Rocky. "Just sit quietly for a moment. I won't be long." She reluctantly left the blonde, after making sure she was comfortable on the couch, and went into the hallway to find Leo.

"What the hell is that?" he asked angrily, pointing towards the now shut door to his office.

Jo pushed him further away, out the front door of the building and into the cold night. "Will you shut up? She's a friend of mine and she needs help."

"Then take her to a bloody hospital. Christ, Jo, it was bad enough you dragging in your little tarts that OD'd when you dumped them. Now you're bringing me vagrants?"

"Look, Leo." She turned away from him, watching the snow swirling around the orange glow of a streetlamp. "I know I owe you, and I know this is unreasonable, but she's really important to me."

"She's a—"

"I know what she is, Leo. I can't explain it. But I know one thing. Tonight is the last night she will spend on the streets."

"So you're into rescuing tramps now? That's a new slant for you, Jo. Scraping the bottom of the barrel, aren't you?" He took a couple of steps and was face to face with her. "Have you broken all the little tarts' hearts in London? None left? Had to cast your net into new waters?" His voice dripped with sarcasm.

Jo's head hung low. She knew his words were close to the truth. "Will you please just help me this one last time? I won't come here again." She looked up at him. Half of his face was lit by the light from the open door. She saw the regret in his eyes.

"I would have given you anything you asked for," he said quietly. "Anything."

She reached out a hand and gripped his arm gently. "I know, Leo. I'm sorry."

He swallowed hard and put an arm around her shoulders. "Let's go see to your friend."

When they arrived back in the office, they found Rocky with her head back against the couch back, eyes closed. Both hands were lying in her lap, and she looked pretty well relaxed.

Jo rushed to her side, pushing the blonde's damp hair out of her pale face. "Rocky?" she asked quietly.

"Muscle relaxants, they work quickly." Leo went to a large cabinet at the rear of the room and pulled out a large pair of scissors. "As this isn't an emergency department, we're going to have to make do. We need to get her out of the sweatshirt." He handed the scissors to Jo. "You can...um, get her out of her top."

Jo took the scissors and then grasped the sweatshirt. She slit the sleeve enclosing the injured arm and then up the body of the shirt itself. Between them they managed to ease it off Rocky's good arm. Beneath that was the shirt. That was unbuttoned and carefully removed without the need of the scissors. A large smile crossed Jo's face when she found that the last garment that Rocky wore was the thermal vest she'd bought her a couple of days before. Beneath the white material, the misplaced shoulder was even more evident. "Can you manage if we leave this on?" Jo asked pointing at the white vest. Rocky was just about oblivious to what was going on around her, but Jo really didn't want her undressed in front of Leo.

"Yeah, that should do." Leo put a hand on the shoulder, feeling for the joint. "Can you go round the other side?" Jo stood and went to Rocky's good side. "Hold her steady."

Jo put her arms around the almost boneless blonde and held

on. She closed her eyes, not wanting to see what was going on. But almost lost whatever food she'd had that day when she heard the joint re-seat itself in its correct position.

Rocky groaned in her delirium, and Jo gathered her gently into her arms. "Shh, it's okay. It's over now."

"Looks like we have another problem here," Leo said, lifting the hem of the vest.

Jo peered past the slumped head that rested on her shoulder to see what Leo had found. There was a slowly spreading stain of blood on the vest. She looked then at the discarded sweatshirt on the floor and saw a small stain on that too.

"It's not a big cut, but I think I'll put a couple of stitches in it." Leo straightened quickly and left the two women alone.

"What did you do to yourself?" Jo asked, her lips brushing the blonde hair.

Leo returned with some more equipment. "Can you hold up the vest?"

Jo reached around and pulled up the thermal vest, baring Rocky's side to Leo's gaze. "Yeah, just a couple of stitches." He swabbed the area clean and quickly inserted two stitches, closing the small wound. Rocky flinched once, but was still at ease from the effects of the muscle relaxants. He placed a dressing over the wound and stood, watching as Jo lowered the garment once more. Rocky was slumped heavily against the tall woman, who was also nearing the end of her reserves.

Leo sat on the end of the couch, the oblivious blonde between him and Jo. "You look awful, Jo."

"Thanks," she chuckled, but her attention fixed on the blonde in her arms.

"Do you want me to call you a taxi?"

Jo shook her head. "No. Just help me get her into the car. I'm taking her home."

Leo and Jo managed to get Rocky into her shirt, but the sweatshirt was a lost cause. Jo took off her leather jacket, which she'd worn the whole time, and draped it around Rocky's shoulders.

"What can I do for her?" Jo asked as they took the steps slowly. Rocky was more aware, but whether it was shock or tiredness that kept her silent, Jo wasn't sure.

"Cold will help. If you can, crush some ice and put it in a plastic bag, then wrap it in cloth. Here," he handed her a small pill pot. "Painkillers. Give her one every four hours or so, or as she needs them." They reached the car and Jo held Rocky with one arm while disarming the alarm and unlocking the car with the remote with the other.

Leo opened the car door, and Jo lowered the blonde into the passenger seat. Rocky fumbled with the seat belt with her right hand until Jo placed her hands over the seated woman's hands and buckled her in. She closed the door and turned to face Leo. "You're a good friend, Leo. Thank you." She leaned forward and kissed him on the cheek.

"I'm sorry for shouting at you."

"Well, it's," she looked at her watch, "nearly 4am. You had every reason to shout."

Leo scrubbed his face with his hands. "Give me a call in a week or so, and I'll take a look at the stitches."

"I will," she said and got into the car.

As she drove down the street away from Leo, she watched him in her rear view mirror. He stood for a while then turned and made his way back into the building.

She looked to her left at the blonde, who was sitting quietly. "You all right?"

"I feel a little woozy."

"You'll be fine. But it may hurt once the relaxants wear off. Leo gave me some painkillers."

Rocky was silent for a moment. Then she took a deep breath. "You can drop me near to the park if you want."

Jo turned incredulous eyes on the small figure. "You don't really think I'm taking you back there, do you?"

"It's where I belong."

"Like hell it is. You're coming home with me. You have a serious injury, which needs to be treated, and a hole in your side. I have painkillers, which you're going to need later. They will make you groggy. You could freeze to death in your sleep." She viciously changed gear, the engine howling in protest. "No way are you going back there."

Rocky looked out of the window, away from Jo. "Don't I get a say?"

"Not tonight, no."

The blonde head dropped, her fatigue evident. "I don't sound very grateful, do I?"

Jo was silent.

"Thanks," Rocky said.
"Anytime," Jo said.

Chapter
12

Jo parked the Merk outside her front door and looked to her left at the hunched figure. "Looks like you're in a lot of pain," she said to the blonde, who raised her head wearily and looked out of the snow-smeared window. Rocky was clutching her injured arm, the hand of her right arm cradling the elbow of her left, supporting it. "I'm sure Leo should have strapped you up. We'll find something when we get in."

"Is this where you live?" Rocky asked, as Jo opened her door.

"Yeah, this is it. Stay there while I open the front door."

Jo keyed in the security code and pushed the door open, pushing across a doorstop to make sure it didn't close again as she went back to help Rocky out of the car.

"All right then, let's get you inside." She eased the injured girl out of the car and steadied her as she swayed. Jo pulled the jacket more securely around Rocky's shoulders as they made their way through the now heavy snow and into the house.

At the threshold, Rocky stopped. "I can't."

Jo's arm was draped gently around the smaller girl's shoulder, taking care not to rest heavily on the injured one. "You can't what?"

"I can't go in."

Jo turned the blonde carefully, so that her back was against the opened door. She held her by the tops of her arms, her hands feeling the shaking through the leather jacket which was still draped about her shoulders. "Rocky, there's nothing to be afraid of in there. It's my home, and you're welcome here."

Rocky looked to her right, up the short flight of stairs that led to Jo's home. "It's been so long," she said, her eyes fixed on the door at the top of the stairs. "I've been out there so long." She looked back into the bewildered blue eyes. "I'm not sure I can do it, Jo."

Jo shook her head gently. "I'm trying to understand. Really I am." She took a deep breath, her hands gently running up and down the shaking arms. "I just want you to be warm for a while. Warm and comfortable. With no worries, no pressures. Just you and me." Rocky's head slumped forward. With a gentle hand, Jo lifted her chin, her own eyes watering when she saw the fear that misted the girl's green eyes. "What do you say?"

Rocky closed her eyes. "Ow?" she said, and wiped away the tears that started to fall, a small smile finally gracing her features.

"I need to call Leo," Jo said and turned the girl, walking her slowly up the stairs. "I think I may need to sue him."

"Jo, he did more than could be expected." She waited as Jo pushed open the door at the top of the stairs and felt Jo push her gently into the warmth of her home.

"This way," Jo said and led her into the lounge, sitting her on the sofa. "I'm going back down to put the car in the garage and get your painkillers from the glove compartment. Just sit tight." She pulled the jacket from Rocky's shoulders and threw it over a chair, leaving the blonde alone with her thoughts. When Jo returned, she found Rocky standing in the middle of the lounge holding her arm tightly. "What's the matter, is it hurting more?"

Rocky shook her head.

"So what is it?" She walked towards the girl, placing the pot of pain pills on the low coffee table.

"My boots are dirty, but I can't reach to take them off." Rocky peered at the boots in question, hating the small dark smudges they had left on the spotless carpet.

"Come on, sit down."

Rocky peered at the ivory coloured sofa. "Jo—"

"It's okay, don't worry. Please, sit down before you collapse." She could see the signs of strain in the pale face and didn't want this to be more of an ordeal for the girl than it needed to be. Rocky sat, still holding on to her injured arm. Jo knelt at her feet and started to pull off the scruffy boots.

"Jo, you don't need to do that." Rocky peered down at her but sat back quickly when pain seared through her shoulder.

"Yes, I do," Jo said and cupped the back of Rocky's calf with

one hand while easing the boot off with the other. She repeated
the procedure with the other foot. "There," she said, sitting back
on her heels. "I'm going to find something to strap up that shoulder with." She climbed to her feet and left the blonde alone again.
When she returned, she handed Rocky a glass of orange juice and
a pill. "I think it's okay to take another now." Then Jo picked up
the phone and dialled a number from memory. It rang for a while
before it was answered.

"For Chrissake, Jo, now what?"

"Leo, how did you know it was me?"

"Because no one else would think they could get away with
waking me twice in one night. What is it?"

Jo sighed. "I'm worried about Rocky's shoulder. I think you
could have done more."

"Of course I should have bloody well done more. I probably
should have x-rayed it. I probably should have packed you both off
to the local hospital. I put it back in, and I gave you some pain
pills. Both could get me struck off if it became public."

"I'm sorry."

A long sigh from the doctor. "So what was bothering you?"

"Shouldn't it be strapped up?"

"Actually, yes. I meant to tell you that. I didn't really have
anything there that would do. Not in the office anyway. Yes, get a
scarf or something, and strap her arm across her stomach. Not too
tight, just to stop it from moving around. But saying that," he continued, "every day, just get the shoulder moving a little. Not so it
causes her huge amounts of pain, just to keep the muscles from
seizing up."

"Anything else?"

"Cold is good. Ice, like I said before, or a packet of frozen
peas, inside a t-shirt."

"Okay, Doc. Thanks."

"Can I please go back to sleep now?"

"Yeah, good night, Leo."

Her answer was the dialling tone, so she replaced the phone
in the cradle. When she turned back towards her guest, she found
Rocky valiantly trying to keep her eyes open. "Be right back," she
said to the sleepy woman. She found a scarf, not quite remembering where it came from, or whether it was even hers, and returned
to the lounge. "Right then, let's see if we can work this out." She
eased Rocky's good arm down, supporting the injured one as she

wrapped the scarf around it. Then she wound the makeshift sling around the blonde's neck, being careful that the weight of supporting the arm wasn't put upon the injured shoulder.

After she finished, she looked at her friend, who returned her look with sleepy green eyes. Jo sat in the corner of the sofa and gently pulled the unresisting woman around, so that she leaned back against her chest. Then she reached down and picked up the bag of frozen peas that she had taken from the freezer. She thanked her housekeeper briefly, as she wrapped them in a thin t-shirt and eased the package below the scarf and onto the injured shoulder. With Rocky reclining, there was not so much pressure on the sling, and so the package sat snugly without causing the blonde further pain.

"I can't sleep here." Rocky's voice was slurred, no doubt testament to the pain pills she'd just taken.

"Just rest for a while," Jo whispered into soft hair.

The blonde head nodded slightly. "Okay, but I won't be able to sl—" she murmured as she fell asleep.

Jo tightened her grip on the small blonde, buried her face in her hair, and fell asleep herself, a smile of contentment on her face.

Jo woke with a start, taking a moment to reorient herself. A blonde head rested on her chest, the gentle rise and fall of the smaller woman's chest indicating she was still deeply asleep. The tall woman tried to stretch beneath the comfortable weight but found she couldn't. And, for the umpteenth time in the past few days, she found herself stiff and uncomfortable after spending too long sleeping on the sofa.

She eased herself to a sitting position, the girl in her arms, still soundly asleep, sat up with her. With great care, she managed to get out from beneath the blonde. Holding the seemingly boneless girl, she reached across, took a large plump cushion from the armchair, and put it behind Rocky, then settled her on it. She made sure that the injured girl's arm was in a comfortable position, and then with a long lingering look at her guest, she made her way upstairs to the bathroom.

After a short visit to the bathroom, she went into her bedroom, shedding clothes as she went. She selected some looser items from drawers and the wardrobe. Pulling on a pair of sweat

pants and a large t-shirt. She went back downstairs. After putting
her head through the lounge doorway to check on Rocky, Jo made
her way to the kitchen, filled the kettle, and turned it on.

Jo slumped on the chair at the small kitchen table. She felt
like she'd slept only a few hours for the past few days, though she
knew that wasn't so. Up until the previous weekend, her life had
been completely undemanding. She'd had fun and thought little of
the consequences. And now, a woman who she'd had no knowledge of only days ago was the focus of her entire life. For the first
time in her life, she was putting someone else's well-being before
her own. And in a strange way, it made her feel worth something.
She'd never felt that before, she realised. Never thought of herself
as some kind of benefactor. She knew she would have a time of it,
trying to persuade Rocky to let her help her. What must the
blonde think? Here was some crazy rich woman babbling on about
dreams and premonitions. But hadn't Rocky said she felt something too? So maybe it wasn't so crazy. Maybe this was the point
in her life when her reason for being was fulfilled. She certainly
hadn't found the purpose of her existence up until that point.
Unless you count...No, she decided not to go there.

The kettle automatically turning itself off startled her slightly,
and she wearily stood and retrieved a couple of mugs from the
small cupboard. She smiled as she saw the two objects in her
hands. Even subconsciously she was already thinking of her and
the girl now asleep on her sofa. She suspected Rocky would sleep
longer so she put one mug back and put a tea bag into the remaining mug. It was then that she heard the cry. Forgetting the tea, she
rushed back into the lounge, finding the girl struggling to sit up.

Rocky's face was glistening with the effort, white as chalk.
"No!" she screamed, her good arm flailing in front of her as if to
ward off an imaginary attacker.

"Rocky, please." Jo tried to approach the distraught woman
carefully, not wanting to scare her further. Because that's what she
saw in the pale face: fear, pure unadulterated terror. Rocky was
weakening, and Jo managed to get hold of her arm and gently
push her back down onto the sofa. But that just seemed to galvan-
ise the blonde, and she pushed up against her apparent attacker,
crying out in rage and pain as she did so. Jo knelt beside the sofa,
one hand holding Rocky's good arm, the other stroking her face.

"Hey, what's all this about?" she asked, watching the eyes
darting beneath tightly shut eyelids. "Shh, you're safe here." She

pushed damp hair off Rocky's forehead.

"No, not again. I can't..." Rocky pushed up again, but was weakening. "Please, don't...I can't..."

"Rocky, baby. It's Jo, you're safe here." Jo kept repeating the phrase over and over, and eventually the blonde started to relax. Jo thought she was probably exhausted rather than convinced that she was safe. As she waited for Rocky to be still again, she traced a thin scar that ran for a couple of inches above a pale eyebrow. She felt Rocky's shirt and realised it was drenched with sweat. She knew she had to get the girl out of her clothes but to do that she would have to wake her.

"Hey there," she said and took a limp hand in her own, rubbing the palm with her thumb. "Rocky?"

Green eyes fluttered open and tracked dazedly to Jo. For a moment, utter confusion was evident in the pale face, then she recognised the woman smiling warmly at her, and the small body relaxed once more.

"I'm..." Rocky croaked and coughed, wincing against the pain in her shoulder.

"Stay still. I'll get you some juice."

Rocky did as she was told, passing a shaking hand across her sweat-drenched face. Her head was thumping and she knew she'd had one of her nightmares. They always left her shaking.

"Here you are," Jo said as she reappeared, a glass of orange juice in her hand. She placed the juice on the low coffee table and helped Rocky to sit up.

Rocky slumped back against the sofa, holding on to her injured arm with her good one once more.

"Painful?" Jo asked as she handed Rocky the juice.

Rocky merely nodded, taking the juice from Jo and quenching her raging thirst. "Not used to this," she said as her voice returned.

The tall woman eased herself onto the sofa, next to her friend. "Used to what?" She took the glass from Rocky, noticing the shaking in the small hand.

"The warmth...made me sleepy."

Jo shrugged. "That and the pills." She took a deep breath. "You okay?"

Rocky had been gazing at her, unashamedly staring. "Yeah." She looked away, suddenly finding the fire extremely interesting.

"Rocky, you were screaming." Jo reached out and once again

took a shaking hand into her own. "And now you're shaking."

"Just confused when I woke up here. That's all." She closed her eyes against the throbbing headache, which was intensifying rapidly.

"You were terrified, Rocky." Jo gripped the hand tighter as Rocky attempted to pull away. Then she reached across with her free hand and cupped a flushed cheek. "You're hot. Your clothes are drenched through. We need to get you changed into something dry." Panic-filled green eyes turned towards her. "Hey," Jo said quickly. "There's nothing to be afraid of. Just let me help you."

Rocky's head dropped. "This is really hard." She looked back up into gentle blue eyes. "I've been alone so long. Haven't had to depend on anyone."

"And I've never had anyone depend on me. But then," she leaned forward, brushing her lips against the blonde's, "I've never cared about anyone else before." When she leaned back she saw Rocky's eyes were shut, a dreamy look on her face. But Jo put that down to the drugs. "Come on," she said. "Let's get you out of those clothes."

Green eyes snapped open, and Jo winced. "That sounds all wrong, doesn't it? I don't mean it like that. Well...I mean, I would like...it if you would..." Jo sighed long and hard. "Look, I'll help you for as long as you need me. But if you're not comfortable with something, just say. Sound good to you?"

Rocky nodded shakily and allowed herself to be carefully pulled to her feet.

"Come on, I'll find something for you to wear." Jo headed up the stairs, smiling to herself when she heard the blonde following.

Rocky stood outside Jo's bedroom, watching as her friend rifled through her drawers trying to find something for the smaller woman to wear.

"This might do." Jo held up a plain white t-shirt, which was large even on her. She estimated it would come down to the smaller girl's knees. She threw that on the bed and opened a smaller top drawer, throwing some briefs onto the bed next to the t-shirt. Rocky was still standing outside the door. "You can come on in."

Rocky entered, looking around the room as she did so. "This is nice."

"Thanks." She took the blonde gently by the shoulders and pushed her down onto the bed. Rocky was too tired to resist and sat quietly watching with sleepy eyes as Jo started to undo the knot holding the sling in place. She held the injured arm in place as she threw the scarf into a corner. "Okay, let's think about the best way to do this. Hold on." She ran down the stairs and looked through the drawers in the kitchen, finally finding what she was looking for—a large pair of scissors.

Rocky hadn't moved, and Jo knelt down again in front of her. "The shirt should be easy to get off, but the thermal will be more difficult," Jo said. Rocky nodded, bending her good arm as Jo eased the shirt off. "We'll leave the thermal on for now. I think we'll do the trousers next."

"No." The word was little more than a whisper.

Jo ducked to see into watery green eyes. "Rocky? Sweetheart, we need to get you out of these damp clothes."

"It's okay. I'm used to it."

"But tonight you don't have to be used to it. And tonight you're sick. And tired. And hurting." She ran her fingers through damp blonde hair. "Please?"

"You don't understand." Tears squeezed from between tightly shut lids.

"What don't I understand?" She waited patiently, but Rocky just shook her head. "Hey," she whispered and got up from the floor and sat beside the sobbing girl on the bed. She carefully put her arm around Rocky's shoulders and gently pulled her against her chest. Jo supported Rocky's injured arm with one hand, the other rubbing the heaving back. She rested her cheek against the blonde hair and let the girl cry herself out. When she was finished, she pulled away from Jo and looked up at her with tired green eyes.

"Are you going to tell me what's wrong?" Jo asked, wiping away tears with her fingers.

Rocky nodded and pushed her hair out of her eyes. "It's just...my clothes, they're...well, they're dirty."

Jo cocked her head to one side, waiting for Rocky to continue.

Rocky took a deep breath. "I don't get to change very often."

Realisation hit Jo, and she felt suddenly ashamed that she had put the girl through this without thinking about it. "Did you think that would bother me?"

Rocky shrugged. "Everything you have is so nice." She looked around the room, at the quilt and at the clothes Jo had put out for her to wear. "So clean."

"Rocky," she said, pulling the pale face back so that Rocky was looking at her again. "I didn't think twice about bringing you back here. I know where you've been living for the past five years, and I know the consequences of that. I'm not going to judge you because you have dirty trousers on." She smiled, relieved to see the smile echoed in the face of the blonde. "So, will you let me help you?"

Rocky nodded her head and stood shakily. Jo stood as well, and they faced each other for a moment. Rocky looked suddenly very vulnerable, standing there in her thermal vest and huge trousers.

Jo turned her attention to the old leather belt, which held the very large pair of trousers up. There was no button or zip, and once they were lowered Jo was faced with another similar pair of trousers. "Okay, step out of them." Rocky did as she was asked and waited while Jo struggled with the button fastening the top of the second pair of trousers. "The button's stiff," she said as she managed to get it open.

"Army surplus," Rocky said. "I always tried to get it if I could."

Jo cast a quick glance up as she lowered the zip of the trousers and pulled them down. Many times before, she had undressed women in this room. But how different this occasion was. This time there was no ulterior motive. There would be no seduction, no night of blinding passion.

"Sexy, huh?" Rocky asked with a small smile. She looked down at herself, now dressed in her thermal vest and long johns.

Jo sat back on her heels. "Looks good to me." She smiled up at the blonde, pleased to see that she appeared to be relaxing. "Ready?" she asked, hooking her fingers in the waistband of the long johns.

Rocky nodded, and the white garment was pulled down over slim legs. Rocky stood now in nothing but a white vest, dark blue briefs, and thick, grey army socks.

She swallowed hard, seeing the shapely legs only inches from her face. "Um, there you are." She stood quickly and picked up the scissors. "I'm going to have to cut the vest off." Rocky had started to shiver, and Jo knew it was time to start hurrying. She didn't believe the girl was cold but knew the ordeal was starting to take its toll on the blonde.

"I'll cut it from the back," Jo said.

Jo turned the blonde and carefully started to cut the vest from the hem to the neck. When it was open at the back, she pulled it forward and off. Trying hard to avert her eyes from the expanse of creamy white skin in front of her, she reached for the t-shirt lying on the bed. She opened the neck and drew it over the blonde head. "Can you get your arm through?" she asked.

Rocky tried, and, as the shirt was so big, she managed it with comparative ease. When she was in the t-shirt, Jo turned her and retrieved the makeshift sling. Positioning Rocky's arm against her stomach, she refastened the sling.

"There, how's that?"

Rocky smiled up at her; there were tears in her eyes. "Thank you," she whispered.

"Come on." Jo pulled back the quilt and urged Rocky into the bed. "You get some rest. I'm going down to get one of your pain-killers."

Rocky snuggled into the thick quilt, her eyes fluttering closed as her head hit the pillow. When Jo returned, Rocky was asleep. Jo lay on top of the quilt next to her friend. For a long moment, she watched her sleep. "When you wake, you will tell me about your nightmares," she told the sleeping girl, smoothing away the soft blonde hair from a warm forehead. She settled down beside Rocky, lying on top of the quilt, and kept watch. She lay in wait for the demons that had come for the girl on both occasions she had slept in Jo's presence.

And when they came, she would chase them off.

Chapter
13

Jo rolled over as she woke and found herself face to face with an angel. Rocky was lying on her back, her face turned towards her host. Jo felt a pressure on her hand and looked down to see a smaller one gripping it. Craning her neck to see the clock beside the bed, she found it was close to noon. She was surprised that the girl had slept so long. She'd expected the night demons that haunted the small blonde to pay her a visit. But she saw that the sleeping face looked relaxed though pale.

Jo enjoyed the moment, feeling free to watch the girl sleep. Her gaze fell upon soft lips slightly parted in sleep. She remembered the photograph she'd had, how she'd studied it in great detail, committed to memory every facet of the face before her. Then she looked down at the small hand curled around her own. The image blurred. Jo blinked her eyes rapidly, confused at the appearance of tears. Her gaze returned to the pale face of the blonde and found misty green eyes regarding her thoughtfully.

"Hi," Rocky said concern evident on her face. "You okay?"

Jo nodded, swallowing tightly. "Yeah, I'm fine."

They regarded each other for a long moment, the blonde not moving from her reclined position. Nor did she move as the dark-haired woman dipped her head and brushed her lips briefly against those of the smaller woman.

Jo pulled back, looking for any discomfort from Rocky. The small hand left her own, and she felt a pressure on the back of her neck, pulling her back down. Trying to keep the majority of her weight off the blonde, she gave in to the gentle tugging. The meeting of their lips was more insistent this time, the contact more solid. Both sets of breathing became ragged. Only a small gasp of pain from the smaller woman made Jo back away. "I'm sorry," she whispered, pushing dishevelled blonde hair off Rocky's face.

"It's all right. Just forgot about it for a moment then."

Jo chuckled and stood, walking around the bottom of the bed. She sat on the edge of the bed to Rocky's left and handed her the pain pill she'd put there the night before. "You'd better take this now." She helped her sit up and gave her the glass of orange juice. "I'm going to pop out for a while. Is there anything you want me to get you?"

Rocky shook her head, peering into the bottom of her now-empty glass.

"I'm going to go to the chemist, get some dressings for your side. I'm sure I could get some waterproof ones, then you could have a bath or a shower."

Green eyes looked confused. "My side?"

"Yeah, you have a couple of stitches in it."

"I do?"

Jo nodded. "What happened exactly?" She stood and went to her wardrobe, pulling out a pair of jeans.

"At the leather works?" Rocky asked.

Jo looked up from the drawers she was rifling through and nodded.

The brow beneath the fair hair furrowed as Rocky thought back to the previous night. "I was looking for wood," she began. "It was colder than usual, and I needed a lot to make sure the fire lasted through the night. I wasn't really concentrating and just about walked into a bunch of guys. I think it was a drug deal." She looked up to find wide blue eyes regarding her. She shrugged. "I ran back into the factory. I hid from them until they gave up. I was back in a part of the factory I've never been in before. When I tried to get back out, I fell through the floor," she finished in a matter-of-fact voice.

"Something must have gone right through your jacket and everything else to have cut your side," Jo said, hopping from one foot to the other as she pulled her jeans on.

"I didn't know it had. I hit the bottom pretty hard, and I knew I'd hurt my shoulder. I managed to get to my feet, and I found an old rusty ladder. I think I was down in the boiler room or something. I got out. The old boys found me and went and got Edna. Don't remember much after that."

Jo pulled on a sweatshirt. "Well, Edna got in touch with me and, more by luck than judgement, I managed to find the factory." She sat on the edge of the bed and pulled on her boots. "Right, then," she said, standing. "I'll be as quick as I can. Is there anything you need before I go?"

"No, I'm fine."

Jo hurried over to the bed, leaned down, and kissed Rocky on the forehead.

"Thanks for looking after me," the blonde said.

Jo's answer was a dazzling smile, and then she was gone. Rocky listened to her footsteps as she descended the stairs, and then heard the front door close. She snuggled back down into the quilt and drifted off to sleep again.

Rocky woke with a start. She knew she hadn't been asleep long, but the nightmare had come quickly. She had the same feeling of panic as always, the tightness in her chest and the thumping pain in her head. She tried to rise, but quickly fell back onto the bed, the pain in her shoulder excruciating. She knew she couldn't take another painkiller for a while, so she eased herself carefully out of bed and made her way to the bathroom.

As she exited the bathroom she heard a buzzing noise. She carefully descended the stairs, the pain in her shoulder making her dizzy. She went into the lounge and then the kitchen. The noise sounded again, and she followed the noise until she found a grey box with a flashing red light on it at the top of the stairs. There was a small black button next to the red light. Below the black button was a white button, with the word "open" on it.

The buzzer sounded again, causing her to take a step back. Maybe she had to do something, maybe there was a security system and Jo had forgotten to reset it. Had she set it off by walking through the house? Again the buzzer sounded, and this time she pressed the black button next to the flashing light.

"Jo?" the tinny voice asked. It was a woman.

Rocky remained silent, staring at the box in horror.

"Jo, you've changed the bloody code. Open the door."

Rocky backed away from the wall, holding her injured arm with her right hand.

"Come on, Jo. It's been days. I know you didn't mean what you said."

Rocky approached the box and spoke into the small holes at the top of it. "Jo's not here," she said quietly.

"What? Who the hell's that?" There was silence for a moment. "Look, sweetie, whoever. You just push the little white button and let me in. Then we'll see about finding you the exit door. You obviously don't know the rules. If Jojo goes out then you're meant to be gone before she gets back. It's a kind of rule with her little sleepovers. I'm surprised that she didn't explain to you." There was a sigh. "It's just good fortune I came along before she returned; saves everyone a lot of embarrassment. Now, be a good girl and open the door." She waited. "Come on, sweetie. Be good and open the door. Now don't start thinking you're any different from any of the other sweet little things she has up there."

"She told me to wait," Rocky said, more to herself than to the disembodied voice. She slumped against the wall and slid down it, staring up at the talking box with tear-filled eyes.

"Very well. You just believe that. But when she tires of you, remember this little chat. And I'll be here, waiting to give her what you couldn't."

Rocky listened to the sound of footsteps and then a car door slamming. She struggled to her feet and went in search of her stuff.

Jo parked the car in the garage and reached across for the large bag of shopping she'd put on the passenger seat. Then, taking the stairs two at a time, she made her way up to her home. It was silent in the house, and she guessed that the blonde was probably still asleep, so she climbed the next set of stairs to the upper level. The bedroom was empty, the quilt pulled back, and the t-shirt and the scarf she had used as a sling were in a heap on the floor.

She picked up the t-shirt and ran out of the room. "Rocky!" she shouted, throwing down the garment and descending the stairs quickly. She went into the kitchen and then the lounge. Rocky was nowhere to be found. She had gone.

"Shit!" was all Jo could manage, as she ran down the stairs and out into the courtyard, using her remote control to open the garage door. Once inside the car, she gunned the engine and sped out into the cold, damp day. She automatically headed for Whitechapel, that being the only connection she had with the girl.

And she hadn't gone far before she saw a familiar hunched figure. Her gut clenched as she saw the people that passed Rocky were giving her a wide berth. She parked the car slightly ahead of Rocky and got out. The blonde was struggling so much with her two bags that she didn't notice Jo until she almost walked into her.

"Rocky?" Jo asked, putting out a hesitant hand to stop the girl's unsteady progress. Rocky looked up at her, and Jo was alarmed at the pale, sweaty face and glazed eyes that met hers. "Rocky, you're ill. What d'you think you're doing?" She tried to take the two heavy bags from the shorter woman, but Rocky pulled away from her.

"Leave me alone, Jo," she said, staggering back so that her arm collided with a wall. She gasped in pain, dropping one of her bags.

Jo made a grab for her as the blonde's knees buckled, and they both ended up in a heap on the wet pavement. "Oh God, Rocky. What were you thinking?" Jo's voice was strained as she tried to keep her friend from toppling onto her side.

"What's wrong with her?" Jo turned to see a policeman exiting his patrol car. "Is she bothering you?"

Jo tore her eyes from the blonde, stood, and faced the officer. "No, she's not bothering me. I'm trying to help her."

The policeman looked from her to the crumpled figure on the pavement. "Has she been drinking or taking illegal substances?"

"No!" Jo's tone was somewhat outraged, and the policeman raised his eyebrows in a warning gesture. Jo sighed. "No," she said again, calmer. "She's not well, and I'm trying to help her. Will you help me get her into the car?" She pointed to the Merk, its indicators still flashing, parked illegally on double yellow lines.

"Wouldn't you rather I called an ambulance, Miss?"

"No, really. She's a friend. I can help her."

The policeman turned his back on her. For a moment, Jo thought he was just going to walk away and leave her. But then he reached into the car, said a few brief words to the driver, and returned, pulling on a pair of gloves. A small crowd had gathered around the slumped figure by the time the policeman reached down and pulled Rocky none too gently to her feet.

Seeing an expanse of uniform filling her vision, Rocky pulled back. But in her weakened state, she was no match for the man, who was a good few inches taller than Jo. He guided her towards the Merk and put her into the passenger seat. Jo threw her bags into the boot, thanked the policeman, and quickly sped away.

Jo pulled savagely on the handbrake as the traffic in front of her came to a halt. A delivery wagon had stopped, and the driver jumped out. He didn't seem to have any concerns that he was blocking the road as he disappeared into the shop to which he was delivering.

Jo shifted in her seat to face her passenger. "What were you thinking, Rocky? Look at you, you're in agony." There was not much sympathy in her voice.

Rocky didn't answer, just pulled off her hat and threw it into the back of the car.

"I told you I wouldn't be long."

"I know." Rocky's voice was strained. The pain in her shoulder had intensified, and she was feeling nauseous.

"So why did you run? I really don't understand. I thought I'd made it clear you were welcome in my home."

Rocky gingerly supported her injured arm. "I don't want to be a burden, cramp your style."

"My style?" Jo was incredulous. "What are you talking about?"

"I don't want to be in the way." The blonde turned pain-filled green eyes on the driver; the pain wasn't all physical. "If you want to take someone back to your place, I wouldn't want to stop you doing that."

"Rocky, what are you talking about?"

Rocky looked at her. *Tell or not tell?* Well, she wouldn't be around Jo much longer. "You had a visitor."

"Who?"

"I don't know. A woman."

Jo closed her eyes. "Did you let her in?"

"No, I spoke to her on the intercom thing."

Jo took a deep breath, suspecting to whom Rocky had spoken. "So what did she say?"

"Why is it so important?" Rocky asked quietly.

"Because it drove you out of my home!" Jo's voice rose, causing Rocky to shrink back. Seeing the movement, Jo reached out, placing a gentle hand on a trembling thigh. "I'm sorry. I think I know who you spoke to."

"It doesn't matter." The blonde looked down at the hand on her thigh.

"But don't you see? It does. Whatever this person said to you caused you to leave. I want to know."

A blast of a horn behind her made her look up to see that the car that was parked opposite the delivery wagon had moved and she could now drive through the gap.

Rocky missed the warmth of Jo's hand on her thigh and looked across at the driver, taking in the tense lines of her face. "I shouldn't have gone like that." Jo didn't look at her, but Rocky saw the muscles in her face shift as she clenched her jaw. "I'm sorry, Jo. You've done so much for me. I shouldn't have believed her."

Jo sighed loudly. "Whatever it was she said was probably true. Up until a couple of days ago, I didn't care about anyone." Jo steered the car off the road, coming to a stop in a small side street. She took the car out of gear but left the engine running. She turned to face Rocky. "I want to help you, Rocky. I've never done anything to help another soul in my life. There are people I know who would laugh in your face if you told them I was helping you. The person you talked to today was one of them. I'm asking you to trust me. Will you do that?"

Rocky bowed her head and nodded. "I shouldn't have doubted you." She looked up and reached across and took Jo's hand. "I'm sorry."

Jo gave her hand a squeeze. "Let's go home." She put the car into gear and pulled out into the traffic again.

As Rocky hadn't really gone that far, it was only a few minutes before they arrived back at Jo's home. But when they arrived there was an unpleasant surprise awaiting them. "Trixie," was all Jo said as she got out of the car and walked around to help Rocky out. Trixie had unfolded herself from her own car as the Merk glided into the courtyard.

Rocky looked a state. Her hair was in disarray and her face was pale and pasty as testament to the pain she was feeling. She concentrated hard on not falling to the ground as she stepped out of the car and didn't notice the tensing of her friend.

"Oh my God. What is that?" Trixie stared in utter disbelief at the woman Jo was helping.

Jo ignored her and opened the door to the house. She turned to Rocky and ducked her head. "Can you get upstairs? There's something I need to do." Rocky nodded. "Okay, you go on and go sit in the lounge. I won't be long." She watched the blonde as she slowly climbed the stairs, then turned to the woman who was leaning casually on her car.

Trixie was smiling and shaking her head. "Oh, Jojo. Even for you, this is kinky."

"I think you'd better leave, Trix. Before I do something we'll both regret." Jo's voice was low as she approached the woman.

Trixie folded her arms across her chest, the smile never leaving her face as her sometime lover came to within inches of her. "Jo, baby, if you had told me you wanted something a little younger, I could have helped you. Found you something at least a little more hygienic."

Jo's hand didn't move that quickly, so Trixie didn't flinch as the taller woman's fist took hold of the front of her very expensive Kashmir coat. "Listen to me," she hissed. "I'm helping a friend. Something alien to you, I know. But I want you to try very hard, and just maybe you'll be able to believe that I can. Now, I want you to go away. Find one of your other little friends to play your games with."

Trixie placed her own hand over the one pressed into her chest. "She won't satisfy you the way I do, Jo. You know that. She won't let you do the things I let you do." Trixie smiled, seeing the blue eyes close. "Admit it, Jo. You want me. Now."

Jo pushed her away and took a step back. "No more." Jo backed further away.

Trixie followed, like a panther stalking its prey, looking very much as she did the first night they'd met. The blonde had spotted Jo, made her a target, and later that night had taken her home. She reached out an immaculately manicured finger and traced the tense jawline. "Jojo, why so tense? You know I have a cure for that."

Jo was standing with her back against her own car now. She reached up and took the hand into her own, pulling it to her lips.

Trixie smiled a smile of triumph, but it soon left her lips as her fingers were bent back. "Jo! Stop it!" she screamed as the pain in her hand drove her to her knees.

Jo bent to speak into the ear of the now sobbing blonde. "I'm not going to fight you, Trix. I want you to go and get in your car and drive away." Again the voice was a low hiss. "I don't want you to come here again, because if I see you anywhere near me, I will hurt you." She gave the woman's wrist one more savage twist before releasing her.

Trixie scrambled to her feet. "You bloody pervert," she cried as she got into her car. She lowered the window as she started the engine. "This isn't the end of this," she screamed as she drove from the courtyard.

Jo stood in the drizzling rain and looked down at her shaking hands. Then she got into her own car and drove it into the garage. Suddenly the need to be with Rocky was overwhelming, and she took the stairs two at a time in her effort to get back to her house-guest.

Rocky was sitting on the sofa again. She had obviously not even had the strength to remove her jacket. She turned weary eyes onto Jo as the tall woman rushed into the room.

Jo dropped to her knees in front of Rocky. "Are you in a lot of pain?"

Rocky nodded. "My fault though." She looked into the blue eyes of her friend. "What happened downstairs?"

Jo sighed. "I told Trixie to stay away."

"I don't want to cause trouble between you and your friends."

"Trixie wasn't what I would call a 'friend'. We slept together, that was all." She looked up at Rocky, waiting to see the disgust in her face.

"So you used each other?" the blonde asked.

"I suppose we did."

"Did you enjoy sleeping with her?"

"Yes, I did."

"But you didn't want to be with her?"

"Not in a relationship, no."

Rocky chewed her bottom lip. "Are you in a relationship with anyone else?"

"No, I'm not."

"Do you want to be?"

"Yes, I do."

Rocky smiled. "Anyone I know?"

Jo chuckled and shook her head. "Why aren't you angry? I just told you I slept with someone I'm not particularly fond of because she's good in bed."

"It's not for me to be angry. How can I be angry with some-one who is changing their whole life to keep me safe?"

"I'm not—" Jo began.

Rocky raised a hand. "So you regularly help homeless peo-ple?"

"You know I don't."

"Exactly my point." She reached down and took Jo's hand. "I'm glad I'm the one you're saving."

Jo smiled. "Come on." She got to her feet and then helped Rocky. "I got some waterproof dressing for your wound. I want you to have a nice relaxing bath, and then we'll have something to eat. How does that sound?" She took Rocky's jacket and hung it in the hall, then turned the blonde in the direction of the stairs. In the bedroom, Jo gently turned Rocky to face her. "Do you want a painkiller?"

Rocky shook her head. "No, not yet, they make me sleepy."

"Okay. Listen," Jo searched for the words. "I'm going to help you undress. Are you okay with that?"

Rocky considered her reply. "I can't manage on my own, and I can't think of anyone else I'd rather have helping me."

"I was worried. You've been so independent for so long."

"I know, and I thought it would be hard, letting someone else do everything for me."

"Is it? Hard, I mean." Jo pushed Rocky gently back onto the bed and started to take off her boots.

Rocky looked down at the top of the dark head. "No, it's not hard." She smiled. "I'm enjoying it actually."

Jo looked up at her, a lopsided grin gracing her features. "Well, don't get too used to it." She reached for the tattered shirt, the only thing Rocky was wearing beneath the jacket. She unbuttoned it very slowly and, when the last button was undone, she sat back on her heels. "You okay?" she asked quietly.

Rocky nodded, and Jo pushed the shirt back off the slim shoulders, being careful not to jar the injury. Rocky watched Jo's face as the shirt fell onto the bed behind her. She watched Jo's eyes leave her own and drop to take in her naked form. She was fascinated as Jo's eyes almost changed colour and her mouth dropped open.

"Jo?" she asked, feeling strange that she felt no embarrassment being under this woman's scrutiny.

"My God, you're beautiful," gasped Jo, looking back up at her. "But I knew that all along." Jo leaned forward, her lips meeting Rocky's, her hands going to the waistband of the tatty trousers.

Chapter
14

Jo pulled one side of the waistband of Rocky's trousers down and leaned in to peer at the wound. It was still covered by the dressing that Leo had applied and there was a small amount of blood staining it.

"I'm going to pull the dressing off," she warned the blonde.

Rocky had placed her good arm on the tall woman's back as Jo knelt between her legs.

"Hold on. Ready?" she asked as she glanced up at the pale face. Rocky nodded, and Jo slowly pulled the dressing off the wound. She stopped when she heard a hiss of pain. "Sorry."

"Just pull it quickly," Rocky said, trying to see what Jo was doing.

"I'm worried I'll pull on the stitches. Hang on." She leaned in closer to get a better look beneath the pad. The stitches were small and precise, exactly what she would expect from one of the wealthiest plastic surgeons in the business. "It looks okay." And with that, she quickly pulled the dressing away. She held Rocky steady with one hand and examined the wound. To her inexperienced eyes it looked awful, but there was no bleeding.

"Right then," she said, standing. She reached into a bag on the bed. "These are supposed to be waterproof." The pads in the packet were large squares of lint, with a waterproof backing. She placed one gently on the wound and smoothed down the edges. "How's your shoulder?"

"Painful," she said.

"A bath will help." Jo took a step back. "Do you want me to help?" She gestured towards Rocky's trousers with a waving hand.

"Well..." Rocky stood shakily and tried to ease the trousers down with one hand. She couldn't remember how she'd got them on. She'd been upset and angry and had ignored the shooting pains in her shoulder as she pulled on the two pairs of trousers before. Now, in the warmth of Jo's presence, she wanted nothing more than to let her new friend help her. "Um, could you?"

With a smile, Jo stood in front of her and undid the second pair of trousers. Then she pulled both down over slim hips and held Rocky's hand as the blonde stepped out of them. Jo handed Rocky her robe. "Sit for a moment while I run the bath."

Rocky did as she was asked and listened to the sound of water running into the huge bath in the next room. She pulled the robe around her shoulders, holding it with her good arm.

Jo poked her head around the door. "You ready?"

Rocky nodded and followed Jo into the bathroom.

Jo helped her into the bath again trying hard not to let the perfect body revealed to her distract her from her task. She looked down as the blonde relaxed back against the tub. "I'll, um, leave you to soak for a while," she said as she backed out of the room.

Jo went downstairs and pulled a chair out from beneath the table in the kitchen. She rested her elbows on the table and her head in her hands. "Oh, heaven help me," she said, remembering the body she'd just left in the bath upstairs. "She has no idea what she does to me."

She scrubbed her face vigorously with her hands and stood, opening the fridge door. "Would you like me to cook something?" she called, loud enough for the woman upstairs to hear.

"If you're hungry," came the distant reply.

"Are you hungry?"

"I am if you are."

"Well, I am."

"Okay, I am too."

Shaking her head, Jo picked out some eggs, some bacon, and some mushrooms. She'd seen someone else make an omelette once and was sure she could do it.

"Jo?"

She put all the things down on the table and went to the bottom of the stairs. "Yeah?" she called up.

"Could you help me here?"

Jo swallowed. "Sure," she said tightly and ascended the stairs. She stood outside the door. "What was it you wanted?"

"I don't have a washcloth."

Jo went to the airing cupboard and pulled out a washcloth and a couple of large towels. Pausing before she entered, she knocked on the door and pushed it open when she heard Rocky invite her in.

"This is wonderful," the blonde said, relaxing in the deep water. She had sunk down so that she was completely beneath the water, just the tips of her knees showing apart from her head. "I haven't had a bath in years." She looked up at the dark-haired woman, taking in the look of shock Jo couldn't keep from her face. "I had showers. Don't think I've been all these years without washing."

"Oh, I didn't," Jo said quickly. "I could tell that you'd washed. I mean, your skin it's so..." Jo cleared her throat. "It's just obvious." She placed the towels on the floor and handed Rocky the washcloth.

A small hand emerged from the water and took it from her.

Jo sat on the edge of the bath, one hand trailing in the water. "Rocky?"

Rocky said nothing, but green eyes peeking from beneath damp hair found Jo's gaze. She inclined her head slightly.

"How did you manage? Out on the streets."

Rocky closed her eyes, and Jo thought she wasn't going to answer. Then the blonde head nodded slightly, and she took a deep breath. "When I first got there, I was terrified. I met Edna almost immediately. She took me under her wing. She and some of her friends." Rocky soaped the cloth absentmindedly. "I couldn't claim benefit. I was only fifteen, and they would have sent me back or into care. Either way they would have been informed and I didn't want that." Jo opened her mouth to ask a question. "Don't stop me now, Jo."

Jo nodded.

"So I went with Edna. She didn't ask me why I was there, just accepted that I had to be there. Pretty soon after, a guy called Tito tried to get me to go on the streets for him. He had a load of young girls working for him. Edna tried to protect me, but in the end, he got to me. I knocked him out. Right hook, right to the jaw. We had to get out of there then and came to Whitechapel. I've been there ever since. Old Dougie said I punched harder than Rocky, and they just started to call me that." Rocky grew quiet, looking down at the cloth in her hands and remembering her old friends.

Jo felt an overwhelming sympathy for the girl, who suddenly looked very small, very vulnerable in the bath. "Let's get you out before you start getting cold."

Rocky looked up, tears falling from her chin into the water.

She handed the cloth to Jo who soaped it again and gently applied it to the blonde's back and shoulders. When she'd done as much as she thought she should, she handed the cloth to Rocky and stood up. "I'll go and find you something to wear." She left the bathroom, angrily wiping away the tears as she went.

Jo was laying a t-shirt and some underwear on the bed when Rocky appeared in the bedroom. "There's some stuff for you to put on." She bent and took a pair of sweatpants out of a drawer. "I'll leave you to get dressed. If you need me just shout." She left the room, closing the door behind her, and made her way back down the stairs to the kitchen.

When Rocky arrived in the kitchen, looking swamped in Jo's clothes, she found the taller woman peeling large open mushrooms, removing the dirty skin and dirt. "Hi. Take a seat in the lounge. I'll come in and we'll change your dressing for a dry one and put your sling back on."

Rocky did as she was told and sat gingerly on the sofa. Her shoulder was throbbing. Jo came in and made short work of changing the dressing on the wound and settling the injured arm into the makeshift sling. She gave Rocky a glass of orange juice and a pain pill.

"It makes me sleepy," the blonde complained.

"You need it. Don't tell me your shoulder isn't hurting." Jo stood and watched until Rocky took the pill, then returned to her omelette creation. She brought the hot food in a little later and balanced a tray on Rocky's lap. Jo placed a fork in her hand. "I cut it up for you," she said, placing a plate with a couple of buttered bread rolls on the seat beside her. Jo sat in the armchair with her own tray and tried her omelette. Her eyebrows rose. It actually tasted like an omelette. She looked up and was inordinately pleased to see the blonde tucking in with gusto.

When they finished, Jo took the trays out to the kitchen and settled herself on the sofa next to Rocky. "How do you feel now?" she asked.

"I feel good. Kind of out of it. Must be the pills." Rocky eased herself back against a large cushion and squirmed for a while before finding a comfortable position.

"Will you tell me your real name, Rocky?" Jo couldn't meet the green gaze, instead watching her hand as it worried the hem of Rocky's t-shirt.

"No one's called me anything but Rocky for so long."

It was obvious that the girl was dredging up bad memories, and Jo silently berated herself for bringing up the subject while her friend was still recovering from her injuries. "I'm sorry," Jo said, reaching out and taking Rocky's free hand. "Forget I asked."

"No, it's okay," the blonde said, almost in wonderment. She had kept this secret for so long, living with it gnawing away at her. And now she found herself willing to give up her past. Willing to share the pain.

"Michelle."

"Michelle?" Jo asked.

"My name. Michelle Kersey."

Jo leaned over and gently kissed the blonde. "Hello, Michelle. It's nice to meet you."

Rocky put her hand behind the dark head, pulling Jo into the kiss. It was only when the taller woman felt her flinch that she pulled back, finding that her hand had sneaked under the hem of the t-shirt and was caressing smooth skin. Jo blushed; Rocky chuckled.

"Come here," Jo said, leaning back into the arm of the sofa and gently turning and pulling the blonde so that she rested against her chest. She was careful to position the injured arm so there was no strain on it, and then she settled her arms around Rocky's middle. "So, Michelle, are you going to tell me who you are?"

Jo felt the head under her chin shake. "It's been so long since anyone has called me that. You know, my parents only called me Michelle when I was in trouble. They used to call me Shelly."

"Where are they now?" If it were possible to pull words back into your mouth, Jo would have done so immediately. She felt the small body in her arms stiffen, and Rocky tried to sit up. "Hey, I'm sorry. I shouldn't have pushed," she spoke softly into dampened hair, her lips brushing an ear.

Rocky relaxed again. She was quiet for a long time, and when she began to talk it was in hushed tones. Her voice almost strained with the effort it took to tell her tale.

"I grew up in Cornwall, near Tintagel on the north Cornish

coast. My father had his own business and was very successful. Though the headquarters was in London, he ran it from home and would only spend a few days a month away." She took a deep breath. "We were very happy. I was an only child, and I wasn't exactly spoilt, but I didn't want for much." She took hold of Jo's hand, intertwining her fingers with the longer ones. "I loved it there. It's such a beautiful place." She turned slightly. "Have you ever been there?"

"No, I haven't," Jo said softly.

"You must." She squeezed the hand held within her own. "We must. I'd like to go back one day. Will you take me?"

"Of course," Jo whispered. "I told you I'd take you anywhere you wanted."

"I've been waiting a long time to be happy again." The blonde head rested back against Jo's collarbone. "I don't think about them often, because it hurts so much. I missed them for such a long time, and that hurt. So I wanted to forget them, but I never could. And I hated myself, because I wasn't strong enough to forget them." She sighed. "I survived by not feeling, not feeling the pain or the loneliness. Not feeling the loss of my parents." She pulled the hand up that she was holding and brushed her lips against the knuckles. "You made me feel, Jo." She pressed the hand to her cheek. "The first time I saw you. All those feelings came rushing back. At first I was angry with you. I didn't want those feelings. I had taken five years to work out how to bury them so that I could just get through the days. And along you come and turned it all on its head."

They sat quietly for a long moment, comfortable in each other's presence. Then Rocky spoke again.

"We'd gone out for a drive, taken a picnic. We stopped by the river; it wasn't that far from where we lived. It was a beautiful day, quite late in the year though. October, I think. But it was a sunny, blue sky. We stopped beside the river. We were eating our picnic, and I went down to the riverbank. There were rocks, which created a path across the river. I couldn't stay off them. I was jumping from one to the next. Dad was shouting at me to get off them. I didn't, of course. I fell and hit my head. They both jumped in after me. Dad got me out, but Mum got into difficulties. He put me on the bank and went back for her. It was so calm, hardly a wave. They never came back." Rocky felt the arms tighten around her, and it gave her the strength to go on. "I waited for them. It got dark, and then someone found me. If I had gone for help, maybe..."

"You were hurt?" Jo was holding onto Rocky now with desperation, almost feeling the girl reliving something she probably hadn't spoken of in years.

"Someone found me and called an ambulance." The pain pills were making her tired, and she fought to stay awake. "I wanted to tell them where they were. But I was so tired. My head hurt. They put this thing on my face, and I couldn't talk. I tried to tell them."

"I know you did." Rocky was becoming more upset, and Jo held her close. "Shh, now."

"It was my fault."

"It was not your fault, don't say that." She pulled the trembling body back against her own. "Rest now."

"They were the only people who loved me." Rocky's voice trailed off. The pain pills and the effort of reliving the moment she lost her beloved parents were finally getting the better of her.

"Not the only people," Jo whispered into soft blonde hair. "Not any more." Jo held Rocky as the blonde drifted into a troubled sleep. She listened to the sounds of discomfort coming from the woman in her arms and debated waking her. But she thought not; she would let Rocky sleep.

She thought back to her own childhood and tried to imagine losing her parents. Her life would have differed greatly from that of her new friend's. Her parents tended to show their love with material things. Though she was not neglected, she never knew the kind of love that Rocky had described. But not knowing that life could be any different, she was happy with the attention she got from her parents.

Rocky started talking in her sleep. "Please." The word came out as a gasp; the pain behind it and the tension in the body in her arms scared Jo. "Oh, God." Rocky's head was moving from side to side; her free arm came up to protect her face. "No, no more."

"Rocky," Jo said gently, her mouth very close to the blonde's ear. "It's Jo. It's all right."

"Not again," the blonde gasped, the pain in her voice evident.

"You're safe here. Rocky, you're not there anymore." She gently pulled the small hand to her lips, kissing the palm. But it was wrenched from her grasp as the small woman tried to sit up.

Rocky screamed in anger and pain when she was held in strong arms.

"Rocky, no! You're safe here. Don't go back to that place." She held on, burying her face in soft hair, wrapping her arms around the trembling body. "Rocky, come back to me now. Wake up."

Rocky's fight continued; she pushed back against the body behind her.

"Please, Rocky, wake up."

Slowly the struggling calmed, and the blonde lay in Jo's arms, dragging air into her lungs as if she'd been pulled from a raging sea. "I'm okay," Rocky said in a shaky voice as she came to full awareness. "Let me sit up."

Jo reluctantly released her hold on the blonde and sat back. She watched as Rocky moved away from her and wiped away her tears with a shaking hand.

"How long was I asleep?" She turned glazed green eyes on the stunned looking woman.

"Not even half an hour." Jo moved a little closer, rubbing the trembling back gently. "Are you okay now?"

"It takes a while." She was now rubbing her forehead with the heel of her hand. "I'll be fine in a minute."

"Does this happen often?"

Rocky turned to regard her.

Jo held her hand up. "Sorry."

"No." Rocky sighed. "Don't be. I think talking about it tonight brought back some bad memories. Things I've tried not to relive for a while."

"I shouldn't have made you..."

Rocky looked at the stricken face, her guts twisting as she realised Jo was taking the blame for her nightmares. She turned on the sofa and, lying on her right side, laid her head on Jo's lap, feeling a tentative hand come to rest on her head. She felt the hand start to smooth her hair and looked up into concerned blue eyes.

"It felt good to tell you," she said quietly. "I need to remember them. They were everything to me."

"Will you tell me what happened next?"

Rocky closed her eyes, revelling for a moment in the feel of the hand, gentle on her scalp. Jo's other hand found her free one, and held on.

"I woke up a couple of days later in the hospital. I'd had an operation to relieve pressure on my brain." She paused, seemingly collecting herself for the next part. "They'd found the car and had identified me by that. They found my parents' bodies the day I woke up. I was alone in the hospital for over a week."

Jo looked down at the strained face and pushed blonde hair away from closed eyes. "Is that why you don't like hospitals now?"

"Yeah. I was terrified. I thought I was going to be there forever." Rocky snuggled closer, relieved when Jo's grip on her tightened.

"Why wasn't someone informed earlier? Your parents had family, didn't they?"

"Oh they were informed. My mother's sister had moved to Leicester when she married someone from that part of the country. They had some checks made to find out first if there was anyone else who could take me on." She looked up at the woman holding her, seeing more compassion in those blue eyes than she'd felt in the many years since her parents' death. She'd kept the pain inside, allowing only Edna a tiny glimpse of it. But she finally felt she could unburden some of the crippling weight of her torment. She looked away from the eyes, which urged her on, focussing on the material close to her face that covered Jo's stomach.

"They took me up to Leicester a month after the accident. They put my parents' house on the market as soon as they could and took me to their place. I loved living in Cornwall, but they took me away." She looked up again. "Have you ever been to Leicester?"

Jo shook her head, not trusting her voice. She wanted to remain strong for Rocky, but never in her life had she felt the pain that she was feeling now. And it was for someone she'd known only a few days. But how she wished she could turn the clock back. She wanted to be there on that riverbank, holding the injured and confused girl. She felt an irrational feeling of guilt, and then anger.

"Jo?"

Jo managed to unclench her jaw.

"You okay?" Rocky asked, struggling to sit up. Jo helped her, and then sat back against the arm of the sofa.

"Yeah, I'm fine. Just getting a little angry that you were alone for so long." She shrugged and rubbed her face vigorously, screwing her eyes shut.

"Don't get angry because of me; it's past now," the blonde said, reaching out a tentative hand and closing it around Jo's hand. She felt the tension in her friend, amazed that this woman would feel anger for something she had no control over. "There was nothing you could do. Nothing anyone could do."

"But why did you end up here, living on the streets?" That was it; that was the question Jo had wanted to ask since she first saw the picture in the gallery. "What could be so awful, that you would choose to live with nothing?"

Rocky opened her mouth to speak, but nothing came. Nobody had ever asked her that question before, and though the answer was easily within her grasp she found she couldn't speak the words. Her voice when she found it was small and broken. "I can't."

And Jo accepted it, shifting across the sofa to take the blonde in her arms. She knew that Rocky had revealed more to her in an afternoon than she had to anyone else in the past five years. And she knew that the toll taken upon the girl had been great. She felt the small body sag against her. Jo did her best to show that she was strong and would be strong for as long as Rocky needed her to be.

"Are you tired?" Jo asked, feeling Rocky's fatigue.

"Yeah," was the simple answer.

"You want to lie down?" Rocky's head nodded against her chest, so Jo stood, pulling the blonde with her. She led Rocky up to the bedroom and helped her out of the sweatpants, leaving her in the t-shirt. She pulled the quilt back and gestured for the blonde to get in.

Rocky climbed in but caught Jo's hand as she tried to leave. "Stay with me?"

"Okay." Jo sat on the edge of the bed.

"No, in here." Rocky held back the quilt.

Jo contemplated for a moment, in truth wanting nothing more than to lie down and just close her eyes for a while. "Are you sure?"

Rocky nodded and watched as Jo took off her sweats and carefully eased into the bed beside her, lying on her back.

"Would you hold me?" The question tore at Jo's heart, so she merely held out her arm and let the blonde head rest on her left shoulder as Rocky eased herself onto her side. Then Jo wrapped her arm around Rocky's back being sure to support the injured limb. Rocky said nothing more, and Jo listened to her breathing as it changed becoming deeper and then evening out in sleep.

The dark-haired woman stared at the ceiling and prayed to anyone who might be listening to give her the strength that this woman obviously thought she had. Because if she hadn't the strength, she wouldn't be able to handle failing Rocky.

And if she failed her she could lose her.

And if she lost her, she would not survive.

Not now.

Chapter 15

Jo was not familiar with the feeling of another body in her bed. True, she had entertained many women in the very spot, but they usually knew to slip out of the bed quietly when Jo turned over and presented them with her back. She was comfortable in the knowledge that she had always satisfied her bed guests. She herself was rarely dissatisfied with her choice of partners for the evening. So it didn't take much movement from the blonde lying half on top of her to wake Jo from her pleasant slumber. The past few days had taken a lot out of her, however, and the heavy weight of sleep wouldn't immediately relinquish its grip.

"Jo?" The word pierced through the veil of sleep, and the pain behind the word nudged her out of its depths a little further.

"Mmm?" she mumbled, pulling the body closer, her foggy mind not hearing the gasp of pain as she did so.

"Jo," the voice said again. "It hurts."

She felt the body pull away and heard the gasp that the movement induced. "'S 'kay," she said and rolled over, nearly falling when the edge of the bed appeared before she expected.

She somehow managed to get to the bottom of the stairs, without fully opening her eyes. She found a glass and then the fridge. Up to that point she hadn't turned a light on in the house, and she squinted against the light the fridge produced when the door was opened. She poured a glass of orange juice, taking a sip herself before refilling it. Then she collected the small pot of pain-killers from the table and made her way back up the stairs. She stumbled through the bedroom and sat on the edge of the bed beside the blonde.

Rocky felt a hand from behind lifting her. She sat up and felt a pill being pressed to her lips. Then she felt the cold rim of the glass as it was tipped gently. She swallowed the juice and the pill and heard the glass get set down on the bedside cabinet. Then she listened as Jo padded around the bottom of the bed to the other side and slipped under the covers beside her. She rolled over and resumed her position, using the taller woman's shoulder as a pillow. Rocky felt the long arm gently fold across her shoulders and heard Jo's breathing immediately even out. A smile crossed the blonde's features, and she wondered at the fact that her new friend could do what she just did whilst apparently asleep.

They hadn't moved at all when Jo woke up next. The weight on her arm was comfortable, and she looked down at the face of the girl sharing her bed. She had a vague memory of being woken in the night, but the memory skittered away in the reality of the here and now. Rocky was deeply asleep and did not even stir as Jo eased her arm from its place as the girl's pillow and slipped out of bed. With a long lingering glance at the sleeping girl, she made her way downstairs.

The phone rang as she sat on the sofa with a cup of tea she'd just made. She picked it up. "Yeah?" she said as she placed the mug on the low coffee table.

"Really, dear," her mother said, "is that the most appropriate way to answer the telephone?"

"For me? Yeah." *Mother baiting is such an underestimated sport.* A loud sigh emanated from the receiver. "Was there something you wanted?" Jo asked.

"I was just wondering if you'd be flying up to Cumbria with your father and I?"

Jo closed her eyes, covering her face with her hand. "Um…"

"I didn't catch that, dear. You know I'd prefer it if you would fly with us. I don't like you driving all the way up there."

"I'm not sure."

"Not sure, dear? I would rather you got up there a little earlier than Christmas Eve. Last year you could barely stay awake during the service on Christmas morning."

"I'm not sure I can get there this year, Mother." Jo waited for the outburst she knew was about to come. It was a tradition passed down through the generations, and no member of the family had missed a Christmas at Collingford Manor in centuries. Even her sister would arrive from across the Atlantic rather than suffer the wrath of her mother.

"Joanna, I shall be there in half an hour." The voice was replaced by the dial tone.

Joanna stared at the phone in her hand, and then placed it gently on the cradle. "How d'you forget about Christmas?" she whispered to herself.

It was actually twenty-three minutes before Jo's doorbell rang—a new record for her mother. She knew who it was by the insistent ringing, so she pressed the entry button and resumed her seat on the sofa, awaiting her fate.

Marianna Holbrook-Sutherland was pulling off her gloves as she entered the lounge. "Joanna, dear, you look dreadful."

Jo stood and embraced her mother. "Thanks, Mother, love you too."

"First the episode in the gallery, and now I find you looking like you haven't slept for days. You really should take more care of yourself." She folded herself elegantly onto the armchair, regarding her daughter's slumped form. "Now, what's this about you not coming up to Collingford?"

"I have a problem here." Jo curled up on the sofa, hugging a cushion to her chest.

"And this problem can't be solved in little over a week?"

"I don't think so." Marianna was being uncommonly reasonable, and it unnerved her daughter.

"Can you tell me what the problem is?"

Jo looked at her mother warily. "I have a friend who is unwell, and I'd like to stay with her while she recovers." Jo expected her mother to laugh at her, much the same as Trixie had.

"Is this person here?"

"Um, yes, she's—" Jo jumped to her feet as Marianna stood. "Where are you going?"

The slightly shorter woman made her way purposefully out of the lounge and glanced in the kitchen. She turned back to her daughter. "I want to meet this person who is obviously more important to you than your family."

Jo stood on the bottom stair and blocked her mother's path to the bedrooms. "She's sleeping. I'd rather you didn't wake her."

"Exhausted is she?" Marianna took a step forward. "Joanna, step aside please."

Jo bowed her head and allowed her mother to climb the stairs. "It's not what you think," she said quietly and looked up as her mother turned on the stairs to regard her daughter. Marianna nodded slightly and resumed climbing, stopping outside the partially opened door of Jo's bedroom.

Jo caught up with her mother and pushed ahead of her. The light from the open doorway illuminated the dark room. She looked up from the sleeping form to see her mother standing at the bottom of the bed. Jo put a finger to her own lips when she saw her mother was about to say something.

So Marianna walked around to stand beside her daughter. "What happened to her?" the older woman asked.

"She fell. Hurt her shoulder." Jo was smoothing away hair from Rocky's eyes when her hand was captured by a smaller one and pulled towards the sleeping woman's chest. Jo looked at her mother and gently pulled her hand out of Rocky's grasp.

"She looks very young, Jo."

Jo sighed. "Yes, she is."

"Would she not be better with her own family?" Marianna asked as she approached the head of the bed, pushing between Jo and the sleeping girl.

Jo watched in fascination as her mother leaned over the slumbering form and mirrored her own actions, smoothing soft blonde hair away from where it had fallen once again to tangle with long eyelashes. "She has no family. Her parents were killed some time ago."

Marianna took a deep breath and then grasped hold of her daughter's arm and pulled her from the room. Once outside, she quietly closed the door. "Your friend, Beatrice, called me this morning."

Jo crossed her arms in a defensive gesture. "Trixie? She called you?"

"Yes, she did. She tells me you have taken a vagrant into your home." Marianna held her hand up as Jo opened her mouth to object to the description. "Wait." She watched her daughter lean back against the wall, her features guarded. "Someone in your position, of your background, has to be especially careful in the company they keep. I want to know that you are satisfied that the girl in there, in your bed, is all she claims to be."

"She doesn't claim to be anything. She didn't want to come back here. It was only when she got injured and was physically incapable of staying on the streets that she agreed to come home with me." Jo's tone was defensive and a little confrontational.

"And then into your bed?" Marianna raised an eyebrow in question.

"It's not how it looks."

"Really?"

Two identical sets of blue eyes bored into one another.

"Jo?" Both women were startled by the voice that drifted from the bedroom. Jo was first to move, followed by her mother.

Rocky was blinking up at the two women standing beside the bed. She thought she must have suffered a head wound at some time, seeing the double image in the dim light. "Jo?" She tried to sit up, and Jo helped her, putting the extra pillows from the bed behind her to cushion her back against the headboard.

Jo stood at the head of the bed beside Rocky while her mother sat on the edge of the bed. "Hello, dear. I'm Joanna's mother."

Rocky reached out with a shaky hand, taking the one offered to her. "Hello."

"Joanna tells me you had a mishap."

Rocky looked up at her friend, who nodded slightly. "Um, yes. I had a fall."

Marianna reached out and put a gentle hand beneath Rocky's hair, feeling her forehead. "Are you taking medication?"

"I'm...um, taking some painkillers."

Jo's mother nodded and turned to her daughter. "She should be eating if she's taking any type of painkiller."

"We've eaten," Jo said defensively. "We had an omelette."

"Jo cooked it," Rocky said, looking up at her friend adoringly. "It was very nice."

"My daughter doesn't cook, dear. No wonder you're not looking well." She turned slightly towards Jo. "Joanna, get me my phone book please."

Jo looked from her mother to her friend.

"Run along, dear, it's in my bag. This poor child requires food, and I doubt you have anything in your refrigerator that would produce the kind of meal I have in mind."

Jo still made no attempt to leave.

"Your friend is quite safe with me." Jo slowly left the room, and Marianna turned back to the girl in the bed. "Has my daughter been looking after you?" she asked. "It would appear that she has made you very comfortable." In order to emphasise what she was referring to she patted the bed.

"She's been wonderful. I still have a hard time believing I'm here."

"Oh, yes, I understand you are homeless. Is that a temporary situation?"

"Is everything all right in here?" Jo asked, as she reappeared a little out of breath and handed her mother the small black book.

"Everything's fine, dear." Marianna took the book from her daughter and reached for the phone on the bedside cabinet. She found the number she wanted and dialled. "Sandor, darling. I need a delivery... For three... No, at Joanna's. You have the address? I trust your judgement, darling... Sounds delightful... And a good wine? Fabulous. Bye." Marianna ended the call and turned to her daughter. "We have an hour and a half, which will be a little after one. Perhaps we can all go downstairs, and you two can tell me exactly what has been going on the last few days."

It was a couple of hours later that Marianna watched in fascination as her daughter cut up some of the food on her friend's plate as they sat at the small table in the kitchen. She took in the look of shy adoration on the blonde's face and the look of patient concern on her daughter's.

"Rocky is an unusual name, dear." Mariana sat back, pushing her plate away and refilling her glass with the wine that had arrived with the meal.

"It's a nickname." The blonde remembered the raised eyebrows when she had told Jo's mother her name. "It's the only name I've known for the past five years."

"Is that how you prefer to be known here?" Marianna asked.

Rocky regarded the food on her plate. "My name is Michelle." She looked up. "You may call me that if you want."

"Michelle is a beautiful name," she said with a smile.

Rocky blushed. "Thank you."

She turned to her daughter. "So, Joanna." Her smile faded as did her daughter's. "I'm assuming that you won't be travelling to Collingford for Christmas."

"I won't, I'm sorry." Jo held her mother's gaze, hoping she wouldn't cause a scene in front of the blonde.

"I can't say I'm not disappointed. This will be the first year the whole family has not been in attendance." Marianna stood and extended her hand towards Rocky. "Michelle, it's been a pleasure meeting you."

Rocky took the hand, shaking it gently. "Thank you for the meal."

"It was rather enjoyable. Sandor never disappoints." She went from the kitchen to the hall, picking up her coat and shrugging into it. Jo followed her out.

"Thank you for understanding." Jo helped her mother into her coat, settling it on shoulders as broad as her own.

Marianna turned back to face her. "I want you to bring her up to Collingford—" She held her hands up as Jo began to protest. "Not for Christmas. Bring her up in a couple of months. I'll arrange to be there. I have something I want you to see. It belonged to my great grandmother's sister. I've always kept it because my grandmother brought it with her when she married your grandfather. She gave it to me some years ago. I do believe you are ready to have it now."

"I don't understand."

"You will." She embraced her daughter. "Now, I must go. I have an interior decorator to meet."

Jo shook her head. "You're redecorating the London home again?"

Marianna laughed. "Of course, dear. It's been over a year."

She walked her mother to the door and watched as the chauffeur opened the car door and allowed her mother to slide into the back. Marianna gave a brief wave as the car pulled away and then was gone, leaving a bemused daughter looking at the empty courtyard while large flakes of snow gently fell and covered the ground.

When Jo went back upstairs, she found Rocky piling the plates into the dishwasher. "Hey, let me do that." She eased the blonde back into the chair and finished the job for her.

"Your mother is nice," Rocky said simply.

"Yeah, scary, isn't it?"

"Why d'you say that?"

Jo sat in one of the chairs again. "She's never accepted any excuse for not making it to Collingford for Christmas. I've driven up there through blizzards to make it before now." She chuckled. "Rather that than face the wrath of my mother."

"So what was the difference this time?"

Jo reached across and took Rocky's free hand. "You, I think. I don't really know why." Jo took a deep breath. "She wants us both to go up there after Christmas."

Rocky gently pulled her hand from Jo's. "Jo, I can't. I—"

"It'll be all right. You'll be with me."

"I don't mean that. As soon as my arm is better, I'll be leaving."

"But, I thought..." Jo looked down at the tabletop, her stomach clenching, her temples beginning to throb.

"I can't live off you, Jo. And there's nothing I can do." She looked at the bowed head. "What you've done for me has been wonderful, but I can't stay."

"I want you to," Jo said, her voice breaking. She looked up, tears pooling in her eyes. "Will you promise me something?"

Rocky nodded.

"Will you stay with me over Christmas?"

"Of course. You've chosen me over your family." Rocky looked puzzled.

"Good." Jo looked relieved. "That's good."

"But then, in the New Year, I'm going back."

Jo nodded tightly. No way, she decided, absolutely no way. And she had a couple of weeks to change the blonde's mind.

Later that evening, they sat together on the sofa, watching the television and talking about past Christmases. Rocky seemed to enjoy telling her new friend about her past now. The memories she kept locked away now washed over her, and Jo smiled as she watched Rocky animatedly tell her of the yearly ritual of buying a Christmas tree.

"And they always let me choose it. So, of course, I always chose the largest one I could."

"D'you want to get a tree now?" Jo asked suddenly.

Rocky was taken aback. "Now? It's late."

"It's only just after 7. We could get one somewhere I'm sure." Jo was up and making her way to the door. "Come on."

"We can't go like this." Rocky spread her good arm and looked down at her baggy clothing. And then up at Jo, who was equally relaxed in sweats and a t-shirt.

"I'll get you a jacket. It's going to be crazy out there this close to Christmas. No one will take any notice." Jo reached a hand out, and Rocky felt the hair on the back of her head prickle as a feeling of déjà vu swept across her. She lost herself in the blue gaze and was suddenly enfolded in long arms, her head resting against Jo's chest. "You okay?"

Rocky heard Jo's voice as it rumbled through her chest next to her ear. "Yeah, must be the painkillers."

"Let's go then. Maybe some fresh air will do you good."

So half an hour later, they found themselves trying to find a parking space in their local B&Q DIY store. The place was packed. And Jo was right; no one took any notice of the two bizarrely dressed women, especially the one in the huge army boots and oversized leather jacket.

"Let's see what they have left," Jo said and made her way through the throng towards the decorations. They still had plenty of everything, unlike years before when they would run out of decorations a couple of weeks before Christmas.

Jo started grabbing handfuls of everything. She got a few large strands of each colour of tinsel, draping it around Rocky's shoulders. Then she started grabbing boxes of balls of different colours. She realised she couldn't carry everything and so went in search of a shopping trolley. Rocky waited patiently, covered in tinsel until Jo returned. She gave a sheepish smile to two small children who stared at her.

At last Jo reappeared, pushing a trolley ahead of her, which had a mind of its own. Her boxes of decorations were already inside it, and she unwrapped the blonde from the tinsel and placed that in as well. "We need ceiling decorations," Jo said and disappeared again. Rocky wandered over to a set of shelves and found some small decorations—a few table decorations and a garland to go on the front door.

"Put them in the basket," Jo said, peering over her shoulder and then was gone again. Rocky placed them in the basket and then wandered to the next set of shelves. There was a nativity scene there, all boxed up. Jo was at her shoulder again.

"Do you want to get that?"

Rocky turned to her. "We weren't a particularly religious family, but we always had one of these." She looked back at the box. "I used to set it up. It always sat on a small table."

Jo reached past Rocky and took the box, setting it in the basket. "And you will this year, too," she said quietly. "Come on, let's go find a tree."

They had to go outside to the garden centre, to find a tree, where they were disappointed. The few sorry bushes that were left were in such a sad state that even the low prices couldn't persuade them to buy one. So they decided on a six-foot artificial tree, one of the more lifelike examples. It was two women with glowing faces that arrived back at Jo's house over an hour later and unloaded their packages.

"I can't believe this," Rocky said, looking at the decorations spread across the floor.

"I've never done this here. Don't really know why not." Jo sat cross-legged beside the blonde. "Never had anyone to share it with before, I suppose."

Rocky raised a hand to her shoulder.

"Is it hurting?" Jo asked, standing and going to the kitchen. She returned a moment later with the pain pills, handing the blonde a couple.

"Just a nagging pain. I'll just take one, I think." She swallowed it with the juice. "Can we put this up now?"

Jo chuckled. "Of course we can. I'll get a chair from the kitchen."

With Rocky's expert guidance and as much help as she could give one-handed, they had the decorations up in a couple of hours.

"Turn the lights off," Rocky said as she sat on the sofa.

Jo did so, leaving them in the glow from the tree lights and the fire. "It's beautiful," Jo said as she settled on the sofa next to the blonde. Then she turned to her companion. "But then, so are you." She put an arm around Rocky's shoulders and gently pulled the smaller woman against her.

"I'm so happy," Rocky whispered.

"Good. I want you to be happy." She bent and kissed the blonde head. "I want you always to be happy."

Rocky was quiet for a moment. "I didn't think I'd ever be happy again after my parents died."

"I'm sorry."

"No, please don't be." Rocky pulled away, looking up at the beautiful profile in the dim light. "You've done so much for me, and I still don't know why."

"It makes me happy, too. Maybe that's why. A picture in a gallery—that's all you were to me for a while. But now, the reality is so much more than I could have dreamed of. Please, Rocky," she cupped soft cheeks in her hands and looked into misty green eyes, "believe that there is something that drew me to you. I don't know why or how. I'm just thankful that you're here." She leaned forward and brushed her lips against even softer ones. "Please don't leave me."

"You want me to stay?"

"More than anything."

Rocky smiled and it was the most beautiful thing Jo had ever seen. "Then I'll stay." Rocky's smile was mirrored, and she found herself pulled into a loving embrace, sinking into a security she hadn't known for many years. And as she revelled in that security she knew it was time to unload the demons that still haunted her. It was time to tell Jo the rest of her story.

Chapter
16

It had been the most wonderful week for both of the young women. They had grown more confident in their blossoming friendship, falling into an easy routine together. Rocky had reluctantly agreed to Jo buying her some clothes. Although Jo didn't mind the blonde borrowing her things, the difference in the women's sizes made for a strange look for the shorter woman. As Rocky's shoulder healed and she became more independent, Jo asked her if she would prefer to sleep in the guestroom.

"Do you want me to sleep in there?" Rocky asked.

"I want you to sleep wherever you're comfortable."

"I'm comfortable with you. If you're comfortable with me."

"That's settled then," Jo said.

"Looks like it."

And that was that. Jo had immediately turned away from Rocky, so that the blonde couldn't see the look of relief that crossed her face.

So it was a surprise when Jo woke in the early hours of the morning to find herself in an empty bed. She lay there in silence for a while, listening for any sound that might tell her Rocky's whereabouts. But she heard nothing except the sound of the wind outside. So she slipped out of bed and went in search of the blonde. After checking the bathroom, she descended the stairs, seeing a pale light emanating from the lounge.

She hadn't realised how shaken she was at Rocky's brief disappearance until she found her, sitting on the floor in front of the illuminated Christmas tree. The fire's artificial flames also added to the gentle glow reflecting off blonde hair. The girl was so deep in thought that she didn't see Jo come into the lounge and jumped slightly when the taller woman knelt on the floor next to her.

"Hey there," Jo said quietly.

Moist green eyes met her own. "Hi." She wiped away a tear and reached for Jo's hand. "Sorry, didn't mean to wake you."

Jo squeezed the small hand. "No problem." She watched the blonde head turn away from her. The Christmas tree lights reflected off the tears escaping from green eyes.

"What is it?" Jo felt a little helpless, but was relieved when Rocky snuggled up against her. She made them both comfortable, sitting on the floor with their backs against the sofa.

Rocky was quiet for a while, seeming to draw comfort from the nearness of her companion. "I had a nightmare," she said simply.

"You haven't had one for a few days."

Rocky nodded. "I know. I was stupid enough to think they were going to stop for good." Her voice was a little muffled, and Jo had to strain to hear her. "But I think I'm always going to be reminded."

"Reminded of what?" She ducked her head, wanting to see the blonde's face. But Rocky just burrowed deeper into Jo's embrace.

"Jo?"

"Yeah?"

"I'm going to tell you something now, and I want you to promise me you won't interrupt." Rocky looked up, finding confused blue eyes looking back at her. Jo started to speak, but the blonde shook her head gently. "No. Please, Jo. I want you to hear this, but it's going to be hard, and if I stop I may not be able to find the words again."

"Okay." Jo's voice broke on that single word, for she felt the small body in her arms trembling and knew the fear that Rocky had of the words she was about to speak.

Rocky took a deep breath and began. Her voice was devoid of emotion; her breath hot through the thin t-shirt Jo was wearing.

"A week after I had been admitted to the hospital, my Aunt Susan and Uncle Ron turned up. Susan is my mother's sister. They told me I was going home with them to Leicester. My parents had been buried the previous day. I wasn't taken to the funeral." Rocky felt a flinch from the woman holding her, but Jo kept her promise and kept her silence. "They took me to Leicester.

"About a fortnight after I got there, Ron began coming to my room at night. At first he just touched me, and I pretended to be asleep. But then he started climbing into bed with me. He raped me on a Saturday night after he and Susan had been out to a dinner party. I remember smelling something on his breath, but I didn't know what it was. He hurt me and, when he had finished, he walked out of the room without a word. I didn't cry. He would come to my room most nights after that. But I was numb then. So I'd let him do what he wanted to do.

"They wanted to send me to school, but I was diagnosed as being depressed so they kept me at home. That just meant he had more opportunity to rape me. He would come home in the afternoon and take me on the living room floor. I never fought him. I know I should have. He started to want to do things..." Her voice broke, but the arms around her tightened and she swallowed. She continued, saying, "I had to get away. So I collected as much as I could carry and left." She focused on the clenched fist of her friend as it rested on her thigh, fascinated by the whiteness of the knuckles. "I didn't try to stop him, Jo," she said as she smoothed her friend's rigid hand and opened it, finding Jo's nails had cut into the skin of her palm. "I'm sorry."

The breath left Jo in an explosive cough. Almost as if she had been holding it throughout the telling of Rocky's suffering. She buried her face in soft blonde hair and cried, berating herself for not being able to find the words to ease Rocky's terror.

Rocky looked up again, her mouth opening in surprise at the look of pure hatred on the face above her. She tried to extricate herself from the tight grasp. "I'm sorry," she said again. "I'll go."

Those two words snapped Jo out of the place she had gone to, and she found herself looking down into terror-stricken green eyes. "Go?"

"I didn't stop him. I let him do it." She was still squirming, vainly attempting to untangle herself from long arms.

Jo held on tighter. "I won't let you go," Jo said resolutely. "Never." She cupped a flushed cheek in her palm. She felt the blonde relax again. "Never," she whispered again.

Jo watched the artificial flames of the fire. It had taken her some time to calm herself, and she knew she was no good to

Rocky unless she was there for her, strong for her. But at that moment, she didn't feel terribly strong. She found it hard to comprehend how the small blonde, now resting peacefully in her arms, had survived what she had gone through. She'd been orphaned and then raped by the very people who should have been there to help her grieve. But she hadn't had the chance, and Jo wondered if she had ever actually grieved for her parents.

"Jo?" The voice was very small, and the taller woman ducked her head, pulling Rocky closer to her own body.

"Yeah?" she whispered.

"I'm sorry for being so much trouble."

Jo tightened her hold. "You're no trouble."

There was silence for a few more moments, then she felt as well as heard Rocky draw in a long shaky breath. "I would understand if you wanted me to go," the blonde quietly said.

"I don't want that."

"What about your friends?"

"My friends?" Jo rubbed her cheek against soft hair.

Rocky hesitated. "Jo, I don't want you to stop seeing your friends."

Jo lifted the blonde away from herself slightly, so that she could look into the still tearstained face. "What are you talking about, sweetheart?"

Rocky's eyes slid closed and she ducked her head. "I may not be able to give you what your friends do."

Jo mulled over the statement for a moment before realisation struck her. "Are you talking about sex?"

Rocky didn't look up but nodded slightly.

A brief flash of anger changed immediately to sadness, and Jo reached out to take Rocky's hand. "Rocky, I don't want..." She saw the blonde head snap up. "No, I do want to have s—" She expelled a long explosive breath and closed her eyes. "We've been here together for nearly two weeks," she said quietly. Rocky had relaxed back against her, and she ran her fingers through soft blonde hair. "In that time I've been happier than I've ever been. Yes, I've had a lot of women and, yes, I just wanted them for sex. But when I'm with you..." Jo shook her head, trying to find the right words. "Just being with you fulfils me." She pulled gently on the blonde locks between her fingers, wanting to see the green eyes. "Does that make sense?"

Rocky didn't trust her voice, feeling her throat closing at the sound of Jo's tentative speech. So she nodded and buried her face once again in dark hair.

The two women were quiet for a while, and then Rocky drew in a long breath. "I want to have sex with you."

Jo's hand stilled in Rocky's hair.

"I've only known his hands. Sometimes I wake in the night and I feel him on me. I feel the weight, smell his breath. I feel his hands." She extricated herself from Jo's hold and knelt up, straddling Jo's legs. "I want you to take those memories away."

Jo swallowed hard. "Now?"

Rocky smiled gently and leaned forward to brush her lips against Jo's lips. "No, not now. Now I need you to hold me, tell me I'm safe. Tell me he won't come back." She took a lock of midnight black hair in her fingers, twirling it around. "You were in my dreams before I met you. I'm terrified I'm going to wake up and find myself back out there. In the cold."

Jo lifted her knees slightly, causing Rocky to press against her. She pulled the smaller woman into her own body and held her tight.

Their faces were only inches apart, their breath mingled. Jo tangled her hands in short blonde hair again, and leaned forward, capturing soft lips with her own. The kiss deepened as Rocky's good arm wound around the taller woman's neck, pulling their bodies closer together. They finally separated, both sets of breathing becoming ragged. Jo was framing the blonde's face with her large hands, looking at Rocky in amazement. Rocky searched the blue eyes, worry creasing her brow.

"You know what?" Jo finally asked.

"No, what?"

"I love you," Jo said simply.

"Really?"

"Oh, yeah."

"No one has said that for so long."

"Shall I say it again?" She leaned forward, giving smiling lips another peck. The blonde head nodded. "I love you, Rocky."

Rocky turned her head, kissing the palm of Jo's hand, which still cradled her face. "And I've always loved you. When you came to me in my dreams, I loved you then, though I didn't know it was you. But you're everything I dreamed of. When you came into my life I was afraid to hope. It was easier to be numb." She traced a perfect dark eyebrow with a trembling finger. "But now I want to live, and I want you to show me how."

"We have plenty of time." Jo's hands moved down across Rocky's neck and onto her shoulders.

Rocky leaned back and stood. She reached down to the still sitting woman. "Let's go back to bed."

Jo allowed herself to be pulled to her feet and wound an arm around the blonde's shoulders. As they left the lounge, she bent to turn off the fire but left the Christmas tree lights on, taking a brief glance at them over her shoulder as they walked out of the room.

Rocky groaned as Jo manipulated her left shoulder.

"How's that?" the taller woman asked.

"It's feeling a lot better, not so stiff. What was that stuff?" She peered around Jo, trying to see what she had used on her shoulder.

"Horse liniment."

"You're having me on." Rocky tried to push past her to see the bottle of foul-smelling liquid.

Jo picked up the bottle and held it behind her back. "Does your shoulder feel better?" she asked, backing away from the curious blonde.

"Yes," Rocky said suspiciously.

"So what does it matter what it was?"

Rocky plopped down on the sofa, pulling the neck of the t-shirt back into place. Jo had pulled the material away and reached into the opening with the liniment on her hand, massaging it into the blonde's injured shoulder gently. She disappeared into the kitchen, and Rocky heard the water running as Jo washed the stuff off her hands before returning and plopping herself down next to her.

"So what would you like for Christmas?" Jo asked as she draped an arm around the blonde's shoulders.

"There's nothing I need." Rocky reached for Jo's free hand, holding it within both of hers. "Please don't get me anything. I have everything I want," she kissed the tips of Jo's fingers, "right here."

Jo pouted. "But I'd like to get you something."

"There's nothing I want," she explained. "And besides, I'd just feel awful because I couldn't get you anything."

"I don't want anything."

"Then that's decided." Rocky chuckled and nudged Jo with her shoulder

"Then maybe there's something I can do for you. Something you've wanted to do or maybe see? How about a show or an evening out in a nice restaurant?"

Rocky shook her head, smiling. But then she seemed to remember something. "You know there is something."

"What? Anything, you know that."

"I'd like to go home."

"Home?"

Rocky watched as Jo's smile disappeared. "Hey, just to visit." She squeezed the large hand reassuringly.

"Oh. Right." Jo was embarrassed. The panic she'd felt for a brief moment had taken her unawares.

"I've never been back there." Rocky closed her eyes for a moment, remembering her home. When she opened her eyes, they were watery. "I'd love to show you it."

"Then we'll go." She patted the small hand. "That's settled."

Rocky chuckled to herself. "What have I done to deserve this?"

Jo shrugged. "Why shouldn't you deserve it?"

"Oh, I'm not saying I don't. I must have been good in a previous life or something." The hair on the back of Jo's neck stood on end at the innocent statement. "What?" Rocky asked, seeing Jo's gaze turn inward.

"Just something Edna said."

Rocky's hand flew to her mouth. "Oh my God...Edna." She looked up at Jo. "I haven't been to see her. She'll be worried."

Jo pulled Rocky a little tighter. "Believe me, sweetheart. I'm sure somehow Edna knows exactly where and how you are."

"You think so?"

"I'm absolutely sure. But tomorrow," she leaned in and kissed away the worry lines on the blonde's brow, "we'll go and see her and make sure she's all right. Okay?"

The door buzzer invaded the peace of the small house, and Jo stood, leaving Rocky curled on the sofa clutching a cushion in lieu of the tall woman. She went to the entry phone and pushed the buzzer. "Yeah?"

"Jo? It's Harry."

Jo's face creased into a smile, and she hit the button allowing her friend entry. Then she made her way back into the lounge and to Rocky's side.

"Who is it?" the blonde asked.

"A friend. I'd like you to meet her."

"Not..."

"Trixie?" Jo laughed a distinctively unpleasant laugh. "D'you really think I'd let her up here?"

Harry appeared, framed in the doorway, pulling off a thick, heavy coat. "My God, it's absolutely bloody freezing out." She suddenly took in the scene in front of her and her mouth snapped shut with an audible clunk. "Gosh," was all she could manage.

Jo stood, chuckling to herself, and took the coat from Harry, throwing it onto one of the armchair backs. "Harry, I'd like you to meet Rocky," she said, pushing her friend towards the still seated woman.

Rocky stood as well and took a tentative step towards the other blonde, warily extending her hand. Her experience of Jo's friends had not been encouraging up to that point.

Harry took the offered hand, shaking it gently. "Hi," she said. "I'm glad she found you."

The three women spent a relaxed evening. Harry and Rocky warmed to each other immediately. Of course, Harry really wanted to dislike the other blonde but found it impossible. Her feelings for Jo were such that she was delighted that the dark-haired woman had found someone to cherish. For that was what she saw when she caught a glimpse of Jo watching Rocky as the smaller woman told her the tale of Jo coming to her rescue. She watched as her friend took the smaller hand in her own, kissing it occasionally, then running her fingers along the inside of her arm from wrist to elbow. She seemed to need to be in contact with Rocky every minute they were in touching distance. As the night went on and the sound of the sleet grew louder against the window, Harry decided it was time she left.

"Are you sure?" Jo asked. "It sounds pretty filthy out. You could use the spare bed."

"No, I'm sure. I'll be fine. I have Dad's car." She stood and gathered her coat, slipping it on, and then she turned to Rocky.

The two shorter women faced each other for a moment, and then they were hugging. Rocky somehow knew how special this woman was to Jo, and she felt that there was also a small amount of sadness in the woman she now held in her arms. "I'm sorry," she whispered into her ear.

Harry pulled away and held Rocky at arm's length. "Don't be." She looked up at Jo, who was looking on in confusion. "You've got your work cut out there."

Rocky turned her head as well, and Jo found herself the subject of twin sets of adoring gazes. She shuffled from foot to foot until each of the smaller women extended an arm and she bent slightly, joining in the group hug. Then Rocky backed away as Jo walked her friend to the door.

Harry was buttoning her coat as they descended the stairs to the front door. "She's lovely," she whispered, holding the door catch but not opening it.

Jo nodded. "She is."

"And you're happy." It was not a question.

"I really am." Jo shrugged, seeming to disbelieve it herself.

"I've never seen you like this."

"Like what?"

Harry punched her friend softly on the shoulder. "Like a lovestruck teenager."

"I am?"

"Absolutely." Harry laughed softly at the perplexed look on Jo's face. "But it suits you, so don't go doing anything to ruin it."

"I'm trying really hard."

"And you're doing everything just right by the look on that girl's face." She stood on tiptoes and kissed Jo's chin. "Being in love suits you." Blue eyes went wide, and Harry patted her friend's cheek. "Don't tell me you haven't realised that yet." Harry shook her head and opened the door, letting in a blast of frigid air.

Jo held the door open, the sleet hitting her in the face. "I knew that!" she called out to her friend, who shook her head and folded herself into her father's huge car. Jo watched her leave the small courtyard, and then shut the door against the wind and rain. She stood for a moment with her back to the door. "I knew that," she said again to herself. "I just didn't know it was written all over my face." By the time she'd returned to the lounge her grin was of epic proportions.

"Knew what?" Rocky asked as Jo sat next to the blonde and resettled her arm around her shoulders. "What were you shouting about?"

"Something Harry said."

"She loves you very much, doesn't she?"

Jo nodded. "She was my best friend...is my best friend," Jo corrected.

"Did you and she ever..." Rocky waved her hand around, trying to get her question across without saying the actual word.

Jo leaned away from Rocky, peering down at her. "Have sex?"

Rocky sighed. "Yeah."

"No, we didn't. I didn't know she felt that way until a short time ago. But I'm glad we didn't. It would have ruined our friendship."

"Do you think us having sex would ruin our relationship?" Rocky looked down at the large hand she was holding in her own. But that same hand extricated itself from hers, moved up to her chin, and tilted her head up. She found herself pinned by eyes as blue as the summer sky.

"Make love," Jo corrected. "I've only ever had sex in the past, but I would make love with you." She pulled Rocky closer, pressing her cheek against the blonde head when it rested back against her chest.

"Jo, please don't make promises you can't keep," Rocky whispered, closing her eyes as tears threatened.

Jo reached down again, needing to see Rocky's face. A gentle hand urged the smaller woman to look up again. "Sweetheart, when we make love I will give you my heart. Please believe me."

Rocky searched Jo's eyes, looking deep into the blue gaze for any sign of a lie. She found none. "I believe you," she said, hearing the wonder in her own voice.

Chapter
17

"All sorted," Jo announced and threw the cordless phone onto the sofa. "I've found us a cute little hotel just outside Tintagel."

"Really?" The blonde looked up from the Christmas tree. She was placing on it some more decorations that they'd bought earlier that day. She rose and crossed the room, fitting herself neatly at the taller woman's side as she sat on the sofa. "Thank you," she said, leaning in and giving Jo a peck on the cheek.

"I'm looking forward to it. Never been to Cornwall."

"You're joking." Rocky chuckled, elbowing Jo gently in the ribs.

"Nope. I've seen the South of France, quite a bit of Spain, the States, Egypt, but I've never been to Cornwall."

Rocky shook her head. "Then I'm glad you'll be with me when we do see it. I can show you some beautiful places."

Jo wound a long arm around her friend. "I'm sure you can. We'll leave the day after Boxing Day."

"Wow, that soon?" Rocky became quiet.

"What's wrong?" Jo gave the blonde a gentle squeeze.

"I'm scared of the memories." Rocky rested her head against Jo's shoulder, her eyes finding the flames of the fire.

"But they're good memories."

"Yes, they are. But it's been so long, I'm scared I'll just remember the..."

"The river," Jo finished for her.

"Yeah, the river." She ran her hand along Jo's thigh, feeling the soft fabric of the sweatpants she was wearing. She herself was in a similar pair, with a white t-shirt that matched the one Jo was wearing.

Jo looked up at the clock; it was a little before midnight. "It's nearly Christmas," whispered the taller woman and reached down, bringing the blonde's face up towards hers. "Merry Christmas," she said, dipping her head and claiming soft lips.

After a long moment, they separated, and Rocky gazed into the blue eyes above her. "I love you, Jo." She shifted around until she was straddling Jo's lap and wound her arms around the dark head, holding on for all she was worth as the taller woman clasped her tightly. Jo's lips found her neck, her hands disappearing beneath the t-shirt and smoothing their way up her sides and then to her back. Rocky cupped Jo's face and forced her lips away from her neck so that she could claim them again, pushing her body hard into the one below her. She felt large hands caressing every inch of her back, and she leaned back into them. Rocky looked down into the face of the woman who had so recently come into her life. Jo's eyes were half closed, her skin glowing in the light from the fire and the lights on the tree. And Rocky's heart clenched at the sight. She reached behind her, her hand closing on one of Jo's hands, which had come to rest on her hips. She drew the hand round to the front, looking at it intently. "Will you be gentle with me?" she whispered.

Jo's eyes closed, knowing exactly what it was that Rocky was asking and offering. "Rocky, maybe we should wait. I shouldn't have—"

The blonde placed trembling fingers against soft moist lips. "Who's sitting on whom here?"

Jo didn't trust her voice, so she just nodded. Rocky was cast in the golden glow from the fire, which danced in her hair. Never losing eye contact with Jo, she slowly peeled the t-shirt off then gathered the large hand again and placed in on her breast.

Jo couldn't understand why she could no longer see. Then she realised her eyes were filling with tears. She blinked them away and took in the sight in front of her. The most beautiful sight she had ever seen. She watched her own hand as if it belonged to someone else. It was being lovingly cradled in a smaller one; the thumb of that small hand brushing against her knuckles as it was pressed into soft flesh. She looked back up into the blonde's face and saw a host of different emotions in the green eyes. She saw love and hope, but she also saw fear. For the briefest of moments, she tried to pull her hand away from the inviting softness it was nestled against. "I don't want to hurt you." She didn't realise why she said those words—hurting the gentle woman was the furthest thing from her mind.

"You won't." Rocky now had both of her hands holding Jo's against her flesh. "I want you," she whispered. She leaned forward, pressing her lips against Jo's and running her tongue across full lips.

Jo's free hand cupped the back of the blonde head, pulling Rocky deeper into the kiss. And Rocky, feeling Jo's other hand kneading her breast, released it and clutched onto the white t-shirt her friend still wore.

Jo was halfway up the stairs, the blonde's legs wrapped around her waist and her own arms holding Rocky close, before she realised they'd left the comfort of the lounge. She didn't stop to wonder from where she'd got the strength to carry them both up the stairs, and she didn't care. She staggered into the bedroom and deposited them both onto the bed, covering the smaller form with her own. She rose up enough to pull the sweatpants off the blonde, and then eased herself back down, pulled once more into position by Rocky. She felt small hands pulling at her t-shirt, and allowed it to be pulled over her head and thrown to some dark corner of the room.

Both women sighed at the sensation of flesh on flesh. But in the back of her mind, caution still ruled for Jo. "You okay?" she asked between kisses.

"I'm great," came the breathy whisper.

Jo ducked her head and took a hardened nipple between her teeth and flicked it with her tongue. She felt small hands tangle themselves in her hair, but they weren't pulling her head away from the torture, which confirmed that the blonde was enjoying what Jo was doing to her. Jo raised her head again to look into the face of her lover. Her lover. She'd thought about this moment even before she'd met the woman that she now held naked in her arms. She let her hands roam across skin as smooth as silk. She felt the muscles beneath that skin tremble as her hand made its journey down across taut breasts, across a quivering abdomen, and then to the very edge of silky curls. There she stopped, watching the blonde's face very carefully for any signs of discomfort. Her hand detoured, coming to rest on Rocky's hip.

Rocky let her hand fall from Jo's head to her shoulder, then she tentatively cupped the taller woman's breast, rubbing her thumb across a hardened nub. She looked shyly into blue eyes. "Is that nice?" she asked.

Jo swallowed hard. "Very nice," she gasped.

"Tell me what to do," she whispered, watching her own hand as it caressed one breast to alertness before switching to the other.

"You're doing fine," Jo ground out between gritted teeth.

"I've never loved anyone like this before." Rocky closed her eyes, not wanting to remember those terrifying nights shared with a man who used her, but not being able to completely shut away the memory. "I never thought I could. I thought he'd taken that from me."

"Maybe we should stop," Jo said, however she didn't make any effort to move away from the girl.

"No, please."

Two small words, but to Jo as important as any she'd ever heard. She moved her hand from the gentle curve of Rocky's hip and looked deep into green eyes as her fingers danced over slick heat. She watched in fascination as full lips parted at the first true contact between them and hungrily possessed those lips already swollen from the passion that had gone before. She felt Rocky's arms holding onto her, pulling her down to crush the small body beneath her own. Jo pulled back, needing to see the face of the woman she was loving. Because that was what she was doing. For the first time in her life and in her bed, she was putting the pleasure of another person above her own. And she desperately wanted to see the face of her lover when the moment came. She felt short nails dig into her shoulders and the hips of the woman beneath her buck as her hand drew out the blonde's pleasure.

Rocky's eyes were tightly shut, and Jo ducked her head, kissing a flushed cheek. "Open your eyes, sweetheart." She needed Rocky to know it was her touching her; that it was her loving her. Green eyes fluttered open, looking slightly dazed. "Say my name." Jo needed to hear it, needed to know that Rocky knew where she was and whom she was with.

"Oh God, Jo," Rocky gasped.

Jo smiled down at her, venturing a little deeper, watching carefully the face below her. Rocky's hips bucked again as Jo gently entered her. With her free hand, Jo swept away sweat-slickened hair from the blonde's brow. Her lips followed her fingers across the damp face, kissing her eyelids, the tip of her nose, and then lips, which were whispering Jo's name over and over. Then, with a gasp, Rocky's back arched and her hands clutched at the tall woman's shoulders.

Jo held still and savoured the delicious feeling as the blonde's body released its passion. She carefully withdrew her hand, letting it rest at the edge of blonde curls, her fingers idly teasing the soft skin there. Again she pushed away damp blonde hair from the face of her lover, watching as green eyes refocused on her. She was delighted to see a small smile on the lips she had kissed only moments before.

"Why can't I move now?" Rocky asked quietly in a voice full of wonder.

Jo chuckled and managed to pull the quilt from beneath the boneless woman and roll her beneath it. Then she slipped out of her sweatpants and joined the sated woman. She pulled Rocky over so that the blonde was on top of her and tucking her head beneath her chin.

"Comfy?" she asked.

"Oh yeah." Rocky listened for a moment to the strong heart beating beneath her ear. "Jo?"

"Yeah?"

"Love you."

"Love you, too." Jo held her tight.

"Merry Christmas."

Much later, Jo was awakened by Rocky moving away from her slightly and lying on her back. Jo turned onto her side, watching the girl in the pale light coming from the landing. Rocky seemed to be at peace, one hand lying relaxed beside her face which was turned slightly towards her lover. Jo couldn't resist tracing an eyebrow, partly hidden beneath pale hair. She shifted closer, watching the sleeping face. Her thigh shifted across the blonde's and her hand found the gentle curve of Rocky's hip. Dipping her head, she kissed the hollow of her throat moving down to take a hardening nipple into her mouth.

She smiled into the warm flesh when she heard the sharp intake of breath from the blonde and ran her hand up from Rocky's hip to cup a firm breast, feeling the hardness of the nipple against her palm. She moved her thigh slightly, trying to settle it between the legs of her lover but met with resistance. She rose up onto her elbow to look down at the blonde. Rocky was lying still, her eyes half open, so Jo leaned across her to turn on the small bedside lamp.

"Hey," she whispered, gently trying to turn the blonde's head towards her. Rocky was rigid however her muscles trembling with the effort of resisting Jo's touch.

"Rocky?" Jo's voice was tinged with the beginnings of panic and she reached for Rocky's hand, finding it clenched and unyielding. "Rocky, please." She knelt at her side now, putting both hands on the blonde's shoulders and shaking gently. "Rocky, it's me. It's Jo." She knew what was happening now. Rocky was back there, back with him. And she didn't know how to convince the girl that she was safe and hadn't returned to her nightmares. She should have known better and admonished herself for touching Rocky when the blonde was vulnerable.

"Rocky, I'm sorry." Her voice cracked. Her hands were shaking as she caressed a flushed cheek, but then she withdrew her hand quickly, not knowing if her touch would be rejected. She looked into eyes that held no recognition. "Rocky, come back to me," she whispered.

She watched as the vacant green eyes closed and held her breath as she waited for Rocky to return from wherever she had gone. Suddenly the blonde's chest heaved as she resurfaced, dragging in huge breaths as a drowning woman would do. She reached frantically for Jo, holding on when the long arms pulled her in and grounding herself in the touch and feel of her new lover.

"I'm sorry. I'm sorry." Jo repeated over and over, holding on tight, burying her face in damp blonde hair.

"It was him," Rocky choked out. "He came for me. He'll never leave me."

"No, it was me. It'll always be me. He'll never touch you again, I promise."

"I'll never be free of him," Rocky sobbed into Jo's chest, and the taller woman felt helpless, guilty that her own need had brought about the blonde's despair.

Jo held on tight, not knowing what to do except to give the woman in her arms the security of knowing that she was there and would always be there.

It was Rocky who woke first, hearing the heavy rain hitting the window. She was still wrapped in the long arms of her sleeping lover. She remembered waking earlier, feeling hands and a mouth on her, and she was back there. A scared child believing that, if she pretended to be asleep, the torment would stop and she'd be alone again. But then there was the voice, breaking through the hurt and the anger, the voice of her lover.

Jo had shown her how love could be, how sex could be. And she had repaid her by freezing. In those first panic-filled moments as she awoke, she couldn't tell it was Jo's hands. She just knew someone was touching her, caressing her, just as he had. He would come to her room in the dark hours, lift the quilt and touch her body. And she would let him. She would close her eyes very tightly and hope he would maybe grow tired of an unresponsive body and leave her alone. He never did.

And now, when she wanted to give her body to the woman she had grown to love, he had come to her. He had intervened as if he had been there in the bed with them. The memory of him still haunted her, and she wondered if it would ever leave her. And would Jo grow tired of the constant battle with him? Would she want to take him on, for that is what she would have to do?

Rocky looked across at the woman holding her tight, even in sleep, their faces only inches apart. There were faint worry lines across the forehead beneath the silky black hair, and she frowned, knowing she was the source. Jo hadn't told her much of her life before she had come into it. Rocky knew that her lover had led a mostly carefree existence, which even Jo was beginning to find unfulfilling. And now suddenly Jo had someone to look after, to provide for. Someone who couldn't give her body without a struggle. Surely Jo wouldn't want to persevere with such a difficult relationship.

Tears sprang from green eyes, and Rocky put a hand over her mouth, not wanting to wake Jo with her sobs. She looked at Jo, pushing dark hair away from the sleeping face.

Blue eyes fluttered open, widening when they took in the moist green eyes staring at her intently. "You okay?" she asked huskily, not moving and tightening her hold slightly.

Rocky nodded, never breaking eye contact for a moment. "I'm sorry."

"Don't be."

"It was really stupid." She tucked her head below Jo's chin, not wanting to see the annoyance in her lover's face.

"If anyone was stupid it was me. You told me about what happened. I shouldn't have touched you when you were asleep." She kissed the top of the blonde head. "You gave me so much last night, more than I imagined. I can't begin to tell you how much that meant to me."

"But..." Rocky paused, unable to voice her fears.

"But what?" Jo swallowed hard, worried that she had gone too quickly and lost Rocky's trust.

Rocky listened to the rapid heartbeat beneath her ear. "Tell me about your life before we met."

Jo went very still, closed her eyes, and held on tight to her lover. "Why?"

"I want to know."

Again Jo swallowed hard. "It's not pretty."

"I think I know that."

"I didn't care much for other people's feelings. I took what I wanted and threw them away. People like Trixie. She has a reason to hate me. I used her...like I used many others." She paused for a moment, her hand wandering idly across the smooth back of the woman she held close to her. "But you know what?" She felt the blonde head move against her chest. "I enjoyed it. I knew they wanted me. I knew I could use them and they'd still come back for more. So I did."

Jo rested her cheek against blonde hair. "The night before I saw your picture in the gallery, I picked up a little blonde...brought her back here and fucked her brains out. She told me she just wanted sex. I was happy to oblige. I never even knew her name."

"You're so much more than that, Jo." Rocky's voice was small.

"I wasn't then. It was all I was good for." She kissed the blonde head. "You give me a purpose."

"And if I'm going to wake up screaming every time you touch me?"

"Then I'll just go on until you recognise it's me. We can't let him win."

"Sometimes I think he already has, and I worry you'll lose patience with me."

"Never. Have a little faith, huh?"

Rocky sighed deeply. "I worry that I'm not going to be

enough for you. Those women wanted you because..." She fought her own embarrassment, never having spoken of such matters before. "They wanted you because you're good. And I think they maybe made you feel good too."

Jo thought about that for a moment. "Yes, they made me feel good. But just being with you makes me feel wonderful. I didn't think I could be with another person just because I enjoyed their company. But with you that's exactly how I feel. Don't get me wrong, you excite me, and I love the feel of your body beneath my hands. But sex will never be the most important part of our relationship." She reached down, tipping the blonde's head up with a gentle finger, smiling down into moist green eyes. "We can learn all about love together. I'm just as new to that as you are to...other things."

"So you'll show me how—"

"I'm sure I don't need to show you how to make love." She kissed the tip of Rocky's nose. "But I'm willing to let you practice as much as you like."

Rocky let out a half sob, half chuckle. "You're sacrificing yourself for me?"

Jo nodded, not wanting to betray herself by having her voice break on the words.

"Thank you," Rocky whispered, brushing away hot tears, which were running from blue eyes across Jo's face.

After a few moments, they both fell asleep, relaxed in each other's arms, free of nightmares and haunting shadows.

"Good morning," Jo said, placing the mug of tea on the bedside cabinet and sitting on the edge of the bed next to a dishevelled blonde. She leaned across the sleepy woman and gave her a gentle kiss on the lips. "It's Christmas."

Rocky raised her head slightly, looking at the clock on the radio alarm. "It's halfway through Christmas. Why didn't you wake me?" She sat up, pulling the quilt up to cover her nakedness.

"I thought you needed it. You didn't move when I got up, and you were using me as some sort of mattress this morning."

"Sorry." Rocky leaned across and grabbed the mug, sighing as the warm liquid soothed her throat. "Oh, that's bliss."

Jo patted a quilt-covered knee. "Anyway, hurry up, take a shower, and get dressed. I want you to see something."

Rocky put the mug down with an audible thump. "Jo, you promised me. No gifts."

"I don't think you'll mind this one."

Rocky threw the quilt back and stomped out of the bedroom. Jo watched her go, grinning to herself as Rocky treated her to a vision of angry nudity. "Cute dimples," she called after her.

Half an hour later, Rocky descended the stairs, still towelling her hair. She flopped down on the sofa and looked around the room for whatever it was Jo wanted her to see. "Well?" she called to her friend who she assumed was in the kitchen.

"In here," Jo called.

Putting the towel around her shoulders, she reluctantly made her way to the kitchen. The first thing she saw was the food. The small table was groaning under the weight of the Christmas feast. Then a movement caught her eye, and she looked towards the sink and burst into tears. Edna was just turning towards her, drying her hands with a small hand towel.

"Now is that any way to greet me?" the old woman asked, causing the teary-eyed woman to launch herself into her arms. She looked over Rocky's shoulder at the tall woman, giving her a little wink of the eye. Edna managed to pry the blonde away from herself and held her at arm's length. "Look at you now."

"It's so good to see you, Edna," Rocky snivelled.

"And you too, dear." She guided Rocky towards the table. "Let's not let this get cold. Young Sandor has outdone himself." She smiled at Jo, whose gaze was riveted on the delighted features of her lover. "What a nice young man."

Jo was slicing the turkey, placing slices on each of their plates. "He is," she agreed. "This is a gift to us both from Mother."

Rocky merely nodded, still sniffling slightly and obviously unable to take everything in.

Jo paused in her serving to remove the damp towel from the blonde's shoulders. "Don't want your shoulder seizing up."

"Thanks," Rocky said, her voice a husky whisper. "How long will you stay?" she asked Edna, who was digging into her Christmas dinner with great gusto.

"Jo has asked me to stay a while, and I have agreed," she managed between mouthfuls.

Rocky looked up at her lover, who was just sitting after filling her own plate. "When did you do all this?"

"You sleep a lot."

"Not that much."

Jo shrugged. "A few mornings ago, I slipped out of bed, went down to Whitechapel, and managed to find Edna." She looked across at the old woman. "She didn't take much convincing."

"I can't believe you did all that when I was asleep." Rocky was shaking her head, pouring gravy in huge quantities across every part of her meal.

Jo shrugged. "Are you happy?" she asked, popping a sprout in her mouth and grimacing at the taste.

Rocky looked from her friend to her lover. "Stupid question," she said. "I'm spending Christmas with the two people I love the most. How could I not be happy?"

Edna looked across at the blonde. She never thought she'd hear Rocky speak of love. But she could see the evidence of it on the girl's face, and she decided it suited her.

Jo poured wine into each of the three glasses. "Let's make a toast," she said.

Rocky stood quickly, picking up her glass. "I want to," she said quietly. "To Jo," she raised her glass. "The woman who saved me. The woman I love. I owe you my life, and I will repay you every moment of every day."

"To Jo," Edna raised her glass, clinking hers against Rocky's and waiting for a speechless Jo to join in.

"Every moment of every day," Rocky repeated and sat again, reaching across the table for her lover's hand.

Chapter
18

"Please." The voice was little more than a whimper, and Jo looked to her left at the sleeping blonde slumped in the passenger seat of her car.

"Shh." She reached across and took Rocky's hand, which was resting on the large road atlas of Great Britain held precariously on her lap. "It's okay. You're safe here," she whispered. She held Rocky's hand as the young woman calmed and then, realising she had slipped back into a more peaceful sleep, tried to pull her hand away. The blonde was having none of it, however, and Jo decided that she could manage for a while one-handed.

They had decided to drive to Cornwall the easy way. Straight along the M4 to Bristol, then down to Cornwall on the M5. It was monotonous and not terribly scenic, but Jo didn't want to make the journey any longer by getting lost. Rocky had offered to navigate and had pulled the map out soon after leaving London. She was asleep within an hour however, and, though Jo missed her chatter, she was happy to let her sleep.

Jo had managed to talk Edna into looking after her house while they were away. They'd had a wonderful two days over Christmas, but the only way the old woman would stay longer was if she thought she was doing Jo a favour by watching the house. In truth, the house had an adequate alarm system, but they both so much wanted Edna to have some time without having to worry about where she would sleep or where the next meal was coming from that they opted not to tell her about it.

Jo glanced down at her sleeping companion. She frowned at the obvious exhaustion Rocky was feeling, due partly to the new-found aspect of their relationship and partly to the dreams that woke her frequently during the night. Jo sighed deeply, holding on to the limp hand a little tighter. She'd promised the blonde that she would help her through her nightmares, but was she herself contributing to them? She also worried that the blonde would decide staying with her wasn't worth the pain of the once buried feelings.

She glanced up at one of the huge signs. The West, was all it said.

And what would Cornwall hold for them both?

Suddenly Rocky jumped beside her, and the atlas fell from her lap. "Ugh," was all she managed as she sat up and looked groggily around her.

"Hi, welcome back." Jo chuckled at the confused look on the blonde's face.

"Where are we?" she asked, reaching down to retrieve the map from the floor, but not relinquishing Jo's hand. She looked out of the window, trying to spot a signpost.

"Just gone past the exit for Bath. I think we get off at 20."

"Okay." Rocky's voice was very small, and she looked down at the map, her finger plotting a route for them once they got off the motorway. "We could go all along the north coast road."

"That sounds nice."

Rocky nodded, her finger finding the village of Tintagel. "It is, it's beautiful. Of course, this time of year you won't be able to see much, not like on a clear summer day."

"You miss it, don't you?"

Rocky nodded, not looking up from the map.

"Hey," Jo said, taking her hand again. "Everything's going to be fine."

Rocky nodded again and turned slightly in her seat so that she could face Jo.

Jo glanced at her, noticing her eyes drooping closed again. "Tired?"

"A little." Rocky dropped the map on the floor and used both hands to grasp Jo's hand.

"Go back to sleep for a while then. I'll wake you if I need directions." When she heard no answer, she looked down to find the blonde already asleep, still holding on to her hand with both of hers.

It was some time later, that the monotonous motorway changed to roads with hedgerows on either side. And it was this view that Rocky awoke to see. She looked around, and then up to Jo, who was chuckling at her.

"I don't know how you slept so long scrunched up like that."

Rocky twisted around so she was sitting straight in the seat, rolling her stiff shoulders. "Painfully," was all she said as she spotted a sign for Minehead.

"I got off the motorway at Bridgwater." Rocky was scrubbing her face and scratching her head frantically. "Let's stop for a while, stretch our legs," Jo said and spied a lay-by up ahead with a refreshments trailer in it.

Rocky just about leapt out of the car as it ground to a halt, walking briskly towards the trailer. She was reading the small menu on the blackboard next to the serving hatch. She felt a warm presence at her back and leaned back into Jo's taller frame.

"You hungry?" a low voice enquired, Jo's warm breath hot in the blonde's ear.

Two hands came to rest on Rocky's hips, and the blonde could feel the heat from them even through the denim of her jeans. Rocky couldn't hide the shiver that ran through her body and cast helpless eyes at the large woman who had appeared at the hatch to take their order. "A hot dog and a cup of tea, please," Rocky squeaked. She heard a chuckle behind her and felt Jo's body shift, causing her to stumble back a couple of steps before she felt strong hands on her shoulders holding her in place.

"Me, too," she heard Jo say.

"Onion?" the woman asked as she cut through two rolls in preparation.

Jo leaned forward again, the blonde in front of her apparently struck dumb. "Onion?" she breathed into Rocky's ear. The blonde head shook, and Jo looked up at the woman. "One with, one without, please."

"Tea for you?" the woman asked, wondering exactly what was going on in front of her.

"Please," Jo said. "We'll just be over there." She nodded at a break in the hedgerow, which gave a view across the fields. She guided Rocky across, her hands still on the smaller woman's shoulders.

Rocky allowed herself to be guided to the gap in the high

hedge, oblivious to the fine drizzle that was falling. "God, Jo," she whispered as they went behind the trailer.

"Mmm?" Jo snaked her arms around Rocky's waist pulling her closer.

"You make me feel..."

"What?" she rested her chin on the blonde's shoulder.

Words failed her. "So much, I feel so much."

"Is that good?"

"Oh yeah." She covered the hands circling her waist with her own and leaned back, enjoying the moment.

"Hot dogs!" The woman bellowed, startling both of them. They disentangled themselves from each other and made their way back to collect their food.

Another two hours passed before they arrived at the windswept and very damp village of Tintagel, known most famously for the ruined castle built on an outcrop of the dramatic North Cornish coastland. Over the years erosion had eaten away at the rock and a bridge had to be built to enable visitors to visit the ruins. A precarious path down the cliff face, difficult under normal circumstances and considered impossible in the weather conditions that Rocky and Jo encountered, reached the ruins. It was the legend of King Arthur that drew sightseers to brave the windswept path. Geoffrey of Monmouth first wrote of Tintagel as the birthplace of King Arthur, and from there the legend grew, the small village prospering from the steady stream of visitors that wanted a brief taste of mythical history.

And it was here that Rocky grew up.

The snow they had left behind in the east had turned to rain in the west, and the wind blew in off the coast making it feel almost as cold as London. Jo pulled their cases out of the boot of the Merk, looking up at the pleasant little hotel she had booked them into. Rocky had walked away to look at the view from the cliff edge that ran parallel to the hotel's drive.

An elderly man came out of the hotel, pulling an overcoat on as he came. "Miss Sutherland?" he asked. Jo hadn't used her full title when booking.

"Good," she looked at her watch, "afternoon," she said, putting the bags on the ground and slamming the boot closed. She reached out a hand, which the man took, shaking it vigorously.

"Good for ducks maybe." He bent and picked up the bags. "I'll take these in, and we'll be sure to put the kettle on. I expect you could both do with a hot drink."

Jo smiled at the man. "Thanks, we'll be there in a minute." Jo walked up behind Rocky, who was shivering in the cold wind, which held rain and probably spray from the sea far below. This time she didn't touch Rocky. She just let her have this moment of contemplation.

"I always loved the sea when it was like this." She looked down at the rocks below, watching as they disappeared beneath the waves before the sea receded to gather itself again and repeat the process. Jo stood alongside the blonde, and Rocky took her hand. "You can just see the tip of the outcrop that the castle ruins stand on from here." She pointed along the coast to her left, pulling Jo around slightly so that she could follow her directions.

"I see it," Jo said, squeezing the small hand in her own. "Come on, let's go inside." Rocky nodded and allowed herself to be pulled along into the hotel.

The elderly man who had met Jo was taking their luggage up the small flight of stairs. It was a small hotel of twelve rooms and they appeared to be the only guests.

The hotel register was pushed towards Jo as she approached the reception desk. "Good afternoon, Miss Sutherland. Was your trip uneventful?" The woman was rather splendid, with a mass of pearls about her neck.

"Yes, it was, thank you. With the Christmas holiday being over the weekend, I think a lot of people are still on holiday." She signed the register and handed a credit card to the woman, who processed it and took a key down from some small shelves behind the desk. "I've put you in number three, which is a double room." She looked across at Rocky who was leafing through the tourist leaflets. "We have twin rooms if you'd prefer."

Jo produced her most engaging smile. "I'm sure the double will be fine. We'll be staying two nights at least. Would there be a problem if wc wanted to stay longer?"

"Not at all. As you can see, we are not overbooked." The woman looked at the entry in the register and handed Jo the key. "My husband has taken your cases up." She gestured towards the stairs. "Top of the stairs, first door on the left." Jo and Rocky ascended the stairs but turned when the woman called out to them. "Will you be requiring lunch?"

"That would be nice, thank you," Jo said and ushered the blonde up the rest of the stairs. They showered, changed, and ate a light lunch in the small sun lounge, which had views over the rocky cliffs.

"Where would you like to go first?" Jo asked a thoughtful Rocky.

"I'd just like to go into the village. It'll be pretty quiet this time of year." She pushed away the plate, which had held her sandwiches. "And then I need to go to the church." Jo watched her carefully. Rocky sighed deeply. "I need to see it. Where they are now."

"Okay. We'll drive down there as soon as we've finished here."

Rocky glanced around the sun lounge. "It's very quiet here."

Jo nodded, pushing her chair away from the table and standing. "It would be since we're the only guests."

"We are?"

Jo nodded, giving the blonde a wink before turning away and leaving the sun lounge.

"Jo, what have you done?" a bemused blonde asked, following hard on the heels of her friend.

The small church just within the boundary of the village stood strong against the wind and rain that assaulted it with persistent intensity. Jo left the engine running as both women looked at the forbidding high wall that surrounded it and the small graveyard.

Without a word, Jo reached across and took Rocky's hand. "You up to this?"

"Probably not, but I've thought about it a lot since I met you." She looked from their linked hands up into concerned blue eyes. "You gave me the strength to remember them. And now I need to go and say goodbye."

"You want me to come?"

Rocky shook her head and eased her hand out of Jo's grasp. Taking a deep breath, she opened the door and stepped out into the storm. Before she closed the door, she ducked down looking back into the car. "Just give me a few minutes."

"Okay," Jo said quietly. Jo watched her through the rain-slicked windscreen, switching on the wipers for a couple of passes so she could see her lover more clearly. She positioned the Merk so that she could see through a part of the wall that had collapsed.

Rocky pulled up the collar of the waterproof jacket that Jo had bought her, but her head and legs were still becoming quickly drenched with the freezing rain. She vaguely knew where her grandparents had been buried and knew her parents would be close by. Stumbling slightly, she came across the white headstone. It said simply: Michael and Annabelle Kersey. Rocky's legs suddenly felt weak, and she staggered backwards. Behind her she heard the Merk's door slam, and she turned to see Jo striding towards her around the other headstones in the churchyard. She shook her head at the advancing woman. "Not yet."

Reluctantly Jo nodded and walked slowly back to the car.

Rocky turned back to the gravestone. She ignored the rain seeping down the back of her collar and stood, arms held limply at her side.

"I should have come before, I'm sorry." Her voice was small, broken. "So much has happened, and I couldn't get back. I didn't want to forget you, but it hurt so much to remember, and I was so alone. I had friends, good friends. But they couldn't fill the place you left in my heart." She pushed wet hair out of her eyes. "But now I've met someone who is giving me the strength to remember you. I think you'd like her. And I don't think you'd hate me for loving her. I hope you can hear me now. I want you to know how happy I am. I know you're together, and I know you love me. I love you. Always."

Jo watched the hunched figure of her lover. When she saw the slumped shoulders heaving as sobs racked the small body, she could stand it no longer. Slipping in the mud and wet grass between ancient graves, she made her way as quickly as possible to the distraught blonde and took the unresisting body into her arms.

The taller woman looked down at the gravestone. "Michael and Annabelle," she said quietly. "Your name was a mixture of both of theirs." She felt the blonde head nod against her chest. "Come on, let's get out of the rain. We can come back here again, any time you want."

Rocky allowed herself to be led out of the churchyard. Across the street was a small café, and Jo steered them towards that. A small bell rang as they entered the café, and a woman appeared behind the counter.

"Oh my goodness!" she exclaimed. "What a filthy day. Sit down. I'll get Katy to take your order."

"Thank you," Jo said, settling Rocky at a table. "You

wouldn't happen to have a towel we could use, would you?"

"Of course, let me get one from upstairs." She disappeared for a moment and then returned with a large, fluffy, blue towel.

"Thanks." Jo took it from her and started to dry Rocky's hair. "Look at me," Jo said. Rocky looked at her with slightly dazed eyes. "You okay?" the dark-haired woman asked. Rocky merely nodded, not trusting her voice.

Jo smiled at her and carried on gently drying the soaked, blonde hair. "Look at you," she gently scolded. "Let's get that jacket off." She leaned forward, pulling down the zip on the front of the jacket and then easing it back off the blonde's shoulders.

"Shelly?" a voice behind them asked.

Jo looked up to see a young woman standing behind her lover. Rocky turned herself, shrugging her way out of the wet jacket.

"Kate," was all Rocky could manage. She stood, taking a step forward, hugging the girl fiercely.

Jo tried to look away, to give what were obviously old friends a moment. However, she couldn't take her eyes off the anguished look on the face of the girl holding on to her lover.

When she'd finally composed herself, Kate reluctantly let go of the blonde. "They said you were dead."

Rocky wiped a hand across her face. "Who said?" Rocky sat heavily on the chair, feeling a gentle hand on her arm as she did so.

Kate looked at a loss standing there in front of the two seated women, shaking slightly. She ran a hand through short brown hair and looked back at the woman behind the counter. "Can I have a moment?"

The woman nodded, and Kate sat with her friend. Kate nodded at Jo, who smiled back, then her gaze found her old school friend again. "It was a couple of months after the accident. A man came here looking for you. Said you'd disappeared." She looked down at the floor. "Then a few months later, he came back and said he had to clear out your house, that you were presumed dead."

Rocky covered her face with her hands, then reached across and took one of Jo's hands.

Kate looked at Jo. "I'm sorry..."

"No, my fault." She reached across with her free hand, offering it to the girl. "Hi, I'm Jo."

"Kate," the still tearful girl said. "We grew up together."

Rocky looked up at her friend. "It's really good to see you, Katy."

"Where did you go?" she asked.

"It's a long story. I can't tell it right now."

Kate nodded. "That's okay, Shelly. It's just good to know you're okay." She stood. "I'll just go and get you some drinks, then maybe we can talk."

Rocky nodded and watched her friend disappear behind the counter.

An hour or so later, Jo and Rocky walked towards the Merk, still parked beside the wall. Their clothes and hair were still damp, and they wanted nothing more than to get back to their hotel and test out the large bath they'd seen in the bathroom of their suite.

"So you went to school with Kate?" Jo asked as she unlocked the car with the remote on her key ring.

"Yeah, we were really close." Rocky slid into the passenger seat. "I didn't think about people like that. I should have gotten word to her." She looked across at Jo, who was inserting the key into the ignition. "Did you notice how quiet she got after she first saw me?"

Jo started the car and waited for the de-misters to work on the windscreen. "Yeah, I think it was all a little too much for her to take in."

"I wouldn't blame her for hating me." Rocky pulled her seat-belt on and sat forlornly with her head bowed.

"Now why would she do that?" Jo asked, becoming a little annoyed with her morose lover. She looked across at the dejected figure. "Hey," she reached out and took one of the cold hands that were clutched together in the blonde's lap.

"I was thoughtless," Rocky said quietly. "Didn't think of any-one but myself."

Jo squeezed the hand she held. "You had to do what you did to save yourself." She shook the hand. "Hey, look at me."

Reluctantly, Rocky looked up, and moist green eyes locked with Jo's gaze. Jo turned in her seat to face the blonde.

"You survived, Rocky. And now you have all the time in the world to go back and find some of the life you left behind." She raised their joined hands to her lips, kissing the knuckles of her lover. "And I for one am very, very grateful you survived." She leaned across and her lips found the blonde's. In that moment Jo managed to show just how grateful.

There was only one pay phone in the small village, and the young man that stepped into it managed to take his eyes off the Merk long enough to take a small piece of paper from his wallet. He keyed the numbers on that paper and waited while he heard the dial tone change to a ringing tone.

"Hello? It's Paul Langley...You asked me to let you know if Michelle Kersey ever showed her face here again...Yes, I'm looking at her right now...No she's with a tall woman, never seen her before...Don't know...They're in a Merk—nice one, silver, soft top...Yeah. X1 JHS...You'll send the money? Okay, bye."

He slid out of the phone box as the Merk, which had only gone a few yards since he saw the women get into it, drove away again and disappeared into the rainy gloom.

It was getting dark as they arrived back at the clifftop hotel.

"So you're telling me that they opened up just for us?" Rocky asked as she leaned in, testing the temperature of the water filling the bath.

"Yeah. All the hotels that were open over Christmas were fully booked. They didn't take too much persuading."

Rocky sat on the edge of the bath. "How much did it cost?"

"Does it matter?"

Rocky nodded. "I don't want you spending all your money on me."

Jo leaned her hands on the shoulders of the smaller woman. "I have lots of money."

"Not the point," Rocky said, but she was rapidly losing her resolve to be angry with Jo as she felt her lover begin to unbutton the still-damp shirt she wore.

"There won't be any room service, but I've ordered us an Indian meal which will be delivered in an hour or so. Mrs. Maple is going to bring it up."

"Mrs. Maple?"

"The woman at reception."

"And the old man who helped with our luggage?"

"Mr. Maple."

The shirt was removed and thrown onto the bathroom floor. Then Rocky was gently eased to her feet, and Jo knelt, undoing the laces of the black leather boots she wore. "I can do that," the blonde protested.

Twinkling blue eyes looked up at her through ebony hair. "I know," Jo said with a smile.

"So you talked them into opening?" Rocky asked, as Jo eased off her shoes and then turned her attention to the button-down fly of her jeans.

"Yep," she said, undoing the top button. "They said they'd do it." The second button popped open. "But they could only provide light meals." Another one gave under expert fingers. "And no room service." She stood as the jeans fell to pool around Rocky's feet. She bent to kiss the lips of the half-naked woman in front of her. "I love you," she said as she pulled back.

"And I love you." Rocky decided to return the compliment and turned her attention to the zip of Jo's fly.

The bath had taken longer than they thought, and Mrs. Maple had called them twice on the phone to tell them their meal had arrived and was in the microwave heating for the second time. The old man tried valiantly to avert his eyes from the long legs that emerged from the bottom of a long t-shirt when Jo opened the door to allow him to bring the meal into their room.

"Mrs. Maple and I will be in the lounge if you need anything, dear," he said as he set the plates down on the small table.

"Thank you," Jo said, giving a smirk to her lover, who was more decently covered than she was.

"You should put more clothes on," Rocky scolded when the old man left, shutting the door gently behind him.

"Why? If you've got it, flaunt it. That's what I say."

Rocky looked at the limbs in question. "You've just got...so much of it."

The meal was, as most Indian meals are, hot and spicy, and they had to call down a couple of times for more orange juice and Coke. But every time, it was the elderly man who made the long trek up to room number three. Then it would take a few moments from an unrepentant Jo to usher him out of the door again. The last time he took the dirty plates and cutlery with him.

"You know what it does to him," Rocky said as the door closed. "You should have put something else on this time."

"Why? I'm comfortable."

"You know why."

Jo chuckled and eased into the warm, comfortable bed, watching Rocky as she turned on the TV and then joined her in the cosy nest.

"This is nice," Jo said as she wound an arm around the blonde, who sank easily into the embrace.

"It is."

"You okay?" Rocky nodded but remained silent. "So why do I feel like there's something wrong?" Jo asked, turning her head slightly and kissing soft blonde hair.

"I'm still waiting to wake up." She looked up at her friend, her heart missing a beat when she looked into eyes as blue as the summer sky. "It's like a dream." She laid her head on Jo's chest. "You're like a dream."

Jo lay there, the blonde resting comfortably in her arms, enjoying the moment and the comfortable silence that surrounded them. It almost made her jump when Rocky spoke again.

"I'm scared of losing you." The blonde's voice was very small, very pained.

"You won't, I promise."

In the snowy midlands, a man picked up the phone, dialled a number, and waited for it to connect. "John? Yes. I need you to run a check on a car for me...Silver Mercedes convertible. Registration number X1 JHS. As soon as you can...Let me know." He replaced the phone in its cradle and sat back. "Happy, happy day," he whispered to himself.

Chapter
19

Rocky woke with a start. For a brief moment, she didn't know where she was. A television cast a flickering glow across the room. She looked to her left, the presence at her side demanding her attention. Jo was still asleep, flat on her back. She was on her stomach right next to Jo. Their hands were tangled together between them.

Rocky gently turned onto her side. The dark-haired woman stirred but didn't awaken. Many nights, when she was woken by her dreams, Rocky would do this—just lie there in the silence of the night watching Jo. They were both naked. Rocky pulled gently on the quilt, which Jo had pulled up over them when their skin started to feel the chill of the evening. It slid down the long body, and she watched in fascination as the dark nipples responded to the fabric of the quilt cover as it slid across them.

Jo sucked in a deep breath, exhaling loudly. Rocky smiled to herself as she pulled the quilt away from her lover's body. She looked up from the flesh she had uncovered to Jo's face, to find two very blue, very dazed eyes looking back at her.

"Hi," she said quietly.

Jo attempted to speak but had to clear her throat first. "Why are you awake?"

Rocky reached out, tracing the soft flesh of Jo's cheek, running her hand down, following a smooth jawline. "I'm not sure. Active mind, I think."

Jo captured the roaming hand, bringing it to her lips and kissing the fingertips. She pulled slightly, settling the blonde on top of her and holding on to her loosely.

"This is nice," the blonde said, relaxing onto the living mattress, revelling in the feeling of silky skin against her own.

"Yes, it is," Jo breathed into her ear, her own hands wandering across the planes of Rocky's back.

"Jo?" Rocky suddenly pulled back, sitting up astride Jo's knees, leaving the brunette's hands empty. Long arms flopped back onto the bed. The blonde looked down at the woman, and her hands traced the taut abdomen watching as the muscles beneath the skin tightened at her touch. "You're very beautiful."

Jo swallowed. "So are you."

"You know, I still don't know why you chose me." Rocky's hands found Jo's navel, the tip of her finger dipping into it. She had received such pleasure at Jo's hands in the past few days, and her lover had never asked anything of her in return. Now she wanted to show Jo how much she loved her. Green eyes looked into the flushed face. "I'm not sure I know what I'm doing here."

Jo opened her mouth to disagree but clamped it shut again as a tentative hand then found her breast. "Is this nice?" Rocky whispered as her finger brushed across already tense buds. Jo nodded quickly. "And this?" She squeezed the aching nipple between two fingers, feeling the body beneath her react.

"I didn't ever think about loving another woman," she said quietly, watching her own hand as it caressed Jo's body. "But then I didn't think much about love for a long time." She brought her other hand up to join its mate. Now both breasts were enjoying the attention. She cupped the soft mounds, her short nails raking gently across the sensitive skin. "In my dream, you came and took me away, to somewhere safe and warm." She still cupped Jo's breasts in her hands but now caressed both nipples with her thumbs. "The fact that you were a woman didn't surprise me. Why was that?" She tore her eyes away from her own hands when she received no answer, to find Jo's eyes tightly shut. "Jo, are you listening?"

Jo's eyes shot open. "Um, yes, I'm listening."

Rocky sighed. Her hands drifted downwards, along the outside of Jo's now highly aroused breasts, and came to rest on her hips. "I want to make you feel the way you make me feel." Her hands moved inwards, her thumbs tracing the sensitive skin at the juncture of long thighs. She smiled to herself when she heard Jo's breathing increase, the chest she had been loving so tenderly only moments before rising and falling rapidly.

She ran her hand through soft curls, marvelling at the feel of them. "Anyway," Rocky continued. "You're just going to have to tell me if I'm doing anything right." She traced patterns across the twitching abdomen, circling a perfect belly button and tracing the edge of the dark patch of hair. She looked down, and, cocking her head to the side, ventured further. Jo's hips bucked so violently that Rocky was nearly thrown from the bed. She quickly withdrew her hand from the place she had found that elicited the reaction.

"Sorry," Rocky said steadying herself with both hands on Jo's stomach.

"Don't be," Jo squeaked.

"Did I hurt you?"

Jo shook her head tightly.

"I want to do it right." Rocky's hand once again found the place, and she watched closely as blue eyes fluttered closed. "Tell me what you want," she whispered.

Jo's mouth opened and closed, but no coherent sound was forthcoming.

"So this is okay, then?" She'd never felt such softness, and she felt her own body reacting to the new feelings she was experiencing.

Jo's hands grasped onto the sheet beneath her as Rocky's tentative touch drew out her pleasure. Her hips rose, encouraging the blonde in her efforts, feeling the touch become bolder, deeper. And when a hot mouth enveloped her nipple, she took two handfuls of soft blonde hair, holding her lover in place.

Even in her inexperience, Rocky knew Jo was nearing the edge, and she desperately wanted to see her. She raised her head, struggling against her lover's hands, which attempted to keep her in place. Desperately, Jo grasped for Rocky's free hand, pressing it to her aching breast. Rocky gazed upon the face of her lover as Jo came. She'd never seen anything so beautiful; never had Jo looked so beautiful. She eased her hand away from the warmth and softness of her lover's pleasure and pressed her body gently down onto the gasping form below her. Gently pushing damp hair from Jo's forehead, she kissed the tip of her nose, her closed eyes, and then her slightly swollen lips.

Though her arms felt heavy, Jo clutched at the woman who had just given her more pleasure than she'd ever felt. True, she had experienced much in her time, but never felt such emotion. She had finally given her heart. True, she had allowed others to touch her, but this was so very different. And as she held her lover, whose fingers were at that moment making small patterns across her lower abdomen, she realised she had finally made love. It wasn't sex. It was love. Rocky's tentative, nervous hands had drawn out the woman in her, and for that she would be forever in her debt. To the other women who had taken her body, she had been nothing more than a conquest. A notch on a bedpost, a name to be whispered. And she hadn't cared. Until now. The hand on her stomach had stopped its torturous movement, and she looked down at the face of her lover, relaxed in slumber. Her tears surprised her. Why on earth was she crying? This was quite probably one of the most wonderful moments of her life. And here she was snivelling like a baby. She tightened her hold on the blonde.

"What?" Rocky's voice was sleepy. She looked up, alarmed at the tears she saw coursing down her lover's face. "Jo?"

"I'm fine," she said quickly, wiping at the tears with her hand.

"You're crying." Rocky propped herself up on one elbow, catching a tear as it made its way across Jo's cheek.

"I'm happy," Jo sniffed.

"I'm glad." Rocky leaned forward and kissed Jo, trying to put into that kiss the love and respect she felt for this woman. Trying to convey her thanks for the gift Jo had given her. "I love you so much," whispered the blonde.

Jo merely smiled, knowing her voice would fail her. She pulled Rocky tightly against her own body and dragged the quilt from where it had fallen to the side of the bed to cover them. Two sets of breathing fell into a rhythm as they fell asleep, holding on tightly to one another, both secure in the knowledge that they had found one more piece of their soul. One more part of the jigsaw that might one day make them complete. The TV played on. Its silver light picking out the forms on the bed, bathing them in an eerie glow and highlighting the matching smiles on sleeping faces.

They say when two English men, or women for that matter, meet, they will discuss the weather. And the day that greeted the lovers proved that point. Though dark clouds gathered in the distance, the sky over the small village of Tintagel was blue and the winter sun shone fiercely. It was still frigidly cold, but the sun cast the village in a new light, and Jo could imagine the woman walking beside her growing up there.

They had parked the Merk in a small car park and walked slowly through the village, looking at the places that Rocky was rediscovering. The long walk down to the cliff face to the ruins of the castle, was made carefully, the path still damp from the rain that had fallen in the previous days. They surveyed the ruins, hand in hand.

Rocky felt the large hand squeezing her own. "You okay?" she asked, squinting against the sunlight, which brought out the slightly auburn highlights in her lover's hair. Jo's eyes were closed, her lips slightly parted. A furrow marred her forehead. "You feel it too," Rocky said, moving around in front of the taller woman, and reaching up to brush away the ebony hair that had blown across the angular face.

"I feel sick," Jo said simply.

"I used to." Rocky leaned into the shaking form, winding her arms around Jo. "There's something magical here...something old...it used to call to me." She rubbed her hands up and down the rigid back. "Take deep breaths."

Jo did so, and the colour started to return to her cheeks. She took a deep breath and looked down into concerned green eyes. "What was that?"

Rocky shrugged slightly. "I've never been sure. Some sort of echo of the past." She squeezed tighter, feeling Jo return the embrace. "You believe in reincarnation?"

Jo snorted, a most unladylike sound. She looked down, seeing the serious expression on the beautiful face of the woman holding her.

Rocky smiled up at her. "I think I've been here before."

Jo looked over the blonde head at the ruins. "Well, you have," she said simply.

"I have," Rocky conceded. "Many times." She turned her back on Jo, gazing out at the sea battering at the tiny outcrop to which the ruins clung. She felt Jo's arms encircle her from behind. "But it's more than that. I feel I've been here before that."

"In another life?"

Rocky nodded, closing her eyes and feeling the salt spray gentle on her face. "And I think you were too."

Jo looked down at the ruins, trying to imagine what it would have looked like in its prime. "Must have been quite a place."

"Fit for a king." Rocky's voice was almost lost on the wind.

"Or a queen?" She bent her head and kissed the edge of the

blonde's ear.

Rocky chuckled. "D'you think we were here once? Together?" She felt the woman behind her take a deep breath.

"I've never really thought about that kind of thing. Never thought about anything much before I met you."

Rocky thought about that statement for a moment. "Why was that?"

Jo seemed to shift uncomfortably behind her, and Rocky waited patiently for her answer. "I didn't need to think. Everything was done for me. My parents already had two successful children, and when I showed no ambition, they didn't push me." Jo laughed gently. "And I loved them for it." The tall woman looked at the storm clouds gathering, starting to hide the sun. "Now, with you, I see so much I want to do. I want to do well for you, make you happy. I want you to be proud of me."

"I am."

"But you don't—"

"No, please." She turned again in the circle of Jo's arms to face her lover. "No, I know what you've turned your back on. I know you've given up that life for me. All of a sudden, you have someone with more emotional baggage than she can handle looking to you for some sort of support, and you're giving it without asking for anything in return." She looked up shyly into blue eyes. "You're my hero," she said, watching as a blush spread across Jo's face.

"I'm not."

"Yes, you are."

"Can we agree to disagree about that?"

Rocky shrugged. "If you like, but I'm right."

Jo looked down at her for long moments. "Where now?"

The blonde head eased forward and rested against Jo's chest. "Back to the graveyard. I need to say goodbye."

Rocky watched the changing landscape as they left Cornwall and then Devon. By the time they reached the M4, they had started to see small pockets of snow that had resisted the slightly warmer weather. The further east they went, the worse the weather became. As they passed Swindon, they hit the first light snowfall.

"You're quiet," Jo said, studying briefly the tired profile of the blonde.

Green eyes turned in her direction. "Just thinking."

"Good thoughts?"

Rocky nodded. "Oh yeah, I was thinking about you."

Jo's face creased into a smile. "Really?"

"I was just wondering where we'll be in a year or so from now."

Jo reached across and took her hand. "Where would you like to be?"

Rocky looked down at their linked hands, turning Jo's over and studying it intently. "I think I'd just like to be wherever you are." She watched the larger hand curl around hers and squeeze. "But..." The sentence hung in the air between them.

"But what?" Jo tore her eyes from the increasingly heavy traffic she was encountering to look down at the girl slumped in the passenger seat. "We have all the time we need. What's bothering you?"

"I'm finding it hard having to rely on you for everything. This trip, the clothes, everything. I was so used to fending for myself... It's just hard," she finished weakly.

"It's no big deal," Jo said, matter-of-factly.

"It is to me."

"Okay then, we'll enrol you in the college. What would you like to do? They have plenty of courses."

Rocky looked at her as if she'd sprouted another head. "I couldn't do anything like that!"

"Why not?" she asked simply.

Rocky was obviously trying to come up with a reason, but her jaw snapped shut as she realised she didn't have one. "I don't know," she said quietly.

"How about computers or something?" Jo gave her hand a little shake, realising that, at last, Rocky was starting to think a little positively.

"Maybe."

"See?" She raised their linked hands and kissed the blonde's knuckles. "I want you to be happy, sweetheart."

"I am," Rocky said.

Jo pulled into the courtyard and parked the car in front of her house. No sooner had they opened the boot than the front door opened and Edna greeted them. "I saw you drive in. I put the kettle on."

Jo heaved the bags out of the boot and threw them inside the front door. "You go on up, I'll bring these," she said and gently pushed the blonde towards her elderly friend.

Rocky followed Edna up the stairs and into the kitchen, pulling off her jacket and hanging it in the hallway as she went.

Edna stood against the sink, watching Rocky as she settled into one of the kitchen chairs. "How was it?"

"It was...hard." The blonde planted her elbows on the table and cradled her head in her hands. "Too many memories." She looked up at the woman from beneath pale hair. "But I'm glad I went."

The shrill whistle of the kettle interrupted them, and Edna turned to make the tea just as Jo stumbled into the hall with the bags.

"Come in here and sit yourself down," Edna called through the door. "I bet you drove the whole way without stopping."

"I was worried about the weather, didn't want to be out in it too late," Jo said as she sat, depositing a kiss on her lover's cheek as she passed.

"They do say it's going to get worse in the next few days. Cold front coming from the east." She put two mugs of tea in front of the two women. "I'll go gather my things."

Jo's eyes snapped up. "You don't have to go yet, Edna."

The old woman placed a gentle hand on the brunette's shoulder. "Yes, Jo. I do. It's been a pleasant few days here, but I've been out there too long." She shrugged and smiled at the confused look on Jo's face. "It's what I'm used to." She padded away quietly.

Rocky looked across at Jo. "You can't understand it, can you?"

Jo shook her head. "It's the worst winter for years, sub zero temperatures, and she'd rather be out in it than here. No, I don't understand."

"Same old story," the blonde said.

Jo shrugged.

"The feeling of imposing, of being a burden."

Jo leaned towards the blonde. "You," she pointed a finger in Rocky's direction, "are not going back out there."

"No, I know," she said with a small smile. "But I have something Edna doesn't."

"What's that?"

"You."

Jo chuckled and leaned across capturing the blonde's lips. "That's true," she said, her breath warm on Rocky's mouth.

"I'm ready," Edna said, dropping her bags just outside the kitchen door. "I'll need to find another trolley. I don't think mine will be where we left it."

Jo leaned back, away from the blonde and turned in her seat to face the old woman. "Can I finish my tea?"

Edna huffed and settled herself in the spare kitchen chair, watching as Jo and Rocky sipped their tea as slowly as they could.

It was an hour later that Jo opened the door of the car and allowed Edna to settle herself in the passenger seat. The tall woman turned back to the blonde framed in the doorway. "Are you sure you won't come?" Jo took a couple of steps back towards Rocky.

Rocky nodded. "Yeah, I'm sure. I don't think I want to go back there yet." She turned Jo in the direction of the car. "Besides, I have three days of washing to sort out."

Jo resisted the gentle pushing and turned back, gathering the small woman in her arms. "I won't be long."

"Make sure you're not." She frowned slightly. "Shouldn't you take a jacket?" she asked noticing Jo only had a sweatshirt on along with her jeans and sneakers.

"I'm fine. I'll be gone an hour at the most." She ducked her head and nipped at soft lips. "I love you," she whispered.

"Love you, too." Rocky gave her a shove and stepped back into the doorway, wrapping her arms around her in an attempt to keep out the cold. "Now go," she said, with a smile. Jo pouted but slowly got into the car.

The blonde waved to her friend as the Merk pulled slowly out of the courtyard. Then she closed the door and made her way straight to the laundry room. She had just emptied the contents of their travel bag on the floor when the doorbell rang. "What have you forgotten now?" she muttered under her breath as she reached for the handle and opened the door. Before her stood a nightmare—a smiling nightmare.

"Michelle," the tall man said, reaching for her.

Rocky felt her knees unlock, and she staggered backwards, tripping over the bottom stair. She sat heavily, watching as the man quietly closed the door and turned back towards her. "It's been so long," he said as he crouched in front of her and cupped a cheek already wet with tears. "I've missed you so much."

Her mind struggled to comprehend what was happening. It couldn't possibly be, could it? She'd been so careful and had stayed away. Surely by now he thought her dead. But no, here he was. He'd come for her.

"I searched for you," he said, pulling her to her feet and crushing her in an embrace. "I knew I'd find you. I never lost faith." He kissed blonde hair and held her at arm's length. "Now we can be together again."

"No." Her voice was little more than a whisper.

"No?" His smile never faltered. "Michelle, I forgive you for leaving me. Whatever it was that made you leave, we'll sort out. We'll be happy again."

"I was never..." Her objection died on her lips as he crushed her to his chest again.

"Is there anything you need to take?" he asked.

Rocky managed to pull away from him. "I can't leave."

"And why is that?" he asked patiently.

"My...friend."

"The tall woman I saw leave a moment ago?"

Rocky nodded and realised he had waited until she was alone. He smiled again, the same smile she had seen in her nightmares. "I waited for her to go, because I knew seeing you alone would be safer. I wouldn't want anything to happen should she object to you choosing to leave with me." He waited a moment for Rocky to think about what he was saying. "Would you rather we waited?"

"Would you hurt her?" Rocky asked, her voice breaking.

"If she came between us, Michelle, I would have to."

Rocky closed her eyes. "I have to get a coat. That's all I have."

"Very well." He followed the girl as she ascended the stairs and stood in the hallway as she reached for her coat.

Rocky hesitated then bypassed her own coat and took Jo's jacket from the hook. She draped it over her arm and turned back to the man. "Can I leave a note?"

"I'm sorry, Michelle. A clean break, I think that would be the best." She nodded and took the hand that he offered. "Let's go home," he said and led her down the stairs and out of the house.

Chapter
20

It was nearly two hours before Jo returned to her house, and she almost had a head-on collision with a Red VW Beetle as she turned into the courtyard. Both cars skidded in the snow, and Jo peered through the snow-smeared windscreen to see her friend behind the wheel of the dumpy car. She waved at Harry, indicating she should reverse. When she did, Jo eased the Merk across the slippery courtyard and flipped the remote for the garage door.

"Where were you going?" Jo asked as she closed the garage and opened the front door.

Harry parked the car and locked it. "Home," she said. "There was no answer, so I was giving up. Just came round to see how your trip went."

"Rocky's up there." She stood back, holding the door open, and allowed the smaller woman to pass her and go on ahead.

"Well, maybe she didn't hear me."

Jo shrugged and climbed the stairs behind her friend. "Rocky!" she called as she got to the top and walked past her friend. She looked back at Harry. "Hold on, I'll go find her."

Harry went into the lounge, pulling off her coat as she went. She heard Jo's footfalls upstairs, going from room to room. She sat on the sofa and used the remote to turn on the TV. The weather forecast was on, and with the present conditions made for interesting viewing. She heard Jo pass the lounge and go back down the stairs.

A few moments later, Jo appeared in the doorway, an unreadable expression on her face. "She's gone." She moved across to the large armchair and slumped down in it.

Harry watched as Jo sat quietly, her hands folded in her lap, her eyes fixed on the Christmas tree. The lights weren't lit, so she stood and walked over, leaning behind the tree to turn them on at the wall socket. Then she returned to her place on the chair.

"Maybe she had to pop out," Harry said and almost winced when she saw the pain in the blue eyes that settled on her.

"I would have done anything for her." Jo's voice was strangled. "Anything she wanted."

Harry stood and took a couple of steps across the room so she could sit on the arm of Jo's chair. "Why are you so sure she's gone?" she asked, laying a gentle hand on Jo's taut shoulder.

Jo covered her face with her hands, so Harry had to strain to hear what she said. "She would have left a note. And things she said...in Cornwall."

"Like what?"

Jo leaned her head against the back of the chair, suddenly incredibly weary. She sighed. "She didn't like being a burden." Tears rolled down her cheeks. "I should never have left...her alone."

Harry was at a loss. She'd witnessed for herself the absolute joy her friend had displayed in the company of the small blonde, and now she was witnessing utter despair. "I've heard sometimes, that these people can't handle going back to a normal life—" Harry was cut short when outraged blue eyes turned on her.

"What the hell do you mean, 'these people'? You're talking about Rocky. She's a person, someone I came to know and love, and you're talking about her like she's some kind of statistic. Jesus Christ, Harry." Jo looked away from her.

"I'm sorry." Harry slipped her hand from Jo's shoulder but remained sitting on the arm of the chair. "You...d'you want to go looking for her?"

Jo shook her head. Her anger had gone as quickly as it arrived, replaced by a sense of resignation. "No, if she wants to disappear she knows how to do it. She did it successfully for five years." She sighed. "I don't know what I did wrong."

"Nothing. You did nothing wrong."

"It was too fast. Everything. I should have waited, let her do things at her pace." She massaged aching temples with trembling hands. "Just something else in my life I've fucked up." The ringing of the telephone interrupted Jo's self-loathing. "Can you get that?" she asked Harry. "Whoever it is, tell them I'm asleep, or dead, whatever you like."

Harry sighed, gave Jo's shoulder a squeeze, and reached across to the low coffee table for the phone. "Hello?" Harry listened, but she could hear only breathing. Uneven breathing. She put her hand over the mouthpiece. "It's a breather."

Jo reached out. "Give it to me." Harry handed Jo the phone and returned to her seat on the sofa. "Who is this?" Jo listened carefully, hearing the breathing, hearing the caller take in a long shuddering breath. "Rocky?"

No answer, just the sound of ragged breathing.

"Rocky, sweetheart, is that you? Please, talk to me. Tell me where you are." She still heard nothing. Then suddenly a beep. She recognised it as the sound a cell phone makes to warn the user that the battery is getting low. "Rocky, you have my phone?" Jo stood and went into the hall. Her jacket was gone, and she knew she'd left the phone in the pocket. She slid down the wall, the palm of her hand pressed to her forehead. "Rocky, whatever is wrong, we can work it out. Please, tell me where you are."

"I'm sorry."

"Baby, don't be sorry. Just come home."

"I can't. I'm sorry."

Another beep. "Rocky, I love you."

Silence for a long moment. "I'm...sorry."

"Are you in London?"

"No."

"I don't understand, Rocky. I thought you were happy. Was it something I did?"

"I have to go."

"Go? Go where? Please, tell me where you are."

"He's waiting for me."

The breath was sucked from Jo's chest, and she expected her stomach to expel its contents at any second. "Who's waiting for you?"

"I just needed to say goodbye."

"He found you?"

Silence. Then, "He said he'd hurt you."

"He can't possibly hurt me more than I'm hurting right now." She waited a moment, then did something she'd never done before. "I'm begging you, Rocky."

"I'm sorry."

"I love you, sweetheart."

Silence.

"I'll find you."

"No."

"I will find you."

"Please, Jo. He'll hurt you, he'll—"

The line went dead, and Jo threw the phone across the hall-way, watching with satisfaction as it broke into two parts.

Harry appeared at her side, crouching down next to her trembling friend. "I'm guessing that was Rocky."

"He's got her."

Harry winced at the pain she heard in Jo's voice. "Who's got her, Jo?"

Jo turned red-rimmed blue eyes on her friend. "Her uncle, the man she ran away from."

"Jesus, I didn't know."

"What do I do now?"

Harry stood, looking down at the slumped woman. "You go get her."

Jo laughed, wiping her wet face with both hands. "Sounds simple." She leaned her head back against the wall. "She went with him." She sighed, a sound of finality.

"What if she didn't have a choice?"

The image of her lover being dragged from the house suddenly burned itself into her consciousness. "Oh my God."

"Jo, do you know where he lives?" Harry reached down and pulled the taller woman to her feet.

"Leicester, somewhere. I don't even know his name." Jo pulled her hair back from her face. "I don't know what to do."

"Hey, calm down." Harry could see her friend was about to break down. "Think hard. Did she ever mention his surname? Was he an uncle on her side of the family?"

Jo shook her head. "No, it was her mother's sister's hus-band."

"Didn't she have any personal things, something that may have had an address on?" Harry so much wanted to give her friend some hope. Never before has she seen the once carefree woman so distraught.

"No, she had nothing, apart from...her bags!" Jo said, and flew down the stairs into the laundry room. There in the corner were the bags that Rocky had carried with her for the five years that she survived on the streets of London. The blonde had been meaning to go through the contents but had always put it off, not wanting to confront the memories that lay within.

Jo opened the bags with something approaching reverence. She reached in, carefully pulling out the jumble of clothing that was inside. There, wrapped in an old shirt, she found a bundle of photos and letters. The photos she put to one side. One day she would go through them with Rocky—of that she was now determined. The letters were all still in their envelopes. She didn't open them. But on the front was an address. An address in Leicester.

"I've found her," she whispered. "72 Forest Lane, Leicester."

Rocky's heart rate increased as the large car pulled up to the front of her uncle's magnificent house. As Chief Constable of the Leicestershire Constabulary, he reaped the rewards the position bestowed upon him. His position and standing in the local community was spotless, and none of his friends and colleagues knew anything of the niece he'd used his rank to hunt down. And it was mainly this that caused Rocky to run rather than seek the help of the authorities. Her word against the top policeman in that part of the country would probably not have much credibility.

So now she was back. Back at the place that haunted her dreams and her memories. She remembered the small room, with the window overlooking the garden and its covered swimming pool. The room with the bolt on the door—the outside of the door. She watched him as he walked around the front of the car, and then the wind and snow blew against her face as he opened the door.

"Come along, Michelle. Your aunt is waiting to see you again." He held out a hand, and when she didn't move, he leaned across, unsnapped her seatbelt, and pulled her out into the falling snow.

She still clutched Jo's jacket in her arms, holding on to that last connection with the woman who had started to ease her out of the darkness. Finding Jo's phone in the pocket when she'd persuaded him to let her go to the toilet in a motorway service station had been a blessing and a curse. She'd stood with her back to the mirror in the rest room and pressed the pre-set button she knew was Jo's home number. She'd just wanted to say goodbye and that she was sorry. But hearing Jo's anguished voice had been too much for her. If only she'd just left it, she'd have had the smiling memory of her lover as she got in the car earlier that day. The failing battery had put an end to the call, and she'd looked at the small device for a very long moment before slipping it back into her pocket and returning to the man waiting for her outside.

That same man led her into the house. They were met in the hallway by his wife, Rocky's aunt. Susan was much more like Rocky than her own mother was. Short and blonde, she was the complete opposite of her tall dark husband.

"Michelle," was all she could say, and she gathered the blonde into her arms.

No other words passed between the two women, both knowing their lives were about to change in very different ways. Susan had prayed he would never find her niece, for she knew she couldn't protect her sister's child against her husband's weaknesses. To her shame, she remembered how she would lie awake on the nights he would leave her bed and creep across the landing. In the morning, she wasn't able to look at the sweet blonde child. She would fail her now, as she had failed her five years before. He took Rocky's hand and pulled her up the stairs. She looked back down at her aunt, who turned away and closed the lounge door quietly behind her.

"Your room hasn't changed. We kept it as it was for when you came home." He opened the door and stood aside for the blonde to enter. When she didn't, he gave her a shove, and she stumbled in.

Rocky spun to face him. "Don't touch me," she whispered.

"Michelle." He took a step towards her. "I know you're tired. Let me help you get something more comfortable on."

He tried to pull the jacket from her arms. "No," she said, pulling away from him.

"Don't be a silly girl, give me the jacket." He managed to get a hold on the sleeve of the leather garment and pulled it forcefully out of his niece's hands, throwing it onto the bed. Rocky looked from it up to her uncle. "Now then," he said.

Rocky closed her eyes as he began to unbutton her shirt. "No," she said quietly.

"What's that, Angel?" His attention was on undoing the buttons, which was difficult with the newness of the shirt.

She knocked his hands away, still hating the nickname he'd given her all those years ago. "Don't touch me." She tried to back away, but he pulled her towards him by the front of her shirt and he ripped it open, losing patience. Buttons scattered across the room and bounced off the walls. He stripped the checked shirt off her shoulders, leaving her standing in her jeans and white t-shirt.

"You used to wear such pretty clothes," he said, advancing on her again. He reached out and traced her cheek, down to her chin, and across her neck. She flinched away from him.

His hand cupped the back of her head, and he dipped down. His lips found hers, and he sighed feeling the softness he remembered. But this time, the lips were responsive. Before, in those days when he'd first brought her back from the hospital, she had been like a corpse in his hands, but he still couldn't resist her. From the first moment he'd laid eyes on her in that hospital bed, he'd been smitten. And nothing and no one would keep him from her.

Then he realised that the response he was getting from her was not one of complicity, but one of rejection. She was pushing against him, then his bottom lip was between her teeth and she bit down hard. He pushed her violently away from him, his hand reaching for his mouth. Rocky bounced off the wall but stayed on her feet. He looked from the blood on his hands to the girl standing before him She looked like the girl he'd brought home over five years before, but something new was behind the green eyes.

"I don't understand, Michelle." He pushed the door closed behind him, cutting off any route of escape for her. Then he approached her again. His hands were heavy on her shoulders; the pain of her recent injury flared with the weight of them. They smoothed down the outside of her arms, and took both her hands in his. He tugged her towards him, released one of her hands to begin lowering the zip on her jeans.

"No!" she screamed and tore her hand from his. She beat on his chest and his face, landing a blow on the bridge of his nose. He attempted to catch her flailing arms and was hit a couple more times. Her feet kicked out, catching his shins. He finally threw a punch at her, catching her across the side of her face and sending her crashing into a low chest of drawers. She scrambled to her feet and launched herself at him. His police training took over and he turned her around, pulling an arm across her throat. He felt her start to weaken in his arms and pulled her closer against his body.

"You're upset, I know that." He could feel her slump against him. As she lost consciousness, he lowered her onto the bed, and arranged her limp form on the bed. His fingers smoothing the growing bruise on her left cheek. "You sleep. I'll be back later. Things will be better once you've rested." He left the room, turning off the light, and slid the bolt into place.

The weather was getting worsen, and Jo managed to encounter every traffic jam and accident as she made her way up the M1 after having battled her way around a part of the notorious M25. In places the traffic, though considerably lighter than usual, came to a mind-numbing crawl. But when she finally managed to get through the hold up, she exceeded the speed limit, driven by her fear for Rocky. She estimated that her lover had been in the hands of that man for up to five hours now, and she dreaded what she would find when she got there.

As she got off the motorway, she saw a petrol station and pulled into it, needing some kind of guide to Leicester, since she had never been there before. She tore through the doors, startling the teenage youth behind the counter. It had been very quiet as the evening drew on, the dreadful weather keeping all but the fool-hardy from venturing out.

"I need a street map of Leicester," she said breathlessly, looking across the shelves. He pointed wordlessly, and Jo snatched an A-Z off the shelf. She walked towards the counter, looking at the back of the book for the price, which she couldn't find. She threw a ten-pound note onto the counter. "Enough?" she asked. He nodded dumbly, and she turned on her heel, the draft from the closing door causing the note to flutter to the ground.

She almost lost control of the car as she turned back onto the street, cursing like a sailor before she managed to get the Merk pointing in the right direction again. She soon came to a halt however, as the evening traffic gridlocked in the horrendous weather. She flipped on the light and looked up the road name on the envelope. Forest Lane. She found it, but then took a while to work out where it was in relation to where she was at that moment.

It was actually on the outskirts of Leicester. She looked up, hoping to find a street sign that would help her on her way. It was hard to see in the driving snow, but she just made out a sign, which, thankfully had a name on it she recognised. She was on her way now.

However, it was nearly two hours later that she found herself still about a mile from the road for which she was looking. Snow drifts, accidents, and a few wrong turns had turned the trip into a nightmare. The entire time, her imagination was playing horrible tricks on her. From what Rocky had told her, she knew the man wanted her for one thing and one thing only. The amount of time she was taking gave him plenty of time to do just what he wanted to do. And what would she do when she got there? Maybe she should call the police. But then, Rocky had never done that, and there must have been a reason for that. But he was a criminal, surely. He had raped a fifteen-year-old girl.

Jo closed her eyes for a moment as she came to a halt in front of red lights. The image of her lover as a young girl being repeatedly abused caused her stomach to tie into knots, and she thought for a moment that she might actually throw up. She turned into Forest Lane and, as she did so, her nervousness grew. What was she going to do? Just walk up and knock on the door? She pulled the car over to the kerb and threw open the door. Leaning out of the car, she lost the contents of her stomach. She wiped her mouth with the back of her hand and sat back in the seat, bringing her breathing under control.

Jo looked through the wet windscreen at the high hedge, which lined the street. Behind that was the house which she hoped held her lover. Shutting the door, she put the car back into gear and turned into the long driveway leading to the house. The house was dark, which surprised her with it being only a little before 10pm There were no other cars in the drive so she drove right up to the door.

A security light came on as she walked to the door, bathing her in a harsh light and catching the heavily falling snow in its beam. Her hand hovered over the doorbell for a moment before pushing it. She automatically took a couple of steps back when a light in the inner hallway came on.

The door opened and, for a moment, Jo thought it was Rocky standing before her. "You must be Jo," the woman said.

"I am." Jo took a step forward, feeling the heat emanating from the house. "Is she here?"

The woman nodded. "Come in." Jo hesitated for a moment. "He's not here," the blonde said, understanding Jo's reluctance to enter.

Jo passed the woman and walked into the hall, stamping her

feet on the welcome mat to remove the snow, which was packed beneath the soles of her shoes. "Where is she?" Jo asked, looking around the hall and into the lounge, which she could just see through an open door.

Her gaze drifted upwards, towards the stairs. "She's in her room." Jo started up the stairs, but a hand on her arm stopped her. "I didn't want this to happen," Susan said.

"But it did." Jo didn't really want this conversation now, but she'd wondered more than once how Rocky's aunt could let her husband abuse a grieving child. "How could you let him touch her like that?"

"You don't know him."

"You could have called the police." Jo looked up the stairs, wanting nothing more than to go to her lover.

Susan chuckled wryly. "She hasn't told you then?"

"Told me what?"

"Ron *is* the police." Susan leaned back against the wall. "She always thought they wouldn't believe her."

"He's with the police force?"

Susan nodded. "You could say that. He's the Chief Constable of the Leicestershire Constabulary."

"Shit," was all Jo could manage. "So it would have been her word against his?"

"Yes." Susan sighed, bowing her head. She looked back up at Jo. "I was so very afraid of him then. When Michelle came to us, he became obsessed with her. I didn't realise at first what he was doing and, when I challenged him about it, he flew into a terrible rage. He beat me. I know I have no excuses." She walked past Jo and started climbing the stairs. "We talked for a long time this evening after he had gone out. She told me about you, and she told me she loves you very much." She looked back down at Jo, who was following her. "He hasn't touched her...in that way." She watched Jo stop dead and bow her head.

"Thank you," the dark-haired woman whispered and resumed climbing the stairs. Jo winced when they reached Rocky's room and she saw the large bolt, obviously designed to keep the blonde in the room.

Susan stopped again and turned to face Jo. "Something happened tonight which caused my husband to leave the house. He's gone to one of his usual haunts, seeking what he feels I can't provide. What he thought Michelle could." She looked at the closed door. "She fought him, Jo. Something he'd never come up against before, not from Michelle, at least."

"Did he hurt her?" Jo was pulling the bolt back and turning the doorknob, but before she could open the door Susan had pulled her back again.

"Yes, he did. I'm sorry. But I spoke to her after he left the house. She told me he didn't have sex with her. I think her fighting him threw him." She leaned across to see into the room. "She may be a little groggy, I gave her one of my sleeping pills. They're not very strong, but she didn't take it long ago, so it'll still be working. She was almost hysterical after he left, calling for you. I tried to call you—Michelle gave me your number—but I just got your machine." She took Jo's hand, squeezing it gently. "You need to take her away, Jo. And then we both need to go to the police."

Jo nodded, realising what this woman was about to lose. "Yes, we do. Thank you."

Susan nodded towards the room. "Go to her," she said and backed away.

Jo took a deep breath and crept into the room. She didn't turn the light on and stood a few feet from the bed for a while, watching the small figure sleep in the light that filtered into the room from the landing. Rocky was lying on her side, curled in a tight ball. She had her back to the door and to Jo.

Jo crouched at the side of the bed and reached out with a tentative hand, curling it around her lover's shoulder. "Hey," she whispered. The reply was a soft whimpering sound, and the blonde pulled weakly away from the hand that was on her. "Rocky, baby. Come on." She pulled Rocky onto her back, ducking back as the blonde's arms flailed.

"No," the blonde said, her voice little more than a gasp. "Don't touch me."

"Open your eyes, baby." Jo cupped a warm cheek in her hand, waiting for the green eyes to open. When they did, they took a few moments to focus. Rocky stared blankly at her for long moments. Jo traced the bruise she found on Rocky's cheek, barely visible in the dim light. There was also a cut near the corner of her eye, which had bled a little. *Probably caused by a ring.*

Green eyes were blinking at her, then filling with tears. She reached shaky arms towards Jo, who gathered her up into comforting arms. "You came," was all Rocky said.

Jo held her close, burying her face in soft blonde hair. She tried to reassure her lover, but her throat closed and she settled for just holding her, revelling in the reality of having her lover back. She managed to pull away from Rocky and looked around the room. She saw her leather jacket lying on the floor and reached across for it. "Come on," she managed after clearing her throat. "Put this on. We're leaving." She sat Rocky up and pulled the jacket around her.

"He'll hurt you," the blonde said, swaying as Jo zipped the jacket up. Rocky looked even smaller, engulfed as she was in Jo's leather jacket.

"No, he won't." Jo stood, pulling Rocky to her feet. She wound an arm around the blonde and started to walk her out of the room. As they reached the doorway, Rocky's knees buckled, and Jo, surprising herself, bent and picked the small blonde up, cradling her against her chest.

Susan approached them, brushing hair away from her niece's face. "I'm so sorry, Michelle," she whispered to the groggy woman. "I'll never let you down again." She looked up at Jo. "You must get her away from here. I'll try to keep him away from the room for as long as possible."

Jo nodded, and, not knowing what to say to the woman she'd hated for a while, she turned with her lover in her arms and made her way carefully down the stairs. At the bottom of the stairs, Susan hurried past Jo and opened the front door, and then went on ahead, opening the passenger door of the Merk. Jo settled Rocky into the seat and buckled her seatbelt. She turned back to the woman shivering in the doorway. "You need to get away from here," Jo said.

Susan nodded. "I know. I will."

The two women regarded each other for a moment across the roof of the Merk. The wind howled, driving the snow through the glare of the security light. With a quick nod, Jo got into the car, started the engine, and drove carefully down the drive. Susan watched them go and then quietly closed the door. She went up the stairs and closed and bolted the door to Rocky's room. Then she went downstairs and sat in the lounge, awaiting the return of her husband.

Chapter
21

Jo had never before encountered such weather. As she picked her way carefully through the almost deserted streets of Leicester, her attention was repeatedly drawn to the hunched figure beside her. Rocky was fighting against the effects of the sleeping pill that Susan had given her, almost desperate to stay awake. She was fearful that sleep would only return her to the horror she has so recently escaped.

Jo reached across when the blonde head slumped against the window for the umpteenth time. "Go to sleep," she said, smoothing her hand against a denim-covered thigh. Rocky captured the hand, but Jo had to pull it away quickly when the need to shift down a gear presented itself. "Sorry," Jo said. "The weather's getting worse."

"Can we stop?" Rocky's voice was strained, and she shifted uncomfortably in the seat.

"If you want," Jo said and steered into the small car park of a darkened "Little Chef," which had obviously closed early due to a lack of customers. The wheels briefly skidded on the slight incline but then caught, and Jo eased the car behind a large sign, hiding them from the street. She turned to the smaller woman who quickly undid her seatbelt and crawled across the gap between them. Jo found herself with an armful of sobbing blonde. "Hey," she whispered into soft hair. "It's okay. We're okay."

"I was so scared," Rocky sobbed into Jo's chest.

"I know, shh." Jo held on tight, letting Rocky know she was there and that they were both safe.

"I can't believe you came for me."

Jo slipped a hand beneath the leather jacket and rubbed a trembling back. "Tell me what happened."

Rocky was quiet for long moments, and Jo thought she wasn't going to answer. "I don't know how he found us." The sweatshirt Jo was wearing muffled her voice. "He waited until you left, then rang the bell. I thought it was you." She was quiet for a while, her hands tangling in Jo's shirt. "He said he'd hurt you. I had to go."

Jo closed her eyes, realising what Rocky had sacrificed for her. "How did you know to take my jacket?"

Rocky pulled away from her, wiping at the tears that dampened her cheeks. "I just took it because I wanted something of yours." She laid her head on Jo's chest and relaxed into her lover when she felt the long arms enfold her again. "I didn't know the cell phone was in there until I put my hands in the pockets when I was walking across to the loo."

Jo tightened her hold. "I'm glad you found it."

"Yeah, me too." Rocky's voice was husky. "Can we get out of here now?"

Jo looked through the windscreen at the worsening weather. "I think we'd better. I'm going to stop to try and get some fuel, then we'll find the motorway and get as far as we can." She gently pushed the blonde across to the passenger seat, and waited while Rocky refastened her seatbelt. "If we have to, we'll find a hotel." Jo eased the Mercedes back onto the road.

"What do we do then?" Rocky switched her attention from the passing houses to her lover. "He knows where you live."

"We go to the police."

"Do you think they'll do anything?"

"They have to if you make a complaint."

Rocky looked down at her hands folded in her lap. "They won't believe me."

Jo looked across at her, sensing an attitude of defeat about the blonde. "Susan is going to help us. We'll be fine." Rocky nodded slightly, not entirely convinced. Jo managed to find the motorway in what was possibly close to blizzard conditions. Theirs was one of a few vehicles trying to find their way using the three-lane road, which looked more like a toboggan run than a motorway. The three lanes had been narrowed into one and a half by the snow banking up against the metal central reservation.

"This is scary," Rocky said, leaning forward in her seat, one hand on the dashboard.

"I know, but we'll get as far as the next exit and then get off."
Jo peered into the gloom, following the track made some time earlier by a snowplough, which had cleared the middle lane. The further she went the more confident she became, and she increased
her speed slightly.

"Jo," the blonde said, her nervousness clear. "Let's stop. This
is crazy."

"It's okay. There's nothing else about. Look," she said glancing at the illuminated clock on the dial. "It's well past midnight.
No one in their right mind is out in this." She shot a wicked grin
at her companion, who, despite her nervousness, couldn't help but
smile back. "I want to get as far as I can."

"That's great, just let's get there a little slower." Rocky
winced as the wheels of the Merk hit the snow bank on their left.

"Ye of little faith," Jo chuckled, trying to lighten the mood as
she increased the speed.

"Jo!"

"Don't worry." Jo looked across at the blonde, who was peering beyond the bonnet of the car. The snow was getting lighter, the
flakes smaller now, swirling around in the beam of the headlights.

"Shit!" The blonde threw herself back into her seat.

Jo's eyes tore themselves from Rocky just in time to see the
abandoned car in their path. She braked and swerved but was only
propelled off one snow bank into the other. The car skidded into
the parked vehicle, coming to rest on its right side wedged
between the snow bank and the bumper of the abandoned car.

Rocky was first aware of a pain across her chest where the
seatbelt had held her against the seat during the collision. "Bloody
hell, Jo! Watch that last corner," she joked weakly, turning her
head slowly towards her lover. It was dark in the Merk, just the
quiet sound of the radio breaking the silence. The engine was dead
but the ignition still on, causing the headlights to illuminate the
now light snow.

"Jo?" Rocky reached across and down to where her lover lay
unmoving. "Hey, Jo." She nudged the brunette's shoulder, beginning to panic when there was no reaction. "Come on, we need to
get out of here." She reached up and switched on the small interior light, breathing a sigh of relief when it flickered on.

Rocky managed to unbuckle her seatbelt, bracing her arm
against Jo's seat so as not to fall onto the obviously injured
woman. She managed to get her foot against the driver's door and

eased herself down, the steering wheel digging painfully into her back. The deflated air bag hung limply across it. She could see the snow bank packed against the window on which Jo's head was resting. The glass of the windscreen was cracked but not shattered; the driver's window was intact. But the canvas roof of the car was torn and buckled out of shape. Rocky reached down with a trembling hand and pulled back the hair that obscured her lover's face.

"Oh God," she breathed as she found hair sticking to Jo's face. The sticky substance, she immediately realised, was blood. Her lover was bleeding from a cut, which must have been inflicted when her head hit the window beside her. She couldn't see the wound, but could feel warm blood on her hand and saw it congealed beneath Jo's head on the glass. She reached behind her with her right hand, opening the glove compartment. Its contents spilled out, but she managed to grab the small box of tissues Jo kept in there. "Jo?" she asked as she tried to mop away the blood from the side of the slack face. "We have to go. It's getting cold here; we need to get out of here."

Jo could hear her lover, but she sounded far away. Besides she was much too tired to wake up and answer her. But the voice was insistent. And she found she couldn't resist the pleading sound of the blonde's voice. She decided she'd just go and see what it was that was scaring the blonde, then she'd go back to sleep.

Rocky watched as the blue eyes fluttered open then quickly closed again. Jo groaned and her face tightened, and Rocky ran gentle fingertips across a tense cheek. "Careful, take it slowly," Rocky said, relieved when Jo's eyes seemed to focus on her and track her as she leaned back for more tissues.

"What?" Jo tried to talk, but a stabbing pain in her head cut short the sentence.

"Shh, just lie still for a moment. Then we need to try to get out of here."

Jo tried to lift her head from its sticky place against the window, but gave up quickly. "You go," she mumbled. "Go find help."

"Not without you." She leaned down and managed to undo the buckle of Jo's seatbelt. "I want you to try to pull yourself up."

"No," Jo slumped back, pulling herself out of Rocky's grasp.

"Come on, sweetheart." Rocky pulled again at her shoulders. "We need to get out of here or we'll freeze to death. The engine's dead, and the roof is bust."

Jo managed to open her eyes again. "Can't see you very well."

Rocky bit her bottom lip. "There's a lot of blood. It's getting everywhere." She leaned in close, Jo appeared to be having trouble focusing and blinked glazed blue eyes rapidly. "We're going to have to climb out of my door."

"Why? What's going on?" Jo looked around then reached for the door handle. "The door's broke?"

The blonde smiled down at her lover. "Jo, the car's broke." She leaned down and gave the groggy woman a peck on the lips. "Now, I'm going to climb out, then I'm going to reach down for you. But I won't be able to pull you out on my own, you're going to have to help me."

"I can do that." Jo sounded annoyed now. Why was Rocky treating her like a kid?

Rocky sighed and turned in the tight space then reached up and opened the passenger door, which was now above her. She pushed the heavy door up, but it wouldn't stay and kept slamming shut again. Wedging her back against the door, she pushed again, and then reached down for Jo. "Jo," she said. There was no reaction from the woman, and Rocky nudged her shoulder with her foot. "Jo, come on, we need to go."

The dark head turned in her direction, the side of Jo's face painted in crimson. Rocky almost sobbed in relief when Jo reached out a shaky hand to her and put her free arm below her to lever herself away from the door she lay against. Then the tall woman managed to untangle long legs and use them to get herself out of the awkward position in which she'd woken.

Rocky held the door open with her back and pulled her lover up. She was relieved that the snow appeared to be stopping, only a few flakes were being blown about in the slight breeze. The sky was clearing and a full moon cast the deserted motorway in an eerie blue light.

Jo pulled herself up, her feet slipping slightly in the blood she'd left on the window below her. Using her arms, she pulled herself up and out of the car, before jumping to the ground. Rocky managed to manoeuvre herself out from beneath the bulky door and quickly scrambled to her lover's side.

"Hey, well done," she said, cupping Jo's face. She still had a wad of the tissues from the box in her hand. In the moonlight, she parted dark, blood-slicked hair and looked for the wound. She found it, a gash about an inch long, just above her hairline, which still oozed blood that flowed down the side of Jo's face and along her neck. She placed the wad of tissues against the wound and took Jo's hand. "Can you hold that?" Jo nodded and lifted her hand slowly to hold the makeshift dressing. "Just wait a mo. I'm going to try to see where we are."

"Okay," Jo said quietly.

Rocky squeezed her shoulder and then left quickly, scrambling up a nearby embankment. Beyond the ridge was a flat field, and beyond that she could just make out the dark shape of some sort of building. The moon shone brightly on the newly laid snow, and it looked like a simple two or three hundred-yard trek to the house. She slid back down the embankment to find Jo patiently waiting, still holding the padding to her head. It was soaked through with blood. "There's a house over there."

Jo nodded slightly, wincing as the movement caused her pain. "Okay, go get help then. I'll wait here." The feeling of exhaustion was overwhelming and, to her groggy mind, it was the best option for her to wait while her lover got help.

"Oh no. You're coming with me." Rocky bent down and caught Jo's free arm. "Come on."

Jo allowed herself to be pulled to her feet and swayed slightly as Rocky pulled her arm over her shoulders and then started pulling them up the embankment. Jo stumbled frequently and struggled through the thigh-high snow. She suddenly pulled away from Rocky and threw up painfully. The blonde put an arm around her lover's waist and held her as her body heaved.

"Jesus," Jo rasped, trying to get her breath.

"You okay?" Rocky asked as she wiped Jo's face with her sleeve.

"Can't see a bloody thing."

Rocky peered into blue eyes turned violet in the moonlight and noticed a glassy look to them. One eye seemed to react quicker than the other, and she surmised the taller woman might have a concussion.

"Let's keep moving. It's not far now." Rocky looked ahead to the house. She could see no lights on, and prayed that the occupants had just gone to bed and weren't away. But she resolved she would find a way in. That was their only hope for survival. She couldn't feel her feet, and she could feel the cold tightening about her chest like a steel band. Both of their jeans were getting soaked, and she knew from her time on the streets that it would be very easy for them to freeze to death in a very short time.

It was only another twenty yards or so, but the snow had banked. Rocky found it increasingly difficult to pull herself and her lover through the deepening snow. Luckily for them, the snow had stopped falling completely. The moon shone bright, with just a few silvery lined clouds making a slow trek across an otherwise clear sky. It was quiet, until the silence was broken by the sound of a barking dog. This strengthened her resolve, and she pulled Jo's arm tighter around her shoulders and hauled them both through the snow. The house was part of a small farm. The main farmhouse stood a little way away from a large barn and a number of smaller buildings.

Jo was flagging and becoming heavy, and by the time Rocky reached the door of the farmhouse she could no longer hold her lover up. She allowed Jo to slide to the ground and lifted an incredibly heavy arm to knock on the door. The barking became louder, and she heard muffled noises behind the heavy wooden door. The door slowly opened, and she was faced with a growling, but rather small, dog. She followed the leash, which she found was held by a woman. In one hand was the leash, in the other what appeared to be an ancient oil lamp.

"Good grief, Jasper," the woman said, tugging back on the leash. The dog stopped barking immediately. She was dressed in a tweed skirt, the thickest green cardigan Rocky had ever seen with a roll neck sweater beneath, and green Wellingtons—a vision of English aristocracy in all its eccentric wonder.

"Please," was all Rocky could manage to say at first. The woman looked from her down to the other woman who was slumped at the shorter girl's feet. "We crashed our car." Rocky crouched down to try to lift Jo to her feet. "My friend is injured, and we're both freezing."

"Well, get her in here," the woman said without further ado. "Can't have travellers popping their clogs on my door mat." She pushed the door open further, and the heat immediately flushed Rocky's cheeks as it left the house. She managed to get Jo to her feet, but she was just about incoherent. They stumbled into what appeared to be the kitchen. "Bloody power's out." The woman pulled a chair out from beneath a pine table and gestured for Rocky to sit Jo in it. "Lucky I have the Aga—keeps it nice and warm in here."

Rocky eased her friend into the chair and then held her when she appeared to be about to slump to the floor. Behind her the woman was filling a kettle at the sink, then she placed it on the hot plate on the Aga.

"Jo." Rocky crouched in front of her lover who appeared to be slipping into unconsciousness. "We need an ambulance. Can I use your phone?" she asked without taking her eyes from Jo's pale face.

"Phone's down as well, I'm afraid. Snow on the lines brought them down apparently." She left again for a moment and returned with a cloth and some slightly warm water she'd drawn from the tap. "If she's taken a bump on the noggin, she should be awake for a while after."

Rocky nodded and started to gently try to wake Jo. "Hey there," she said quietly. "Jo, open your eyes for me." There was no reaction, and Rocky turned to the woman. "She won't wake up."

The woman pushed Rocky out of the way and pushed back on Jo's shoulders, sitting her up straighter. "Come on, girl. You're not doing yourself any good like this." She gave Jo a slap on the face, causing the blonde beside her to wince. Another slap and the blue and somewhat glazed eyes opened. "Hello, dear. I'm Joscelyn, but everyone calls me Joss."

"Joss," Jo repeated, trying to focus on the woman and place her in the events of the past few hours. Her eyes tracked to the left, settling on the fuzzy form of her lover.

Joss gently turned Jo's face back towards her. "That's right, dear. And who might you be?"

"Jo." The injured woman blinked rapidly, obviously having trouble seeing what was only a few feet from her. Rocky knelt beside Joss and wrung the cloth out in the water, then used it to start washing the blood from Jo's face. Jo seemed to relax at the familiar touch of her lover but winced when someone examined the wound on her head.

"This cut isn't too large. Not bleeding much now. I've seen worse on a hockey pitch. Bloody Bunty Adams caught me on the ear in 1958. Never been the same since." She chuckled at her own joke and left the two women alone for a moment while she rifled through a drawer. She brought a bottle of antiseptic and couple of clean towels over to them and pressed one on the wound, which had all but stopped bleeding. "How did she do this?" she asked as she poured antiseptic on the towel and pressed it to the wound.

Again Rocky winced when she saw her lover's face contort with the pain. "I think she must have hit the car window when we collided with the snow bank."

"What make of car was it?" Joss peered at the wound, giving Jo a brief smile as she changed the dirty towel for a clean one.

"Um, Mercedes." Rocky was now undoing Jo's soaked footwear, pulling them off along with the socks.

"No wonder. Bloody German car. Wouldn't have happened in a Jag." She bent to see into Jo's face. "You hear me, girl? British car next time."

Jo nodded mutely, wondering who this person was and where in the hell they were. "Rocky?" She reached out a hand, relieved to feel it enfolded by her lover's smaller ones.

"Rocky?" Joss repeated. "Good grief, girl. Who on earth gave you a name like that?"

"It's a nickname," Rocky said, vigorously rubbing Jo's frozen feet. "My name is Michelle."

"Ah, much more civilised." The dog started barking, jumping up at the door. "Jasper, stop that!" Joss walked across the kitchen, peering through the drawn curtains to see outside. "Looks like we've got another visitor." She turned back to them. "Good job I put the kettle on."

Rocky got up stiffly from her place at Jo's feet. "There's someone out there?"

"Looks like it, dear." She stood aside and let Rocky peer out into the night.

The full moon highlighted everything beyond the farmyard, even giving the figure struggling along the same tracks they had made only twenty minutes or so before a long shadow. And there was no mistaking the figure.

Rocky's chin slumped to her chest, and she turned away from the window. Then she rushed across to Jo, kneeling at her feet. "I have to pop back to the car," she said cupping a still-chilled cheek. "I want you to stay here and keep warm." She leaned forward, her hand going behind Jo's head and tangling in dark hair. Her lips found her lover's, and she kissed her long and softly. "I love you, Jo."

Jo looked confused, and her mouth opened and shut without any words forming.

"You shouldn't be going out there, dear," Joss said, suddenly realising the nature of the two girls' relationship.

"Joss, please listen to me. That man is coming here to get me. But I'm scared of what he'll do to her." She looked across at Jo, who was trying focus on them. "So I'm going to try to get out there and lead him away. I've got a cell phone here." She took the phone from her jacket pocket. "I think Jo's got a charger in the car. Hopefully I can get a message out."

Joss was about to protest, but Rocky had already opened the door and closed it quickly after her.

The cold hit her hard as she stepped into the farmyard. The night was so still she could already hear his laboured breathing as he struggled through the snow. She knew he'd see her immediately in the moonlight, so she ducked down behind a long wall. There was about fifty yards between her and a small clump of trees, and she decided she would make for them. As she broke clear of the wall, she saw his head turn in her direction. It was hard pushing through the snow, but she fixed her attention on the trees and only half heard the sound of her uncle as he changed direction and attempted to cut her off.

"Michelle!" he called, falling headlong into the snow.

She kept going, glancing back to see him pick himself up and continue towards her. Her chest was hurting, dragging in the frigid air which then plumed into the still night as she exhaled. She fell, her bare hands sinking into the snow, her knees hitting something hard buried beneath the whiteness. She ignored the pain in her legs and dragged herself to her feet again.

He was close behind her now. She passed the first tree and was inside the small wooded area. The snow wasn't so thick on the ground here, and she managed to pick up speed. The trees were closely bunched together, and she ran blindly, hearing him curse as his wider frame had more difficulty negotiating his way. She suddenly felt something slam into her back just as she cleared the trees. There was a sharp slope and they both tumbled down it, sliding through the snow and onto a relatively hard surface. He had landed about four feet away from her, and she lay for a moment, staring up at the clear sky, breathing hard. She looked to her left to see him sitting very still, looking at her.

"Why did you run from me, Michelle?"

She sat up then stood on shaky legs. "I can't go back with you, Ron. You need to leave me alone."

"I don't understand." He stood and started to walk towards her but was stopped by a loud cracking sound. They had fallen onto a frozen lake. He was closer to the centre, where the ice was thinner. "I can't let you go, Michelle," he said, sliding his foot carefully across the ice.

"Go back home, Ron. Please. Go back. You have a home and a wife waiting for you."

"I couldn't make Susan understand," he said, sliding another foot nearer. "She wouldn't listen."

Rocky backed away, reaching the bank and safety. "Is she all right?"

"She wouldn't listen, Michelle. I tried to make her understand, but she couldn't see what we mean to each other. But it's all right now. She won't come between us again."

Rocky felt sick, her chest tightened, and she felt the sting of tears. She turned and started to scrabble back up the bank. She heard the crack and a splash and turned to see a hole in the ice where Ron had been. There was no sign of him.

Then suddenly he appeared, just his head and shoulders. He clawed feebly at the ice, trying to get a grip but was being pulled back down into the icy depths by his sodden overcoat. "Help me," he gasped.

Rocky was trembling as she watched the man fight for his life. She took a step back.

"Please!" he cried, hanging onto the edge of the ice.

She looked around for anything that she could throw to him. Some rope or a long branch. There was nothing that she could see. She took off the jacket, feeling the cold assault her bare arms, having only a t-shirt on beneath. She held onto one jacket sleeve and threw the other towards him. He grasped for it, but it didn't reach him. She edged onto the ice, crawling on it, feeling it through her jeans and against the palms of her hands.

It gave way, and she found herself up to her thighs in freezing water. Again she threw the jacket towards him, and this time he managed to get a grip on it. She wound the leather sleeve around her hand and pulled back, watching as the man she hated pulled himself from the ice. He got his knee onto the edge and was pulling himself up when it collapsed under him once more. He went backwards; the force of his weight disappearing beneath the ice again pulled the sleeve from Rocky's frozen hands. She waited for him to reappear. He didn't.

Rocky managed to turn and pull herself out of the water. Then she looked back at the hole in the ice, black and still in the moonlight. She started to shake and was suddenly aware of the awful pain in her legs and hands. She knew she was freezing, and she knew she had to get back to the farmhouse. But her body betrayed her. She crawled on hands and knees up the small slope, collapsing halfway to the top.

She looked around, trying to get her bearings, but nothing looked familiar. She was tired now and wanted nothing more than to just sit for a while and get her breath. The adrenaline rush had gone, and there was nothing but exhaustion left in its wake. She curled into a ball, and her last thoughts as she drifted off were of her lover.

Chapter
22

Jo watched the fuzzy figure approach. She tried to focus on the person but failed. The voice when it came was not the one she wanted to hear.

"Here, drink this tea, dear. You need something warm in you." Joss watched carefully as the younger woman took the mug from her with shaking hands. "Can you manage?"

"Yes, thanks." Jo took a sip of the warm sweet tea, then looked around through bleary eyes. "Where's Rocky?"

"She went back to the car." Joss sat in a large, plump chair next to the stove, picking her mug of tea up from the hearth where she'd put it moments before.

"She what?" The mug fell to the floor and shattered as Jo lurched to her feet.

For a woman who has seen the top of the hill and is on the way down the other side, as she often put it, Joss managed to move quickly. "Now you sit back down, girl. Your marbles haven't settled yet."

Jo found herself back in the chair. "It's freezing out there." She cast her blurred vision across the floor, looking for her shoes.

"Well, she'd seen someone out there, so whoever it was is probably helping her." Joss turned away from Jo and started picking the remains of the mug up from the hard, stone floor.

"Someone out there?" Jo put the heel of her hand to her forehead, trying to lessen the thumping headache she'd had ever since entering the warm kitchen.

"Yes, dear," Joss said from the floor. "Said he was coming for her, and something about you. Didn't make much sense." She walked across to a small bin and threw the shards of china into it. "Shall I make you another?" she asked.

"Joss." Jo struggled to her feet, steadying herself against the table when the floor beneath her apparently shifted. "We need to go out and find her. I think she may be in trouble."

"We're not going anywhere, dear. We'll wait for her to come back." She tried to push back against the dark-haired woman but found herself pinned by blue, slightly out of focus eyes.

"If the man is who I think it is, he raped her when she was fifteen, two weeks after her parents had been killed. Do you really want to wait here while he takes her back with him?" Jo gripped the older woman's shoulders, steadying herself as fear and her injury threatened to take her to the floor.

"Good grief," Joss said, paling. "She said she didn't know what he'd do to you."

Jo closed her eyes. "I think he threatened me. He thinks I've come between them."

"And you love her very much?"

Jo's throat tightened, and she could only nod her answer.

"I'll get you some Wellies," Joss said matter-of-factly.

She brought Jo a thick pair of socks and a pair of Wellington boots. Then she found her a coat and a woollen hat. "Probably not what you're used to, dear, but it'll keep the cold out." She opened a cupboard and pulled out a double-barrelled shotgun. Reaching into a drawer, she took a couple of shells from a box. "Haven't used this in a while, but it's been kept clean." She looked up at Jo, who appeared to be shaking her head slightly, trying to clear her vision. "You ever used one?"

Jo nodded, recognising the sound of a shotgun being loaded. "My parents have pheasant shoots on their estate."

Joss's head snapped up. "Estate?"

"Not now, Joss," she said, shrugging into the coat.

The woman, her curiosity now seriously piqued, called for the small dog, which had been curled up in a basket beside the Aga. "Come on, Jasper," she said, bending and attaching the leash to his collar. The animal pulled her towards the door, not caring that the conditions probably would not be comfortable for a midnight walk.

The door opened, and they were both pleased to find that the wind hadn't picked up and the night was still and calm, the blanket of snow thick and even. Jo took a hold of the other woman's coat and followed her out into the darkness.

Joss didn't make for the field that they had crossed to get to the farmhouse, instead she made her way towards the barn. "Damned if I'm going to be trekking through the bloody snow. We'll get Bessie out."

Jo was too tired and in too much pain to argue, so she followed where the woman dragged her. The moonlight was enough to see by, and she hauled open the door of the barn. Inside, about half a dozen cows regarded them then went back to munching on the feed that was in a long trough along one wall. In the corner, a large lump was covered with a tarpaulin. Joss pulled back the tarp to reveal an ancient piece of machinery.

"This is Bessie," Joss said with a certain amount of pride in her voice. "She'll go through anything." Bessie was a twenty-year old Land Rover. She sat for most of the year in the barn, but Joss went out every couple of weeks just to turn the engine over. And a young man came up from the village every six months to check it over.

"The hunt goes across my land in the summer, and I like to go out and take a look. Haven't been able to participate for a few years now—bloody hip gave out in '98." She loaded Jo into the passenger seat, and Jasper jumped up onto the younger woman's lap.

Joss started the engine and switched on the lights, startling some of the cows. "Good girl," Joss said, tapping the steering wheel. Then she drove out of the barn and across the snow-covered courtyard.

Jo peered out, relieved that her vision appeared to be clearing. "Where do we start?"

"Well, it's a good clear night, we'll try to find their tracks." She slowed to a halt and leaned across and opened the door beside Jo. "Go on, Jasper," she said, and the small dog leaped out of the car, almost disappearing in the deep snow.

"Is that a good idea?" Jo asked, watching as the dog disappeared and then reappeared a few feet away.

"He loves the snow. If there's anything out there out of the ordinary, he'll find it."

They watched the dog for a moment, easily making out his dark form in the moonlight. He found the tracks that they'd made earlier, and then veered off, following another set of tracks.

"He's off," she said and spun the steering wheel to follow the dog. The wheels of the old vehicle spun in the snow for a moment but then caught, and Jo had to hang on as the Land Rover bounced across the rutted field.

Even over the top of the ancient engine, they could hear the excited barking of Jasper. "He's found something. Looks like it's in the copse. We won't get Bessie through there."

Jo was out of the Land Rover before it had stopped and was following the sound of excited barking. She heard the Land Rover move away but ignored it and made her way through the small stand of trees.

"Rocky!" she called, stopping for a moment to listen, but she heard only the excited barking of the dog. "Where are you, you bloody beast?" The dog was suddenly in front of her, barking maniacally. "What?" she asked it, feeling ridiculous. She saw the lights of the Land Rover through the trees, and followed as Jasper took off again, darting between the tree trunks. She cleared the trees but saw nothing. To her right, Joss was getting out of the Land Rover and walking towards her, torch in hand.

"Find anything?" she asked, coming to stand next to the tall woman.

Jo shook her head and looked down towards where Jasper was excitedly dancing around what looked to be a tree branch half way down the slope at the t. All she could see was a dark outline on the snow.

"What is it, boy?" Joss trained her torch on the dog, and the sight that greeted them froze both women. The dark shape they could see was Rocky's jeans, her white t-shirt and pale arms blending into the whiteness on which she lay.

"Oh my God," was all Jo managed and she slid down the slope, coming to rest beside her still lover and the dog, who was licking Rocky's unresponsive face. "Rocky," she breathed and turned the blonde over. Damp hair fell across the blonde's face, her head lolling limply towards Jo. The dark-haired woman brushed the hair away, her fingers trembling as they encountered cold, marble-like skin. She cupped the pale face in her hands, the moonlight making her lover look even paler. Rocky's eyes and cheeks seemed almost sunken, giving her the appearance of a corpse.

Jo gathered the small body into her arms. "Oh Jesus, Rocky," she sobbed, rocking the limp body, praying she would feel just the tiniest response from the woman. "Come on now, wake up," she breathed, looking down into the face of the blonde. "Don't you do this to me. What were you thinking?" She crushed her to her own body once more.

She looked up towards Joss, who was picking her way cautiously towards them. "She's frozen. I don't know if she's breathing." The moonlight reflected off the tears that streaked her face, and she tore her coat off. Jo gathered the limp form into her arms and tried her best to cover the frighteningly cold body with the heavy coat. "We need to get her inside," Jo said, and she tried to pick her up. But the limp body merely slipped through her hands and back onto the snow again. "I can't..." Jo said, trying again, her frustration getting the better of her. She sobbed at her own helplessness.

Joss gently pushed her aside. "Jo, calm down." She looked down at the girl, who looked small and frail. "Hold this." She handed Jo the coat and reached down for Rocky's arms. "It's all in the technique," she said as she pulled on the blonde's arms and then bent her shoulder into Rocky's stomach so that she fell across Joss's back. "There," she said, straightening and looking at Jo, who was staring open-mouthed at her. "Well, come on, girl, we don't have all night." She turned and Jo followed, her eyes never leaving the sight of her lover's limp body across the shoulder of her new and very dear friend.

"Get in," Joss said as they reached the Land Rover. Jo silently did as she was told, and Rocky's freezing body was deposited in her lap. Then the coat was thrown over them both. Joss ran around the front of the vehicle and gunned the engine, taking a moment to negotiate the slope, not wanting them to end up in the lake.

"I can't believe you did that," Jo said, pulling Rocky close and burying her face in damp, blonde hair.

"What, dear?" Joss was peering out into the night, being careful not to run over her excitable pet who was feeling very pleased with himself.

"You just picked her up, like she was a baby." She tipped Rocky's head back so she could see into her face. It was slack and very pale, and her tears began again as her fear for her lover grew.

"I've worked this farm for the past twenty years, five of them on my own. That little slip of a thing weighs a lot less than a hay bale." Joss chuckled to herself as she pulled into the courtyard. She didn't take Bessie back into the barn, instead parking right outside the kitchen door. By the time she had got round to open the passenger side, Jo had opened it herself and was standing with Rocky in her arms, so she just opened the door and let the younger woman carry her lover into the warm room.

Jo collapsed to her knees in front of the Aga and lowered Rocky to the floor. "What now?" she asked. Joss was pulling off her coat. She knelt next to Jo and felt for a pulse at the blonde's throat. "Oh God, she's dead," Jo said, bending forward and burying her face in her hands.

"Nonsense, girl." Joss straightened. "Get her out of those wet clothes, then get yourself out of yours."

"What?" Jo asked, but she started to unlace Rocky's ankle boots.

"Body heat, dear. She doesn't have much of that at this moment, but you do." She filled the kettle at the sink and then placed it on the hot plate on the Aga. "We need to warm her up slowly."

"Why don't we just put her in the bath?" Jo asked as she pulled off sodden socks and threw them across the room.

Joss watched the socks sail across the floor. "Too much, too quickly. It would be too much of a shock for her. I've seen this before; my husband used to like to climb a bit. Did Everest with him one year."

Jo was pulling at Rocky's damp and freezing jeans, but they resisted her efforts. She felt a hand on her shoulder and looked up to see Joss. "Slow down. She needs you now."

Jo turned back to her task. "I'm scared, Joss." She managed to pull the jeans off, the cold skin of Rocky's legs feeling unfamiliar under her hands. She pulled Rocky to a sitting position and pulled off her t-shirt, then cradled the small woman against her chest.

Joss squeezed her shoulder, and then left the room, returning quickly with a few blankets. She placed them on top of the Aga, and then turned to Jo. "Skin on skin is the best thing for someone with hypothermia." She saw Jo open her mouth to speak. "That's all it is, Jo. She's not going to die today."

Jo nodded and stood shakily, pulling her sweatshirt over her head and adding it to the damp pile of Rocky's clothing. Then she quickly kicked off the Wellingtons and stripped out of her jeans.

"Sit on that chair," Joss said, pointing to the plump armchair beside the Aga. Jo did so, and Joss got her hands under Rocky's arms and lifted her into Jo's lap. Jo gasped as her lover's cold skin made contact with hers, but then Joss was covering her with the now-warm blankets, tucking them around the two women.

"You hold tight. She's going to start shivering soon, as her body starts to warm."

Jo wrapped her arms around the small body, kissing the top of the blonde head. "Always," she said quietly.

Jo thought she must have dozed for a while, for she was woken with a start when the blanket was pulled back slightly.

Joss had a hot water bottle, wrapped in a towel. "Here, hold this against her stomach."

Jo did as she was asked and watched as Joss knelt at their feet and slipped a pair of soft, warm socks onto Rocky's feet. Then she repeated the process with Jo. "I'm never going to be able to thank you enough for this," Jo said as the older woman stood and stretched her back.

"Nonsense, dear. It's been a jolly good piece of excitement for me." She pulled up one of the wooden kitchen chairs and sat near the Aga, pouring hot water into a teapot. "Since Hugh died, it's been a little quiet around here. I keep the farm going, but only have a few head of cattle." She put the lid on the pot and sat back in the chair. "You mentioned an estate?"

Jo smiled. "Collingford," she said quietly.

"Good grief, you're Joanna Holbrook-Sutherland."

"Yeah," Jo said warily. Her reputation amongst England's upper class was not good.

"You caused quite a stir a year or so ago." She leaned forward and patted Jo's knee. "Good for you, girl. Those damn pale, skeletal young things down in London need shaking up. Saw that article in the Times. You were making headlines for a while there."

"Yes, I was," Jo said, ducking her head and pulling the still limp girl closer to her chest. Jo suddenly remembered why Rocky was now unconscious in her arms. "Joss, the man..."

Joss was pouring tea. "There was a hole in the ice on the lake."

"You think he went through?"

"I could see no sign of him."

Jo looked down at the woman on her lap, who was just beginning to move slightly. "Oh, baby, what happened out there?"

Joss stood. "Right then, Jo. We're going to try to get this tea in her. It's only just warm, not too hot. But it'll help warm her from the inside."

Jo gave the mug in Joss's hand a concerned look. "Won't she choke?"

"Probably, a little. But you'd be surprised what the body does out of instinct.". Joss smiled suddenly. "Unless of course you'd like to try another way of getting it into her." Jo frowned, obviously not completely understanding. Joss grinned. "From the other end."

"Oh my God," Jo said, smiling for the first time in a while. "She'd kill me."

"That's more like it, girl." She took a couple of steps towards the two women in their cocoon of blankets. "Now, open her mouth." Joss placed a towel beneath Rocky's chin and waited while Jo gently prised open her lover's mouth. She poured a small amount of tea into the blonde's mouth, then rubbed her throat, which in turn caused Rocky to swallow. The second attempt wasn't as successful, however, and Joss found lukewarm tea dripping from her face when it was coughed up forcefully by the unconscious woman. Jo winced, but the older woman just returned to her task. After a while, the whole mug of tea was inside Rocky, and the weak shivering was becoming more insistent.

"Now you drink yours, dear," she said, handing Jo a mug. "She's going to be shivering so hard soon, you'll have a job holding on."

Jo took the mug, draining it quickly, then handing it back to Joss. "I'll never be able to thank you enough for this," Jo said, pulling Rocky closer to her body when her shivering threatened to make her slide to the floor.

Joss stood and pushed the hair back from the blonde's forehead, pleased at the slight warmth she now felt. "I should be thanking you two. I was just sitting here in front of the stove, trying to sleep. It's the only warm room in the house. Haven't had this much excitement for years."

Suddenly Jo's head snapped up from its place resting against the blonde head. "Did you see anyone else out there? My God, I forgot..."

"Jo, shh. I saw a hole in the ice, remember? Rocky's legs were drenched. I've lost livestock in that lake in winters before now, I know the signs. Something went through the ice. I told you that," she said gently, knowing that Jo's concussion was responsible for the repeated questions.

Jo looked down at Rocky. The realisation of how close she'd come to losing her, to the ice and to hypothermia, suddenly crushed down on her. But the feel of the small woman shivering against her gave her the knowledge that she was alive and, for now, that was all she needed. Rocky suddenly gasped, her teeth chattering as her body finally started to do its work. Her arms drew in about her own body, her fists clenching painfully. Jo held on, smiling down at her lover as the green eyes opened and looked dazedly around the room.

"It's okay," Jo whispered into a nearby ear.

"Sssso cccold." She was almost incoherent, and threatened to slip out of Jo's grasp.

"I know, baby. But you're warming up, that's why you're shivering so much."

Rocky tried to talk again, but it was just too difficult. She didn't seem to have any control over the spasms that rocked her body or the chattering that echoed through her head.

"We just have to wait it out, sweetheart. You'll feel better soon." Jo jumped when she felt a small, shaking hand brush against her breast beneath the blankets. "You're feeling better already, eh?" She smiled down at her lover, who returned the smile somewhat shakily.

Rocky eased her head against Jo's chest, relaxing into the feeling of warmth and security she found there. She would tell her lover what had happened at the lake later. She remembered everything. From the feeling of the cold water that encased her legs, sucking the feeling and strength from them. To the look on her uncle's face as he tried to pull himself out of the freezing depths.

The shaking continued, and she felt Jo's hold around her tighten. The tears came then, not just for herself, but for her family. Now she suspected she was the only one left. She had no family left. She had lost so much, yet she had found so much more. She had found her heart and a reason to live. She looked up. Jo had her eyes closed and looked exhausted. "Jo?" she managed.

Blue eyes opened. "Yeah, sweetheart?"

"Dddon't leave mme."

A look of shock and then anguish crossed the angular face. "Never, Rocky. Never." She pulled the damp blonde head against her chest again. "Try to sleep," she said, looking across at Joss, whose tears mirrored her own.

Chapter
23

Joss watched the two women as they slept sharing her favourite chair by the Aga. The younger one, the blonde, had seemed to recover quickly once she woke. The other, Jo, had held her closely, the exhaustion on her face evident. Jo had waited until Rocky fell asleep though, before giving in to it herself. But even then her face never quite lost the tension Joss had become accustomed to seeing there. So she watched them. She watched as the smaller woman became restless, and, in her sleep, Jo rubbed a hand up and down the girl's back, soothing her. Rocky would quickly calm, and the two of them would slip back into a carefree slumber.

Joss opened the heavy curtains and bright rays of wintry sunshine slipped across the bare floor. She turned towards the sleeping women and watched green eyes flutter open. She saw the panic in the blonde's face, until she took in where she was and who held her so tightly.

"Good morning," Joss said quietly. Rocky just smiled. Then a look a discomfort crossed her face. Joss crossed the room. "What is it?" she asked, feeling the blonde's forehead with a cool hand.

"I need the loo," Rocky said huskily, her throat scratchy.

"Hardly surprising, dear, after all the tea I made you drink last night." She pulled back the blankets and helped the younger woman to her feet, replacing the covers over Jo carefully and tucking them around her. "We must let her sleep. She was exhausted last night."

She wrapped Rocky up in her coat, the blonde was too cold and too miserable to worry about being naked in front of the woman. "It's freezing in the rest of the house." She led her along the hallway and pointed to the correct door. "I'll put the kettle on, and then whip up some breakfast."

When she returned to the kitchen, she found Jo to be restless, mumbling in her sleep. "Don't be a silly goose. She's just gone for a moment," she said, laying a hand on the dark head. Jo calmed, snuggling down into her warm nest. Joss watched her for a moment, brushing aside ebony hair to better see the edge of the small wound disappearing into the dark hairline. The bruise extended to Jo's temple. Joss wondered at the strength of the sleeping woman who had gone out into the night in search of her lover with what surely must be a mild concussion.

Joss was pouring tea when Rocky returned to the kitchen. The blonde glanced at Jo before making her way to the table and pulling a chair out.

"There, dear. The Englishman's cure for all that ails you, a nice cup of tea."

"Thank you," Rocky said, shivering slightly after her trip to the small bathroom. She wrapped her hands around the warm mug. "What time is it?" she asked.

"It's a little after 11. The phone's still out, I'm afraid."

Rocky nodded, sipping her tea. "I'm sorry we've caused you so much trouble."

"Not a bit of it, dear. No trouble at all."

Rocky turned to look at Jo. "Do you think she'll be all right? She looks very pale."

Joss followed Rocky's gaze. "I'm sure she will be. She stayed awake for a while last night, after you'd dropped off. Her eyes didn't look as glazed." Then her attention was on the blonde. "What about you, how do you feel?"

"I feel...numb."

"Do you want to tell me what happened?"

Rocky closed her eyes and shook her head gently. "I don't think I can."

Joss reached across and patted her hand. "That's all right, dear. If it's too difficult for you—"

"No, it's not that," Rocky said quickly. "It's all a bit of a mess. I remember going out there. I remember running through the trees."

"There was someone out there, someone Jo was very afraid you would meet."

Rocky looked over at her lover, thankful that she appeared to be peacefully asleep. "Yes. My uncle." She rubbed her eyes with the heels of her hands then sat back in the chair, her head back, her eyes closed. Her eyes suddenly snapped open. "My God, he went through the ice."

"Yes, he did, dear." Joss watched carefully as the woman in front of her crumbled.

Rocky sobbed into her hands as the memory of the past night returned. "I tried, Joss. I tried so hard. But he was so heavy. I couldn't hold him. I threw him the jacket, but it slipped from my hands." She cast stricken eyes on the older woman. "I didn't want him dead, I just wanted him to leave me alone. I thought going with him would be for the best. I was afraid for her."

Joss looked up towards the dark-haired woman and found herself regarded by two very aware blue eyes. Jo shook her head slightly, and Joss turned her attention back to the blonde and waited for her to continue.

"I can't believe I just left her. I thought she'd just put it down to experience. I mean, we've only known each other a few weeks. I thought maybe I was just a passing fancy, a bit of a distraction." She looked up at Joss, smiling through her tears. "But she came for me. She didn't give up on me." She took the tissues that Joss offered and wiped her face of the tears that were flowing freely. "When he turned up here, I knew he would never give up, never give us peace. I thought I could lead him away. Maybe find another house. Just as long as she was safe, nothing else mattered."

"You mattered." Jo's voice broke on the last word. Rocky spun in her seat, taking in the tear-stained face of her lover and with two strides threw herself into the woman's arms.

Joss cleared her throat. "I have to go and feed the chickens," she said. Calling Jasper, she pulled on her coat and left the two women still locked in their embrace. The cold of the morning hit Joss. The snow was crisp, the sky blue, and the sun shone brightly. It was a beautiful morning. She looked across the field towards the tracks her guests had made the previous night. She stood for a moment, trying to imagine the fear Rocky must have felt as she went out to face the man who had been her rapist.

With a shake of her head, she made her way to the chicken coup but stopped suddenly when she heard voices. She looked across the field to see two policemen struggling through the snow. She looked back at the house, and then set off across the field to meet them.

It was almost half an hour later when Joss returned to the farmhouse. She found her two guests to be asleep again. Jo's face was showing the strain, even in sleep. She couldn't actually see Rocky, just the top of a tousled blonde head, which peeked from beneath the blankets.

She laid a gentle hand on Jo's shoulder. "Jo," she said quietly, watching as blue eyes opened, taking a few moments to focus on her. "The police are here."

Jo cleared her throat, looking beyond her friend, but seeing no one else in the kitchen. "They are?"

Joss nodded. "They've just gone back to get their car, then they'll be coming here. They're going to want to take you both back to Leicester."

Jo looked down at the blonde, who was waking. "Hey," she said, her lips brushing the soft hair of her lover. "The cops are here."

Two green eyes emerged from behind the blanket then scanned the room. "Are we in trouble?" she asked, her voice muffled by the covering.

"Your clothes are here," Joss said, handing them the dry clothing. Wordlessly, they both dressed in front of the Aga.

"Rocky," Jo said, pulling on her jeans. She waited until the blonde had pulled on her t-shirt. "I want you to hide."

"No." A shake of the blonde head.

"Please, there's nothing to connect either of us to him. It could all go down as a tragic accident." Jo glanced from her lover to the dark forms approaching the door, her eyes registering sudden panic.

"I'm tired of running, Jo. I want it over with." Rocky turned from her lover as the two men were let into the kitchen by Joss.

"Good morning," the first policeman said through the door, taking off his cap. He wiped his feet on the small mat, and then made his way fully inside. "At least the snow has stopped." He took in the uneasiness of the two younger women facing him, completely disregarding the older woman in the room, who was busy getting extra mugs from a cupboard beside the sink.

"Sit yourselves down," Joss said, placing the mugs on the table. The first officer into the kitchen, the older one, sat down. His companion, however, remained standing just inside the door.

"We're making house to house enquiries," the older man said, "trying to establish the whereabouts of the owners of the vehicles that have been left on the motorway." He pulled out his notepad and was just about to read out what he had noted down when Jo spoke.

"The silver Merk is mine. We've been here all night. I would have reported it, but the phone lines are down." The words came out in a rush, but if the officer thought there was anything amiss, he didn't show it.

"Have you seen anyone else? There are a few vehicles abandoned not far from here."

"No," Jo said quickly.

Rocky, who had been watching the exchange, quietly took a step forward. "Jo," she said and turned to the officer. "There was an accident last night," she said to the policeman. She heard Jo sit in the chair behind her, and Rocky pulled out another chair from beneath the table. "I think I need to make a statement." The crackle of a radio interrupted them, and the younger officer stepped outside to take the call, talking into the mic on his shoulder as he went.

"What is the nature of this statement?" the officer asked, pulling out his pen.

The other police officer put his head around the corner. "Sarge?"

"Excuse me a moment, ladies."

Jo stood quickly, turning Rocky and the chair she was sitting on to face her. "What are you doing?" she hissed, her hands on the blonde's shoulders.

Rocky shrugged out of Jo's grip. "Something right for once. I can't run from this."

The door opened, and the two officers walked back into the house. The older officer once again pulled out his notebook. "Can I have your name, miss?" he asked the blonde woman.

"Michelle Kersey," Rocky said quickly.

"And where were you at around midnight last night?"

She looked to Jo, who sank back into the armchair beside the Aga, then turned back to the officer. "I think we were travelling about that time."

"And where were you before, during the evening?"

Rocky bowed her head, speaking so quietly the officer had to strain to hear her. "I was at my uncle's house."

"Rocky." Jo's voice held a warning.

"And your uncle is?" the officer asked.

"Ronald Schumacher."

The officer stood. "Michelle Kersey, I'm arresting you on suspicion of murder. I am now going to caution you. You do not have to say anything, but it may harm your defence if you do not mention when questioned something you later rely on in court. Anything you do say may be taken down and used in evidence." He took a pair of handcuffs from his tunic, and the other officer closed in as he reached for the blonde.

"Wait a minute," Jo said, standing quickly. "Whose murder?"

"Susan Shumacher was found dead at her home in the early hours of this morning. Ronald Shumacher's car is currently next to yours on the motorway." He fastened the cuffs around the wrists of a very docile Rocky and pushed her back down on the chair.

"Is there any need for that?" Jo asked, taking a step towards the officer who had cuffed her friend. "She's no threat to you."

"Procedure, ma'am," he said, though Jo had enough experience of the police and their arresting procedure to know that this wasn't entirely true.

"He's in the lake," Rocky said, looking down at her cuffed hands. The younger officer took down what he assumed to be a confession. "He chased after me. We both fell onto the lake." Rocky closed her eyes. "He fell through the ice." She looked up at the policeman, her eyes tired now and filling with tears. "I couldn't hold him. He was too heavy."

"I think it would be better if you waited until we reached the station." The officer looked to his colleague, who nodded and slipped out of the house again to make another call on his radio.

"Then you'd better take me, too. I was with her the whole time," Jo said, standing. She wasn't going to let them take the blonde anywhere without her.

"No, Jo," Rocky sobbed.

The policeman repeated the caution to Jo and cuffed her as well.

Joss got out a couple of thick coats and covered both women for their walk to the car. "Another officer will be up to take a statement from you, Mrs..." he waited for her to provide her name.

"Carmichael, be sure to spell it correctly," she said, pulling the coat securely around Rocky. Joss closed the door gently when they'd left, looking back at the now quiet and empty kitchen. And she wondered at the fact that two souls who had visited her so briefly had made such an impact on her.

The rest of the day passed in a blur. Jo and Rocky were searched before being placed into the police car. The car then pulled away and headed back toward the motorway. Once they arrived at the accident scene, Rocky was placed into a separate car. A tow truck was just hitching up the Merk, ready to tow it away to be examined. The dark BMW was still there, a couple of officers standing guard until another tow truck could be called. At the police station, they were processed and fingerprinted, and then led to different interview rooms.

Jo was allowed to call her mother, giving her a brief description of the previous evening and was assured that Marianna would be there as soon as possible. She told her near hysterical daughter that she would arrange for two lawyers to be there within a couple of hours.

"Do you need a doctor?" the officer asked Jo in the interview room, when they were finished.

Jo shook her head. "No," she said quietly. "I don't think so." She looked up at the man, remembering his look of surprise when he'd opened the file and seen a printout of her record. She'd been arrested a few times in London, for offences ranging from a breach of the peace to being drunk and incapable. And most of those occasions had been recorded in the tabloids.

The plain-clothes officer stood and walked around the table. "You said you suffered a head injury. I think we should get someone to look at it."

Jo shook her head again. "Just something for my headache."

"I think we're finished here," he said, switching off the tape recorder. "We're going to want your clothes. For forensic tests."

Jo nodded. "Can I see Rocky?"

"Not just yet. She's still being interviewed, I think."

The officer nodded to the policewoman who stood just inside the door. "Take Miss Holbrook-Sutherland to one of the holding cells and give her something to wear." He turned to Jo. "We'll give you some bags. If you could place your clothes into them, we'd appreciate it." Jo nodded and followed the tall policewoman out of the interview room.

The thing they'd given her to put on after she'd stripped out of her clothes could only be described as a white boiler suit, which appeared to be made of some kind of strong paper. She'd seen forensic investigators, on the odd occasion she'd watched the news, wearing something similar. She sat on the narrow cot, her back resting against the wall, crinkling her nose at the faint smell of antiseptic. Her thoughts drifted to Rocky, wondering how she was coping and hoping that her lover wasn't admitting to something she hadn't done. She knew Rocky's first reaction was to feel guilt for all that had happened in the past few weeks. From not letting her old friends know she was still alive to Jo's anguish when she left her, albeit reluctantly.

She knew her mother would arrive soon and smiled to herself, wondering if the few officers in the police station knew exactly what was heading in their direction. More than once her mother had bailed her out of a cell in one police station or another. And she was slightly proud of herself this time, comfortable in the knowledge that, for once, she hadn't actually done anything wrong.

She closed her eyes and must have drifted off, for she was suddenly woken by the muffled sounds of a commotion outside her thick cell door. She looked at her watch, but that was one of the items confiscated earlier so she had no idea how much time had passed. It had taken over an hour to get to the station from the motorway, a large number of roads were still being cleared of the snow that had fallen the previous day. People were venturing out for the first time in a couple of days, and the roads were clogged. She estimated it to be early evening.

The interview had taken a couple of hours. Jo had told him everything that Rocky had told her. About the death of her parents and the rape by the man charged with her care. The man who was probably his boss. She hoped, she prayed, that Rocky was telling the same story, again wondering whether her lover was somehow taking the blame for the deaths of her aunt and uncle.

She stood and put an ear against the door. She heard another door open, footsteps, the door slamming shut, and then footsteps receding. She settled back down on the cot, lying down this time. "I love you, Rocky," she whispered to the stark white ceiling, before closing her eyes.

Again she was startled awake, this time by her cell door opening. She was led out by the policewoman and taken to the interview room again. Inside were her mother and another man.

Marianna took a couple of steps and embraced her youngest child. "Are you all right, dear?" she asked, pushing the hair off Jo's forehead to see the bruise better at her temple.

"I'm fine. Where's Rocky?" she asked, looking around.

"Rocky is still in her cell." She turned to the man with her. "This is Howard Mayfield, Chief Constable of the Avon and Somerset Constabulary."

Jo took the offered hand, shaking it. "Hello." She turned quizzical eyes on her mother.

"I called Cordelia," she said, easing herself into one of the chairs. "It would seem Michelle's uncle was already under investigation."

Jo's face screwed up in confusion. "Cordelia?"

"Yes, dear. You know Cordelia. Her daughter, Rebecca, was a friend of yours."

Jo winced. "Yeah, I remember."

"Her husband, Charles, is with the Home Office. I managed to have a little chat with him."

The Chief Constable pulled out a chair for Jo to sit on. "Joanna," he said, once she was seated, "I have spoken to the Duty Sergeant, and we have arranged bail for you and Miss Kersey. As you were both arrested, we will have to go through the formalities. But for now, we're releasing you both into the custody of your mother." He sat in the one remaining chair. "We'd like to come and see you both at a later date to take a more detailed statement, especially from Miss Kersey."

Jo frowned. "I thought she was interviewed earlier."

"There was a small problem. It would seem Miss Kersey became hysterical. The officer in charge of the interview called a doctor, and she was sedated. She's sleeping in a holding cell now."

Jo was on her feet instantly. "What? Where is she? I want to see her. Now!" She made her way to the door.

"Joanna, please. Michelle is fine." Her mother placed a tentative hand on her daughter's shoulder, feeling the tension there. "A doctor administered the sedative for her own safety. The two lawyers I asked to attend are here, and everything is being sorted out."

Jo turned towards her mother. "She can't deal with this," she said, scrubbing her face with both hands. "She's been alone so long, now all of this..." She slumped back into the chair. "Maybe it would be better if I'd never found her." She leaned forward, her elbows on her knees, her head in her hands.

"Now, now, dear. You know that's not true."

Jo straightened in the chair. "So he killed Susan?"

The older policeman, who had stood briefly when Jo had jumped up, sat again. "Susan Shumacher was found dead in her home early this morning. Two officers had gone there after the abandoned car had been found on the motorway. A number of items from the house have been sent for forensic tests."

"You said he was already under investigation?" Jo asked.

"Yes, we've had a number of complaints against him, regarding harassment and sex with underage girls." The grey-haired man shook his head. "It would seem he thought his position would prevent any investigation being undertaken."

"Arrogant sod," Jo said between clenched teeth. She turned to her mother. "I need to take Rocky home."

The door opened, and the policewoman poked her head around it. "Miss Kersey is here." The door opened fully, and the policewoman led in a very groggy, very dishevelled Rocky. She was dressed in the same white overalls as Jo and stumbled into the arms of her lover when she saw the invitation open to her.

"Sweetheart," Jo said into soft blonde hair.

"I'm sorry," Rocky mumbled into the strange material of Jo's clothing.

"We're going home." Jo pulled her close, placing an arm around her shoulders. "We can go now, right?" she asked the policewoman.

She smiled. "Yes, we just need your signatures and an address where we can contact you."

The two women shuffled to the Duty Sergeant's desk and filled out the forms. Jo helped Rocky with hers while the two lawyers watched proceedings carefully. Marianna hovered in the background, speaking in hushed tones with the Chief Constable and watching the way her daughter's attention was fixed completely on the small blonde woman. Rocky was suffering; both Marianna and her daughter could see that. Her eyes were unfocussed, and dark shadows marred the underside of them. She'd said nothing since the muffled apology, just following instructions to sign her name and nodding mutely when told of her obligations not to leave the country and to inform them should she move from the address that Jo had given them. Rocky allowed herself to be led through the police station and out of a back door. There, waiting with its engine running, was the magnificent Rolls Royce in which Marianna had travelled down from Collingford.

Jo eased Rocky into the cavernous interior. The smell of leather reminded her of her childhood and the joy of riding in the old vehicle. She slipped into the long seat beside her lover and pulled the unresisting blonde into her arms. Rocky snuggled into the hold, relaxing immediately and falling asleep almost at once. Marianna got into the back sitting opposite her daughter. She was handed a couple of tartan rugs. She took one, covering the two younger women. The other she put over her own legs, then she sat regarding her daughter.

"She's exhausted," Marianna said as the car pulled out into the road.

"Yes, she is." Jo leaned Rocky back a little so she could see into the sleeping face. "I wish I knew what happened back there." Rocky scowled in her sleep, so Jo pulled her in close again.

"I spoke to the police woman, nice young woman. She said Rocky became very upset during the questioning, so they decided to let her take a break. When they took her to the cell, she became hysterical, so they called a doctor. Apparently it's standard procedure."

"Yeah, standard procedure." Jo looked up from Rocky to her mother. "I wish this was all over. I don't know how much more she can take. She's so full of guilt."

"Guilt? She has nothing to feel guilty for."

"You try telling her that." She ducked her head, giving the sleeping women a peck on the cheek. "I am going to spoil her so badly when we get home."

Marianna leaned forward and patted her daughter's knee. "I wouldn't expect anything less from you, dear." She leaned back in the seat, watching the passing scenery for a moment. "Olivia's gone back to Seattle, but your brother is still at Collingford."

"Is he?" Jo shrugged. She hadn't seen her brother in months. She thought for a moment. "Does Father know about all of this?"

"Yes, he does, dear."

"And?" Jo asked cautiously.

"And he's perfectly happy with you both coming to stay for a while. I told him how much she means to you, and you know you're your father's favourite. He just wants you to be happy. As I do."

Jo smiled, the first time for a while. "Thanks, Mum. I love you."

Marianna mirrored her daughter's smile. "Now, go to sleep. It'll be a few hours until we arrive. The traffic's awful." Jo nodded and, taking a secure hold on the blonde in her arms, settled down to join her in sleep.

Chapter
24

However many times Marianna viewed Collingford, it would always take her breath away. She remembered the first time she was brought here, as a twenty-one-year-old by her future husband. The house was quite simply breathtaking. As they arrived along the long and winding driveway, its illuminated form rose out of the darkness like a landlocked Titanic.

As the Rolls drew in front of one of the large doors to the side of the house, the door opened and a tall man walked out to meet the vehicle. The chauffeur greeted him. "Good evening, M'Lord," Jonathan said as he opened the door at the rear of the Rolls.

The man he greeted was a good half foot beyond six feet. His hair was a sandy colour, greying at the temples, and his eyes as blue as his daughter's. Jeffrey Holbrook-Sutherland reached into the back of the car and helped his wife out, bending to give her a peck on the cheek. "Good grief," he said, peering into the back of the car at the two sleeping women. "What on Earth are they wearing?"

Marianna sighed. "They took their clothes at the police station." She pulled on her husband's arm. "Now, Jeffrey, darling, they're both exhausted. You're going to have to wait until tomorrow to talk to Joanna about what's gone on."

"Of course, dear," he said smiling. "Now, let's see if we can't rouse your daughter." He leaned into the car, grasping Joanna's ankle and shaking it gently.

Marianna chuckled as she made her way into the house. He always referred to Joanna as "her" daughter when the girl got herself into trouble. But she knew he adored his youngest child and would go to any lengths to make sure she was happy. She had just handed her coat to her maid, when Jo entered the huge hallway. Then she saw a sight that brought an instant smile to her face. Her husband entered, cradling the still sleeping form of the small blonde in his arms. Marianna thought she looked like a child, dwarfed by her tall husband. But then she realised that Rocky was little more than a child and wondered at how her daughter's friend had survived so much at such a young age.

"Where are you putting us?" Jo asked, stifling a yawn.

"In your usual room," Marianna said. "You'll find some clothes in the bureau. I sent Kate out to get some things for you both. I hope I estimated Michelle's size correctly."

Jo took a step forward and hugged her mother fiercely. "Thank you so much," she said, finding her eyes filling with tears. She heard her father making his careful way up the stairs and started to follow him. Halfway up the stairs, Jo turned. "Any chance of something to eat? We just had some pretty lame sandwiches at the police station."

"I'll be sure to send some up. You go on up. The fire is lit in the room, and there's plenty of hot water." She started to turn away. "Oh, yes, I'll also be calling Dr. Morris tomorrow to get him to look at you both."

"We're fine, Mum," Jo insisted.

"Humour me, dear."

Jo chuckled tiredly and gave a small nod. "Goodnight," she said and turned back up the stairs.

When Jo arrived in the huge bedroom, her father had just placed Rocky on the bed. She watched as he carefully arranged her on the incredibly soft bed covering so that she would be comfortable. The huge four-poster bed, with its canopy, almost swallowed up the small woman.

"Your mother's told me a lot about this little girl," he said, and Jo watched in fascination as he gently pushed away blonde hair from the sleeping face. She joined her father, gazing down at the blonde. "She's important to you?"

"Very," Jo said. She looked up at her father. "I don't say thank you enough."

Jeffrey leaned down and gave his daughter a kiss on the cheek, pulling her into a heartfelt embrace. "You're growing up, Joanna. Never thought I'd live to see the day." He held her away from him, his hands on her shoulders. "I think you may have to accept some responsibility for this girl. Do you think you're up to it?"

Jo looked down at Rocky then back to her father. "Yeah, I think I am." She hugged him again. "But you know what? I like it." She disentangled herself from his embrace and sat on the edge of the bed. "I like having to think about someone else but myself for once. I like wanting to make sure she's happy."

"That's what I felt when I met your mother." He leaned against one of the bedposts. "It's a wonderful feeling, having someone be a part of you. Is that how you feel about Michelle?"

"That's exactly how I feel." Her hand had found the blonde's, her thumb lightly caressing the back of the small hand. "It means so much to me that you understand."

He leaned down and patted his daughter's thigh. "Sounds like your food is here. I'll be in the library if you need me."

"Okay, Dad. And thanks." He left her with a smile, passing the maid as she entered laden with a tray full of food.

Jo let the girl place the tray on a small table and then quietly closed the door as she left. She turned back, regarding the silent form on the bed. Rocky was curled up on her right side, one fist tucked beneath her head. She still wore the white overalls the police had provided them both with. She looked peaceful enough, but as Jo sat on the edge of the bed beside her, she could just make out a small crease of worry between the fair eyebrows.

Jo went to a large bureau, opening a drawer and finding a selection of different colour t-shirts in there. She pulled out a couple and went back to the bed. Easing Rocky onto her back, she began unfastening the top of the strange garment she was wearing.

"Hey," she whispered as green eyes blinked open. "I'm undressing you again." She smiled down, but the smile wasn't mirrored back at her. She stopped what she was doing. "You okay?" Glassy green eyes tracked from her lover and across the room, taking in the antique furniture and then the magnificent decoratively plastered ceiling. "We're at Collingford," Jo said, reaching out slowly and caressing a flushed cheek.

"Why am I so tired?" the blonde asked in a very small voice. She seemed incapable of moving at all and just watched as Jo resumed undoing the fastenings on the suit.

"They sedated you, back at the police station. Plus, we haven't had a lot of sleep in the past forty-eight hours." She leaned forward and eased Rocky to a sitting position and pulled the top of the suit down so that it pooled about her waist. Rocky leaned her head onto her lover's shoulder, sighing deeply as she felt the long arms encircle her.

They sat like that for a while in comfortable silence, until Jo felt the weight in her arms become heavy again as Rocky slid back into sleep. She patted the blonde's back gently. "Hey, I want you to eat something first. Neither of us had much all day." She snagged one of the t-shirts and pulled it over the blonde head, helping the groggy young woman get her arms through the sleeves, and then settled it about her.

"You get the rest of it off then slip into bed. I'll get the tray."

Jo pulled her suit off and slipped into the other t-shirt, before getting the tray and balancing it on the bed. Then she plumped up the huge pillows and placed them against the dark, intricately carved headboard. She jumped up into the bed, which was as antique as the rest of the furniture in the room and much higher off the ground than modern beds. She eased under the thick quilt and leaned against the pillows she'd piled against the headboard. Rocky had dozed off, and Jo shook her gently, waking her again.

"Come on, come up here." Jo pulled the blonde up so that she was sitting with her back against the taller woman's chest. "Try eating something." She handed Rocky a sandwich made with some of the ham cured in the huge kitchens of Collingford Manor.

"I'm not hungry," she said, pushing away the offered snack. "Just tired."

"Okay." Jo wasn't going to force her. "You want a drink? There's some hot chocolate here."

The blonde head nodded, and Jo carefully handed her the mug, watching over Rocky's shoulder to make sure she didn't spill any down her. Then she picked up a mug for herself, closing her eyes at the taste, which reminded her of her childhood again.

"Don't remember coming up here. Did I sleep all the way here?" Rocky asked, handing back the half-finished mug of hot chocolate to her lover.

"You did. You're completely wiped out, sweetheart." She reached down for the plates of sandwiches again. "You going to try this?" she asked, holding the snack in front of her lover's face.

Rocky shook her head. "Don't feel so good, just want to sleep." She turned slightly, taking a handful of Jo's t-shirt and snuggling into the embrace.

Jo was left holding the sandwich, but she too had lost her

appetite, so she placed it back on the plate on the tray. She tucked the blonde head of the already sleeping woman under her chin and settled back into the plump pillows.

She dozed for a while but awoke when she felt the tray lifted from near her legs. Her mother was smiling down at her. "I thought you were hungry," Marianna said.

"I am, just too tired to eat." She blinked sleepily up at her mother, who sat on the edge of the high mattress.

"Your father was quite taken with Michelle." She gazed affectionately down at the sleeping blonde, seeing the death grip she had on her daughter.

"Good, I'm glad." She thought for a moment, chewing her lip. "Will you and Father be at Collingford a while?"

Marianna considered the question. "We could. Is there a reason you ask?"

"I'd like to stay for a few months. Just give her time to rest, to have somewhere where she feels she could maybe belong."

"I've already thought of that. I'd love you both to stay. You could help me with the arrangements for opening the house in the spring." She smiled when she saw her daughter's eyelids start to droop. "We can talk in the morning, dear. You rest now, and tomorrow we'll take Michelle for a tour of the house, if she's up to it." She made Jo slide down further into the bed and pulled the quilt around the sleeping pair, noticing that the blonde didn't stir or relinquish her hold as her daughter made herself comfortable. She closed the door quietly on her way out and made her way down to the library to speak to her husband.

Bright sunshine woke Rocky, and she turned her head away from the annoying light. Then she found soft hair tickling her nose and opened her eyes cautiously to find herself buried beneath the ebony locks. Her head was resting on her lover's shoulder, her hand on the warm skin of Jo's stomach. She reached up, carefully brushing the hair from her face. Then she moved slightly away from the sleeping woman, wanting to see her fully and enjoy the experience of watching Jo in sleep. There were dark shadows under the blue eyes, now closed, the dark lashes brushing against slightly flushed cheeks. Full lips were parted, showing the edges of perfect teeth.

Rocky couldn't resist. She leaned forward, brushing her lips against those of the sleeping woman, delighted when her lover responded unconsciously. She settled back down in her favourite place and closed her eyes to the light that wanted to pull her from her lover's embrace. She felt the arms tighten about her as she relaxed again, and Jo mumbled something unintelligible, though she thought she heard a couple of familiar words in there. Words they had used a lot lately, words that made her smile. She closed her eyes almost reluctantly, wanting to enjoy for longer the sight of her lover so relaxed in sleep. But she felt the pull to return to slumber, and she was not going to try to fight it.

She woke later, her full bladder nudging her to consciousness. She sat up slowly and finally managed to divert her attention from her still-sleeping lover and take in the magnificence of the room she was in.

A huge fireplace dominated one wall, the embers still glowing. All around the room were obviously priceless antiques, from the huge rug on the floor to the paintings on the wall. At the edges of the rug, she could see the solid oak floor boards, polished over hundreds of years to a mirror-like sheen. There were various small tables and an assortment of chairs and small couches dotted about the room. On just about every surface was a small lamp, those being the only source of light in the room apart from the bright sunshine that poured in through the heavily draped windows.

She eased out of the bed, surprised at how far she dropped to the ground, and padded across to the window. The sight that greeted her took her breath away. The grounds of Collingford Manor were covered with a crisp and even layer of snow. She saw what she assumed to be a gardener, sprinkling a mixture of grit and sand across some of the pathways. The grounds dipped and rose, the snow covering the landscaping for which the manor was famous.

Her bladder complained again, and she pulled the thin t-shirt about her and pulled open the heavy oak door. Rocky ventured out into the hallway. More portraits on the walls, and another collection of small tables, each bearing a lamp, greeted her. The plush carpet beneath her toes was cold to the touch. A house of Collingford's size and age was a cold place, even with the newer heating system installed. She froze when a figure emerged from a room ahead of her.

"Good afternoon," the tall man said, a twinkle of amusement in his blue eyes.

"Afternoon?" Rocky began to back towards her room as the man approached her.

"I'm afraid so, dear." He held out his hand. "I'm Jeffrey. We met last night, Michelle. Unfortunately you were somewhat indisposed."

Rocky smiled, taking the man's huge hand in her own. "Hello, Jeffrey." She shook the warm hand. "Do you work here?"

"In a manner of speaking. Are you lost?" He placed his hands behind his back, rocking slightly on his heels.

"I was looking for the loo," she said, feeling the blush rising on her neck and infusing her cheeks.

"Ah, well, now that I can help you with." He reached out and turned her around, his large hands on her shoulders, pointing her back in the direction of her room.

"But that's..."

"Your room, dear, that's right."

He pushed open the door quietly and edged around the bottom of the bed, taking a brief glance towards the sleeping woman. Then he reached one of the wooden panels on the wall and turned a handle. "There you are, dear," he said pushing open the panel to reveal a bathroom.

Rocky shook her head slightly. "I would never have found that. Thank you, Jeffrey."

"Not at all, dear." He made his way to the door again. "We hope to see you later, maybe for dinner this evening." He smiled back at the blonde. "And be sure to wake my daughter by then, otherwise she'll sleep the day away." He gave her a wink and left, closing the door behind him.

Rocky was left staring at the closed door, her mouth agape. "Oh boy."

Jo came to wakefulness experiencing the most amazing sensation of soft lips against her own. She opened her eyes to find her vision filled with golden hair and soft green eyes.

"'Morning," Jo said, her voice rough.

"Afternoon, actually." Rocky grinned at her. "You think we've caught up with the sleep we've been missing?"

Jo reached up and traced the yellowing bruise and small cut on her lover's face, remembering what they'd just been through. "Are you okay?"

Rocky nodded, smiling down at her. She'd got back into bed after her trip to the bathroom, but this time decided she needed Jo awake. So she'd leaned down and kissed her for long moments until she began to stir. "It's almost like I can breathe again, after holding my breath for a very long time."

Jo chuckled. "Yeah, I know what you mean."

The blonde slumped down beside the taller woman, enjoying the feeling of being pulled closer to the warm body. "There's still a lot to get through though."

"The investigation?"

Rocky nodded. "We still have to do that." She looked up at Jo with watery eyes. "And I have a funeral to go to."

"I'm sorry, sweetheart," Jo said, ducking her head and kissing the blonde's forehead. "Let's just look forward to what we have now."

Rocky closed her eyes, taking a tighter hold of her lover. "Mmmm, look forward. I haven't done that for years. Never looked further than the next day, even the next hot meal." She looked up, falling into blue. "You changed all that."

"I'm glad," Jo whispered. "I'm glad I found someone who gave me a reason to look forward to tomorrow." She chewed on her bottom lip. "Tell me you'll never leave me." Rocky hesitated, and Jo's face showed her consternation. "What is it?"

Rocky sighed, her breath warm on Jo's neck. "There may be some things we don't control ourselves." She looked up, angry with herself that she'd just spoiled the wonderful mood they'd woken in. "Believe me, I want to stay with you. I love you. But_"

"No, stop." Jo swiped away a tear angrily. "It's okay. We'll take one day at a time."

"One day at a time," Rocky echoed and laid her head against her lover's shoulder, missing the look of despair on the beautiful face.

By the time they'd got themselves out of bed and dressed in the clothes that Marianna had got them, it was time for dinner, and they sat with the family in one of the smaller of Collingford's dining rooms. The family lived in a small part of the house, which wasn't open to the public. But the rooms they lived in when they stayed at the house were as splendid as any on display.

Rocky had been introduced to Jo's brother, Jeremy, who took

after his father in the looks department. He had been polite and, in turn, introduced her to his wife. But there was something there that the blonde couldn't quite put her finger on, and it annoyed her. Jo was oblivious to anything going on between her lover and her brother. She spent a lot of time with her father, who told her, in no uncertain terms, that she would be a fool to let the small blonde go. After dinner they all sat in one of the large rooms, talking about the future season and what repairs or preparations needed to be done to the house, which would open at Easter.

"It must be wonderful to be made responsible for such a beautiful house," Rocky said, leaning back against her lover as they sat on a large, plump sofa.

"It can be a headache, dear," Jeffrey said. "Sometimes we would just like to give it over to a trust, but it's been in the family for centuries, and I should imagine I'd suffer some unspeakable curse from my ancestors if I were to let it go."

Jeremy suddenly stood. "Could I show you some of the state rooms?" he asked, walking across to Rocky.

"I'd love that," she said, taking the offered hand and allowing herself to be pulled to her feet. She looked back at her lover. "Are you coming?"

"Not yet. I'll catch you up."

"Okay," she said and leaned down, giving Jo a peck on the lips. She followed Jo's brother as he led her along long corridors, turning on lights as he went.

"The library is one of the most popular attractions," he said, turning the light on as they entered the huge room, every wall covered by shelves to the ceiling bearing books of every size. Rocky heard the door shut behind her, and she turned to see Jeremy standing with his back against the wall.

"You must be pleased with yourself," he said.

"I'm sorry?" she asked, not moving an inch from where she'd stopped.

"You've taken them all in. My sister's always had a soft spot for a pretty face, but I thought my parents had a little more integrity." He took a couple of steps towards her, his footsteps loud on the polished wood floor. "I don't quite know how you managed it, but you've managed to worm your way into one of the most influential families in this part of the country. I've been told that only a month ago you were living on the streets of London on charitable handouts." He smiled, chuckling to himself. "Well, we all know

how you people supplement your income. I hope my sister has
taken you to a clinic of some sort. I understand certain diseases
are rife."

"No," whispered Rocky, tears forming in her eyes. "I've
never_"

"Whatever. Look at it from my point of view. My sister, one
of the wealthiest young women in the country, suddenly finds herself with a little parasite in tow." He circled the woman, who was
frozen to the spot. "Now this little parasite allows my sister to
take her in, and then is drawn into a seedy episode that finds her
being bailed out of a police cell in Leicester." He stopped in front
of her. "And now you're here." He gestured at the magnificent
room.

Rocky looked up at the man towering over her. "She came
looking for me," she croaked, her throat closing around the words.

"And you put up a great deal of resistance, didn't you? It took
you all of a week or so before you were letting her spend her
money on you." He took the edge of a sleeve of her t-shirt. "This
is nice."

She pulled away from him. "I didn't ask for any of this," she
sobbed.

"Oh, look," he grabbed her chin, his thumb passing gently
over soft lips. "You play the part so well I can see how they were
taken in." He brushed away blonde hair from her forehead. "Such
a pretty girl."

"What's going on?"

Jeremy turned to see his sister standing in the opened door.
He took a couple of steps towards her. "Just having a heart to
heart with your little vagrant." He turned back to Rocky. "No
offence."

The walls were closing in on the blonde, and she suddenly
needed to be far away from him, far away from everyone. She
pushed past the siblings, running along the echoing hall, not really
seeing where she was going.

Jo resisted the impulse to chase after the distraught woman,
and faced her brother. "You always were a fucking idiot, Jerry."

"Just looking after the family interests. I thought you had
outgrown the Sunday tabloids." He shook his head. "Aren't there
enough little blonde bitches in London to fuck in those dykey
night-clubs you go to? You had to pull some little vagrant off the
street?"

The slap startled them both. Even as children, in the usual fights that kids have, they had never struck each other. "This has nothing to do with her, does it, Jerry?" She advanced on her bother, giving him no option but to take a step back. Before he knew it, he was backed up against ancient books, the shelves digging into his back. "You've always been jealous of me. While I was out there having a life, you were being groomed to take on this place. And you hated that, didn't you?"

"I'm aware of my responsibilities. Maybe you should consider that sometime, Jo."

She poked him in the chest. "Stay out of my business, Jerry. Or so help me, I'll make your life hell. And believe me, I could do that." She stepped away from him, and he straightened.

"You've made a lot of enemies, Jo. There are people out there who would love for you to fall flat on your face over this." He straightened his tie.

Jo folded her arms across her chest. "Okay, who have you been talking to?"

"Beatrice called me the_"

"Trixie!" Jo almost screamed. "You've been taking to that lying bitch?"

"She was concerned that you were being taken for a fool, and to be perfectly honest_"

"For fuck's sake, Jerry. The woman is a fucking psychopath!" She wanted to hit something, but everything in the room was priceless, and her brother just wasn't worth the effort. "I don't have time for this," she said and stormed out of the library, slamming the heavy door as she went.

Jo started down the long corridor, not really knowing which way Rocky had gone. The whole of the hallway was lit by the lamps, which were on tables between various doorways. The further into the house she went, the colder it got. It wasn't possible to heat every room of the huge house through the winter, so the more delicate antiques were stored away and then returned to the rooms before the house was opened in the spring. She went from room to room, checking through that part of the house, until she returned to the room she had shared with the blonde the night before. Jo pushed the door open and poked her head around it.

Rocky was kneeling on a small oriental rug in front of the fire, staring into the flames. The room was in darkness apart from the glow of the fire.

Jo walked quietly up to her lover and sat crossed legged beside her, facing her. "Hey," she said quietly, her heart almost breaking when the blonde didn't respond. She saw the flames reflecting off the tears that coursed down the blonde's cheeks.

Rocky's chin dropped to her chest. "I can't take any more." Her voice was small, full of defeat.

Jo reached for her, but the smaller woman shied away. "Rocky?"

"I want to go back."

Jo shook her head. "Back where?"

"Back to being no one, back to the place I know."

"Don't say that."

"I can't do this, Jo."

"Let me help you."

"You've done enough already. Your brother was right."

"Please, Rocky, don't do this."

Rocky shook her head, the tears drying on her cheeks. "Just help me get back to London, and I'll be out of your way."

Jo was silent for a long time, watching the slumped form of the blonde, golden in the firelight. "Okay, but I want you to do something first."

Rocky looked at her for the first time since she'd entered the room. She nodded. "Okay."

Jo lifted her chin in challenge. "Tell me you don't love me." A sob escaped Rocky's throat, but Jo didn't move. "Tell me you don't love me, and I'll get the damned Rolls and get Jonathan to drive you there right now."

Rocky clutched her stomach and bent over, her forehead nearly touching the ground. The sight of her lover in such pain propelled Jo forward. She gathered the blonde up and pulled her into her lap. They sat like that for a long time, the silence broken only by the crackling of the fire and the shuddering sobs of the blonde. Jo rocked them both, waiting until the sobs died down, her own tears dripping from her chin onto soft blonde hair.

"I know it's hard," Jo whispered at last. "But as long as we stay together, we'll get through it." She kissed Rocky's temple. "Okay?"

The blonde head nodded. "I'm so tired," she said. "It's been so long. All I see are the people that have been hurt." She looked up at Jo. "Because of me." She wiped at her face. "If I'd stayed away, Susan would still be alive."

"Oh no, don't you go blaming yourself for that." Jo tightened her hold, suddenly realising how much the blonde must have been agonising over her aunt's death. "You can't possibly blame yourself for the actions of a lunatic."

"But if I'd just stayed away_"

"No, Rocky. You have as much right to live a happy life as anyone. And I want to be happy." She smiled down at the blonde. "And you make me happy."

"But your brother, I don't want to cause_"

"My brother is an idiot, and if Mother finds out about this he'll probably be disinherited."

"You see," Rocky said, shrugging out of her lover's embrace in her frustration. "I'm causing problems in your family now." She closed her eyes in anguish, pushing damp hair back from her face.

Jo reached for her hand. "Jerry got a call from Trixie. We'll be fine once we've both calmed down. This isn't our first disagreement, and it won't be the last." She squeezed the small hand in her own. "Please, Rocky. Trust me."

Two simple words, thought Rocky. *Trust me.* She looked into the blue eyes of her lover and knew she could. "I always will," she said and allowed herself to be pulled to her feet.

Jo led her to the bed, and they settled on top of the quilt. "Don't scare me like that again, okay?" Jo whispered as she settled her arms around the blonde.

Chapter
25

"Joanna, dear. I'm sure killing your brother would only bring you short term satisfaction." Marianna looked over her copy of Horse and Hounds at her squabbling offspring. Her youngest looked about ready to beat her eldest to the point of death. Jeremy was pointedly not looking at Jo as she carried on her tirade. But he felt the weight of her words and flinched occasionally when she threw her more colourful language in his direction.

"I have the family's good name and the future of Collingford to consider," Jeremy said, shifting uncomfortably in the plump armchair.

His sister's knees touched his own as she stood over him. "And we are no threat to that," Jo growled.

"You are not the eleventh Lord Collingford yet, Jeremy," Marianna said, folding up her magazine and dropping it onto the plush carpet. "And, until you are, you will leave the reputation of the Holbrook-Sutherland name, and Collingford, out of this conversation. Your father and I are satisfied that Michelle has no ulterior motive." She looked up at Jo, who backed away and slumped down onto another armchair. "Now, Jeremy, I wish to talk to your sister. It's late, and I'm sure you're tired."

Jeremy let loose an explosive laugh. "You're sending me to my room?" His eyes found his sister's smirking face. Marianna said nothing, merely smiling at her eldest. Jeremy stood. "Very well. Good night, Mother." He turned to his sister. "Joanna."

Marianna looked across at Jo as the door was shut quietly behind her departing son. "Don't look so pleased with yourself."

"Well, he was a jackass," Jo grumbled. "I never said a thing when he got that tart pregnant in '95."

"Where is Michelle?" Marianna asked, trying to divert the conversation away from her son.

"She's asleep," Jo said, suddenly finding the crackling fire interesting.

"She's exhausted." Marianna ducked her head, trying to see into Jo's face. "What is it?"

Jo sighed, suddenly feeling very tired. "She wanted to go back to London. To be no one again." Jo looked up at her mother. "After she fell asleep, I went into the bathroom and threw up. I never thought anyone would have that kind of hold on me."

"You talked her out of it I assume?"

"Yeah, I did." She shook her head gently. "But if he says another word to her, I swear_"

"I don't think he will now. He knows how your father and I view family members insulting our guests." Marianna looked up at the clock. "It's nearly midnight. Do you think it's too late to wake Michelle?"

Jo frowned. "Wake her? What for?"

"I told you back in London. I have something I'd like you to see."

Jo rubbed her forehead with the heel of her hand. "I remember." She cocked her head to the side. "You gonna tell me what it is?"

Marianna smiled and shook her head. "No, I want you to both see it." She chuckled at her daughter's confused look. "It's nothing spectacular. Just something I thought of the first time I saw Michelle. It's a curious coincidence, nothing more."

"I'll see if I can wake her, but she was really out of it when I left."

"That's fine, dear. If you can't, it will wait." She stood and walked to the door with Jo. "Meet me in the library," she said as Jo left her and started to climb the stairs.

The bedroom was quiet when she entered it, save for the soft breathing of the blonde woman on the bed and the crackling of the dying fire. She walked to the hearth and took a large log, carefully placing it on the glowing embers. Then she made her way to the bed and to the person who had suddenly become the most important thing in her life. She had come to realise that as she lay holding the blonde after Rocky had fallen asleep. And her anger had grown at her brother's outburst earlier in the evening. So she'd eased out from beneath her sleeping partner, gone in search of Jeremy and told him exactly where he could stick his opinions.

She climbed onto the bed, brushing blonde hair away from the sleeping face. Green eyes opened and focused on her. "Hi," she said to the groggy woman.

"Hi." Rocky's voice was hoarse, and she cleared her throat. "Is it morning?"

Jo chuckled. "Nope, just about midnight."

"Why are you up?"

"Couldn't sleep." She traced a fair eyebrow, smiling when the blonde's eyes closed dreamily. "I've been talking to mother, and she has something to show us."

Green eyes drifted open again. "She does?"

"Yep." Long fingers wound in blonde hair, massaging Rocky's scalp. "But if you're too tired, it can wait."

Rocky smiled, grabbing the hand that was threatening to send her asleep again. "I'd like to see."

"Okay." Jo slid off the bed and eased the quilt off the blonde, who was still dressed in sweat pants and a t-shirt. "Let's go see what it is." She stood and swayed for a moment, the floor appearing to tilt beneath her feet.

"Jo?" The blonde was at her side in an instant, easing her into one of the plump armchairs by the fireplace. "Are you okay?"

"Goodness," the dark haired woman said, holding a hand to her suddenly throbbing head. "Everything phased out there for a moment."

"Hardly surprising. You've got a hole in your head, remember?"

Jo screwed her face up, pulling the willing blonde down onto her lap. "Not exactly a hole."

"It was a nasty cut. If you'd have gone to hospital, they probably would have put stitches in." She parted dark silky hair to look at the still angry wound.

"But we didn't, and it's fine now. It hurts, but it's healing." She pulled Rocky's hand away from her own head and kissed the fingers. "I've got a hard head. I'm just tired. We both are."

Rocky nodded gently and stood, reaching a hand down to Jo. "You okay to go now, or do you want to sit a while?"

Jo took the offered hand, letting the blonde pull her to her feet. "Nope, let's go and see what this mysterious thing is she wants to show us."

They walked hand in hand through the silent old house, Jo leading the way to the library. When they got there, Marianna was sitting at one of the large reading tables.

She gestured to two empty chairs. "Sit down," she said, putting on a pair of spectacles. Noticing Jo's lopsided grin, she looked at her over the top of the glasses. "Something wrong, dear?"

Jo shook her head. "Never thought I'd see the day," her daughter said, nodding towards the probably horribly expensive spectacles.

"The light is dreadful in here," she said, by means of explanation, and turned her attention to a large book she had on the table in front of her. "I brought this with me from Greece. It's very old and very delicate." She opened the book and turned it so that the two younger women could see its contents. Each delicate and faded page held a drawing; each drawing was of the same subject.

Jo looked from the drawings to her mother. "Who drew these?" she asked. She looked at Rocky who was staring at the image looking back at her from the pages of the ancient book. Her own image. The hair was longer, the face a little rounder, but otherwise, it could have been her.

"The likeness is uncanny, isn't it?" Marianna was watching the blonde carefully.

"It looks like me, Jo," Rocky whispered.

"There is some likeness." Jo looked up at her mother. "Who did this belong to?"

"It belonged to an ancestor of yours called Evelyn. Whether or not she drew the portraits I don't know, but each picture is signed at the bottom with an 'E.' There was also a bundle of letters with the book, written in broken English." She pushed the bundle, tied with a piece of faded blue ribbon, towards Jo. "Most of the letters were returned unopened. I did open a couple." She smiled across at the confused looking women. "They are love letters."

Jo rubbed her aching forehead. "So let me get this right. This person, Evelyn, wrote love letters." She looked down at the sketches in the book. "To her?"

"I do believe that to be the case. Back then it would have been a terrible scandal. Every effort would have been made to keep them apart." She gestured towards the letters. "One of those letters is in a different hand. It would seem the recipient didn't know they were being sent back without her opening them. She sent a letter to Evelyn, asking her why she hadn't written to her."

"I don't understand this," Rocky said, looking again at the pictures in the book.

"Michelle, it would seem that many years ago, a member of my family fell in love with a beautiful, young blonde woman, the woman in those drawings. It would appear that their love was thwarted at every turn. I also believe that Evelyn may have killed herself. My grandmother and my great grandmother would never talk of her." She looked at Jo. "I didn't ever want to see anyone in my family suffer like that." She reached for both the younger women's hands. "I believe in Fate. I was given this book and these letters for a reason, by a very wise old woman—my grandmother. As soon as I saw Michelle, I knew why." She reached across and carefully turned the pages of the book, until she found a particular image. The young woman staring from the pages was a mirror image of the young blonde that had first captivated Jo in the gallery in London.

Jo sucked in a breath. "Have you ever shown me this?" she asked. "When I was a kid or anything?"

"Never, Joanna. You've never seen this." She smiled at Rocky. "But as soon as I saw you, dear, I thought of this book."

Rocky pulled the book closer. The face staring out at her was similar to her own. The sketches were obviously drawn with a certain amount of affection. She turned the page and drew in a quick breath at the image she found there.

Unlike the other sketches, which were just head and shoulders, this showed the subject in full, lying on her back on what appeared to be a bed. A sheet was gathered about her waist, showing her upper body in all its glorious nudity. Her right arm was above her head, her left extended towards the artist, a red rose clasped gently in her hand. This was the only shock of colour in the whole book, the red rose.

Rocky's trembling fingers traced the delicate lines of the picture. "I think they found love," she said quietly. "I don't think Evelyn drew this from imagination. This is something she saw." She looked up at Jo, who had moved her chair closer and wrapped a long arm around the blonde's shoulders. "I think she drew this after they'd made love."

Marianna smiled across at the pair, wondering at the contrast in them. "You both look tired," she said. "You can look again in the morning."

Rocky carefully closed the book and slid it back across the table to Marianna. "Thank you for showing us the book. It's beautiful."

"Yes, it is," Marianna said, resting her hand on the old leather cover. "I do hope I'm wrong about Evelyn. Maybe we can go back to my family's home in Greece one day. The family histories are well kept there."

Rocky leaned into her lover. "Well, I'm going to believe they found a way to be together." She looked across at Jo's mother. "And I'm going to believe they found happiness." Her gaze turned to the woman next to her. "Like us."

"I do so hope you're right, Michelle." Marianna picked up the book and the bundle of letters. "We'll open these one day," she said, removing her spectacles. "But now, I must go to bed. Too many late nights are catching up with me, and I meet with the estate managers tomorrow."

"Already?" Jo asked. "I thought you didn't do that until the New Year."

"It is the New Year, dear."

"It is?"

Marianna chuckled. "Joanna, it's the second of January. It was the first yesterday."

"So New Year's Eve was the night..."

"The night at Joss'," whispered Rocky.

Jo shook her head. "I completely lost track, what with everything going on. My God." She ducked her head and kissed her companion. "Happy New Year, Rocky."

"You two go on to bed. We'll talk more in the morning, after my meeting. I'll be sure to leave instructions that you're not disturbed."

"Okay, Mother, whatever you say," Jo said, getting to her feet and pulling the blonde with her. The walk to their room, past walls covered with the portraits of her ancestors, was made in companionable silence. Jo pushed the door open, and Rocky wandered into the room, seeing the fire glowing warmly. She pulled Jo to the bed and pushed her down on it, crawling onto her lover's body and lowering her head onto the dark-haired woman's chest.

They lay like that for long moments, Rocky listening to the strong heartbeat of her lover and the even rhythm of her breathing.

"Jo?"

"Yeah?"

Rocky raised her head, looking down into the blue eyes glistening in the firelight. "Thank you."

Jo raised her hand, brushing blonde hair out of her lover's eyes. "For what?"

"For saving me."

Rocky's human mattress chuckled. "You were managing pretty well without me." She was quiet for a moment. "Sometimes I wonder if I've brought you more heartache than joy. Maybe_" Her musings were cut short by a warm mouth silencing her words. She pulled the blonde closer, her hands tightening on the t-shirt the smaller woman wore, pulling it from the waistband of the sweatpants and finding the soft warm skin beneath.

When the kiss ended, the blonde rested her forehead on her lover's chest. The shirt that Jo wore muffled her voice. "Jo, please don't ever underestimate what you've done for me." She lifted her head, looking into aroused blue eyes. "What you mean to me."

"So much has happened." Jo pulled Rocky back down, settling the blonde on top of her.

"It has. And for a moment there, I wondered if it was worth it." She closed her eyes, listening to the rapid heartbeat beneath her ear and feeling the trembling hand that was tangled in her hair. "I'd gotten used to the emptiness, learned to live with nothing." She reached for Jo's free hand, which was still moving in gentle circles against her own back. She pulled the hand to her lips, brushing a kiss across the knuckles. "And it was like an explosion of feeling when you came into my life. That's the only way I can describe it."

"I'm sorry."

Rocky heard the hitch in Jo's throat and squeezed the woman tighter. "No. Don't be sorry, Jo. You gave me back my life, gave me a purpose." She released Jo's hand and brushed ebony locks back from the bruise that surrounded the cut on Jo's head. "And you came for me." Her eyes filled with tears. "You could have been killed." She felt the arms around her tighten. "And you saved my life."

"I didn't—"

"Yes, Jo. You did. I couldn't have gone on just existing much longer. My whole aim in life was working out where the next hot meal came from. It was getting harder. All I had was the dreams."

She pulled away from Jo slightly, raising herself to look into her lover's face. She smiled, looking into the moist blue eyes, knowing she would never tire of the joy of seeing them. "You're my life now."

"You wanted to leave," Jo said, her throat closing on the words.

"Wanted is the wrong word, Jo. I thought I should." She lay down again, taking a lock of silky dark hair and winding it around her fingers. "I never want to cause you pain. I won't come between you and your family."

"You never will, because you're a part of me now." Jo rubbed her cheek against the blonde head. "If you'd gone tonight, I would just have followed you."

"You would?"

"Of course."

They were quiet for a while. Then Rocky disentangled herself from Jo and knelt on the bed. "What will we do?" the blonde asked.

Jo put her arms behind her head, suddenly finding herself without the comfort of Rocky's body to hold. "When?"

"When all this is over, where shall we go?"

"Where do you want to go?"

"Wherever you are." She looked across the room into the fire. "It's nice here."

"You want to stay here?"

Rocky shrugged. "I'm not really sure. It's too much to think about now." She crawled to the bottom of the bed and sat on the edge, her legs dangling. Jo watched her for a moment then followed her. She used the flat of her hand to brush fine blonde hair away from the back of Rocky's neck and kissed the skin she uncovered. "What's up?" she asked, her lips warm on the blonde's neck.

Rocky let her head fall forward, enjoying the attention Jo was giving to her tense neck. "Nothing, just tired."

Jo settled herself behind Rocky, her long legs on either side of her lover. "We don't have to make any plans yet. We'll just see what the New Year brings."

Rocky felt Jo's arms surround her, and then the taller woman's hands cupped her breasts. She leaned back into Jo and felt the hands leave her for a moment, only to return immediately, but this time on her bare flesh beneath the t-shirt. She tipped her head to the side when she felt soft, warm lips nip at her neck. One of Jo's hands released a breast, smoothing down across a quivering stomach. The hand eased beyond the waistband of the sweatpants Rocky was wearing, pausing there for a moment, before venturing onwards.

The blonde's hips bucked as the hand found its goal. "Easy," Jo whispered into Rocky's ear, her breath warm. Jo smiled when a smaller hand pressed down on her own, separated by the fabric of Rocky's clothes.

"I never thought I could do this," Rocky whispered, her breathing starting to labour.

"Shh," Jo's stroking became deeper, her hold on the blonde firmer. "Don't think, just feel. This is me. Us. No one can take this from us."

"Oh God, Jo." Rocky threw her head back, feeling Jo's mouth on her again, taking her earlobe between her teeth and biting down gently. "Don't let me fall."

"I won't." Jo felt the body in her arms tense and held on as Rocky's climax built. Her knowledgeable hands drew out the blonde's pleasure, leaving Rocky limp and sated in her arms. She moved backwards across the bed, pulling her lover with her, until they were lying side by side, their heads on the plump pillows.

"He's gone," Rocky whispered.

"Who's gone?" Jo asked, moving damp hair away from the blonde's eyes.

"My uncle." Green eyes opened, tired but smiling. "I thought he'd always be there. I didn't think I'd be able to have anyone touch me without feeling him. But he's gone."

Jo smiled. "I'm glad, Rocky."

They lay in silence for a while, Rocky's fingers smoothing across the larger hand she'd captured. "Jo?"

Jo's eyes were closed, but her mouth twitched into a smile. "Yes, sweetheart?"

"I don't want to be Rocky anymore."

Blue eyes snapped open. "You don't?"

The blonde studied the hand she held closely. "No. Rocky was someone I became. Someone who suffered. Someone I was when I was hiding." She brushed Jo's knuckles against her lips then raised her eyes to look into concerned blue ones. "I want to be Michelle again."

"Anything you want."

"Shelly. My family called me Shelly," she said, closing her

eyes as the memory of her family caused her a sudden moment of pain.

"Do you want me to call you Shelly?"

She sniffed. "I need you to. I want my life back."

Jo gathered her into her arms. "I love you, Shelly." She smiled. "And now I'm going to show you just how much," she said as she pushed her lover back onto the bed and began to pull her t-shirt off.

Other Books from
RAP

Darkness Before the Dawn
By Belle Reilly
ISBN 1-930928-06-8

Chasing Shadows
By C. Paradee
ISBN 1-930928-49-1

Forces of Evil
By Trish Kocialski
ISBN 1-930928-07-6

Out of Darkness
By Mary D. Brooks
ISBN 1-930928-15-7

Glass Houses
By Ciarán Llachlan Leavitt
ISBN 1-930928-23-8

Storm Front
By Belle Reilly
ISBN 1-930928-19-X

Retribution
By Susanne Beck
ISBN 1-930928-24-6

Coming Home
By Lois Cloarec Hart
ISBN 1-930928-50-5

Madam President
By Blayne Cooper and TNovan
ISBN 1-930928-69-6

And Those Who Trespass Against Us
By H. M. Macpherson
ISBN 1-930928-21-1

Restitution
By Susanne Beck
ISBN 1-930928-65-3

You Must Remember This
By Mary D. Brooks
ISBN 1-930928-57-2

Bleeding Hearts
By Josh Aterovis
ISBN 1-930928-68-8

Jacob's Fire
By Nan DeVincent Hayes
ISBN 1-930928-11-4

Full Circle
By Mary D. Brooks
ISBN 1-930928-25-4

A Sacrifice For Friendship
By DS Bauden
ISBN 1-930928-30-0

Broken Faith
By Lois Cloarec Hart
ISBN 1-930928-40-8

The Road to Glory
By Blayne Cooper and TNovan
ISBN 1-930928-27-0

These and other
Renaissance Alliance titles
available now at your favorite booksellers.

Alison Carpenter, known on-line as Midgit, lives a short distance from the beautiful city of Bath, England. She has been writing since 1997, but *Cold* is the first piece of work she had enough confidence in to submit. She has a fan-fiction site, which hosts numerous authors:- Midgit's Small Corner of the Xenaverse-http://midgit.co.uk

Alison may be reached at a.e.c@blueyonder.co.uk

Printed in the United Kingdom
by Lightning Source UK Ltd.
101932UKS00002B/54